Secrets and Spies

A Delafield & Malloy Investigation
Book 3

Trish MacEnulty

PRISM LIGHT
PRESS

978-1-7375751-4-6

Published by
Prism Light Press

Manufactured in the United States of America.

"Why fear death? It is the most beautiful adventure that life gives us."

— *Peter Pan*, produced by Charles Frohman,
who died in the sinking of the *Lusitania*

“I think one may attribute as much of [the saboteurs’] activity to the dramatic instinct, as to their cupidity or their real patriotic zeal.”

— NYPD Captain Thomas Tunney,
Throttled

Contents

Society Notes

by Louisa Delafield

Friday April 30, 1915

The wind ruffled the roan mare's black mane as she lifted her head and sniffed the air. It smelled damp and smoky, so different from the dry air of the west where she had run with a boy on her back, a boy who had loved her and who had tried not to cry when she was put on a train along with hundreds of others of her kind. The boy cried anyway, and the roan mare must have sensed his sadness and feared what it meant.

When it comes to horses, gentlemen and ladies of society tend to favor thoroughbred racers. However, they've taken an interest in a different sort of horse these days — the war horse. A fund-raiser by a group of distinguished individuals including Mr. Jack Morgan, Mr. and Mrs. Albert Vanderbilt, Mr. and Mrs. Harry Payne Whitney, and Mrs. Alva Belmont, has rounded up approximately 1,050 horses, which will be sent overseas to do their part in the British war effort. The horses, all sturdy steeds, have been shipped from farms and ranches around the country and will be used for the transport of soldiers and artillery. They will also haul ambulances and supply wagons. Not only are the horses able to travel through mud and across rough ground, they also raise the morale of the fighting men.

I visited the corrals and found the horses ready for duty. When a ripple of skittishness ran through the herd, a roan quarter horse, 15 hands high, took charge, calming the others with soft whinnies and neck nuzzling. Fortunately, I had a sugar cube in my pocket to offer her as a reward. They may be mere animals, but they are more like us (and in some ways much better) than we care to admit. Most of these horses will not survive the battles to come, but because of their sacrifice, many more of Britain's young men will someday return to hearth and home.

Chapter 1

Louisa

Louisa noticed the muffled laughter as she wended her way through the maze of desks, but didn't pay it much heed until she reached her own desk and saw that a bucket of oats had replaced her trusty Remington typewriter. Hands on hips, she turned to look at the culprits, and that was when the muffled laughter turned to guffaws.

"Mr. Stephens, thank you so much for this delightful gift, but I'm not hungry at the moment," she said, looking over at the police reporter, who was surely the instigator of this juvenile joke. "Would it trouble you too much to return my typewriter?"

"Lovely piece you wrote, Miss Delafield," Mick Jones, the barely mediocre sports writer, called out. "Pure poetry."

"I'm so glad we're neighbors," Billy Stephens said, drawing out the "neigh," as he brought her typewriter over to her.

"And please," Louisa said, indicating the bucket of oats, "find a better place for this."

The men continued to act foolish as they were wont to do, and Louisa sat down at her desk and ignored them as she was wont to do. She had gone out on a limb with that story, but she'd been moved by the sight of the horses and especially that gorgeous roan mare with the black mane. She could still feel those velvety lips on her palm as the horse took the sugar cube from her hand. She'd always loved horses and remembered her own heartbreak when, after her father's death, they'd had to sell the pair of black geldings that pulled their carriage. Families all over the country must be feeling a terrible sense of loss as they gave up their horses for a senseless war across the ocean.

"Where's your sidekick?" Billy asked, nodding toward the empty chair where Ellen Malloy usually sat.

"She's off to Ireland to visit her sick father," Louisa said. "She leaves tomorrow so I gave her the day off to get ready."

Billy rubbed his chin and then asked, "What boat is she taking?"

"The *Lusitania*," Louisa said.

Billy went to his desk and returned with the morning's newspaper. He opened it to her column.

"Mr. Stephens, how long are you going to harangue me about this column? I know it's not my usual society fare. I may have gone a little — " she said.

"Look at the advertisement," he interrupted.

She read the small print from the Cunard Ocean Steamships' advert aloud, "...vessels flying the flag of Great Britain or any of her allies are liable to destruction..." She looked up at Billy.

"But the *Lusitania* is a passenger ship with mostly American citizens," she said. "I'm sure Germany would never provoke Wilson. This advertisement is just a bluff." And yet she felt extremely uneasy, thinking of Ellen crossing the Atlantic in the middle of a war, neutrality or no neutrality.

Suddenly the newsroom grew quiet.

"Oh, my," Billy said. He lowered the paper and whistled under his breath.

Louisa looked up. All the men were watching as a young woman zigzagged through the warren of news desks toward Louisa. She wore a stylish gray chenille hat with a navy bow, a smart gray jacket trimmed in navy velvet, and a flared skirt that landed a few inches above her ankles and carried a parasol. Louisa surmised in a glance that the woman was perfect for the job, and her heart sank like a stone. The last thing she wanted was to actually hire a replacement for Ellen — even temporarily.

"Miss Delafield?" the woman asked, her voice light and lilting. "It's me, Phyllis Wolfe."

She stood at Louisa's desk, dewy and glowing. Louisa was only 26, but she suddenly felt old and tarnished.

"I'm here about the position as your assistant," the young woman continued. "I sent you a letter."

Louisa patted her unruly hair and forced a smile to her lips, but it took another few seconds to wet her mouth enough that she could open it.

"Please have a seat," she finally uttered.

"Miss, you don't want to work for her," Billy said, throwing a glance at Louisa. "We call her Bloody Delafield for all the murders she digs up. Sometimes literally." He was referring to the poisoning of a doctor two years earlier, as well as the death of a servant girl and a fellow society writer, all of which Louisa and Ellen had investigated. Even though she wrote these stories under a pen name, the men in the newsroom knew she was the one behind them.

"Don't listen to him, Mrs. Wolfe," she said, emphasizing the "missus."

"Married, are you?" Billy asked in dismay.

"Widowed," she responded. Demurely, Louisa noted. Oh, she was good, this one.

"Mrs. Wolfe was a debutante the last time I saw her," Louisa said, turning her gaze toward the young woman. "Your coming out party took five whole inches of my column."

"Five inches?" Billy said, widening his eyes. Louisa decided ignoring him was the best course of action.

"A long time ago," Mrs. Wolfe said in a world-weary tone and glanced down at her folded hands.

"Not that long ago. Four years, perhaps? You married that artist, Herman Wolfe, soon after the party," Louisa said.

"Eloped," Mrs. Wolfe corrected. "You may as well say the truth. It was quite the scandal. My family cut me off entirely. So we moved to Germany where Herman was from."

"Bad timing, that," Billy said with a grimace.

"It was unfair of your parents to cut you off," Louisa said. The belief of the older generation that they had the right to choose the spouses of their children had always struck Louisa as one of the pitfalls of being in the upper classes. Phyllis had married a destitute artist for love, and she'd paid a steep price.

"But widowhood has restored my respectability, which makes me a perfect fit for the job of assistant to the most respected society writer in America," Mrs. Wolfe said.

Billy barked a laugh and noted, "She'll be great at this job."

"Mr. Stephens, isn't there a paddywagon somewhere you should be chasing?" Louisa asked, glaring at him.

"All right. I know when I'm not welcome." He wandered slowly back toward his own desk. Louisa had a mind to smack him with something but she had no weapon handy. Not to mention the fact that she didn't want to confirm the "bloody Delafield" title. It was true she'd strayed off the society beat more than a few times over the past two years, but she was still first and foremost, "Louisa Delafield, syndicated society columnist for *The Ledger*."

"You know the position is only temporary," Louisa said. "I've promised Miss Malloy her job will be waiting for her as soon as she returns from her trip to Ireland."

"*If* her ship doesn't get torpedoed by the Krauts," Billy interjected from his desk where he had continued to eavesdrop on their conversation. "No offense, Mrs. Wolfe."

"None taken. I'm not German. Besides, I saw that advertisement. It's German bluster. I came over from Liverpool on a cruise liner just last month," Mrs. Wolfe said. "We made it without incident."

"There, you see," Louisa said. "Ellen will be fine." She didn't feel nearly as confident as she hoped she sounded.

The young woman leaned forward, her eyebrows pinched together.

"Ever since the war started, the Germans have taken to disliking Americans intensely. You'd be surprised how many of us were on the boat — all leaving Germany. It was such a relief to step foot again on American soil."

"Their loss," Billy said.

Exasperated, Louisa tossed down her pencil.

"Mr. Stephens, please. I'm trying to conduct an interview," she said.

With an exaggerated sigh, Billy rose from his chair, donned his hat and sauntered off. His broad shoulders moved with the swagger of a man who knows that he's attractive to a certain kind of woman. Louisa was not of that kind.

She turned to the unpleasant task at hand — unpleasant because she dreaded replacing Ellen, who was so much more than an assistant. Ellen was also her friend and confidante. And she was absolutely invaluable when it came to Louisa's darker stories, the one she wrote under her pseudonym, Beatrice Milton. On the other hand, this pert young thing would hardly need any training at all when it came to the society stories.

"If you don't mind my asking, Mrs. Wolfe — why not move back in with your family and let them find you a new husband, one that meets with their approval? It's not easy for a woman to make it alone in this world," Louisa said.

Mrs. Wolfe's eyes narrowed, her face tightened, and her breath sounded almost like a hiss.

"I'll never go back into that cage," she said.

"Cage? Your family?" Louisa was stupefied.

"Marriage," she responded. Again she leaned toward Louisa, this time her hands trembling with emotion as she clutched the bag on her lap. "He turned out to be horrid. I made a vow to myself that I won't be dependent on anyone ever again. And please call me Phyllis. I hate being burdened with his name."

Louisa blinked in surprise at the young woman's frankness, and her heart softened.

"Oh my dear. I'm so sorry."

"Thank you," Phyllis said, straightening her back and regaining her composure as she looked at Louisa with forthright, almond-shaped eyes.

Louisa sighed. There seemed to be no way out. Ellen would be leaving tomorrow, and Phyllis Wolfe had all the necessary qualifications for the job — as long as it stayed within the confines of the society page.

"As you observed earlier, you are a perfect fit for the job of my assistant. You certainly know how to dress the part. You can even cover some of the events for me." Which, she had to admit, was not a function that Ellen with her working-class Irish background could have fulfilled. "Yes, I think you'll do quite nicely." Then she added, "Temporarily, of course."

"Of course." Then Phyllis Wolfe smiled at her so warmly that the whole room lit up.

"I'll see you Monday morning," Louisa said. "Bright and early."

"How early?"

"Oh, by the crack of eleven," Louisa said. Then they both laughed. Completely against her will, Louisa had been won over.

After Mrs. Wolfe left, Louisa returned to her correspondence. To her utter surprise, she saw an envelope from Forrest Calloway, publisher of the paper — and the man she had let slip from her fingers a year earlier. She glanced around to make sure no one was watching. Then she opened the note and read:

> *Dear Louisa,*
> *Would you care to join me to go to a baseball game tomorrow afternoon? If so, please call my house tonight and let Mr. Kimura know. We'll pick you up at one.*
> *Yours truly,*
> *Forrest*

She fought back tears and told herself it meant nothing, but her heart told her she was lying. This meant everything.

Chapter 2

Ellen

Ellen looked out the window from the back seat of the Pierce Arrow at the crowd of cars pulling up in front of the Cunard passenger terminal. People poured onto the sidewalk in front of the pink granite facade: wealthy men in top hats, their wives with their mink stoles wrapped around their necks, children tugging on the hands of their nurses, second class passengers toting suitcases and baskets, the occasional single woman and child, businessmen checking their watches, and burly porters unloading trunks.

As she watched, a cauldron of emotions boiled inside her. When she'd arrived in this country three years ago, near penniless, and bedraggled from weeks in the crowded steerage quarters, she'd never dreamed she'd be going back home in a first-class cabin with the woman of her dreams at her side. She glanced at Hester sitting next to her, and they shared a secret smile.

"Do you realize this is the same pier where they brought the survivors of the *Titanic*?" Hester's married sister, Katherine Murphy, asked. Short, plump and nearly always frowning, Katherine was the exact opposite of the smiling, gangly Hester.

"Katherine, would you please not mention the *Titanic* when we are about to board an ocean liner?" Hester said in mock exasperation.

"Oh, my dear, I'm sure nothing will happen to you and your ... companion," Katherine said, casting a glance at Ellen. "I do find it queer that you chose never to have a lady's maid and yet you have hired Miss Malloy to accompany you on this voyage."

Ellen turned away. She and Hester loved each other, a fact someone like Katherine Murphy could never understand. Not only were they both women, but they were from completely different social classes. None of that mattered to them. She had loved Hester since the moment she saw her sitting in a teahouse in Greenwich Village two years earlier.

She surreptitiously let the backs of her fingers slide against Hester's skirt.

"I told you, Ellen's work for the suffrage movement in New York has been vital. She is the perfect choice to be at my side when I visit Emmeline Pankhurst in London," Hester said.

Ellen snorted and pretended it was a sneeze.

"And how does Louisa Delafield feel about having her assistant snatched out from under her," Katherine said and huffed. As a tireless social climber, Katherine had enormous respect for the city's syndicated society writer.

"It's only temporary, Mrs. Murphy," Ellen interjected. "Louisa will manage."

The motorcar nosed into a vacated spot and Ellen was about to open the door when Hester tapped her on the wrist and gave a subtle shake of her head. Ellen sighed and settled back to wait for the portly chauffeur to make his way around the back of the motorcar and open the door.

"Bon voyage," Katherine called out before the chauffeur shut the door.

Two porters loaded Hester's trunks onto a wagon, and as the Pierce Arrow drove off, Ellen turned to Hester with unabashed admiration.

"Oy, girleen, I never knew you were such a skillful prevaricator," she said.

"It was only a little white lie," Hester said. "I know that you're taking this trip to see your father, but what Katherine doesn't know won't hurt her."

"Especially about us," Ellen said. "Does she not even suspect?"

"Of course not," Hester said. "She couldn't possibly imagine that I love you."

Hester smiled at her, and a shaft of sunlight broke through the clouds. Although the sky was cloudy, the temperature was warmer than it had been in recent days. Spring had finally arrived.

"Ellen, is that Louisa?" Hester asked.

Ellen eyes followed Hester's finger and spotted Louisa at the entrance to the terminal, talking to a handsome gentleman in a gray suit with a pink carnation on his lapel and a tweed cap on his head.

"It is!" Ellen said.

"I believe that's Alfred Vanderbilt she speaking to," Hester said. "Perhaps she's working on a story."

The gentleman bowed to Louisa and walked into the terminal as Ellen and Hester snaked through the crowd to reach Louisa, who broke into a smile when she saw them.

"I thought I'd never find you in this crowd," she said.

"We found you, it would seem. What are you doing here?" Ellen asked.

"I came to see you off, and Suzie sent cookies," Louisa said, holding out a bag to her. Ellen peeked inside and smelled Suzie's famous molasses cookies.

"She's a gem, she is," Ellen said. Louisa's older servant was as much of a friend to Ellen as Louisa herself was.

"Was that Alfred Vanderbilt?" Hester asked.

"It was. He said his mother tried to warn him off getting on this ship. Someone apparently sent a telegram saying it wasn't safe."

"That's all rubbish," Hester said. "The *Lusy* is the fastest ship on the sea."

"I tried to get her not to come," Ellen said to Louisa. "She wouldn't even be going on this trip if it weren't for me."

"I'm not just coming on this trip for you, Ellen," Hester said. "I'm eager to see how the British suffragists are faring in the midst of this war. I can't help it if that coincides with your trip back home to see your father."

Louisa glanced from one to the other and then said, "The ocean voyage will be a lovely getaway for the two of you."

Ellen leaned toward Louisa and said, "She told her sister I'm her 'hired companion.' That's how she's dragged me into first class, but don't think this means I won't want my job when I get back. I don't intend to stay anyone's hired companion."

Ellen loved Hester, but she wished the gulf in their social status wasn't so enormous.

"Don't you worry. I've hired someone, but she knows that she's temporary. You just enjoy yourself. I'm sure the first-class accommodations will be quite luxurious, and your new employer doesn't seem like a slave driver," Louisa teased.

They gazed at each other for a moment. They had been through so much since Ellen had become her assistant. They'd uncovered some of New York society's darkest secrets and been on more than one dangerous adventure.

"Ellen, dear. We must hurry. They're inspecting everyone's bags, and detectives are double checking tickets. So there will be no chance of saboteurs," Hester said.

"Aren't either of you worried about U-boats?" Louisa asked.

"Oh, we'll be as safe on that ship as we would be on Broadway," Hester said, tucking her hand in Ellen's elbow. Ellen shrugged at Louisa. Not one of the passengers hurrying into the terminal seemed the least bit concerned about the German threat.

"Bon voyage, ladies, and, Ellen, I hope your father pulls through," Louisa said.

"I hope he's still alive when I get there," Ellen said. "I've a thing or two to tell him before he makes his way to the Great Beyond."

Then Ellen and Hester headed into the terminal to board their ship.

Having passed muster with the detectives, they made their way onto the pier. The ship was a great monster, black and sleek, its slanted funnels painted wartime gray. Brawny stevedores loaded wagons of cargo onto pallets to go onto the ship, men in blue sailor outfits scurried around, and men in white aprons supervised the unloading of food. How much food it must take to feed almost two thousand passengers and crew, Ellen marveled.

They followed the crowd to the boarding area. People leaned on the rails waving handkerchiefs at those they were leaving behind. A man on the pier cranked a movie camera as passengers rushed past him. Ellen caught the tingle of excitement as they made their way up the plank, and soon they were also leaning against the rail, looking out at the concrete jumble of New York city. A cacophony of sounds filled the air with children laughing and screaming, passengers calling out to their loved ones on the shore, and stewards yelling orders.

Finally, the gangplank was lifted while at the end of the boat a sailor raised a flag. Steam billowed noisily through the ship's funnels. An army of small tugs nudged the great ship along the Hudson River and out to sea.

Hester sighed as they stood together, shoulders touching, and said, “And we’re off.”

Chapter 3
Louisa

Louisa strode into the parlor, looking for her bag, and saw her mother, Anna, staring up at the family portrait over the mantelpiece with the ginger cat on her lap. The grand painting looked incongruous in their shabby Harlem townhome. Louisa's dead father seemed to be looking back at her with a bemused expression on his face. Anna bent her head, casting her eyes down, in an attitude of utter defeat. Louisa sighed. For fifteen years this grief had weighed her mother down. She remembered when Anna was as light and chirpy as a little bluebird. Now, she mostly confined herself to an invalid chair though she was perfectly capable of walking. She said too much exertion gave her chest pains.

So Louisa did what she always did when confronted with the unbearable weight of her mother's sorrow. She created a diversion.

"Mother," she said, "you'll never guess where I'm going. A baseball game."

"A baseball game?" Louisa's mother looked up at her as if she'd just said she was going to fly to the moon.

"Yes," Louisa said, slipping on a pair of white gloves.

"What does one wear to a baseball game?" Anna mused.

"This," Louisa said, indicating the black jumper over a lace blouse with pearl buttons and a Georgette-crepe layered skirt that hit mid-calf.

Suzie came in the room, looked Louisa over, and nodded with approval.

"What do you think?" Louisa asked.

"I think he'll want to kick himself for wasting a whole year being mad at you," Suzie said. Suzie had been there during the fiasco the previous year in Florida when Louisa had fallen for an ill-intentioned Frenchman, who had left her out in a swamp for dead. That episode had not turned out well for him. His lady friend shot him. Thanks to Suzie and Ellen, Louisa had escaped the swamp and solved a murder, but she had lost Forrest.

"Why do you suppose he wants to take you out after all this time?" Anna asked.

"I think it's taken him this long to forgive me," Louisa said. "Oh, my hat!"

She rushed upstairs, found the large black hat with the white bow on her vanity, placed it on her head, and gazed at herself in the mirror.

Had Forrest really forgiven her, she wondered. For the past year, she'd buried herself in her work: writing her syndicated column, covering every society event in the city no matter how minor, and slipping into her "Beatrice Milton" role to uncover a few scandals. Louisa was not without her charms. She was still pretty and had excellent breeding. Men occasionally had the temerity to inquire if they might accompany her to an opera or to a play, but she always turned them down. She was not interested in dalliances. She wondered if she'd been waiting all along for this — an invitation from Mr. Forrest Calloway to a baseball game, of all things.

The doorbell rang. Louisa glanced out the window and saw the Packard parked outside.

She took a deep breath, adjusted the hat to a rakish angle and then walked in a stately manner to the stairs, only to rush down them like a school girl.

The chauffeur, Mr. Kimura, held out a slender, perfectly manicured hand and helped Louisa into the capacious back seat of the dark blue Packard where Forrest was waiting for her with a misty smile. He was twenty years older than she with a bit of a paunch, but the glow of his deep-set mahogany eyes shined into her depths and she had to admit that happiness was seeping through her as she sat near him.

"You look radiant," he said.

"Thank you," she said, settling into the leather seat. "I'm quite looking forward to today. I know nothing about baseball."

"I was afraid you might dread it. Brandy?"

"I don't dread it at all. I donned this playful little frock just for the occasion," she said, smoothing down her skirt. "Yes, I'll have a tiny bit, please."

She was grateful for anything that might steady her nerves. He took a bottle of brandy and a couple of glasses from a basket on the floorboard, poured a glass, and handed it to her.

"Thank you," she said and took a sip, savoring the amber taste on her tongue.

Neither of them mentioned the fact that they hadn't spoken to each other in a year, so when he reached over and squeezed her hand, she thought her heart would burst.

"I enjoyed your piece about the horses," he said. "I found it quite poetic."

Louisa laughed, embarrassed.

“The men in the office will never let me live it down,” she said. “They left a bucket of oats on my desk.”

“I will have them all fired,” he said.

“No, you won’t,” she said and playfully tapped his arm. “Isn’t this a bit daring, the two of us being in public like this without a host of chaperones?”

“We’ll have an entire stadium full of chaperones,” he said.

Yes, Louisa thought, but showing up together would make a certain statement. During their year-long relationship, they had often been together in public at various functions, but to the world at large they seemed nothing more than a wealthy publisher, advising and advancing his star society writer. It was only when Mr. Kimura drove the motorcar around to the back of the house in Grammercy Park so she could enter unseen through the kitchen that they allowed themselves to show their true feelings. Fortunately, except for the rare occasion, Forrest took a hands-off approach to publishing and let his editor make all of the decisions so none of the other reporters had ever accused her of receiving preferential treatment. If she’d still been a member of society, instead of simply reporting on it, she might have had to bear more scrutiny but since the doyennes saw her as little more than a well-dressed servant, her scandalous behavior had escaped their notice. Did today's invitation mean a resumption of their previous relationship or the beginning of something new?

As Mr. Kimura drove to the Polo Grounds, the baseball stadium where a polo stick had never once been seen, Louisa changed the course of the conversation and chattered.

"Ellen is off to Ireland to see her dying father," she said. "So I hired a replacement. She won't be much help with my Beatrice Milton stories. Not like Ellen. But she's ideal for the society beat. I may even send her to some of those ubiquitous weddings in my place."

"Perhaps foregoing the Beatrice Milton stories is not such a bad thing," he said.

Forrest had never liked the fact that she sometimes found herself in dangerous situations, so she dropped the matter.

As the motorcar pulled in front of the main entrance of the stadium, Louisa looked around in wonder at the throngs of men and boys, who all seemed on the verge of hysteria as they milled around.

"Don't worry," Forrest said as Mr. Kimura opened the door to let her out. "You won't be subjected to sitting with the stadium riffraff."

"I'm not a hothouse flower, Mr. Calloway," she said and stepped out of the car.

"Thank you, Mr. Kimura," she said. Mr. Calloway only hired Asian servants, a habit held over from his California past, she supposed. Mr. Kimura bowed and closed the car door behind her.

The brisk spring air made her pull her shawl around her shoulders and tuck her hands into her muff.

The crowd was even louder and more boisterous than she'd expected. As they stepped through the marble facade, the noise and smells of unwashed humanity, spilled beer, and popcorn wafted through the air. The sensations overwhelmed her for a moment, but Forrest led her to a private entrance, which she assumed was for wealthy ticket holders and other VIPs.

They entered the stadium, Forrest stopping to shake hands or otherwise acknowledge various men of means. One of them, tall, with ice-blue eyes and a mustache that curled at each end, stopped Forrest with a gesture.

"Herr Calloway, how are you? And who is your lovely companion?"

Louisa held out her hand, "Louisa Delafield, Count von Bernstorff." She knew exactly who he was. That was her job. His job seemed to be to show up at as many society events as he could fit into his calendar. She felt certain he knew who she was, as well.

"The famous society writer," he said and kissed her knuckles. "You cover much territory these days. I read your piece about the war horses."

"They're heroes already."

"They are indeed, but doesn't this sending of horses to the Allies violate the idea of your country's neutrality?" he said.

"As you observed, Ambassador, I'm the society writer, not the political writer," she said and shrugged one shoulder.

"Of course. I'm not blaming you. In fact, why don't you come to the opera with me and my wife as my guest next Friday night? There is a benefit performance of *Lohengrin* for the German Red Cross. We can meet at the Ritz-Carlton, and go from there."

It was a rather sudden invitation, Louisa thought, but it was well within her beat: an opera and a charity function. Count von Bernstorff was a known social climber, but weren't social climbers the bread and butter of her business?

"That sounds delightful," she said. "I shall put it on my schedule."

The count bowed to them and walked stiffly away.

"What a surprise to see a German count at an American baseball game," Louisa observed.

"He's probably here to report to the Fatherland about the fitness of our young men should we enter the war," Forrest said as he led her to a flight of stairs.

"Do you think he's a spy?" Louisa asked.

"Well, I don't think he's rooting for England to win the war," he said.

They came to a staircase and proceeded up.

"They do have boxes here, I assume?" Louisa said.

"They do, but that's not where we're headed," Forrest responded. "As members of the press, we're entitled to a couple of the best seats in the house. The press box."

Louisa gasped in surprise. Forrest Calloway was publisher of *The Ledger,* hardly "a member of the press," but he had the right to call himself that, she supposed.

"Won't they be shocked when a woman steps foot on their hallowed grounds?" she asked with a grin.

He gave her hand a surreptitious squeeze.

They reached the press box, which was not a box at all but a long row of seats overlooking the stadium. The writers leaned back in their seats, smoking and chatting, taking nips from flasks, waiting for the game to begin. *The Ledger*'s own sportswriter, that lackluster scribbler Mick Jones, looked up in astonishment as they approached.

"Mr. Calloway! And... what a... surprise," he said. The writers turned to stare, gape-mouthed at the two newcomers.

The men shared uncomfortable glances until a snappy fellow in a checkered jacket rose. He doffed his cap with an exaggerated bow and said, "Why, it's our esteemed colleague, Miss Louisa Delafield. I hope I speak on behalf of all the gents here when I say, welcome to the lion's den. I hope you'll forgive us if a few accidental pearls of profanity escape our lips. We are not accustomed to such exalted visitors in our midst."

Louisa recognized the man as the famed sports writer, Damon Runyon.

"Mr. Runyon, I'm sure my delicate sensibilities will survive a bit of coarse language," she said with a laugh. She sat down in the nearest chair, right next to Runyon, and gazed about her while the "gents" resumed their discussions.

The stadium wasn't as glamorous as the new Metropolitan Opera House, but that didn't mean it wasn't gorgeous in its own right. The structure was U-shaped like a giant bathtub with seats for thousands of people — almost all of them filled on this brilliant afternoon. On the back wall was an advertisement for men's hair cream. The tiers were separated by a row of colorful bas-relief sculptures, featuring various baseball teams. Around the rim of the tub, large bronze eagles perched every twenty feet or so, wings outstretched as if waiting to swoop down and pluck an errant baseball out of the air.

On the field a small army of photographers stood behind big, boxy cameras. One of them trained his camera on a powerfully built man in the baggy Red Sox uniform, windmilling his arms on the sideline.

Then the game began. The Yankees in their pinstripe uniforms and blue knee socks trotted out to the field while a Red Sox player swung his bat back and forth. Calloway leaned close to her to explain what each man was doing. There were outfielders and infielders and a pitcher and a catcher and hitters. The game seemed absurdly slow. The men swung the bat at the ball and usually missed, or the pitcher threw the ball and the batter just watched it whizz past. This game was nothing like tennis or polo. But she began to get the rules of the game. After three "outs," the teams switched places. This had already happened twice when Runyon leaned close to her, and said, "Watch this guy. I've heard rumors about him."

A burly fellow in the plain gray Red Sox uniform ambled up to home plate, swinging a bat in his left hand. He was the same one who had been the center of the photographers' attention.

"Isn't he supposed to be the pitcher?" she asked. She looked through a pair of opera glasses. The man had a somewhat doughy face, but there was something determined, something steely about him.

"A guy I know played with him in Baltimore, says he's a real slugger, too. The Sox' secret weapon."

Louisa looked at her program and saw the man's name: George Herman Ruth. Putting down the program, she watched with curious anticipation to see if anything would happen. She desperately hoped that it would.

"Now watch," Runyon continued. "Warhop's winding up. And ..."

As the ball sailed toward home plate, the large left-handed man swung his whole body, and the two objects collided in a terrific smack that stunned the crowd. The ball soared over the field and into the second tier of stands. Louisa gasped. The big man loped easily around the bases as the crowd rose to its feet and cheered. Even the reporters were duly impressed.

"In the third inning, Ruth knocked the slant out of one of Jack Warhop's underhanded subterfuges," Runyon muttered as he wrote hastily on his pad, "and put the baseball in the right field stands for a home run."

Subterfuge, Louisa mused. There must have been more going on down there than met her eyes.

"Ruthless Ruth," crowed one of the reporters.

In spite of the Red Sox' slugger, the Yankees won the game, four to three. She had gathered from the reporters' banter that the Red Sox defense had been "wobbly" that day and that they were still the better team, but the fans leaving the stadium were jubilant, whistling and waving pennants and tossing peanuts into the air.

"That was actually fun," Louisa said. "Though you know Mick Jones won't be able to shut up about seeing me and the publisher in the press box. He's a worse gossip than Mamie Fish."

"I don't care what Mick Jones says," Forrest said. Then he took her hand and asked, "Louisa, would you come over to the house?"

She looked into his eyes. There was nothing she'd rather do. The motor car headed downtown toward his townhome in Grammercy Park.

"Let's have a drink, shall we?" he said once they were in the parlor. "I'll have Mr. Wong fix up a plate of cold cuts and cheese."

"All right," she said.

In his drawing room, Forrest poured a glass of wine for her and a Glenlivet whisky for himself. Mr. Wong brought in a plate of finger foods, for which she had no appetite. She was much too nervous.

"I've missed you," Forrest said.

She inhaled and edged closer, wanting to be near him.

"I have missed you, too," she said. "I thought you'd never forgive me."

"I've been a fool," he said and pulled her into his arms.

"I was the fool," she said, reveling in the warmth of his embrace and the scent of sandalwood soap.

He bent his head and kissed her.

"I want it to be different this time," he said.

"Different? How?"

"No more subterfuge," he said. "I want you to marry me."

She leaned away in surprise.

"Marry you? I thought you were already married," she said.

"I hired a Pinkerton to find her. The divorce was finalized last month."

For a moment Louisa reeled. Marriage. She hadn't imagined he would want to marry her.

"I love you, Louisa," he said. "I've waited this whole year to make sure you had not found another and to make sure that this time we would have an honest relationship. As man and wife."

"But what about my work?" she asked.

"You will have plenty to do," he said, "managing a home, raising children. You might have an advice column for mothers if you like."

Mothers? Louisa's breath left her. She finished her wine in two gulps.

"You have caught me by surprise, darling," she said.

"Louisa, journalism is a young woman's job," he said. "You know you can't continue your Beatrice Milton work much longer. And all those society events. Wouldn't you prefer to go as a guest?"

Of course, she would. The constant whirl of covering social events was exhausting.

"Imagine," he said. "A beautiful home. The finest care for your mother. And of course, you'll bring Suzie."

"We also have Suzie's grandniece, Pansy, with us now," Louisa said.

"She's welcome as well. You'll need help taking care of the babies," he said. He brushed a stray strand of hair from her face with his finger.

Babies. She felt a strange and unfamiliar tug at her heart. Babies. She looked into Forrest's mahogany eyes and truly understood what he was offering her: security, a home, children. What woman in her right mind wouldn't want those things?

"May I think about it?" she said.

"I will give you one week," he said. "Friday night we will have dinner at Delmonico's and then you can promise to make me the happiest man in the world."

"I'm supposed to go to the opera with that dreadful German count on Friday," she said.

"We'll have an early dinner before the opera," he said. His fingers drifted over her skirt. She leaned forward. The kiss was long and deep, and before she knew what was happening, he was hungrily kissing her neck, his hand cupping her breast. Her every nerve was on fire. She had missed his touch, missed the soft roar in her body when he held her breasts or moved his hand between her legs, when he was suddenly inside her. She missed the way they lost themselves in oblivion when that thunder in the body happened.

"Let's go upstairs, my love," she whispered. "Mr. Wong might die of shock if he finds us like this."

Forrest pulled away from her and took a deep breath.

"No, no, I want to wait," he said. "Until I hear your answer. When I have you again in my bed, I want it to be as my wife. Or at the very least as my fiancée."

She stared at him — his dark, lucid eyes, the firm jutting chin, and the widow's peak that gave him an air of dignity. He was right, of course. He deserved a wife, children.

Her racing heart slowed.

"I will let you know in one week," she said. She wanted to tell him yes at that very moment. Phyllis could take over her job, Beatrice Milton could go out to pasture, and Ellen would land on her feet. After all, she had Hester. She thought of how ecstatic her mother would be. They would be wealthy once again. But she held her tongue. She would take her time before making a decision as momentous as this.

Chapter 4

Ellen

Sunday, May 2, 1915

The baked Virginia ham was delicious, but Ellen couldn't wait to feast on her mother's potato croquettes and rashers. Almost three years earlier, she'd announced to her family that she had gotten a job in New York City and was leaving Ireland. It had not been a happy leave-taking. Her father had raged, shouting that she was "na daughter" of his while her mother wailed like a banshee. Yet now her mother's letter said Da was sick and that whenever Ellen's name was mentioned, the man wept for want of seeing her. Ellen's throat tightened, and the longing for her kin felt like a magnetic force pulling at her very bones.

"Mr. Murphy often talks about the whitewashed houses of Ireland gleaming in the sunlight," Hester said. She had an uncanny ability to read Ellen's mood. Affecting an Irish brogue, she added, "And the rose bushes all abloom."

"There must be something in your family blood that attracts you Pennsylvania Dutch to the Irish. Your brother-in-law's origins are as humble as mine," Ellen said. She speared a pearled onion with her fork.

"Yes, but because he's a man he's been able to work his way up to president of my father's company. Whereas, since you are a woman, you are much more limited in your opportunities," Hester said and wiped her mouth with the heavy linen napkin.

"I'm happy enough," Ellen said, reaching under the table to rub the backs of her fingers against Hester's silk dress. She was telling the truth; she felt a contentment with Hester she'd never known possible.

"No woman can be truly happy until we secure the right to vote," Hester said. "I plan to connect with Mrs. Pankhurst as soon as I get to London. The British women are so much more active than our American suffragists. They're willing to get their delicate little hands dirty."

"I'm an alto," Ellen said.

"What?"

"I said, 'tis the choir you're preaching to, my love," she said. Hester smiled and looked heavenward.

"You are right, of course," Hester said as she reached under the table and surreptitiously squeezed Ellen's hand.

After lunch Hester found a cozy spot in the first-class lounge to write letters while the ship's small orchestra played a waltz in the background, and Ellen wandered down two decks lower, where the third-class smoking room and ladies' lounge were located. A good number of the third-class passengers were either Russian or British, but it didn't take long to track down the little cabal of Irish women with their dark woolen dresses and shawls draped over their shoulders, who claimed a spot on the sheltered deck just outside the ladies' lounge. Unlike the filthy old steamer that had brought Ellen to America, the Lusitania's third-class accommodations were spacious and clean.

When Ellen approached them, the women were standoffish, noting the fine cloth on her back and the new leather on her feet. She explained she was a hired companion — "basically a glorified servant" — without mentioning that she shared her employer's bed, and she won them over soon enough with her County Galway brogue and her salacious tales of her former work as a domestic for the wealthy and now thoroughly disgraced Garrett family.

"Did the master really get the poor housemaid with child and then send her off to an abortionist without so much as a never-you-mind?" one of the younger women asked.

They had a great gab fest that afternoon. So the next afternoon and the next, Ellen left the upper deck and joined the Irish women. They shared stories of home, of families on the edge of ruin, of fathers who drank too much, and mothers who slapped the backsides of their wailing brats. "Rightly so!" And more than a few tall tales were swapped as well — of ghosts and fairies, of men driven to distraction by the siren calls of flesh-eating mermaids, and of babies taken in the night only to be found twenty years later still babes. Ellen reveled in this time with her country women, especially with Mrs. McNabb, who was taking her grandson, Seamus, back to live in Ireland after his mam had died of disease in the rat-infested tenements of New York.

In the evenings, Ellen and Hester dined with the "Saloon" passengers, as the first class was called, who conversed airily about their houses, their sports, and their other frivolous pastimes — plays and parties and such. From her work as a lady's maid and then as an assistant to Louisa, Ellen knew quite a bit about society but that didn't mean she had anything much to say to them — with the exception of the Hubbards whose socialist, free-thinking politics she and Hester both found refreshing.

Later in their stateroom, they gave themselves over to an abandon they rarely felt in New York where there were always nosy servants or landladies and where it would not do for one or the other to stay the night.

"I live and breathe ecstasy," Hester had whispered one night, her hair wet with perspiration, her beautiful pale breasts rising and falling with her breath. Ellen ran a finger over Hester's firm nipple. She felt exactly the same.

On the third afternoon on the lower deck, Mrs. McNabb had finished spinning a yarn about the little people, and Ellen thought of her own gran, who believed in fairies and sprites so fervently she could make you see them yourself. After the Hunger, after losing her husband and three of her five children, Ellen's gran had moved to the Claddagh with the two children she had left and swore they'd never live off the land again. She learned how to mend nets, and as soon as her son was old enough, she sent him to work with a fisherman. Her daughter, Ellen's aunt, moved to Galway City once she was old enough, worked as a domestic and eventually married a bookseller. "She got airs, she did," Gran said, somehow managing to be scornful and prideful at the same time. That's what they were sure to think of Ellen, too.

"I s'pose I should be getting on up to the fancy deck for dinner," Ellen said as the sun marched westward.

"I'll stroll with you," Mrs. McNabb said. "My old bones seize up if I don't move 'em."

They crossed the wooden planks of the deck as the ship barreled toward the east.

"You don't believe there's any truth to the rumors about them U-boats, do you?" Mrs. McNabb asked.

Ellen glanced out toward the inscrutable surface of the sea.

"I pray not," she said.

"I do, too. I knew we wouldn't catch fire like them other ships you read about in all the papers," Mrs. McNabb said. "I wasn't worried about that. But the U-boats – that's another kettle of fish."

"Why weren't you worried about the fires, might I ask?" Ellen said.

Mrs. McNabb's voice went low and soft.

"Tom O'Reilly, the husband of my poor daughter what's dead, is a stevedore. He told me that there wouldn't be no bombs on this ship. Too many passengers, too many Irish passengers," she said. Then she leaned in closer. "Some of thems been helping the Germans."

"Irish stevedores? Helping the Germans?" Ellen asked, incredulous. The stevedores worked the docks, loading and unloading ships. It made perfect sense that the Germans would turn to them for help.

"Hush, now. He told me with his own lips. They're not after helping Britain win the war."

Ellen pondered this information. In the newspapers, there were frequent reports of mysterious fires and explosions regularly erupting long after boats carrying supplies to the English and the French had left for their destinations. The police, it was said, suspected sabotage but had been unable to prove a thing, and all along it was Irish stevedores, at least according to Mrs. McNabb. She thought of Paddy O'Neil and Captain Tunney, both staunch Irish-Americans. As members of the bomb squad, they would be interested in this piece of information. But would she tell them when she got back? She sighed. This evil war would turn brother against brother and sister against sister before it was all said and done.

She said goodbye to Mrs. McNabb and climbed the stairs up to the Saloon Deck.

Chapter 5
Louisa

Louisa slept miserably. All night she turned over Forrest's proposal in her head. What would it be like to wake up in his bed every morning? Would she grow tired of his kisses, of his touch? And what would she do with herself if she didn't have her work? She wouldn't miss the debutante tea dances or the endless weddings, but no more verbal sparring with Billy Stephens? No more scheming with Ellen to come up with a Beatrice Milton story? No more flattery from young women longing to be included in her column? Would society suddenly accept her as one of them? In her mind, she'd always been one of them, but she knew that the grand old dames had written the Delafields off the moment her father's name had appeared in the newspapers as a murder victim. When she had finally fallen asleep, her window shades were pale with the dawn light.

She woke up and found the ginger cat kneading the pillow next to her, purring loudly. The grandfather clock downstairs chimed twelve times. Noon. She forced herself out of bed, managed to wash herself, and get dressed, and stumble downstairs where all was quiet.

"I wondered if you were dead up there," Anna said when Louisa came into the parlor.

"Where are Suzie and Pansy?" Louisa asked.

"They're at church, of course. It's Sunday," her mother said. "There are so many Negro churches in Harlem now they have plenty to choose from. I would like some coffee please."

Louisa warmed up the coffee that Suzie had left in the kitchen and carried the silver service to the parlor where her mother waited. Fortunately, Pansy had already been down to the corner newspaper stand and *The Times, The World,* and *The Herald* were all at hand. It was part of Louisa's job to keep up with the competition.

Anna perused *The World* while Louisa opened *The Times*. She looked at the weddings and immediately her mind wandered back to Forrest. If they were to marry, her wedding would be reported in all the papers and she knew her fellow society writers would gush enthusiastically over every detail. Of course, it would be in St. James. She would not have a ridiculously long train like some of these girls did. Her dress would be tasteful with pearls over satin on the bodice and a lace overskirt. She couldn't believe she was thinking about a wedding dress!

She looked at the wedding announcements in *The Times*. She hadn't even covered Mabel Keating's wedding. Well, she was only one person, she couldn't get to all of them. Now that she had Phyllis, she wouldn't have to miss the important ones. According to the article Mabel carried a bouquet of white orchids and lilies of the valley. Mabel was quite young, a recent debutante. Louisa wondered what Mabel would think of marriage. Had her mother told her was to expect?

At least Louisa knew what she was getting into. These young women of society had been closely guarded and most of them had no idea what happened in the marriage bed. She had overheard conversations among some young matrons, and for a few of them it had been quite an unpleasant surprise though they never went into detail. She was glad Forrest had already made love to her. He was a gentle and generous lover, and she had experienced exquisite pleasure with him. She thought with a sense of shame of the one time she'd been with another man — the Frenchman she'd met in Florida last year. Before he had left her for dead in a Florida swamp, she'd been foolish enough to go to his hotel room and had quickly discovered that not all men were like Forrest. There was another side to the sex act, and it wasn't gentle or generous.

The thought made her stomach feel queasy — though she wasn't sure if the queasiness was from the past or the future. Marriage changed everything.

"I do wish we still had our cottage," Anna said, apropos of nothing. "The summer parties were so much fun. So extravagant. Everyone got a gift. And that Mamie Fish! What a card. One year I dressed as an Egyptian princess for a costume party. Suzie helped make it. Mamie found out what I was wearing ahead of time — I think she had spies in every house on the island — so she dressed as Pharoah." She sighed. "We were all so carefree then."

Louisa glanced at her mother, who smiled as she continued to peruse the paper. Then she gazed up at the family portrait, her father so handsome a man with his gray eyes and Roman nose, and her mother a rare beauty, creamy skin and golden hair. With eight-year old Louisa leaning against her seated father, they appeared the perfect family. She turned her eyes back toward her mother. She knew that some women lost interest in amorous pleasures after they had children. Louisa was only twelve years old when her father died, but she somehow knew her parents had not been intimate for years — not that she knew what such intimacy entailed. It wasn't just the separate bedrooms. Most wealthy women had their own bedroom. Perhaps, the clue was in the chaste kiss on the cheek that her father gave her mother every night before she retired. The lack of heat between them. She had not understood adult longings, but she could sense that her parents were not like the couples in the fairy tales.

Now that she was older she realized what those impressions meant, which led her to wonder. If she married Forrest, would her marriage turn cold like that? It was such a risky venture. Of course, one could always divorce, but even though it had become more common, she couldn't bear to think of it. She clasped her hands together and squeezed.

There was another reason Louisa had not married. She had been searching for answers to her father's murder for fifteen years. She'd felt she couldn't marry until she knew what had happened. There had been a few clues here and there. Herbert Markham, the family's attorney who had handled their financial affair, had always seemed to be an upstanding sort, but then his wife, Julia, had mentioned last year that she knew some sort of dark secret. She never said what it was, and later she played dumb and pretended she had forgotten the whole thing. Louisa realized she might never know what had happened to her father or why.

***

The next morning, Louisa walked to the IRT station as usual, but everything felt different. Perhaps because it was early May and the trees were adorned in fresh green leaves, she felt hopeful and more alive. Or perhaps it was because she'd finally made her decision. She would marry. She would now be an item in the society column instead of the one writing it. And she would do it with so much more panache than other women. Not that she wouldn't still be involved in things that mattered. She'd march for suffrage and perhaps hold salons for thinkers, writers, and artists. She would host benefits for the war effort in Europe. After all, the pen was powerful, but everyone knew that money was more so.

She got off the subway one stop early so she could have her Sally Lund bun and coffee at the Knickerbocker and catch up on the other dailies. She had made up her mind, but she would wait till the end of the week to let her editor Virgil Thorn know. This would give her a chance to see what Phyllis Wolfe could do.

As Louisa wended her way through the chaotic crowds at Times Square, a newsy yelled, "Extra! Extra! Sabotage!" He held up *The Herald*, a competitor to her own paper. Every week there was some new outrage — a bomb going off somewhere, a ship full of ammunition catching fire at sea. The police, it seemed, were helpless to stop it. As she walked past the boy, she looked closer and saw the headline: "Horses dead!"

She stopped in her tracks.

"My God!" she whispered, taking the paper from the boy. Her hands shook as she read the lede paragraph.

"Lady. The paper ain't free," the boy said.

She thrust a coin into his hand and immediately hailed a taxi.

"Take me to Pier 32," she demanded. On the way, she skimmed the article. More than half of the horses were dead, infected by something called glanders. She had no idea what that was or how that could have happened. They'd been so frisky and alive.

"Here ya go, Miss," the driver said and flicked his vacant flag up as she paid him.

She rushed past the iron fence and through the gate to the docks. Photographers and police stood glumly outside the corral.

Tom Tunney, a burly New York City police captain, whom she knew well, surveyed the damage.

"What is glanders?" she asked.

"A type of bacteria. German scientists perfected it not too long ago. Someone got in here and put it in their nostrils," he said. "Night watchman came along and scared them off. Some of the horses survived. We've got them on a ship already. These poor dumb creatures here had a horrible death."

She edged forward and saw them — hundreds of dead horses on the ground. Flies buzzed around the bodies and a foul odor simmered in the air. The roan mare lay on her side, belly distended, mouth and eyes open, legs still. Louisa's heart shattered.

These equine soldiers did not have to leave home to go to war. The war had come to them. She turned away, stifling a sob. Anger and a sense of helplessness overwhelmed her.

"I'm at my wit's end trying to uncover these saboteurs," Tunney admitted. "What we need is someone on the inside. Someone to tell us what these Krauts are up to. This isn't the only thing they've done."

"I read about the ship that caught fire at sea last week," she managed.

"'Twas a merchant ship with enough grain and sugar to feed the British army for a month," Tunney said, shaking his head.

"Do you have any idea how they're doing it?" she asked.

"I do not. But you might be able to help, Miss Delafield," he said.

"You and your bomb squad have all the resources of the NYPD and probably the U.S. and British government as well. How could I possibly help?" she asked.

"The ringleader is one of these fancy society men. He moves in circles my men can't breach. But you can." His eyes bore into hers.

She shook her head. She couldn't possibly get involved in this. Forrest would never let her do such a dangerous thing, not if she were going to be his wife.

"My investigating days are over, Captain Tunney," she said. "I'm getting married."

"Are ye? Congratulations," he said, drily.

Louisa took one more look at the horses before quickly walking away.

Chapter 6

Ellen

Thursday, May 6, 1915

"Seamus O'Reilly, would you stop your yakking?" Mrs. McNabb said wearily as her black-haired, dark-eyed grandson waved his hand in her face, jabbering about his daily explorations. "You can't be gadding about the ship like you do."

"But, Gran," he said, leaning on the arm of her deck chair. "You won't believe what I found in the hold. Guns!"

Ellen, who'd been sitting in a deck chair on the other side of Mrs. McNabb, perked up and looked over at the boy.

"Guns?" she asked.

"I saw the boxes and they were the right size for guns and there was loads of them. I know because my da told me what to look for. He says the Yanks are sneaking weapons on board all the boats and they aren't s'posed to be doing that 'cause America is neutral. That's what he said." The boy barely took a breath as he spoke.

"You go on with yourself, now," Mrs. McNabb said. "Grown folks are trying to talk. Can you not find someone your age to play with?"

"I'm off to do more exploring," Seamus said and ran away before she could stop him.

***

Ellen got to the stateroom from her daily visit with Mrs. McNabb and the other Irish women a bit later than usual, and found that Hester had already gone to dinner. Ellen donned her dinner dress. As a "hired companion" she wasn't expected to look glamorous, but Hester had insisted on bringing a few silk dresses for her to wear in the evenings. Ellen didn't much like to accept charity, but to keep up the charade she must play her part. Louisa had taught her that much. She looked at herself in the mirror and decided she was presentable. She had never been a great beauty, but to her own eyes, she looked strong and capable. She was straight-backed and clear-eyed with a strong chin that she held high. Her look had kept her safe on the streets of Galway when she was younger and now served to keep people from questioning her right to be at Hester's side.

Ellen made her way to the dining room, winding through the maze of tables, past the enormous fireplace, and across the plush carpet toward Hester, who sat with the socialist couple they had befriended. Also at the table was an annoying British aristocrat, whom Ellen had dubbed "Lord Fatlip." He constantly flirted with Hester, thinking to make a match with a wealthy American in exchange for a worthless title. Ellen derived no small amount of satisfaction in imagining his dismay if he knew that his intended target was already spoken for by a penniless Irish woman.

"Hello, Elbert. Hello, Alice," she said, sitting next to the American man and his wife.

"It's my comrade in arms," Elbert said with a mischievous twinkle in this dark eyes.

"No, she's my comrade in arms," Alice declared. "We were both at the front lines in Washington two years ago, marching for the vote, weren't we?"

"We all were," Hester said. "That's where Ellen and I met. On the bus."

"The bus?" the Brit said, astounded. "How egalitarian of you."

"I couldn't very well borrow my sister's Pierce Arrow," Hester said. "Besides, we had fun on the bus, didn't we, Ellen?"

"Oh, great fun. If you like having your bones rattled for hours," she said. The life she'd been living at the time — fired from her job, hungry, near destitute, and scared for her life — was a far cry from the absurd luxury of this floating palace. Ellen glanced up at the stained-glass panels in the dome high above them and imagined Louisa describing it in her column. *"Former lady's maid, Ellen Malloy, and her elegant lady lover, Hester French, dined on boiled hake in egg sauce, galantine of veal, and plum pudding in the elegant surroundings of the first-class dining room of Cunard's most elegant ship. They were the very embodiment of elegant elegance."* Ellen stifled a giggle. She was no threat to Louisa when it came to society writing, she thought.

"I do hope you ladies get your vote one of these days," Lord Fatlip said. "But it won't happen while there's a war going on."

"War!" Elbert said. "If we had no governments, we would have no war."

"We wouldn't have much of anything," Lord Fatlip said and downed his glass of wine, before signaling for more.

"I read the booklet you gave me this morning," Ellen said to Elbert with a grin. "I think I'll take it home with me. My da will be happy to learn that Jesus was an anarchist."

"After you show it to him, go and leave it in a pew of the nearest church. That'll give them some fodder for their next sermon," Elbert said and nudged her with his elbow.

"Oh, my," Hester said. "What is that man wearing?"

They turned to look at a heavy-set, bearded man, pompously parading through the room.

"It's a life jacket," Lord Fatlip said. "He thinks we'll be torpedoed while we're enjoying dinner. I certainly hope he's wrong. The ox tongue is divine."

Hester shook her head. "The *Lusy* is the fastest cruise ship in the world — a 'greyhound' or so I'm told," she said. "We'll certainly be able to outrun any U-boats."

"But you can't see a U-boat," he said. "How can you outrun what you can't see?"

"I wouldn't put it past the British government to set us up," Elbert grumbled. "They're desperate for the United States to enter the war."

Ellen spared no love for the Brits. What Irish person did? But even she didn't think they'd be capable of such cold-blooded calculations and she said as much.

"If the Huns take Britain, don't think Ireland won't be far behind," Lord Fatlip said pointedly.

Hester deliberately turned the conversation to the arts community that Elbert had founded, and soon Elbert was telling stories of artists and poets and such.

He even quoted a poet by the name of Walt Whitman – America's greatest poet, according to Elbert. In a sonorous voice he declaimed,

"Beat! beat! drums!—blow! bugles! blow!

Make no parley—stop for no expostulation,

Mind not the timid—mind not the weeper or prayer,

Mind not the old man beseeching the young man,

Let not the child's voice be heard, nor the mother's entreaties,

Make even the trestles to shake the dead where they lie awaiting the hearses,

So strong you thump O terrible drums—so loud you bugles blow."

When he was done, he looked around at their solemn faces. A woman at the table next to them clapped as if the talent show had already begun.

"A pacifist I take it," Lord Fatlip commented.

"Whitman had the misfortune to care for the wounded in our Civil War," Elbert said. "He knew the horrors of war. The pointlessness of it. And can you tell me what is the point of the war you people are currently beating drums for?"

"To keep the Kaiser out of our land," Lord Fatlip said.

"But why did they start the war to begin with?" Alice asked. She and her husband were of a similar mind when it came to war, women's rights, and just about everything else.

Lord Fatlip thought for a moment and then answered, "Aggression. Pure aggression."

"And there you go," Elbert said, dropping his fork on the table in triumph as if his point had been proven and could not be disputed.

After dinner, Hester and Ellen strolled the deck.

Ellen thought back to the day before she'd left New York. She'd been at her rooming house, packing the trunk that Louisa had given her for the journey to see her dying father when Hester appeared in her doorway, waving a ticket.

"I'm going with you," she said.

"Nay, y'are not," Ellen said, hands on hips.

"Indeed, I am. I've got a first-class cabin so you can take your ticket and go get your money back. You'll be traveling with me," Hester said, entering the room and shutting the door behind her.

"What? As your maid? I've done that job before. No thank you," she said.

"I'm too modern to have a lady's maid. You'll come as my hired companion," Hester said.

"Hired companion, you say? I thought only old ladies needed 'companions,'" Ellen said, skeptically. She folded a wool sweater and placed it in her suitcase.

"It doesn't matter. I'll pay you more than Louisa does."

"You won't pay me a cent," Ellen said. Against her will, she was already beginning to like the idea of traveling with Hester. "You know if someone suspects the truth, it won't be good for your reputation. That's what Louisa would say."

"My reputation?" Hester laughed. "Are you worried no man will propose to me if people know about us?"

"Well...," Ellen said, but Hester had already stepped in close, wrapped her arms around her, kissed her deeply, passionately, and before she knew it they landed on the bed and were fumbling their way out of their clothes.

Standing on the deck as the sun set, Ellen let the backs of her fingers brush against Hester's sleeve.

"I'm balmy that you came with me," Ellen said.

"I am, too. I do wish I could come with you to Ireland and meet your parents," Hester said.

"'Twouldn't be right," Ellen said. "What with Da's sickness." She didn't mention that she worried she wouldn't be able to hide their true relationship from her big-nosed mother, who had never understood why she had deserted a potential husband and made her way to America.

"I understand. You must make amends. You must heal the rift with him before he dies," Hester said. "I'll make myself useful in London. Maybe I'll go work in a munitions factory."

Ellen scoffed at the preposterous idea. Gray waves jostled gently below them. The western horizon was shrouded in a thin lace of cloud, creating a flaming red sunset.

"You know what your countryman said about sunsets, don't you?"

"Which countryman?" Ellen asked.

"Oscar Wilde," Hester said and paused. "Overdone."

"Overdone?" Ellen said in astonishment. Then she looked at the sky, which clearly did appear to be showing off, and laughed. "Leave it to an Irishman."

"Are you coming to the talent show?" a man's voice asked.

They turned to see Elbert and Alice walking toward them.

"On our last night, must we endure terrible piano playing and ridiculous magic tricks?" Hester laughed.

"Last night, indeed," Elbert said and glanced at his wife for a sober minute, and they all thought the thing that no one was saying: it might be their last night of living. They were close to Ireland and it was said that U-boats patrolled the waters of the Irish Sea. Ellen glanced at the row of sturdy lifeboats along the ship's side, swung out in preparation for disaster. They looked seaworthy enough. She hoped she wouldn't have to find out.

"Funny," she said. "When we first boarded the boat, no one seemed the least bit concerned about that ad from the German Embassy, but now that we're getting close, people are getting all moidered."

"All what?" Elbert asked.

"That's Irish lingo for worried and confused," Hester explained.

"I suggest we go get snockered," Alice said. "That's my lingo for a good time."

The talent show took place in the dining room, and once again the British aristocrat joined their party of four. This time they were also joined by an American theater manager who wanted to chat with Elbert about books in between numbers, but no matter where the conversation started, it somehow always wound back to the topic of submarines and torpedoes and how cold the waters of the Atlantic must be.

"After all the stars I've managed, submarines only make me smile," the theater manager said drolly.

"You may be smiling, Mr. Forman," Hester said. "But I have no wish to encounter a torpedo."

"Here! Here!" Lord Fatlip said, raising his glass.

When the ship's burly captain took the stage during intermission, he had the rapt attention of his nervous audience.

"Tomorrow we will enter the 'zone of war,' and we have received word of recent submarine activity off the coast of Ireland," he said gravely. He had a clean-shaven face with a large nose and eyes as hard as granite. "There is no cause for alarm, however. As soon as we enter the war zone, we will be under the protection of the Royal Navy. The greatest navy in the world."

He had the look of a man who feared absolutely nothing, and his imposing presence in itself was somewhat reassuring, but Ellen could not shake the foreboding she felt. Worse than dying in the cold Atlantic waters was the thought that she might not see her father before his death. More than anything else in the world, she wanted to look on her father one last time and see pride in his eyes.

The talent show continued, but it met with subdued applause. People were frightened, but what could they do? There was no turning back now. Some of the passengers said they planned to sleep in the lifeboats, but most went back to their cabins for an uneasy night's sleep. Ellen's thoughts wandered from one worry to the next: her da's impending death, the coming separation from Hester, and the fact that somewhere in those dark waters lurked malevolent machines, built for the sole purpose of destroying lives.

Chapter 7
Louisa

Today was the day, Louisa thought, as she tried to tame the beast that was her hair and force it into submission. In Europe, thanks to the war, women were cutting their hair, and she hoped it would start a trend here as well. She would give Virgil Thorn her notice, and tonight she would tell Forrest Calloway that she would be his wife — Mrs. Forrest Calloway. She'd have to get new initials embroidered or engraved on everything from handkerchiefs to silverware. She realized she didn't relish the idea of giving up her name. Her father's name, rather. It was her last connection to him.

The memory of the dead horses invaded her ruminations. She shuddered involuntarily. Those poor creatures. The ginger cat leapt onto her vanity and settled on its haunches among the silver-handled brushes, combs and perfume decanters. Louisa slipped into a green linen dress that complimented her slender figure and chose a wide-brimmed hat with a froth of white lace and feathers on top. Pretty but professional. That was the look she needed today.

"Good morning," she said to Suzie as she entered the small dining room and poured herself a cup of coffee.

"Morning," Suzie answered. She was reading a copy of *The Amsterdam News*, which she'd had to explain to Louisa was not about the city of Amsterdam at all, but was a New York newspaper for Negroes. Louisa wondered why Negroes needed a separate newspaper, but after reading a few editions herself, she realized they covered a fascinating world that newspapers like *The Ledger, The Times,* and *The Herald* largely ignored.

"What's new in our world of Harlem?"

"Colored people from the south keep moving in," Suzie said, folding the paper shut. "You hungry? I got some corn flakes."

"No, just coffee," Louisa said, sitting down with her cup.

Pansy came in, humming a song.

"Good morning, Miss Louisa," she said.

"Good morning, Pansy," Louisa said. She couldn't help but smile every time she saw Pansy. So young and untarnished. "How was the picture show last night?"

"Oh, the movie was terrific. It was called *The Carpet from Bagdad*, and it was about these criminals right here in New York City who steal a carpet and then try to sell it to this antiques dealer, and then the man in charge of taking care of the carpet comes after this woman named Fortune and..."

"Pansy, take a breath. You don't need to tell us the whole story," Suzie said.

"Sorry," Pansy said.

"It sounds like a fascinating story," Louisa said. "Well, I'm off to work. I'll be home early to change because I'll be having dinner with Mr. Calloway at Delmonico's and then it's off to the opera with Count von Bernstorff and his wife."

"Dinner at Delmonico's? Does that mean what I think it means?" Suzie asked.

"It does. It means big changes. For all of us," Louisa said.

"What kind of changes?" Pansy asked.

"Never you mind," Suzie said.

"I'm going to have big changes," Pansy said. "I'm going to be in the motion pictures someday."

"How often do you see colored girls in the motion pictures?" Suzie asked.

"I'll be the first," Pansy said.

Louisa and Suzie exchanged a glance while Pansy cleared off the table, humming and lost in her thoughts of cinematic adventures.

***

The rocking motion of the subway car soothed her. She rather enjoyed the proximity of ordinary people. If her father hadn't lost his fortune when she was twelve, she'd never have been exposed to this other world. She would have lived in that sequestered butterfly cage where the women about whom she wrote existed.

She got out at her stop and climbed the steps to the streets. The first thing she would do when she got in the newsroom would be to go to Virgil Thorn's office and inform him that she'd be relinquishing her duties as the newspaper's society writer. She also needed to pay more attention to Phyllis today. She'd been giving her mainly clerical tasks this week, but now it was time to train her, especially as she might be the new society editor for *The Ledger*. She would have to make sure that Thorn kept Ellen on though perhaps she wouldn't want to stay if Louisa was no longer there.

Louisa placed her hat on the rack in the corner near her desk, patted her hair into place and then strode directly to Thorn's office. He was bent over, marking up a large dummy of the Sunday edition of the paper. Fridays were always frenetic in the newsroom.

"Good morning," Louisa said.

Thorn merely grunted.

"Could we have a quick chat?" Louisa asked.

He glanced up at her, his eyes gray as storm clouds. Virgil Thorn was no softie. Everything about him was angled and severe. He'd come from Fleet Street in London and was as hard-nosed a newsman as one would likely come across.

"Can it wait?" he asked.

"Certainly," she said.

"Come back after I've put the Sunday biz to bed," he said. "About three."

As Louisa walked through the newsroom, she glanced over at the bank of windows across the front of the building. A seagull flew past, and she stopped to watch it. Usually the only birds one saw around there were pigeons. She thought of Ellen and wondered what the voyage had been like and if they had reached Liverpool yet. Fortunately, she'd be in Ireland soon safely away from the war, and Louisa could stop worrying about her.

Chapter 8
Ellen

Morning fog shrouded the ship as Ellen wrapped her arms around Hester's sleeping body and reveled in her lover's warmth. What a marvel this thing between two people, skin touching, the salt taste of flesh on the tongue, breaths comingling like cream in coffee. Hester's chest rose as she made a sleepy moan; then she rolled over to face Ellen. Their mouths were inches apart. They kissed, tongues touching, exploring.

Far below them the steady hum of the ship's engine rooms. A foghorn sounded in the distance.

"That's Ireland, welcoming you home," Hester said, smiling.

"Oh yes, I'm Queen Mab, you know. Queen Mab of Ireland," Ellen said with a laugh.

"You're my queen," Hester said as her fingers drifted down the pale landscape of Ellen's torso and gently brushed the soft red hairs below.

They spent the morning in bed, dozing, making love, dozing again. It would be their last morning together for who knew how long. Ellen did not know how much time she would need to be with her family as her father made his leave-taking. And if the war got worse, would they even be able to get back?

They weren't far from Liverpool now. Ellen pushed up on her hands and looked through the porthole. The thick fog from earlier was slowly dissipating. The Irish Sea lay like a sheet of blue glass surrounding the ship, a few gentle swells nosing against the boat. When she was younger, she had worked at the Salthill resort on the Irish coast during the summers. She and a few friends had taken to swimming in the cold waters after work. It was a happy memory, one she welcomed right now as she would soon face her father's imminent death.

Eventually, they rose and dressed for lunch. Hester didn't have a Gibson girl figure, lustrous hair, or delicate features. She had large, protruding eyes and a rather toothy smile. But to Ellen she was lovely, and she looked especially appealing in the pink cotton dress and matching straw hat she donned for their last day.

Like her father, Ellen hadn't cared much for the moneyed classes – until Hester had defied all her preconceived notions.

Ellen put on her comfortable, plain brown traveling dress. After they reached Liverpool, she'd be on her way home where fancy clothes would be likened to "putting on airs." They made their way to the dining room for lunch. Elbert and Alice were nowhere to be seen, and so they sat by themselves. The mood in the Saloon Dining room was lighter than the night before. A beautiful French actress, surrounded by admirers, laughed gaily. Alfred or Albert Vanderbilt – Ellen could never remember his exact name though she knew he was quite famous – held court at another table with his own set of admirers. A pretty little girl about 11 or 12 years old smiled at Ellen from the table next to them. Everyone seemed giddy with relief to be so close to their destination.

After lunch Ellen found Mrs. McNabb sitting in the lounge downstairs with one of the young mothers.

"I've come to say I hope I'll be seeing you on the boat out of Liverpool," Ellen said to her.

"Of course, you will. And won't your da be proud when he sees you?" Mrs. McNabb said with beaming blue eyes. "You're a feisty one. Pure Irish, you are."

Ellen bade her good-bye, then headed up to the Promenade Deck to look for Hester. She strode along the planks of the Observation Corridor, past the lifeboats. Steam poured out of the four funnels, painted gray to fool the Germans — an idea she found absurd for how could you hide a vessel full of mansions even with the mandatory blackouts. The sun stood high in the sky, radiating a warm white light across the calm water. She walked along the starboard side past the mustached stewards in their jumpers and the old men playing shuffleboard and found a spot toward the front of the ship by the railing. The salt-laden breeze tugged her hair from its pins. A crewman sat perched above them as a lookout.

The trip had been perfect in many ways, she reflected. The silk cocoon of Hester's wealth may have been an uneasy fit, but Hester's presence in that cocoon made it more than bearable. From one of the lower decks, she heard women singing "God Save Ireland," and she smiled. Tickling strands of hair whipped against her cheeks as she looked out at the vast blue. And then she saw what looked like a chimney in the water. She put a hand over her brow and peered at it. A woman beside her gasped, and the crewman above yelled, "Torpedo on the starboard side."

More gasps, and "ohs" and "dear Gods" shot through the air as a cylindrical shadow a few feet under the water silently rushed toward them.

The thud of impact shook the boat so hard that the young man on watch fell from his perch above them to the deck below. His cap skittered into the water, revealing blond hair almost gold in the sunlight. A tower of water spewed into the air through the funnels and sprayed the decks with debris and coal dust. Ellen grasped the rail tightly as her knees buckled. Gasps turned to screams, screams to wails, a terrifying *BOOM* came from below, and then pandemonium as passengers rushed onto the decks.

Ellen looked around. She had to find Hester. She had to get Hester onto a lifeboat. No one had discussed the details of what to do in case they were hit. Now it must be figured out. *She* must figure it out. She pushed her way past frantic women and men, past crew members shouting confused orders, and the crowds all grabbing life belts. She managed to tug a life belt out of an officious crewman's hands.

"Stay calm," the crewman barked.

Ellen wasn't sure if Hester could swim, but she would make sure Hester had a life belt no matter what. If only she could find her. Only action.

She searched the deck, leapt along the stairs to the first-class lounge, and pushed her way through the throngs. The lounge had emptied out by now. She stumbled as the ship listed to one side. Broken plates, food, and glasses littered the floors. Flowers. A child's shoe. A woman's beaded handbag. The lights flickered off. She rushed back to the deck. Hester must be frightened, she thought. Then a memory of Hester during a melée at the Women's March in Washington, kicking the heckling men with her expensive Louis XIV heels flashed in her head. Hester had courage aplenty.

"Ellen!" She heard Hester's voice calling, but couldn't see her.

"Here! I'm here!" she yelled. Other voices were also yelling names.

"Where?"

"This way!" Ellen pushed through passengers milling about on the deck in confusion.

By call and response, they finally found each other. Hester's eyes were wild with terror.

"Oh my God, I thought I'd lost you," she said and grabbed Ellen by the arms.

"Put this on," Ellen said and thrust the life belt over Hester's head. Hester pulled the straps tight with shaking hands, and Ellen helped her buckle them.

"Where is yours?" Hester asked.

"I've swum this water plenty," Ellen said with false bravado. "I'll be fine."

"For God's sake, don't be stupid," Hester said. "Let's find one for you. I can't lose you, do you understand?"

Ellen's breath caught. She knew Hester loved her, but she had not really fathomed the depth of that love.

Not until this very moment — the two of them clasping hands, staring at each other. The hell with what other people might think. Ellen kissed Hester full on the lips.

Then she said, "Let's go."

They made their way through the swarming passengers to the steward handing out life belts, but he was empty handed by now.

"There's one," Hester said, pointing to a bedraggled but viable belt on the deck that had been trampled by the panicked passengers. Ellen snatched it up and put it on.

"This way!" a man bellowed. "Women and children! This way!"

"Don't go to the port side!" someone else yelled. "They can't lower the lifeboats."

They couldn't lower the lifeboats? What a shambles, Ellen thought, as she and Hester were herded toward a lifeboat on the starboard side. Children around them whimpered. Frightened mothers tried their best to comfort them. An officer shouted orders to the sailors, who were manning the pulleys for the lifeboats. Men kissed their wives and told them they would find them later. A woman in front of them held a tiny baby and looked around frantically.

"Jenny! Where's my Jenny?" the woman screamed.

Ellen scanned the deck. She did not see a lone girl nearby. The British aristocrat, Lord Fatlip, ran past, carrying a pair of bedraggled children to the front of the line for the next boat. As soon as he had deposited the two children, he went back for more. Steerage children, Ellen noted, grateful that he did not pay heed to the class of the children.

They finally reached the lifeboat, and the muscled arms of a sailor lifted Hester in. There was room for only one more. The sailor held out his hand for Ellen. She grasped it and was about to hoist herself into the boat when a child's voice cried out behind her.

"Ma!"

"Jenny!" the mother, who was already in the boat, called, reaching out with her free arm. The baby in her other arm stared round-eyed at all the confusion.

"Ellen, get in!" Hester called.

Ellen turned and saw a girl of about eight, tears smeared across her face, a lopsided white bow in her hair. Ellen took one more look at Hester's worried face and then slipped back down to the deck, lifted the girl in her arms and handed her over to the crewman.

"That's all for this one," he yelled. The men lowered the lifeboat from the chocks.

"Let me out!" Hester called in alarm. "Ellen, wait!"

"Go," Ellen said. "I'll get the next one. I'll find you. I promise."

She watched as the small boat swayed precariously. As the stokers lowered it, the tackle in the front became tangled. The boat jerked, and the passengers screamed in terror. Then one of the stokers took an axe and swung it, cutting the rope. Before Ellen's horrified eyes, the lifeboat nose-dived, spilling the occupants into the freezing water below: the mother clinging to the baby, the little girl with the lop-sided bow and Hester, her hands reaching toward the sky. Hester's pink straw hat caught a draft and twirled upward toward the sky.

Ellen's head filled with the sound of her own screams.

Chapter 9

Louisa

She returned to her desk and checked her calendar, remembering the German count's invitation. She thought of Captain Tunney telling her something about a German who frequented society events. In spite of what Forrest had said about Count von Bernstorff at the baseball game, she couldn't imagine that fatuous man with his curlicue mustache as a spy.

Phyllis Wolfe showed up at her desk. Again, Louisa was struck by the young woman's sartorial sense. She wore a navy suit with white piping and a smart navy hat with a single feather. She not only dressed well, she carried herself with a certain fearlessness and an upward tilt of the chin that would be useful when dealing with the New York aristocracy.

"Good morning," the young woman said with a bright smile. "I hope I'm on time."

"You are, indeed," Louisa said.

The two women sat at Louisa's desk and went over the schedule for the following week.

"The season is over now, as you know. But there will still be some charity events, a few weddings and that sort of thing in town," Louisa explained. "During the summer I go to Newport regularly. And Saratoga two or three times. There will be some events on Long Island. The Morgans have a bash around Independence Day. I haven't been to it, but I hear it's fun."

"I'd be more than happy to go out of town if you needed me to cover anything," Phyllis said.

"That might be possible," Louisa said. She couldn't breathe a word of the opportunity Phyllis might soon have before she had told Thorn, so she changed course. "Let's have lunch at the Empire Room in the Waldorf-Astoria. I'll introduce you to Oscar, the *maitre d'*. It's important he knows who you are because you can't even get in at night unless he gives you the nod," Louisa said. If Phyllis was going to take over as society writer, she would need to know who really ran things.

***

Louisa had a meager expense account thanks to the syndicate, but most of the finer establishments gave her a steep discount for the frequent mentions in her columns. It wasn't entirely ethical, but Louisa had long ago decided that if she wanted to do her job properly she must not pay too close attention to scruples. Phyllis, of course, did not know these details as she scrutinized the menu, but she would learn.

"It's a bit out of my price range," Phyllis said.

"Not to worry. It's on me," Louisa said. "Or I should say, on the syndicate. We must be seen at the best places."

"Well, if that's the case, let's have the Beluga caviar," Phyllis said. The caviar was 75 cents, the priciest appetizer on the menu. Louisa hesitated only a moment before agreeing.

"Excellent idea," she said.

Over the caviar they decided on a lettuce and grapefruit salad for Louisa, an endive salad for Phyllis, iced coffees, and macaroons for dessert. Phyllis seemed as fond of culinary pleasures as Louisa, and Louisa enjoyed the younger woman's company. They had both been born into wealth, and they had both lost that exalted status. They were both inside and outside society.

"Miss Delafield," Phyllis began.

"Oh please, call me Louisa," Louisa said. "At least when it's just the two of us. I find it odd when people constantly refer to each other by their surnames. The women in our mother's generation might as well not have had first names. Even their husbands called them by Mrs. Such and Such." She paused and then whispered, with a sly look, "I wonder if they did that *all* the time."

She suppressed a grin, and Phyllis clapped a hand over her mouth.

"Louisa," she whispered. "You naughty thing."

Louisa suppressed a giggle.

Their salads arrived and they regained their decorum.

"How did you become a society writer?" Phyllis asked.

Louisa sighed. She held the linen napkin and thought of her childhood: the formal dinners at their grand house which her parents occasionally let her join, servants busily bringing in food, removing dishes, pouring wine into her parents' glasses. That was to be her life when she grew up.

"I was twelve when my father died and we lost our fortune. I got through college at Barnard on scholarships where I majored in English, but I didn't want to be a teacher. I wanted to be in the world I had been born to. Writing about society was the only way I could see to do it. I loved writing, but the pay was terrible. We were poor as church mice until I got the syndicated column. We almost lost our house at one point."

"How dreadful," Phyllis said. She leaned over and put her hand on Louisa's wrist. "I'm so sorry you lost your father." The fact he had been murdered was unspoken. Everyone knew about it. If he'd simply died, it would not have been nearly so scandalous.

"You know how unforgiving the New York aristocracy can be. However, there are advantages. I'm not expected to live up to the impossible standards they set. Neither are you now. And yet we know their ways, and if they want their names in the paper, which they all do, then they must put on their best face and invite us into their circle on a regular basis."

While they ate their desserts, Louisa and Phyllis talked about the racing scene in Saratoga and the field in the upcoming Kentucky Derby.

"I'm placing a bet on the chestnut filly to win this year," Phyllis said.

"I'm not a gambler," Louisa said. "But I do hope Regret leaves the boys in the dust. She'd be the first filly ever to win the Derby."

Unbidden came the memory of the dead mare at the pier, but Louisa erased the image from her mind. After all, what could she possibly do?

Chapter 10

Ellen

The last thing Ellen saw as the lifeboat plunged into the water was the white bow in the girl's hair as she sank into the depths right behind Hester. Ellen clung to the railing, watching, her mouth open in a silent scream, but no one rose to the surface. She waited, hoping, praying, but the water had swallowed them. They were gone. Just like that.

Ellen sank to her knees clinging to the railing posts and stared at the sea. She'd given her seat up for a little girl who was dead now because of it. Everything went dark. She wanted to let herself fall into the water so she could die with Hester, but the life force was too strong. She couldn't will her hands to release the railings.

Some unforgiveable part of her would keep her alive come hell or high water, and the high water was on its way.

"Help!" someone screamed. It sounded like Mrs. McNabb.

She rose from her knees and stared at the pandemonium around her.

The prow of the *Lusitania* sank incredibly fast, and the slant of the deck made staying upright close to impossible. Everything was off balance. As the ship leaned toward the water, people dropped off the side either intentionally or not. An old man in a straw boater rushed to the rail and threw himself overboard.

"No need to panic!" a steward yelled. "She'll float for at least an hour."

Ellen didn't believe him. This ship was going down fast. She pulled herself along the deck, feet scrambling on the slick surface. Among the hordes clamoring for the remaining lifeboats, Mrs. McNabb stood, mouth agape, wailing. Her grandson was nowhere to be seen. A sense of calm descended upon Ellen. For a moment she could hear her own heartbeat. She would grieve later. Now she must act.

She pushed through the crowd to Mrs. McNabb, who was at this point turning around in a circle, calling out, "Seamus! Where are ya?"

Ellen put an arm around the older woman and said, "Come, let's get you on a lifeboat, Mrs. McNabb."

"But what about my boy, my Seamus?" she asked.

"Where did you last see him?" Ellen asked.

"In the bunks below," she said. "But he weren't there when I just looked."

Ellen glanced around, wondering where a boy might be in a time like this. He wouldn't have stayed below, not if she knew boys, which as a sister of three of them, she did.

"We're going to get you on this boat here," Ellen said, pointing to one of the lifeboats. "And then I'll look for him. We'll find you once we're all safe on land."

She spoke in a strong and assured voice, and Mrs. McNabb allowed Ellen to lead her to the group of terrified but oddly calm passengers, waiting to get on the next lifeboat.

"His name is Seamus O'Reilly," Mrs. McNabb said, weeping as she got on the boat.

Ellen hoped this one would make it to the water without mishap. Then she turned, and ran up the stairs.

She stood for a moment, catching her breath. A boy, she thought, would want to be where the excitement was. A boy would want to go where he could not go before. She reached the uppermost regions of the ship, found the bridge, and looked inside the room. She saw the great wheel of the ship, unmoving, and a row of windows looking out toward the fast-encroaching sea. No boy. Instead, she saw the square shoulders of the captain as he looked forward like a stone statue. She didn't know whether he was in any way to blame for this, but a flame of anger burst in her nevertheless. Then it was quickly extinguished by pity. This stoic man had lost everything.

"You'd better get on a boat, Captain," she said, but he didn't move.

She left him there and looked over the railing at the business end of the deck — the area where passengers weren't allowed. It was all giant spools and ropes and chains as big around as a man's arm — now deserted except for one lone figure staring, transfixed, as the prow nosed into the water.

"Seamus O'Reilly!" she yelled.

He turned and saw her. She realized she must keep the panic out of her voice.

"Come with me," she called calmly. "I've found your grandmother. She's waiting for you." She stumbled down the steps from the bridge and took his moist hand.

The nose of the ship was completely underwater now, the sea swallowing the ship like Leviathan taking in a minnow. She hurried him to the deck where the lifeboats were, but before they could reach it, the last boat dropped into the water with a splash.

A few life rafts floated on the surface. Two crewmen in the water appeared to be helping people into them. A man and a child clung to an upside-down lifeboat. The shadow of the four funnels drifted over the people in the water below as the ship listed.

"Seamus, can you swim?" she asked.

The boy shook his head. She unbuckled her life vest and took it off. He allowed her to pull it over his head. She stood wide-legged on the tilting deck, so she wouldn't slide off. Her hands shook as she buckled the straps.

"There now," she said. "We're jumping in the water, see, and then getting on to one of those rafts."

The boy looked over the side of the boat, blanched, and shook his head.

"I'm na going in there," he said.

"Sure you are. A big boy like yourself. You can't be scared."

"I'm going down with the ship," he said stubbornly. "Like the captain."

"All right. I understand," she said. "But I'm going to jump in. Will you give me a hug around the neck. I'm a might scared."

He reached his arms around her neck. The scent of sweat and fear covered the both of them. She clutched him tightly and then leapt overboard with the boy in her arms. Together they plunged into the icy Irish Sea.

The cold water stunned her. Every nerve ending in her body screamed in shock, and she couldn't hear anything except a wild rushing sound in her head until she bobbed back to the surface. The boy had been ripped from her grip, but there he was, crying and shivering in his life vest, his head above water.

"Move your legs like you're running," she called to him. "This way."

The boy obeyed her and slowly they propelled themselves forward. Moving was good, she thought. The blood in her veins hadn't turned to ice — yet. A man clinging to a deck chair cried out, "Darling, where are you?" The blue body of an infant floated nearby. She turned her eyes from it and headed toward a raft, tugging the boy with her.

The same blond crewman who had fallen from the mast when the torpedo hit was treading water near the raft and beckoned to them. She pushed the boy toward him. The young crewman grabbed hold of the life belt and hauled the boy to the side of the raft. Ellen swam up behind them, and together they shoved the boy into it.

The crewman spit some water from his mouth and said, "You, too, Miss."

She didn't argue. She looped her arms over the side of the raft and with the crewman's help, she hoisted herself up over the edge and landed on the wet surface next to the boy. Their eyes met. He was no longer crying.

"You all right?" she asked.

He nodded.

"Good," she said and sat up in the raft.

The crewman found two more survivors nearby, and she helped him get them on board the wobbly raft. As soon as the raft was full, the crewman squeezed in. He pulled out the oars and handed one to Ellen.

"Paddle hard," he said to her. "Gotta get away from this ship! When she goes down, she'll take whatever's near with her."

The two of them paddled hard past pieces of luggage bobbing in the waves. The bodies of the dead floated around them, some of them face down but most of them face up, staring at the sky. Cries of "Help!" and "Save me!" sounded all around.

"Where's my grandma?" Seamus asked.

"She's in one of the lifeboats," Ellen said, still rowing the small raft. Those on the lifeboats were also laboriously rowing away from the sinking ship. When she could row no longer, Ellen turned and watched as the grand vessel disappeared. The rear of the boat heeled up in the air spilling luggage and deck furniture into the water. As it went down, a foamy vortex surrounded the dying vessel. The tip of the flag pole with the British flag on the aft end of the boat was the last thing they saw. It had happened so quickly, less than half an hour she estimated from the time the torpedo hit till the time the ship disappeared below the surface. So much death in such a short period of time.

They floated on a sea as smooth as glass, squashed together on the rubbery raft. Her damp clothes clung to her, and she shivered. Seamus snuggled close to her. Fortunately, there were no clouds in the sky, and the sun slowly dried them off and warmed them. In the distance, the lighthouse on the cliffs of Kinsale was visible — for all the good it did them. They sat helplessly on their raft, surrounded by the piteous cries of the barely living, the silence of the newly dead, and the screeching seagulls, diving down to peck at unseeing eyes.

Something pink, about the size of a small duck, floated nearby. She reached out with the oar and scooped it up.

"What's that?" Seamus asked.

"A hat," she whispered, clutching Hester's straw hat to her heart.

Chapter 11

Louisa

Louisa led Phyllis down to the newspaper morgue in the basement. The room held the musty smell of old newsprint.

“This is where we bury the bodies of dead stories,” Louisa said, waving her hand at the room full of filing cabinets and shelves of large bound books. “The books contain the older stories. Clips from the past five years are kept in these files.”

“Will I need to come to this graveyard often?” Phyllis asked with a laugh.

“Occasionally. Sometimes an older story helps jog my memory about some event that I need to recall. I go to so many things – balls, luncheons, debutante parties

— that I forget who I am, much less who hosted what," she said, opening one of the cabinet drawers marked Society. "Ellen often finds old stories down here to repurpose for the syndicate."

"Explain to me the difference between your local column and the syndicated column," Phyllis said.

Louisa pulled out one of her columns that described a recent debutante luncheon and said, "For my columns in *The Ledger,* I don't need to impart any lessons. My New York readers will know who's who and what's what."

Then she found a longer piece that had been published by the syndicate.

"My syndicated column is weekly. I draw on what's been happening, making sure to include tidbits about fashion, manners, decorating, and so on. Sometimes I even sneak a little propaganda in there," she said conspiratorially.

"Propaganda?" Phyllis asked.

"Well, as you know, many of our grand ladies are reformers. So if they've had a benefit for women's suffrage, for example, I'll include a few facts about the issue for the less enlightened women in the hinterlands."

"And therefore, you're spreading the message of the suffragists across the land. I see," Phyllis said with a knowing smile. "Very clever, Miss Delafield."

They left the morgue and went upstairs to the newsroom where Louisa identified the different sections of the paper by desk cluster.

"*The Ledger* is mostly a business paper," Louisa said. "So that's the biggest section, of course. But we have a crime reporter, whom you've already had the dubious pleasure of meeting."

"Mr. Stephens, I presume," Phyllis said.

"Correct," Louisa said and then led Phyllis over to a small room in the corner. "In here you'll find the teletype machines. This is how we get the bulletins from the wire service."

"News from around the world?" Phyllis asked.

"Sometimes. Usually it's boring stuff like the daily agriculture report," Louisa said lifting the pages from the machine. She held up one of the sheets and skimmed it, then added, "Or something thoroughly incomprehensible such as the situation between China and Japan."

"Sounds scintillating," Phyllis said.

Louisa pointed to some cubbyholes against the wall.

"You can always make yourself useful by checking the bulletins and delivering them to the in-boxes of the appropriate department. There's a boy who's supposed to do it, but he's often out running errands."

The machine startled both of them by ringing loudly, and clattering violently as a sheet of paper emerged from its mouth. Louisa picked it up and quickly perused it. Then her eyes lost focus. The room felt cold and slowly spun around her.

"Louisa, are you all right?" Phyllis asked, stepping closer to her.

Eyes fixated on the sheet in her trembling hand, Louisa whispered, "The *Lusitania* has been torpedoed."

```
DAY LOCAL 20, --
B U L L E T I N    E O S
WASHINGTON MAY 7,-- (Lusitania) News of
the torpedoing of the Lusitania struck
official Washington like a bomb. While
disposed to await full details before
expressing opinions, all administration
officials realized that the incident was
probably the most serious Washington has
faced since the beginning of the war.
--aj--A209 PM--
```

Chapter 12

Ellen

Under a dark sky, the trawler Blue Bell, which had rescued the people on the raft bearing Ellen and Seamus, brought its cargo to land: exhausted, thirsty, and grieving. War raged in Europe, and now bodies littered the shore on the southern coast of Ireland.

Ellen clutched the woolen blanket wrapped around her with one hand and the boy's cold hand with the other as they staggered onto the quay. On her head the pink straw hat sat incongruously. They were surrounded by bedraggled survivors and townspeople who had come to help. A scroungy dock dog barked at them. Stout old women wrapped in scarves clucked like worried hens. "Poor things," they whispered. A plaintive child's voice called out, "Mama! Mama!" But there was no mother's voice to answer her. Some of the sodden passengers had to be brought off the boats on stretchers. The quiet, cordial fishermen dropped off their load and went back out again.

Town officials directed the survivors to hotels where rooms were ready and waiting.

"Is this your son?" a man in a suit asked her.

Ellen shook her head, no.

"His name is Seamus O'Reilly," she said. "His grandmother, Mrs. McNabb, was on one of the lifeboats."

"Then you'll go to the Rob Roy, and we'll house him with one of the families that's volunteered to help out."

"The boy stays with me until we find his gran," Ellen said, her hand locked onto Seamus so hard her knuckles ached.

"I'm afraid that's not how we..." The man was interrupted by a woman's firm voice.

"That's fine, dearies. The both of you are welcome in our house," the woman said, stepping in and putting an arm around Ellen, as a man in worker's clothing put his arm around the boy. They looked like decent enough folk with their plain manners and their plain clothes, and Ellen was too tired to question their offer. She allowed the woman to lead her down the street.

"Not much further," the woman said. "I've two boys of my own, but we've sent them to the neighbors. You'll sleep in their beds." The thought of a bed at the end of this journey gave Ellen the strength to stay on her feet, swollen and aching as they were in the water-logged leather shoes.

The couple took them to a modest but comfortable house a block away from the quay and showed them to a bedroom with a bed on either side of the room. A few books and toys were scattered about, but otherwise it was clean, and to Ellen the beds looked fit for royalty as she dropped the woolen blanket and sank down on the mattress.

"It's not as nice as the hotels but I hope you'll be comfortable," the woman said. The man stood at the woman's side, quietly observing them with moist eyes. Their rough-hewn kindness ravaged Ellen's poor heart, and she sighed deeply.

"I know it were awful," the woman said softly.

"But yer safe now," the husband added.

Without even taking off her dress, Ellen stretched out onto the bed and fell into a deep sleep.

Chapter 13

Louisa

As the day wore on, Louisa stifled the terror she felt and sent Phyllis scouring through the morgue for articles about Alfred Gwynne Vanderbilt. It was her job to prepare obituaries for the elite members of society who happened to be on board. A heartbreaking task, but it helped stave off the worry she felt for Ellen and Hester.

She'd been through this once before, when the Titanic sunk, but while some of those passengers were acquaintances, none were close friends. She cursed herself for letting Ellen get on board that ship after the warning from the German embassy, but how could she have possibly stopped her from going to see her dying father? And everyone said the *Lusitania*, was the safest ship in the world.

She pondered what to write about the 37-year-old Vanderbilt, a sportsman who was the very definition of "dashing." She'd met him several times over the years and written glowingly about his second wife, a divorcee, yes, but also a woman of intelligence and a keen sense of humor. Some members of society looked down their noses at her, but when one was as rich as Croesus, what did a few snubs matter? Alfred had inherited close to a hundred million dollars and so the two of them did as they pleased. She had parties. Alfred raced horses and cars. He even played a silly game in Britain that involved dressing up as a coachman and tearing around the countryside. He was affable and charming, and if one woman had committed suicide over him, that would not be mentioned in her story. *The Times*, on the other hand, would probably dredge up the whole sordid history.

With Phyllis's help, Louisa compiled short biographies of several eminent passengers on board — a noted philosopher, a playwright, an actress, as well as the inimitable Charles Frohman, who produced *Peter Pan* on Broadway. Then she got to Hester French, daughter of a wealthy Pittsburgh industrialist and sister to Katherine Murphy. Hester was becoming well known as a supporter of suffrage and an advocate for poor women. Not to mention, never to mention, Louisa thought, she was in love with a former lady's maid and Louisa's partner in investigative subterfuges, one Ellen Malloy. Louisa had once gone to a lecture by Havelock Ellis, who described people who loved members of their own sex as "sexual inverts." Others said it was a perversion. Louisa only knew that it was an excellent method for preventing unwanted pregnancies, something she had worried about with Forrest even though he took precautions.

"Phyllis, it looks like we won't be going to any events this weekend, after all," Louisa said. "Why don't you go home? I'll see you on Monday. If you want to, you can get some quotes about Saturday's Kentucky Derby."

"Please may I stay? I want to be useful," Phyllis said, but Louisa merely shook her head. She liked the young woman, but right now Phyllis was a distraction.

"All right," Phyllis said. "By the way, a courier just delivered a note for you."

Louisa opened the note. Count von Bernstorff regretted to inform her that due to the unfortunate incident in the Irish sea he would need to return to Washington tonight. He hoped she would forgive him, but he and his wife would not be going to the opera, after all. No, she thought, and neither would she, tossing the note into the trash and forgetting about it.

By the end of the day, Louisa felt scorched inside. Her jaw ached from grinding her teeth. Every time her mind strayed in the direction of Ellen's fate, she reined it back in. Now, staring at Hester's name on the manifest, she knew she must face the awful prospect.

The newsroom was packed with reporters on phones or reading and sending telegrams and generally milling around, discussing the crisis with a lurid sense of curiosity. Every time the teletype rang, they thronged around it. Thorn paced the room, giving orders to the political reporters to call officials, to business reporters to call company leaders, and to police reporters to check on possible outbreaks of unrest in the city. Then he turned and walked into his office and shut the door. She knocked on the closed door.

"Enter," he said.

She entered. He lifted his face from his hands and stared at her.

"Mr. Thorn?" she said and stepped closer. "Virgil?" She rarely called him by his first name but in this moment she approached him not as his reporter but as his friend. She'd never seen the unflappable editor anything but cool as cucumber salad. Now his eyes were frightened and his face livid.

"I keep wondering, where was the Admiralty?" he said. "They're supposed to protect ships in the war zone. Could they possibly have just let this happen? Are they that desperate to get America involved?"

He wasn't looking for a response. That much she knew. She waited for him to collect himself before speaking.

"What is it, Miss Delafield?" he asked.

"I'm going to see Katherine Murphy. She had a sister, Hester French, on board, and she must be worried sick," she told him.

"Many people have loved ones who are missing," he said.

"Hester was traveling with Ellen. I'll be back tonight."

Thorn rubbed his eyes and then said, "Of course. I forgot that your assistant was on the ship."

"She's also my friend," Louisa said. She went back to her desk, retrieved her hat, gloves, and bag and walked toward the elevator. Someone called her name.

"Delafield."

She turned. Billy Stephens stood a few feet away from her. Instead of his usual smirk, he was tight-lipped and ashen.

"I hope Miss Malloy is safe," he said.

The unexpected sympathy sliced through her shell like a blade. She blinked back the tears that had been waiting for just the right moment to burst out. She couldn't speak, so she nodded at him and walked on to the elevator.

Outside, the fading light of the spring day could not assuage the fear she felt. Tears ran in rivulets down her cheeks. She felt utterly broken. What would she do without Ellen?

"Stop it," she told herself and dug into her bag for a handkerchief. She dried her face and admonished herself to save her sorrow. She must pull herself together for Katherine Murphy's sake if not for her own.

It was near six o'clock and the sidewalks were filled with workers leaving offices and stores, and early birds heading out for dinner. Many of them would not know the news yet. She strode through Times Square and saw a rabble surrounding the public bulletin board. She knew what the bulletins said but still she drew near. In times like these, one wanted the company of others, she realized. Even strangers. A woman cried out in shock. A few men bristled, balled fists at their side. Most of the people looked around in stunned disbelief. She was about to walk away when a youngish man in a bowtie pushed his way through the crowd to read the bulletin.

"*Lusitania* torpedoed!" he cried, and then to the astonishment of those standing near him, he tossed his hat in the air and shouted, "Hurray for Germany!"

The surprised crowd looked at him, aghast. He didn't seem to notice. He chortled happily while New Yorkers around him stirred angrily.

"Shut your damn trap," a man in the flour-speckled apron of a baker bellowed. But the German man waved a dismissive hand at him. Violence brewed as the others in the crowd began circling him. Were it not for the arrival of a policeman who took the man by the arm and roughly escorted him away, he would surely have been beaten by the seething mob, eager for a scapegoat.

Louisa hailed a cab and gave the driver the address of the Murphy's Central Park Avenue apartment. Inside the luxurious pied á terre, she gave her card to the butler, who showed her into a drawing room, which had been decorated in the art nouveau style — sinuous lines and gilt flourishes, all the rage ten years ago. A moment later, Katherine's voice trilled in the hallway.

"Louisa Delafield, to what do I owe the pleasure?" she asked, beaming as she entered. Seeing Louisa's grim expression, she stopped short. "Oh dear. Something's happened, hasn't it?"

Louisa nodded.

"Let's sit, Mrs. Murphy," Louisa said, lowering herself to a nearby settee.

Katherine sputtered for a moment and said, "Of course. Where are my manners? Mrs. Hahn? Sherry, please." Katherine sat down next to Louisa and turned to face her. "From the look on your face I believe that sherry is more appropriate than tea."

Louisa steadied herself and then told her, "The Germans have torpedoed the *Lusitania*. There is no word of survivors yet."

The blood drained from Katherine's face. She was a short, stout woman who always seemed much larger than she was. She gathered her emotional forces and then called out, "John! John?"

Mrs. Hahn entered with a decanter of sherry on a silver tray and set it down. Louisa poured a glass for Katherine.

"Please find my husband," Katherine said to the maid. Her lower lip trembled, but she downed the glass of sherry in one gulp and then placed her hands in her lap to wait for her husband, who entered momentarily. He was a big man with the dark eyes and the thick scowling eyebrows of the Black Irish.

"The *Lusitania* has been sunk," Katherine informed him in a quavering voice, rising from her seat. "And there's no word of survivors."

When he saw the tears in his wife's eyes, he took her in his arms and whispered, "There, there, Mrs. Murphy. There, there."

"Why? Why would they kill innocent people?" Mrs. Murphy asked.

"The Germans have poked a sleeping tiger," John Murphy said. "We'll be in the war before we know it."

Louisa promised to keep them informed of any development. After she left the Murphy's home, she took a cab to her townhouse in Harlem. The residents of Harlem had been mostly Jewish when they'd moved there after her father's death. At the time the properties, which were far from the wealthy enclaves downtown, were reasonably priced, and they'd found a house that was larger than anything else they might have gotten. Now, more and more colored people from the south were moving in. The streets were livelier these days, and there was a new dialect. Living in New York was like living inside a kaleidoscope. Always changing. But tonight even the laughter ringing from the stoops couldn't alleviate her anxiety.

Inside the house, she glanced in the parlor and saw her mother dozing in her chair. Suzie stood up slowly.

"I thought you would be here earlier. Don't you have plans for dinner at Delmonico's?" Suzie asked, quietly so as not to rouse Anna.

Oh no, Louisa thought. She'd completely forgotten about her dinner with Forrest. This was the night that was supposed to have changed her life. Well, it was changed all right.

"You haven't heard," Louisa said. "The *Lusitania* was sunk today. By the Germans."

Suzie gasped. "Oh, dear Lord. Is Miss Malloy safe?"

"I don't know," Louisa said and stepped into Suzie's open arms.

They stood there, holding onto each other, for a long moment.

"I cannot stay," Louisa said, pulling away. "I expect we'll be at our typewriters all night."

"Eat first," Suzie said. "Then type."

Louisa nodded and followed Suzie to the kitchen.

She wondered if she should call Forrest and cancel their date, but she knew Thorn would have already contacted him to tell him about the Lusitania. As publisher he would have to be notified of a story this big. He would not expect her to go out and celebrate while this was going on. She was still a reporter, after all.

Chapter 14

Ellen

The next morning when her eyes blinked open, she had no idea where she was or what had happened. Her muscles ached as if she'd been trampled by horses, and the skin on her face, especially her lips, stung as if a swarm of bees had landed there. She rose up and saw her shoes and stockings on the floor and a clean dress and clean undergarments on the chair next to her. The other bed was empty. All in a rush, she remembered the events of the day before and felt a terrible pressure in her chest.

She got up and found a water closet just down the hallway where she undressed and tried to scrub the smell of sweat, salt, and terror from her skin. She would not think about Hester. Not yet, or she would surely dissolve into a puddle of screaming anguish. She put on the clean clothes and made her way to the kitchen where she found Seamus seated in front of a plate of eggs, sopping bread into the runny yolks.

"There's herself," the woman said. "Can I get ya somethin' to eat?"

"I've no stomach for it, I'm afraid," Ellen said. "Just some coffee, please. Thank you for your kindness. I don't believe I got your name last night."

"I'm Agnes Wright. My husband's Rob. He's out building coffins this morning," she said, her voice heavy with sadness.

"We should go find . . ." Ellen couldn't continue. Agnes set a mug of coffee in front of her and offered some cream.

"My gran," Seamus said, completing her thought.

"Yes, your gran. Finish up, and we'll go look for her, Seamus," Ellen said. She noticed he was also wearing clean clothes though the trousers and the shirt sleeves were a bit short on him. She turned to Agnes and said, "Thank you for the clothes. We'll return them as soon as we can."

"You'll do no such thing," Agnes said. "You've been through enough already."

Again the kindness made Ellen feel raw inside, as if her chest had been sliced open and her heart exposed. She drank her coffee quickly and stood.

"Come, Seamus," she said.

"Go to the hotels first," Agnes told her. "That's where they took most of the survivors. And God be with you."

"Thank you," Ellen said again. If she said the words a thousand times, it would not be enough.

"And don't forget this," Agnes said, holding out the pink hat.

Ellen put on the hat, dry and misshapen now, and left with Seamus in tow. At first he was quiet, but few things are more irrepressible than the spirit of a ten year old. Soon he was peppering her with questions and observations.

"I was born in America, so how can I also be Irish? Will the Americans punish the Germans now? How many torpedoes do you think hit the ship? I heard two explosions. Do you think my gran is looking for me? Maybe she thinks I'm dead. Maybe they'll have a funeral for me and they'll all be crying until I suddenly show up and say 'Here I am! No more crying for the poor wee boy.'" He laughed when he said this.

"Ah, Seamus, must you talk so much?" she asked.

She was so weary she wasn't sure how her feet were still moving. She could have slept for a month. They reached the row of hotels and saw dazed people milling about, all in misfitting or mismatched clothes.

"Has anyone seen my baby?" A tearful young woman pleaded to the crowd. "Curly hair and rosy cheeks."

"You might look in the Cunard sheds," an older man said to her. The woman ignored him and continued to implore the others, had they seen her child? She was not ready to search among the dead and probably never would be.

"Where was the British navy?" a woman with an aristocratic accent asked. "Weren't they supposed to protect us?"

Good question, Ellen thought.

She took Seamus by the hand and led him into the Rob Roy Hotel. It looked like the perfect seaside resort except instead of well-heeled travelers, the stunned survivors of the sunken ship gathered, asking questions of each other.

"How can I make a cable? I must let my parents know I'm safe."

"All our luggage and belongings — gone. What will we do?"

"Has anyone seen Mr. Vanderbilt? He saved my life."

"They're putting the Captain on trial, I heard. How can he be at fault?"

Ellen and Seamus wandered among the groups of people, but they found neither Mrs. McNabb nor Hester. A numb feeling inside her chest held Ellen's fears at bay.

"Let's go to the next hotel," she said. So they went to the next one and the next one and found much the same scene. They saw some passengers that Ellen recognized, but not the ones they were looking for. She stopped a Russian woman she remembered from the third-class ladies' lounge to ask if she'd seen Mrs. McNabb, but the woman shook her head and moaned.

"My husband? Have you seen my husband?" she asked in halting English.

"I'll keep my eyes open for him," Ellen said and led Seamus away. They must go to the quay now to look at the bodies, she decided. She wondered if she should leave the boy here, but no, she decided she could not do that. If his gran were dead, better that he know it now.

"We were brave, weren't we, Miss?" he asked. "We jumped into that water with all our clothes on. And we swam and swam. We must've swum for hours."

As he prattled on, they walked down the street to the Cunard sheds. Plain wooden coffins stretched out across the room with more being brought in through the back door. Agnes' husband was one of the men bringing in the coffins. They set them down, and then another two men would put a body inside. They left the covers off so the survivors could walk through. Fathers, mothers, relatives and friends slowly circulated through the room, looking down at the dead faces, occasionally crying out in recognition and heartbreak.

"Wait by the door where I can see you," Ellen said to Seamus. She approached the coffins and looked in the first one. The pale, bloated body of a woman clung to a dead infant.

"Mother Mary," she said, turning away from the sight. She continued on. What would she do if she found Hester, she wondered. Wouldn't the life jacket have kept her afloat? Had it somehow come off in the impact? Was she still floating somewhere, pulled into that endless horizon?

Ellen walked down the first row. When she reached the end of it, she gasped. In a small coffin, little Jenny lay, cold and blue and bedraggled, a white ribbon plastered along the side of her thin, dead face.

Ellen backed away from the sight, turned around quickly and bumped into someone in front of her. The woman looked up at her. It was Mrs. McNabb.

"Ellen!" the old woman cried and then she looked over Ellen's shoulder and saw Seamus, who had run over to them. She wept openly as she yanked him into her tight embrace. "Oh my boy. Oh my boy."

Then still holding tightly to Seamus, Mrs. McNabb drew Ellen into her arms.

"I thought ya were lost," the older woman said over and over.

"It's all right. Seamus is fine. Aren't you, boyeen?" Ellen said. Ellen was relieved to have found Mrs. McNabb but the warmth of their bodies could not thaw the icy rock in her chest.

"Come," Mrs. McNabb. "Let's celebrate finding each other."

Ellen shook her head and said, "I'll leave you two now that you've found each other. I've still got some searching to do."

Mrs. McNabb hugged her again and then took the boy away from the horror surrounding them. Ellen hoped he would forget this day, this hall of death, but she was not sure it would be possible.

She returned to the grim business of searching the coffins for the body of the woman she loved.

Chapter 15

Louisa

Louisa's eyes blinked open and focused on the Remington typewriter inches from her nose. She swallowed, lifted her head to peer around the newsroom while surreptitiously wiping the corner of her mouth. Apparently she wasn't the only one who had fallen asleep at her desk. Billy Stephens' brown fedora was tipped over his face, and his feet were propped on his desk. If she wasn't mistaken, he was snoring.

"Good morning, Miss Delafield," Thorn said. He stood over her desk and dropped the latest cable in front of her. She cleared her throat and widened her eyes in an attempt to awaken fully. "Shall I read it to you?"

"No, I'm fine," she said. She picked up the cable and read:

"Torpedo boats, tugs, and armed trawlers from Queenstown are all in except the Heron. Landed from these were 595 survivors and 49 dead. Landed from steamers, 52 survivors. Landed at Kinsale, 11 survivors; 5 dead. Total survivors, 648; dead, 45. Numbers will be verified later. Possible Kinsale fishing boat may have a few more. Only a few first cabin passengers saved. It is understood they thought the ship would float. She sank in less than twenty minutes."

"They thought it would float?" she said, incredulous. Were they that naive? Had the second and third-class passengers seen enough of the world to know better than to trust a capricious God? And, of course, Hester and Ellen had been traveling first class.

"No names yet. I want you and Stephens to go to Cunard's office. You go to the first class office. Stephens can check out the second class and steerage offices. You may have to stay there all day, but don't come back without names. Survivors. The dead. Whatever you can get," he said. He walked briskly away.

On her way to the ladies' room, she nudged Billy awake and told him Thorn's instructions.

"Coffee," Billy said. "We can't do this without coffee."

"Stella made a fresh pot," Louisa said, pointing to the percolator in the break area. "I need to freshen up."

In the ladies' room, she nearly fell asleep on the commode, but she roused herself, washed her face at the sink, and examined herself in the mirror. She pinned back strands of unruly hair, and decided that would have to do.

She found Billy at the break table, gulping down coffee. He set his cup down, stuck out an elbow and said, "Shall we, milady?" as if escorting her to a dance. She ignored the profferred elbow and led the way to the elevator.

The morning air tingled with the brisk chill of springtime, but she'd had enough foresight to wear her long linen coat. The streets were not crowded as it was a Saturday morning, and most of the downtown businesses were closed.

"What time do the Cunard offices open?" she asked Billy.

He glanced at his pocket-watch and said, "Seven forty-five. We'll be there by eight if we grab a taxi. Or would you prefer a perambulation?"

"Stop pretending to be a pompous ass," she said. "Smirking is more your style. Hail a taxi, please."

Billy raised his hand to get the attention of a passing taxi driver, but instead of a taxi, a black Pierce Arrow with gold trim pulled up in front of them.

"Well, now, this is service," Billy said, tipping back his hat.

Katherine Murphy sat in the back seat, holding a handkerchief over the bottom half of her face, her eyes swollen and red.

"Get in front with the chauffeur," Louisa said to Billy as she slid into the back seat next to Katherine. She took Katherine's free hand in her own.

"We've had no word," Katherine said.

"There are survivors," Louisa told her. "We'll go to Cunard's and wait for the list."

"Yes," Katherine agreed.

"Twenty-four State Street," Louisa told the chauffeur. He pulled the motor car away from the building.

The Cunard offices were at the bottom tip of the island. The chauffeur pulled in front of the building. Two reporters she recognized from *The Herald* and *The Sun* lounged against the iron railing in front of the building, having a smoke.

"You can wait here, if you like," Louisa said to Katherine. "I'll come out if I have any news."

"Thank you. I'll be here," Katherine said.

Louisa and Billy got out of the car. Louisa looked up at the two pillars at the entrance of the building — they were as big as tree trunks with metal engravings that said "Royal Mail" and "Cunard" at the bottom. Inside the crowd was sparse. A dozen reporters lingered in the hallways among the passengers' family members and friends, obvious by their low voices and somber miens. The minutes crawled by. Louisa hadn't eaten and her stomach growled unpleasantly. At ten a.m. they received word that the survivors at Queenstown would soon be en route for Liverpool.

"No names yet?" Louisa asked the clerk. He shook his head.

At eleven she went outside to report to Katherine that she still had no news and didn't think there would be any until later in the day.

"Why don't you let us take you home for a break?" Katherine asked.

Louisa agreed. She needed to change clothes, force herself to eat something and if possible, take a brief nap. Katherine said she would go back to her apartment to wait for word there.

At home Suzie prepared a light lunch, and they ate together. It was unconventional for a mistress and servant to eat together, but Louisa was no more a "mistress" than she was Queen of England. Even her mother who had been such a stickler for convention had finally realized that Suzie, who had saved them from the poorhouse by assiduously managing their accounts, had as much right to eat with them as anyone.

She thought of Ellen with her wide view of the world. If that wide view were to disappear, Louisa was not sure how she could reconcile the loss.

Rather than going upstairs to rest in her bed, Louisa lay down on the sofa in the parlor and shut her eyes. She drifted in and out of consciousness, memories passing through her mind like wisps of smoke. If Ellen were to die of this most unnatural cause, Louisa's grief would be a monster, a demon sitting on her chest, reveling in her misery. Finally sleep tugged at her consciousness and pulled it away from coherent thoughts, replacing them with randoms words and pictures. Why was she thinking of fish? Then she was out.

"Louisa, wake up. There's someone at the door for you," Suzie said, shaking her shoulder.

Louisa blinked sleepily and asked who it was.

"That Chinese chauffeur."

"Forrest is here?" Louisa asked, confused.

"I don't know, but his chauffeur is," Suzie said.

Louisa struggled to gain full consciousness for the second time that day.

"How long was I asleep?"

"About an hour."

"That makes two hours of sleep since yesterday morning," Louisa said, blinking her eyes. "Tell Mr. Kimura, who is Japanese by the way, I'll be out shortly."

She went upstairs to change her dress. She would not wear something cheery, nor would she wear black. She reached into her wardrobe and pulled out her outfit for the day.

When Louisa came outside in a severe gray dress, she found Forrest's Packard waiting by the curb. Mr. Kimura opened the back door, and she climbed inside where Forrest waited. Being in his presence stirred something inside her and made her feel weepy. She was tired and felt as fragile as china doll.

"I'm sorry I stood you up last night," she said.

"It's all right. You must be devastated," he said pulling her close. Of course, he would remember that Ellen had been on board. Then he muttered, "German bastards."

As he held onto her, it occurred to Louisa that when she'd first learned the news of the Lusitania, she had not immediately gone to Forrest for comfort. She'd turned instead to her work. The realization felt like a punch in her stomach. She couldn't marry him. She was already married. She pulled herself out of his arms.

"I have to get back to the Cunard office to see if there's any news," she said in a strangled voice.

“Louisa, you don’t have to do this,” he said. “Let Stephens and the other men handle the job. Come home with me.”

She shook her head. Her purpose was clear.

“Mr. Kimura, please take me to the Cunard office,” she said.

They did not speak during the drive. When they arrived he put a hand on her arm and said, “Let me know if you hear any word of Ellen.”

She cleared her throat. She must address the unspoken issue.

“Forrest, about your proposal—” she began.

“No need to talk about it, Darling. You’ve other things on your mind right now.” As if he knew. As if he dreaded what she was going to say.

“I need to talk about it now,” she said and then blurted it out, “I can’t marry you. I’m sorry. I wish I had a different answer for you, but this horrible tragedy has made me realize that I can’t give up what I do. I can’t be a wife and a mother. This is too important. Can’t you see that?”

“No, I don’t see it,” he said.

“I know if sounds arrogant as if there were no one else in the world who could write the news. However, I can’t help but believe that I’ve been put here on this Earth to do this, to write about the things that happen to people and the effects these things have. I have a perspective that not everyone has, and I've learned how to be brave, and how to tell human stories, and . . ."

She ran out of words. His face showed no expression whatsoever. She felt a burning sensation in her chest. She didn't know how to make him understand. She took a deep breath and tried again.

"You deserve a wife, one who will make you the center of her world, one who will give you all the children you could ever want. It's not me," she said. She wanted to add that she loved him, but that would only sound cruel because obviously she didn't love him enough, she didn't love him as much as she loved her work.

He turned away from her to hide how deeply she had hurt him.

As much as she loved him, she felt something like relief. It had taken this tragedy to awaken her to the simple fact that she did not want to be married — not to Forrest, not to anyone.

She touched his hand gently before opening the door and getting out of the motorcar. As the Packard pulled away from the curb, she saw Billy Stephens stubbing out a cigarette.

"Do you travel everywhere in chauffeur-driven automobiles, Duchess?" he asked.

"Names?" she responded.

"Not yet," he said.

They went inside the building into a sea of grief and fear.

The first-class office of the Cunard Line was decorated with posters of the company's various ocean liners. One poster featured the routes: New York, Mediterranean, Egyptian, and Adriatic. Another featuring a majestic steamship boasted the "fastest steamers in the world" — The *Aquitania*, *Mauretania*, and *Lusitania*. The fact that this was no longer true made Louisa feel momentarily nauseated. She sat down in one of the few chairs, which a gentleman had vacated for her.

"Are you all right, Miss Delafield?" he asked.

She glanced at him and realized she knew him. He was the Vanderbilt's butler.

"I'm fine, thank you," she said. "Any word on Mr. Vanderbilt?"

"None, I'm afraid."

The jingle of telephone bells rang constantly. Next to her sat a pretty young blonde in a fashionably layered dress and heels, biting her lip and wringing her hands. Louisa would need to begin gathering quotes, she knew, but she didn't want to pry into this young woman's unhappiness.

When she felt better, she went into the hallway where the crowd had swelled to more than a hundred. She realized it was time to do her job and so began asking people for whom they were waiting. Everyone she spoke to seemed almost relieved to share their fears. One man was waiting on word of his father, a jeweler, who had gone to London with a package of diamonds to sell. Another woman was waiting to hear about her brother. A middle-aged man with tears in his eyes said his daughter was on her way to County Galway.

"My friend was going there as well," Louisa said. "I hope they will both be all right."

The saddest figure of all was a young man whose wife and baby were on the ship to visit her family in England. The man's mother stood at his side and said, "It's terrible. We never thought such a thing could happen."

At 3 o'clock she returned to the first class office where the family members were now crowded around the clerk's windows, asking him to check names.

"They got the first list of survivors," the *Times* reporter told her. He shook his head and added, "That boat was as helpless as a ferry."

It was, indeed, she thought.

She overheard the clerk tell one man who looked to be in his 30s that one of his friends' names was on the survivor list, but another was not.

"I knew he was dead before I came in," the man muttered and left.

A moment later they heard a shriek as the pretty young woman who had been sitting next to her earlier threw her hands in the air and fainted. The Vanderbilts' butler and another man helped get the woman into a chair. Louisa sat down next to her and chafed the woman's hands. The butler ran to wet his handkerchief in a water fountain. After he applied the wet handkerchief to her face, the woman came around.

Louisa offered words of comfort, but the woman could not stop crying, only pausing long enough to catch her breath in great gulps.

"We were to be married on June first. He only went to London to finish up some business," she said between sobs. "His name isn't on the list."

The clerk by then had come around and tried to offer solace.

"His name may still be on one of the revised lists," he said.

But the inconsolable woman left the office.

Louisa took her turn at the window.

"Vanderbilt?" she asked. He shook his head. The Vanderbilt butler stood beside her and sighed.

"What about Hester French?" she asked. Again he perused the list and shook his head.

She screwed up her courage and asked, "Ellen Malloy?"

"No, Miss. I don't see her name."

Louisa settled down in a chair. Unlike the young woman who had lost her fiancé, she refused to give up hope. More people came and went, either stricken with grief and uncertainty or weeping with relief if their loved one's name was among the survivors. She continued to collect quotes long after she'd had enough. It passed the time and somehow seemed to help. People needed to talk at a time like this, it seemed.

The afternoon turned into evening and Billy found her.

"I've got names and quotes from second class and steerage," he said. "You good to go?"

Louisa sighed. There was no point in staying. The office would close soon, but they could still receive cables at the office, and she could make her phone calls.

"Hungry?" Billy asked as they left the building.

"No," she answered. "I'm afraid my biggest headline will be 'Vanderbilt feared lost.'"

"We'll grab some hotdogs," he said. She shrugged. She had no argument in her so they stopped at a cart and bought a couple of hotdogs. She had no appetite but ate anyway to keep up her strength.

When they got to the paper, she trudged through the newsroom maze to her desk. She stared at the chair where Ellen had always sat, typing or telling stories of her childhood in Ireland.

She lifted the receiver of her desk phone and asked for the Murphy residence. Katherine's maid answered and said they'd had no word either. Next she called Margaret Vanderbilt.

"All I've heard," Margaret told her, "is that he saved several lives. He gave up his life vest to a woman even though he couldn't swim. His body has not been found. I'm afraid the worst has happened."

"I'm so sorry," Louisa said. "His behavior doesn't surprise me though. There was always something gallant about him."

Margaret's voice broke as she thanked Louisa. Then the line went dead.

The lack of sleep caught up to her, evident in the number of typos in her story.

"Miss Delafield?" She looked up and saw Thorn beckoning her.

She went into his office and sank into the chair across from his desk.

"I've a cable from William French, the American Consul to Ireland."

"What does it say?" she asked.

"See for yourself."

He handed her the cable, and she read:

I am alive. Hester dead, body not found. Ellen

"Ellen is alive," Louisa whispered. She put the cable on the desk, looked down at her lap, and took a deep gulp of air as tears leaked from her eyes onto her dress. Ellen was alive, but Hester was not. This would be hard news for Katherine, and Ellen must be devastated. She brushed away the tears, and went to the telephone to call Hester's sister.

Chapter 16
Ellen

Ellen entered the small house followed by a strapping young man of 20 years. Light streamed through the panes of the window and sprawled across the battered wood table, where Agnes wiped up the crumbs of breakfast.

"And who is this ladeen?" Agnes asked, looking up at the two of them.

"'Tis my brother Martin," Ellen told her. "He found me this morning down at the quay. Seamus is with his grandmother now."

Martin doffed his hat and grinned at Agnes.

"Mam swore Ellen was still alive and sent me here to find her," Martin said. "She was right, of course."

"I did send a cable," Ellen said.

"An' that was after I already left."

"Will you be going home soon then?" Agnes asked as she poured tea into mugs and handed one to each of them.

"We'll be going today right after the funeral," Ellen said.

"Did you ever find your friend?"

Ellen shook her head. Hester, it seemed, was one of the many whose bodies would never be recovered. She took a sip of the tea and then cleared her throat.

"It's been kind of you to take me in. My brother has brought some money. Maybe I could pay something for your troubles," Ellen said.

"I wouldn't hear a word of it," Agnes responded, eyes blazing. "We won't be profiting off the suffering of others."

"I didn't mean any offense," Ellen said. "I know you gave out of your heart."

Agnes immediately forgave her with a warm smile and a pat on the hand.

"I'm glad I could help ya," she said. "Let's draw the curtains now, and we'll be going to pay our respects. Rob, are ya comin'?"

The four of them walked through the town. Businesses had shuttered for the day, and curtains were closed in all the windows. *No one has such an affinity for death as the Irish,* Ellen thought. She glanced over at her brother. He'd been a smart aleck teenager when she left, but now he was filling out and becoming a man. He had short, sandy brown hair, parted on the left, full lips, and the strong, virile features of a man who would not be deterred. He was her favorite of the three brothers, and she was glad he'd come to get her though they hadn't had much time to catch up on family news — only that her da was still alive and faring a bit better, and Michael, the oldest of the three boys, was off fighting with the Rangers in Gallipoli. Her mam couldn't sleep for worrying over him.

"She didn't know you were the one to be worrying about," Martin had said, giving her a thump on the back. Now he plodded beside her in his dirty black boots, holding his hat in his hand as all the men did, unaware that her grief ran far deeper than she let on.

The horses each wore a tall black feather on their heads as they pulled the ornate black hearses. Behind them the Royal Irish Regiment and Connaught Rangers trooped, followed by an impossibly long cortege of mourners, including survivors and many of the local Irish, who did not know the victims but were filling in for the family members and friends who could not be there to send off their loved ones. Ellen and Martin walked along with Agnes and her husband as a brass band played the "Dead March."

For almost three hours, they walked behind the hearses carrying at least a hundred coffins covered in British flags from the quays to the cemetery outside of town where three great pits had been dug by soldiers. Though Hester's body was not in any of the coffins, there were others, others she had recognized in her searches through the temporary morgues— people she'd seen laughing, dancing, eating, drinking and singing; people who a few days ago had been alive; people who loved and were loved, as she had loved and been loved. Two years of happiness. That's what she'd been allotted in this life. It was more than some got, she told herself.

Ellen had placed Hester's pink straw hat in the coffin of a woman who had sung quite prettily at the talent show. Her body had been rescued early on so she was not bloated and misshapen the way some of the bodies who'd drifted into shore had been. Some of the infants were so discolored it was hard to imagine they'd ever cooed and cried. Ellen was almost glad that Hester had stayed out there in the deep like so many others: the Vanderbilt man, the theater manager, the valets of the Saloon class who had served to the end. She imagined Hester's body drifting in that deep blue soup, her bones finally settling down to rest in the dark.

Once they reached the cemetery on a hill speckled with blue and yellow flowers, overlooking the harbor, a

Catholic priest and a Protestant minister spoke in turn. She didn't hear a word. She looked out at the red roofs of the town and the flags flying at half mast, felt the soft, insistent breeze winding in her hair, and listened to the weeping around her. These mourners knew their job. Then that sorrowful crowd sang "Abide With Me," and a dry eye couldn't be found in the county.

When it was all over, she climbed into the passenger side of a delivery truck Martin had borrowed from a friend, and they took the road north. She closed her eyes as soon as they left Queenstown, and somehow in spite of the hard seat, the bumps in the road, and the grinding of the engine, she slept like the dead herself.

***

They stopped at Limerick to buy some petrol. Ellen stood outside the truck, munching the brown bread Agnes had insisted they take with them. Once they started driving again, Ellen looked out at the countryside and saw workers in the beet fields. Life goes on, she thought.

"So what are you doing with yerself these days?" she asked her brother.

"I'm working at the sawmill," he said. "And I've a room of me own in town now. The only one left in the Claddagh with Mam and Da is Gilly."

"You're not thinking of joining the Rangers like Michael, are ya?" she asked.

"No, but I learned a song they sing," he said with a laugh. "Michael taught it to me. Want to hear?"

"Why not?" she said. Anything to distract from the ache that would not leave her chest.

"Oh we don't give a fuck for old Von Kluck. And all his feckin' army," Martin sang in a loud voice.

"I bet you don't sing that song in front of Ma," she said sourly. She didn't like to hear her brother use such language, but she reminded herself she had no authority over him. He was a man now.

"No, indeed, I don't. She'd hang me from the Lynch window," he said, reminding her of the old ruin of a window from Lynch's castle where a mayor hung his own son in defiance of the local crowd. So many things she'd forgotten about, but with every inhalation her native land reclaimed her.

"Mam must be happy you're not joining up. But tell me why. Last I heard you were all about getting your uniform and going off to fight in India or wherever the Rangers were headed."

"I don't have to go anywhere to fight. There's a war here, too, ya know. And in this war, the Germans are not the enemy," Martin said. "England's difficulty is Ireland's opportunity."

Ellen's breath caught, but she kept her concern in check. She may not have loved England, but you didn't take the side of murderers. She thought of what Mrs. McNabb had said about Irish longshoremen helping Germans sabotage boats.

"I know you didn't come up with that pithy quote all on your own, little brother. Who's been bending your ear with this dangerous nonsense?" she asked.

"I'm a Volunteer," he said with unmistakable pride in his voice.

"You mean you're supporting John Redmond now?"

"Not on yer life. Redmond is a compromiser. I'm with the Sinn Féin Volunteers."

"Oh, then you're a Republican, following in Da's footsteps, are you?"

"Seven hundred years we've been under the British thumb," Martin said bitterly. "Sure and they finally agreed to home rule but took it away as soon as the war started. Don't you follow the news over there? Or are you so busy shopping for pretty clothes with all your American money, you don't have time to think about what we're going through here."

Ellen sat up straight as if a flame had been turned up inside her and scorched her ribcage.

"I'm not out and about shopping for clothes. I'm assistant to a journalist and we've investigated the abduction and murders of women," Ellen said, omitting her many mundane duties helping with society news and not mentioning that she'd been traveling in a posh, first-class cabin with the daughter of a millionaire industrialist.

"Yeah, well, the Brits have been murdering us in one form or another for a feckin' long time."

"Enough with the cursing, Martin. I don't like it," Ellen said.

But Martin seemed not to have heard her, so caught up was he in his passion.

"Now old Redmond is telling us to join the army and save our overlords' asses and mebbe they'll throw a few crumbs our way when it's all over."

"You've grown cynical," Ellen said. Ellen had always believed that Ireland deserved to be free of the English yoke, but she thought that Redmond and his ilk were making progress without bloodshed.

"I never saw you back down from a fight." He looked over at her. She turned away from his hard gaze.

"I wouldn't side with the Germans, not after what they've done," Ellen said, staring out the window at a flock of sheep in a field. The vacuum in her heart threatened to swallow her.

"That was a bad bit of business with the *Lusitania*, I'll admit," Martin said. "But they've promised us weapons. Don't you see it's our chance to finally get those English boots off our necks?"

"You're talking about an uprising then?" Ellen said angrily. "You'll all be killed."

"I don't care. Seven hundred years is enough."

They stayed quiet for the rest of the ride, lost in their own thoughts.

As they drove through the countryside, she marveled at how wide open it was. She'd forgotten how endless the sky, how green the hillsides — so vastly different from the crowded city where she now lived. How Hester would have loved this. And yet Ellen had told her not to come to Ireland with her. She'd said it was because of her da's health, but wasn't it really that she didn't know how she'd explain this wealthy "friend" to her family. She'd been ashamed, hadn't she?

She couldn't help remembering Hester's hearty laughter, her soft hand on Ellen's face as they stared into each other's eyes, the smell of her lavender *eau de cologne*. A sob escaped her throat, and then more and more sobs crowded up through her chest, shaking her uncontrollably.

"Elleen!" Martin said, reaching a hand over to her. "Are you all right? I'm sorry. I won't be killed, I promise."

He pulled the truck off to the side of the road, where it coughed to a stop, and pulled his sister into his arms.

"Hush, Elleen," he said. "Hush now." He hadn't called her that name since they were kids and slept huddled together on a mattress on the floor of the cold cottage.

He squeezed her hard as if he could squeeze the pain right out of her. After a few minutes, he let her go. She leaned back against the door of the truck. She could not let her brother see the chasm inside her. No one must know. She must breathe. Sobs banged at the door of her throat but she would not let any more of them out.

"You had better not get killed or I'll kill you," she said. She forced herself to smile and wipe away her tears. He smiled at her, then got out to crank the truck and they headed on.

As they rode onward, she felt she might drown in the darkness of her emotions. It had been better, she realized, when she was numb and could not feel anything. Now that she had opened the door to her grief, would it consume her? No, she decided, as they passed more stone walls. She would be like those rocks. She would feel nothing. And with every ounce of will she had, she hardened her heart.

Eventually they reached the thatched cottage where Ellen had grown up. She remembered the sound of mice scratching through the thatch above them and those mornings when she'd find a dead one, drowned in the leftover fat. She had sat in front of the hearth warming herself on many a winter night as the moon crept over the bay, and she had eaten the salted fish and the boiled potatoes that were the staples of their existence. They were lucky in that though they had little, there was always a bit of food.

Ellen and Martin got out of the truck. Her mother stood in the doorway in her long checkered skirt and black shawl, the flat planes of her face a reflection of Ellen's own.

"Ma," Ellen said and hugged her and looked over her shoulder. "Ma, who is this man standing behind ya?"

"Why that's your little brother, Gilly," her mam said.

"Come here, ya rat," Ellen said and pulled her youngest brother into her embrace. He was nine years younger than she, so they'd not spent much time together growing up and he'd been a bit of a crybaby, but now he was this big, handsome boy. They went inside the hovel. The stone walls were covered in a century's worth of smoke, and her da lay in a bed near the fireplace. He'd been a robust man, a fisherman, but now he was thin and frail and looked like he was ninety instead of sixty.

"Hello, Da," she said, quietly.

His face crinkled, and he reached a hand toward her. "My girl. My darlin' girl."

He'd been a hard man when she was growing up, difficult to please, easy to anger, but when he smiled it was like sunshine drenching the earth. She'd never seen him show weakness or betray any sort of sentiment. He'd never been one to shower his children with praise or affection, and so his rare kindnesses were like pieces of gold the children hoarded. They had feared and adored him. Now he pulled her to him and kissed her. And she felt tears on his face.

Society News: The Prettiest (and Fastest) Filly You Ever Saw

By Phyllis Wolfe
May 9, 1915

Three years ago, Harry Payne Whitney was so disappointed when his horse Jersey Lightning gave birth to a filly that he named the chestnut foal Regret. Yesterday at Churchill Downs, his unwanted filly lived down that name and turned his regret into a cause for celebration as she became the first of her sex ever to win the Kentucky Derby. Beating out her fifteen male competitors, Regret made women and girls around the country proud.

A record crowd came to watch the horse — a sleek beauty with a white blaze down her face — take the title of turf queen. Gentlemen accompanied women in hats "with six-furlong brims," according to one quipster.

The crowd leapt to their feet when Regret snatched the bit and won the race by two lengths.

"Isn't she the prettiest filly you ever saw?" Mr. Whitney asked, standing by his champion, who was draped in a wreath of roses.

Born in New Jersey, Regret was one of several horses from the fashionable East Coast stables to make the journey westward for the race this year. With a whopping $10,000 purse and Regret's win, the once regional race has vaulted onto the national stage.

"I never saw a more enthusiastic crowd," Mr. Whitney, in a stylish pin-striped suit and Homburg hat, proclaimed.

Churchill Downs' energetic manager, Matt Winn, added that the Kentucky Derby will be "an American Institution" after this year.

The win is bittersweet for Mr. Whitney and his wife, the talented sculptress Gertrude Whitney. Mrs. Whitney's brother, Alfred Gwynne Vanderbilt, was on the recently torpedoed steamship, the *Lusitania*. As of this writing, the family is uncertain of his fate.

Chapter 17
Louisa

Louisa sat at the dining room table between her mother, who was reading *The New York Times,* and Suzie, who was reading *The Ledger* while Louisa stared into her coffee cup and tried not to think about the look on Forrest's face when she told him she wouldn't marry him. She knew she had done the right thing — the only thing — but it felt as if she'd put a spike through her chest. Fortunately, she had not mentioned the proposal to her mother.

"Poor Alice," Anna said. "She was quite fond of her brother Alfred. They all were. I wish there were something I could do."

"Why don't you write her a condolence letter, Mother," Louisa said. "I'm sure it would mean a lot to her. After all, you and she were so close when you were younger." Louisa could remember her mother and Alice Vanderbilt chatting in the parlor of their home near Central Park, heading off to tea or sitting together on the beach at Newport, watching the children play.

"I couldn't possibly write to her," Anna said with a shake of her head.

"Why not?"

"Out of the question," Anna said and lifted the paper like a shield in front of her face.

Louisa sighed. Her mother was in her mid-fifties, and she hadn't left this house since they bought it shortly after her father died. The shame of losing husband and fortune in one fell blow cast a long shadow.

Suzie lowered *The Ledger* and asked, "What is a quipster?"

"What are you talking about?" Louisa asked, setting down her cup of coffee. The smell of cinnamon wafted in the air as Pansy brought in a plate of rolls.

"Says right here in your column something about a quipster," Suzie said.

"My column?" Louisa said, confused. "I didn't write a column for today."

"It's right here," she said.

"That's not Miss Louisa's name, Auntie," Pansy said, peering over Suzie's shoulder.

Suzie looked closer and then handed the paper to Louisa, who stared at it in confusion. It was her column, all right, but not her byline. Apparently, Phyllis Wolfe had written the Society Notes column.

"Of all the..." Louisa muttered, skimming through the article.

"Looks like someone is after your crown," Suzie said.

Louisa inhaled so deeply she practically depleted the room of oxygen before getting her bearings and regaining her composure.

"I suppose it's my fault. I did tell her to get some quotes about the Derby." She read the column a second time. The worst part was that it was good. Phyllis even managed to tie the Derby to the sinking of the *Lusitania*. She dropped the paper onto the table.

***

In the chair across from Louisa, Phyllis, hands clasped in her lap, leaned forward with wide, innocent eyes.

"The problem, Phyllis, is that you did this without my permission," Louisa said, trying to keep the exasperation out of her voice.

"I asked Mr. Thorn. He said it was fine. A friend of mine was there and we talked on the telephone. He related the news about the race. Then I was able to get quotes. I didn't ask you because I knew how exhausted you must have been after all those sad stories about the *Lusitania*," Phyllis said. She did sound sincere, Louisa admitted to herself, and writing about the *Lusitania* had drained her.

"Next time, don't worry about my exhaustion. Pick up the telephone and call me first. We do have service at my house," Louisa said.

"Of course. I'm so sorry. I didn't mean to step on your toes. I did hear the good news though. Your friend survived, didn't she?" Phyllis asked.

Louisa nodded. Yes, Ellen had survived. She needed to keep things in perspective. Not only was Ellen alive, but a few days earlier she'd been planning to hand the reins over to Phyllis anyway so she could marry Forrest. A German torpedo careening into a ship full of innocents had changed everything.

"Phyllis, be a dear and make a list of all the upcoming June weddings, names of bridesmaids, groomsmen, and so forth. I need locations, dates, times, and — if you can — find out where the happy couples plan to honeymoon," Louisa said and reached for her hat. Phyllis eagerly took down some notes. She was more than happy to be useful, and Louisa was confident that she couldn't steal tomorrow's column on the basis of a few weddings. Besides, Louisa still had *Lusitania* stories to write, including a write up of one Hester French, sister to Katherine Murphy.

"Nice column, Ace!" Billy Stephens said, grinning like the Cheshire Cat at Phyllis. Did Phyllis blush? He was right, of course. It was as good as anything she might have done.

The abrupt clanging of the telephone on the table in the middle of the newsroom burst into Louisa's thoughts. Billy Stephens wandered over, pulled the receiver off its hook and lifted the candlestick phone to his mouth.

"Stephens here."

Louisa was about to walk away but Billy stopped her.

"It's for you," he said. "Your pal Detective O'Neil."

Louisa took the phone. Paddy O'Neil, a friend of Ellen's, asked her to meet him "at the Old Cathedral at Mulberry and Houston. 2 p.m." Of course, he would want to know news of Ellen, but this sounded as if he had something else on his mind.

Louisa checked her pocket watch. Three hours. She'd have plenty of time.

Louisa's first stop was Katherine Murphy's home on Central Park. She had a vague hope that somehow Hester survived, but if there had been no word, then the least she could do was pay her respects. The maid showed her into Katherine's bedroom, where Katherine, wearing a ruffled baby blue peignoir, sat up in her four-poster bed, handkerchiefs littering the silk bedspread, a writing table over her lap and a stack of cream stationery on the table top. She stared down at the paper, a motionless pen in her hand.

"Katherine?" Louisa asked.

Katherine looked up, her jaw slack and eyes dull.

"I never should have let her go," Katherine said.

"You couldn't have stopped her," Louisa said, foregoing propriety and sitting on the bed where she could place a hand on Katherine's.

"Those damned Germans!" Katherine blurted. She clapped a hand over her mouth. "Forgive my crudeness."

"It's perfectly understandable," Louisa said. "It's war, and wars make us hate each other. It's quite awful, isn't it?"

"But America is not even in the beastly war," Katherine said. "We're supposed to be neutral."

"Neutral or not. We have to do whatever we can to stop it," Louisa said. "Though I don't yet know what that would be."

"If you figure it out, call on me – for anything," Katherine said, her round little chin jutting toward Louisa.

Louisa had not much to give Katherine in the way of comfort. Katherine and Hester were very different, but Louisa suspected that Katherine was proud of Hester and her reformist zeal. She wondered if Katherine knew the real reason that Hester got on that ship. She hoped not. She would hate it if blame fell on Ellen.

Louisa left with promises to check in later.

"I'll be better in no time," Katherine said. "I'm not English, but I can do a stiff upper lip with the best of them. Just not yet."

"When you're ready, I would like to write a profile of Hester," Louisa said, gently. "She devoted her life to others. I think my readers need to know about her."

Tears spilled from Katherine's eyes and she nodded, trying to smile amidst her sorrow.

Flowers bloomed in window boxes and the park was coming to life with songbirds swooping and chirping. She took the IRT downtown, and when she emerged from underground, she found herself in tenement territory, teeming with street carts, and hawkers. Horse-drawn trucks competed with motorcars for the roadway.

She wondered if the "Old Cathedral" wasn't some sort of Irish pub. A couple of little girls with big bright bows on their heads — as if doves had alighted on top of them to rest — skipped ahead of her hand-in-hand for several blocks. Just as her feet began to throb inside her shoes, she turned the corner of Houston onto Mulberry and saw a stately stone church. As she reached the red door, an elderly nun tottered out.

"Good afternoon, Sister," Louisa said and went inside.

Inside the cavernous old cathedral, Louisa found a seat on a wooden pew in the back. At the front of the church, an old man and woman knelt and prayed together. Perhaps, they had lost a loved one on the *Lusitania*. Otherwise, the place was empty, but it had the smell of humanity, of garlic and sweat, mingled in with the smell of stone and incense — as if the church was in constant use. She studied the chancel. A gorgeous stained-glass, rose-patterned window loomed overhead. Below it, Jesus hung morosely on a gold cross. Below all the glitter and gilt, ten carved statues of men in robes looked down upon an ornate white stone altar.

In spite of her Episcopalian upbringing, Louisa was not religious, and certainly not inclined toward the Papists. Yet she couldn't help feeling she should thank God for having spared Ellen from a cold, watery death. She did not ponder why God would save some and let others perish. She merely bowed her head and uttered a "thank you" to whomever might be listening. It was surely her imagination that the light seemed to be brighter when she lifted her eyes, and the dove in the center of the rose window gleamed for an instant.

"How d'ye like our old Basilica of St. Patrick?" the detective asked as he sat down.

"This is a lovely place," she said, gazing around at the arching windows and stone pillars.

"A hundred years this building has been here. Used to have only Irish parishioners, but now the Italians have moved in and not as many of us attend," he said. "Paula still prefers it to any other."

"I believe Ellen told me of it," Louisa said.

At the mention of Ellen's name, Patrick stiffened visibly and looked away.

"Poor girl," he said in a choked voice.

"Paddy, she's safe," Louisa said, placing her gloved hand on his arm.

His head whipped toward her, and his robin's-egg-blue eyes shone.

"You don't say?"

"I received a cable. She survived."

He sighed.

"Well, now, Paula will be happy to hear that. She's been praying for her night and day," he said with a big gap-toothed smile lighting up his handsome face. "Thank you for the news."

"Was that why you asked me here? Why the subterfuge? Why not simply come to my house or to the paper or ask me on the telephone?"

"I'm still undercover," he said. Paddy had been instrumental in helping the Bomb Squad under Captain Tunney prevent the wholesale destruction of a different Catholic church in Midtown. He was quite the hero.

"There's another reason," he continued. "Tunney wants to know if you've changed your mind about helping him infiltrate the Germans? You know, after what happened? But he doesn't want you to be seen talking to him."

"Does he think I'm being watched?"

"No, Miss. But he's certain that he is. They know he's digging into this sabotage business," Paddy said.

Louisa pondered this information. These were dangerous waters, but no more dangerous than the ones Ellen had survived. Hadn't she just been wondering to Katherine Murphy what she might do to help end this madness?

"What does he want me to do?" she asked.

"There's a fella by the name Count von Bernstorff," Paddy said.

"I know him. I was supposed to go with him and his wife to the opera Friday night," she said. "He's the German ambassador. Surely, he can't be responsible for these horrid deaths."

Paddy looked at her with a furrowed brow.

"Miss Delafield, this Bernstorff fella wants his country to win this war. He will do whatever is necessary to make that happen," he said.

The man she had met at the baseball game had been charming and jovial. She couldn't believe that he was involved in such awful business, and yet he *had* made that comment about America's neutrality and the donating of horses to the Allies.

"Tunney wants you to get close to him if you can," he said.

"That shouldn't be too difficult," she said. "He is enamored with society, but I don't see how I could possibly learn what he's up to, if anything. It's not like he would tell me."

"Just be our eyes and ears," Paddy said. "Tunney's desperate."

"All right," she said. It seemed like a paltry way to help but she would try. After the *Lusitania*, she had to at least do that. "How will I communicate with him?"

"He'll find a way. Many powerful people want Germany to be defeated," Paddy said. "You'll be an enormous help, I know it."

She did not know if she'd be any help at all. She desperately wished for Ellen's counsel.

***

By five that afternoon, she'd finished another article about the sinking of the *Lusitania*, this time concentrating on survivors who happened to be in Saloon class. To get her mind off the grim topic, when she was done, she started a column about wedding guest etiquette for the syndicate.

As Phyllis got ready to leave for the day, Louisa swallowed her pride and complimented her on the Derby story.

"Thank you," Phyllis said and beamed. Of course, she was proud of herself. And Louisa realized she shouldn't be mad at the girl. She was ambitious — as she should be.

After Phyllis was gone, Louisa went in to see Thorn. He pinched the bridge of his nose and squeezed his eyes closed as if they ached, which they probably did. He'd also been working on *Lusitania* stories night and day.

"How may I help you, Delafield?" he said.

"Do you remember on Friday before we learned of the *Lusitania*, I said I wanted to speak to you?" she asked.

"I'd forgotten but now that you mention it, yes," he answered. "Was it important?"

"I simply wanted to inform you that I'll be assisting Captain Tunney in uncovering the German saboteurs in our midst. Some of them, he believes, are members of society," she said. "And if you don't mind, I prefer that you not say anything to Mr. Calloway for the time being."

Thorn's face was impassive as his eyes traveled above and behind her. She turned around and saw Forrest Calloway standing in the doorway.

"He won't need to, Miss Delafield," Forrest said.

Chapter 18
Ellen

Ellen leaned out the half door of the cottage to escape the smoke of the turf fire in the hearth. She'd been home nearly a week and was at a complete loss as to what to do with herself. She could stay in the tiny spare room in her aunt's house in the city, but she worried it would seem like she thought she was too good to stay in the cottage with her own folks. Da seemed neither better nor worse, and she didn't know when she might go back to America — not that she wanted to get on another steamer anytime soon.

She spied Martin ambling down the roadway. He came by regularly to update their father on his activities.

"Hiya," Martin said, a cigarette cupped in one hand. "Missed you at mass this morning."

"Since when are you religious?" she asked.

"Ever since the priest came over to our side," he said. "He knows we're in the right."

"If the Brotherhood is so favored by our Lord, maybe I should come to a meeting," she said. She didn't actually want to go to any of their meetings except perhaps as a way to get out of the cottage for a couple of hours.

"Women aren't welcome," he said. "You'd only get in the way."

It took a moment for her to register what had just come from her brother's mouth.

"Is that so?" she said, scornfully. "Then you're more the fools. Women are much better at clandestine activities than you clumsy oafs. I've helped expose a doctor what was sending young women off to the brothels as slaves, and I've infiltrated an anarchist group to find a murderer, which I did by the way and would've brought her to justice if fate hadn't intervened and burned her to death, and I've other stories, too."

Martin stubbed out his cigarette and looked at her thoughtfully.

"Thought you went to America to be a servant," he said.

"Turns out I'm not cut out for servitude," she said. He chuckled and reached for the door. She stood aside to let him pass.

Martin sat on a stool close to their da, speaking in a low voice. He was talking of Mauser rifles. How many they had. How many more were needed. The Irish had been talking for centuries about how to throw the British from their backs, but this sounded like more than talk. How deep was Martin getting into this, she wondered.

Ellen went outside to feed the few rangy chickens her mam kept for eggs. They clucked and stirred up dirt around her feet. Worry nagged at her. The men in her family had been always been Republicans. They carried a lingering bitterness over the famine that had seen the deaths of so many of their folk while Irish food was sent to England. She wasn't immune. That injustice rankled inside her, too. But this talk of guns and revolution smacked of utter failure. And she couldn't abide the idea of taking sides with the Germans. Not after her plunge into the sea.

She shooed the cluckers away and went back to the cottage just as Martin came out, and the sky started to drizzle again.

"I'd forgotten about our land of perpetual mizzle," she said to Martin as he pulled his cap low over his forehead. "It doesn't rain like this in New York."

"Yeah?" he asked. "What's it like?"

"Cold as the dickens in winter and hot as Hades in summer," she said with a laugh, "but at least you can get dry once in a while."

He looked up at the gray sky.

"I'll talk to Liam about you coming to the next meeting," he said, hands in his pockets.

"Don't do me any favors," she said. But then she grinned, and he punched her arm, and she went to smack his head as he dodged her hand.

"Will the two of you never grow up?" their mam asked, leaning over the half-door.

Martin stumbled away, laughing, and called out over his shoulder, "You got a letter, Sis. I left it with Ma."

Ellen rushed in and found the letter. She walked away from the house to a quiet place on a boulder by the bay to sit and read in the soft evening light.

Dear Ellen,

I am deeply sorry for the loss of dear Hester. I know you must be devastated. Hester was a force to be reckoned with, and yet she always seemed to have a smile on her face. She made the world a better place. Her sister Katherine Murphy has pledged to donate a large sum of money to the Women's Relief Fund in her name. I'm sure Hester would have preferred the money go to a suffragist cause, but it's the thought that counts, or so they say.

I met your friend from Galway at the Old Cathedral the other day. He and his wife are happy to know you are safe. I told him all about a new venture I've started, which I'm sure would interest you. I'm learning to make strudel. I know how much you love to bake. I believe we could serve some just desserts.

I look forward daily to your return and hope that all is well with your family and that your father's health has returned in full force.

Your faithful friend,
Louisa

Strudel? Baking? Louisa detested any sort of kitchen work. Just desserts? Louisa was up to something. And it involved the police, hence the mention of Paddy. Strudel was German. Was Louisa "cooking up" an investigation into the Germans. Well, it was about time. Ellen's blood nearly boiled in frustration that she wasn't there to help. Louisa would surely get herself into some kind of trouble without Ellen there to watch out for her. She folded the letter and went back to the house. It was hard sleeping that night with her father coughing and crying out for Mam every so often. She couldn't stop wondering what Louisa was up to back in New York and what Martin was doing with the Irish Brotherhood. She felt utterly useless. A few times her thoughts drifted to Hester, but she clenched her fists when that happened and forbade herself to feel a thing. If she let herself feel her loss, it would suck her down as surely as the vortex that had surrounded the sinking ship.

The next day three ladies showed up in the Claddagh. Ellen, who'd been out walking in the heather with her da's old dogs, Grendel and Merlyn, saw that they were representatives of the stolid middle class, come down to the poor fishing village for some sort of dubious purpose.

When she approached the cottage, she found her mother sitting outside on a crude wooden bench, smoking a pipe and staring at the women who stood with their clasped hands looking at her expectantly. She could hear her mother's voice from the street.

"You've got my oldest boy," Mam said. "I won't give you the others."

"But the men from this village are said to be the hardiest men in the kingdom."

Ellen had noticed that there seemed a dearth of young men in the village.

"You've got my Michael. But you won't get Martin. And Gilly's too young so move on." Mam looked away from them to stare down the road. The ladies glanced at each other and walked away. At the cobblestone road, Ellen stopped them.

"Who might you be?" she asked curiously.

"We're with the Galway Women's Recruiting League," a stout woman in widow's weeds said. "This village has made the county proud. So many fighting men from one small village."

"How many?" Ellen asked.

"Two hundred and fifty," a different woman informed her with a satisfied smile.

"That's a lot of Irish blood to be watering foreign soil," Ellen said.

The ladies marched on to the next cottage without responding. Ellen crossed the dirt yard and sat down next to Ma.

"Martin's got no use for the Army, praise Mary," Mam said. "I may lose Michael, but I won't lose any more."

"Not in this war, perhaps," Ellen said. "But then there's the rebellion. And those boys don't stand a chance. It's a blood martyr."

Mam puffed on her pipe.

"You may be right," she said.

Ellen watched the smoke from her mother's pipe snake into the air and dwindle into nothingness.

***

"You're in luck," Martin told her as they walked along the quay toward the Wolfe Tone Bridge. "Mr. Mellows wants to meet you and learn about your American connections. He thinks you might be some use, after all."

"Does he?" Ellen asked, smelling the salt air and trying as always not to think of Hester. "I'm supposed to be used by the Brotherhood?"

"We all are, Ellen," Martin said. "We're doing this for the Republic. If it's martyrdom, then so be it. We won't be England's slaves any longer."

"You're hardly slaves," she muttered.

They crossed the bridge and made their way to a pub in the city. Ellen's eyes took a moment to adjust to the darkness inside the small room. It smelled of fried food and tired men. At a back booth, a man sat in a rumpled, ill-fitting suit. They sat down across from him, and he studied her curiously as Martin introduced them.

"Will you have a pint, Miss Malloy?" Liam Mellows asked in a gentle voice. He was a smallish fellow with a high, white forehead perched like a cliff over be-spectacled, deep-set eyes. The movement of his hands was slow and thoughtful as he gestured. She sensed an inner strength that drew other men to him.

"No thanks," she said. She wasn't a teetotaler, but she wanted to keep her wits about her. "I'll have tea instead."

Martin went to the bar and got a pint for himself and a cup of tea for Ellen.

"Your brother's a good man," Mellows said, nodding at Martin's broad-shouldered back.

“I’d like him to not get killed if it’s all the same to you,” Ellen answered, gazing steadily into those unflinching eyes.

“I’d like that, too,” Mellows said.

Martin returned with their drinks, and no one said anything for a bit. Then Martin broke the silence.

“Ellen works for a newspaper in America,” he said.

“Are you a reporter?” Mellows asked. “What’s your beat?”

“Actually, I’m an assistant to the society reporter,” Ellen said. Mellows’ eyes flicked over at Martin with a hint of skepticism. “But she also investigates murders, kidnappings, and that sort of thing. That’s where I come in.” She lifted her chin and gazed around the room as if she were getting bored already.

“I see,” Mellows said. “Well, we like having friends in America, especially if they work for a newspaper.”

“Why especially a newspaper?” Ellen asked.

“It never hurts to have a story favorable to the cause every now and then,” Mellows said. “And occasionally we can get a piece of information to our friends through the right news article.”

This second bit of information was interesting. She hadn’t thought of that.

“How so?” she asked.

“We have our ways. When will you be going back?” he asked.

"I'm not sure," Ellen said.

"She's waiting for our da to die," Martin said and took a gulp of ale.

"That's a crude way of putting it, but true," Ellen said.

"Let's talk before you go back, yeah? Maybe you can help us out. Do you know any rich Irish in America, by the way?" Mellows asked. He didn't mince words, she noticed.

"No. I know a peeler and a few servants. That's all," she said. "I did know a rich woman who was sympathetic to a number of lost causes, but she…" Ellen stopped speaking. For a moment it felt as she'd stopped breathing, as if she were underwater, sinking.

"My sister was on the *Lusitania*," Martin interjected. "She was traveling with a lady who died."

"Tragic," Mellows said gently. "I'm sorry that happened to you."

Ellen was thankful that no tears had sprung from her eyes. She did not want to share her pain with a stranger. Then she remembered her conversation on the ship with Hester about how both Hester and her sister had fallen for an Irish person.

"Actually," Ellen said. "This woman, my friend, had an Irish brother-in-law. He's the president of her father's company. He worked his way up from office boy."

"What kind of company?" Mellows asked, leaning forward, interested.

"I don't know. I never even asked," Ellen said. She mentally castigated herself. Why hadn't she asked more questions? How could she have been so incurious about the other people in the life of the woman she loved? "Some sort of manufacturing concern."

"That could be useful," Mellows said with a slight upturn of his mouth. Then he grew serious again. "But I haven't asked if you're willing to help? Do you want to help your country get free of this tyranny?"

Ellen wondered that as well. A month ago, she would have been enthusiastic to help Ireland gain its independence. But she'd lost her confidence. She hadn't known before how one action could shatter your world. A man on a U-boat had uttered the word "Fire" and life had been ripped asunder. How many lives would be shattered if their rebellion turned bloody? It was better left to the politicians.

"I want Ireland's full independence as much as the next person," she said. "But I don't know how I can help you."

"That's a good enough answer for now," Mellows said.

They finished their drinks.

"We're having a meeting in the backroom if you care to join," Mellows said to her.

Ellen followed him and her brother into a room in the back of the pub where they were soon joined by five other men — all working men like Martin, hard-muscled with dirt in the creases of their necks. All of them dwarfed their leader.

"You think you're going to defeat the British army with these few fellas?" Ellen asked Martin while Mellows talked to one of the other men, studying some papers he'd handed over.

"Nah, this is just the information committee."

"Why does he trust me to be here?" Ellen asked.

"Because you're my sister," Martin said. "And also the daughter of Frank Malloy. Rebellion is in your blood."

Ellen sat back and listened as the men spoke in turn. It didn't take her long to realize they were speaking of ways to convince Germany to come to their aid. They believed that old adage: the enemy of my enemy is my friend. She thought of the Irish bodies washed up on the shore, all killed by a German torpedo.

"The British have approximately forty thousand troops in country," said a tall man with a sparse beard on his gaunt face. "Five thousand of those are in Dublin, others scattered here and there with most of them biding their time in County Cork."

"We're outnumbered, yeah," Martin said. "We've only got ten thousand Volunteers and they're unarmed at that."

"I'm telling you we'd have forty to fifty thousand recruits if we were armed," a red-haired man said.

"You may be right," Mellows said. "Pro-German sentiment is high, especially in Galway. But we need to get the weapons in without detection or capture. Ideas?"

"The Shannon Estuary," the first man said, and others nodded.

"We could lay a minefield in the Shannon between Tarbert and Foynes," the red-haired man proposed.

Minefield? Ellen suppressed a gasp. Would they destroy the land and the waterways, too?

"And we can use the canals to Dublin for transport as well as defense," Mellows said, thoughtfully. "Good thinking."

They were planning a war. Ellen's heart thumped so loudly in her chest she was sure they must be able to hear it, but they weren't paying any attention to her. She was just a woman, after all.

Martin laughed. "Their calvary will be useless. Can you see those fat shites on their fat horses in one of our bogs?" The others guffawed. All except Mellows.

"Hold on, boys," Mellows said. "We have to offer the Germans something in return."

They were silent for a moment. Then the tall man spoke up.

"Killany Harbor."

"Why's that?" Mellows asked.

"It's deep. It's impregnable. They could use it as a submarine base."

The floor seemed to wobble beneath Ellen. A submarine base? So that the Germans could slaughter more innocent people? Were they stupid? Or just so blinded by their cause that they couldn't see what kind of devil they were bargaining with.

"Perfect," Mellows said. "Just one problem. Plunkett has already left for Germany to make a deal. And we've no way to get this information to him. He needs it when he makes his proposal to the German foreign office. Sending a cable would be disastrous."

The men looked around at each other, stumped. Martin scratched the side of his face. The red-haired man swayed. Mellows studied them one after the other.

"What about a coded cable?" one of them asked.

"It's too late for that. He wouldn't have a key for the code," Mellows said.

Another silence ensued.

"We could use some kind of courier," Martin ventured.

"I could take it to him," Ellen said. They all turned to stare at her.

"You?" Martin asked, stunned. "You will not!"

"Afraid I'll steal your thunder, little brother?" she asked with a smirk.

"Not a bit," he said. "It's just that... Da..."

"Da would be proud, don't you think?" she said. Then she turned to Mellows. "I could go as Plunkett's wife or fiancée. That wouldn't be so strange. A woman won't be nearly as conspicuous as a man."

As Mellows looked at her, a grin spread across his face. Martin crossed his arms and shook his head.

"I see you've had some time to think about things," Mellows said.

She nodded. But it was a lie. She hadn't thought of anything. She had no idea what she was doing or how she would do it. She only knew she must stop them from making the worst mistake they could possibly make. They must not trade one conqueror for another. There was also the matter of this new-found wrath inside her that had nothing to do with Ireland's independence and everything to do with a woman who smelled of lavender and who once wore a pink straw hat, a woman who was gone now, thanks to a German U-boat.

Chapter 19

Louisa

Woodrow Wilson had not declared war on Germany, and while the sinking of the *Lusitania* was not forgotten, Louisa had written all there was to write about the society members who had lost their lives or managed to somehow survive. She'd attended a dozen memorial services and written a tribute to Hester French.

Life slowly resumed its normal pace. She'd had no contact with Forrest since her encounter with him in Thorn's office where they had reached a deal which she did not find satisfactory at all but was the best she could do under the circumstances. She'd been given strict orders. Any story that was not a society story would go under Billy's byline — even if *she* broke the story. That was the deal she had struck with Calloway and Thorn. Her society column would not be tainted by muckraking.

She drifted in limbo, waiting for Ellen to return, waiting for something to happen. When it did happen, it was not at all what she expected.

The invitation to the party aboard Mr. J.P. Morgan Jr.'s yacht, Corsair III, had a hand-written note from Mrs. Morgan inside: "Mayor Mitchel, especially, hopes you will be in attendance."

It's always nice to spend time on a yacht in the summer, Louisa thought. And if the "boy mayor" of New York City hoped she would be there, then all the more reason for her to attend. She wondered what he could want with her. Maybe he wanted favorable publicity for his idea of military training for the city's young people. It wasn't the most popular idea he'd had.

"Phyllis, you'll have to attend the Wanamaker wedding," Louisa said, interrupting the young woman's typing. "I'm going to a party aboard the Corsair on Saturday."

"Oh, I'm dying to attend the Wanamaker wedding," Phyllis said. "They say the train of her dress is thirty feet long."

"Indeed," Louisa said. Frankly, she was bored with weddings. There were so many this year. Cupid had been active among the restive New York society members who couldn't go to Europe for the summer. "You'll have plenty more, I'm sure."

Louisa handed her the embossed invitation.

"Have you checked out the Summer Register?" Phyllis asked. "With everyone staying home, we'll have more events to cover."

It was true, Louisa mused. Last year some 900 families summered in Europe. Now, everyone was going to the Berkshires or even to the West Coast. And of course, there was always Newport and Saratoga.

"Where are your parents spending their summer?" Louisa asked. Louisa assumed Phyllis had reconciled with her parents since she certainly couldn't have afforded her fashionable wardrobe on her salary.

"On their yacht. I'm not invited. Speaking of yachts, what will you wear to the Corsair party?" Phyllis asked.

Louisa wasn't sure. The party would start at six when it was still light out and included a quick cruise around Long Island Sound. A sailor outfit would be too obvious. But something that suggested a nautical motif might do.

"My white serge dress with the blue embroidered cuffs and hem, I think," Louisa said.

"Very fashionable."

"I do need a new hat though."

She had just written an article about hat fashions this year for her syndicated column. "Hats and dresses must be homogeneous," she had written, "or one will spoil the effect of the other." She had also advised women to have at least four hats for the summer — five if they had a special hobby, such as gardening or motoring. So she was due for one more hat as she only had three.

***

The Corsair III was a sleek old girl with teak wood decks and railings, brass fixtures, and a nose like a spear. Two tall masts stood fore and aft, but it was also steam-powered with a single funnel in the middle. The first Corsair had served in the Spanish-American fiasco. Could this powerful vessel wind up in battle someday as well? She jotted down a note to ask someone.

Lifeboats hung on the port and starboard sides, and for one awful moment she thought of the passengers on the *Lusitania* and how so many of the lifeboats had failed them. Ellen had written to her and described the awful mishap that had killed Hester. What were her final moments like? She buried the thought. She was here to work. She must go downstairs into the saloon and speak to all the ladies, make note of their dresses, sample the copious canapés so she could rave about them, and then add in a comment about the string quartet, which was playing Vivaldi.

"What a gorgeous hat," Jane Morgan said to her. Louisa was pleased. It was a blue silk and chiffon number and had been a bit out of her budget, but the store owner had given her a discount in the hopes of a mention in her column. Mrs. Morgan looked stunning herself in a beaded gown the color of Chinese jade.

"Thank you," Louisa said, notebook in hand, discreetly examining the beading on Mrs. Morgan's dress. "Charles Worth?"

Mrs. Morgan smiled.

"Who else? I'd be happy in old sackcloth, but Mr. Morgan wouldn't hear of it, so we go every year to enrich Mr. Worth. War or no war," she said. Louisa knew the elegant woman wouldn't be caught dead in anything less, but it was nice to pretend men cared about such things.

In the large stateroom, Louisa circulated among the guests, smiling and trading compliments with the ladies. She spotted a Rockefeller, an Astor, a governor's daughter, even a Broadway actress. Her readers would be delighted.

She had just popped a shrimp and cucumber canapé in her mouth when she spied a familiar figure across the room. Forrest Calloway held a drink in his hand and stood at the side of a young woman in a garish crimson gown that plunged in the back to reveal more flesh than all the other women in the room combined. Louisa tried to remember the woman's name. She was the daughter of a cousin of Mamie Fish, neither a nobody nor a somebody, according to the Social Register.

At that moment Forrest turned and saw her. His smile dropped. She turned away abruptly, and busied herself admiring the decor — Empire furnishings, African mahogany, and velvet everything. She hoped her face was not as flushed as it felt.

Suddenly the imposing figure of Jack Morgan stood in front of her. He had his father's heavy facial features and the stance of a bear about to get in a brawl. Like his father he was not fond of publicity, and she rarely had the opportunity to speak to him face to face.

"Thank you for coming, Miss Delafield," he said, gruffly.

"I'm delighted to be here," she said, grateful to have something to occupy her attention other than the presence of Forrest Calloway and that woman-child.

"You need a drink," he said and waved over a waiter. "Bring Miss Delafield a glass of the Rothschild." He turned back to her. She smiled. She was rarely, if ever, nonplussed, but this was one of those rare moments. Jack Morgan was as much a legend as his father had been.

"What do you think of this war, Miss Delafield?" Morgan asked, leaning the bulk of his torso toward her.

"I think it's dreadful," she said. "I also think the British and the French are quite fortunate to have found a friend in you."

"You follow finance then, do you?"

"A five hundred-million-dollar loan would be hard not to notice," she said. "Very generous of you. I'm sure the allies have run quite low on supplies. Your loan will enable them to fight on."

The waiter appeared at that moment with a crystal glass of wine on a silver tray. She took it, sipped, and her heart floated for a moment as the smooth earthy taste slid down her throat.

"How is it?" Morgan asked with a barely perceptible smile under his bushy mustache.

"It's quite nice," she said, savoring the panoply of flavors, which had managed to erase the bitterness in her mouth at the sight of Forrest and the girl. "No, that's an understatement. It's divine."

At that moment, a tall hawkish man, accompanied by a stout woman with pleasant features and a mink stole, its teeth clasping its tail, approached them.

"Nice little boat, Mr. Morgan," the man said. They shook hands, and Morgan turned to Louisa.

"You know our mayor don't you? Hard to believe this youngster runs the greatest city in the world," Morgan said. "And this lovely lady is his wife."

"Good evening, Mrs. Mitchel, Mayor Mitchel," Louisa said. John Mitchel was indeed a young mayor and almost handsome in the starched collar that accentuated his long neck. Those hawk-like eyes were his most noticeable feature.

As they exchanged pleasantries, Louisa felt she had wandered into a play and wasn't sure what her lines were. So she complimented Mrs. Mitchel's dress, asked about her charity work, and made much of John Mitchel's role as a reformer. New York politics had never been so clean.

"You've certainly terrified the overlords of the boroughs," she said gaily. The wine not only tasted wonderful, it cast a glow across the whole evening to match the golden sunset that colored the windows. She didn't care a whit what Forrest Calloway was doing or with whom he was doing it.

"I hope so," Mitchel said. "They're a bunch of incompetent louts."

"Why don't I show the three of you around?" Morgan said suddenly, leading them toward the staircase. She took one quick glance back and saw the back of Calloway's black jacket and the profile of that young woman gazing up at him raptly. Morgan led them upstairs to the deck, all the while spouting facts about the ship too quickly for Louisa to remember them all.

"This way to the bridge," he said. As they passed the ship's brass bell, he pulled the cord and a resounding dong echoed across the water.

"I love that sound," he said.

They entered the glassed-in bridge at the top of the boat.

"This ship was christened by my sister in 1898. It has three expansion steam engines," he said. "Perfect for warfare if needed. The first Corsair served in the Spanish-American War. And this lovely lady is ready to serve if called to duty." Ah ha, the answer to her unasked question.

"Mrs. Mitchel, would you like to steer?" he asked, placing his hand on Mrs. Mitchel's shoulder.

"I would love to!" she exclaimed. "That will give the mayor and Miss Delafield a chance to chat. She glanced meaningfully at the mayor as Morgan led her to the wooden wheel of the ship.

"Shall we get some air, Miss Delafield?" the mayor said, taking Louisa's arm and guiding her out of the room. Something was afoot, she thought.

She stood at the rail next to the mayor and watched the water undulate below them, still carrying the sun's golden patina on its back.

"Looking out at the sea, I can't help but think of those poor people on the *Lusitania*," she said. "They were completely unaware of what fate had in store for them."

"Not fate, the Germans!" Mitchel said. "It's time to stop pussy-footing around. We need to prepare for war. It's coming."

"Are you hoping I'll write favorably of your program to prepare young people?" she asked.

"Actually, no. I'm concerned about something else," he said. "You are aware of what's been happening on the high seas since January of this year, are you not?"

"Only what I've read in the papers," she said.

"In January a steamship in the Erie Basin had an unexplained explosion on board. In February, the steamship Carlton caught fire at sea. And no one knows why the Cressington Court caught fire at sea." Mayor Mitchel said. "It's only getting worse. There have been three more explosions just this month. Someone is placing bombs or incendiary devices in the holds of American ships." He turned to her. "Captain Tunney tells me you are willing to help us to capture these saboteurs."

"I've seen their handiwork with my own eyes," she said.

He looked at her in surprise.

"The horses they poisoned with glanders," she said. "It was a terrible and unforgettable sight."

"Yes," he agreed. "Tunney mentioned you had been there."

The script for this scenario finally became clear to her. Of course, the mayor would be working with the police, and no one would question him being at the same party as a society writer whereas if she were seen talking to Captain Tunney, that might render her useless to their cause.

"I have agreed to help," she affirmed. "But I'm not sure how."

"We believe the saboteurs are being financed by the German Embassy. Do you know Count Johann von Bernstorff?"

"I've met him," she said, remembering the baseball game she'd gone to with Forrest — their last outing together. "Captain Tunney wants me to get close to him, but he's been out of sight."

"That won't last long. Von Bernstorff is quite fond of society, and he'd be flattered to gain the notice of a respected society writer like yourself. He's also quite fond of the fairer sex."

"You don't expect..." She didn't finish the sentence.

"Not at all," he said quickly. "His tastes aren't quite so refined." His eyes passed appraisingly over her.

"That's a relief," she said.

He turned his gaze toward the sea.

"He'll be interested in you for the simple fact you work for a well-known American newspaper," he said. "The Germans are starving for good press. The German-American papers are full of their propaganda, but the American press has been less accommodating."

"We've been downright hostile," Louisa said. "As a reporter I try to stay objective, neutral even, but ever since the *Lusitania*, I find that position almost untenable."

"He's come back to New York and is now trying to win friends. Will you befriend von Bernstorff?"

"I'll try, but then what?"

"Learn as much as you can. Pretend to sympathize with his cause. Keep your ears and eyes open. We need to find out who is making the bombs, how they're planting them, and anything else they're up to. Believe me, ship explosions aren't all these 'divils' are up to."

His sudden shift into an Irish brogue caught her by surprise.

"Not all Irish feel as you do," she said. "I've heard some see this as an opportunity to overthrow their English overlords." At least, that's what Ellen's letter had said.

"I am not my grandfather, Miss Delafield. I am an American," he said. She hadn't mentioned his grandfather, a notorious Irish radical, who had supported the

Confederates during The Civil War. She didn't need to. It was understood that for some Irish, independence was all that mattered.

When the yacht returned to the dock, Louisa was one of the first to disembark. She had managed not to encounter Forrest Calloway for the rest of the trip by staying up on deck. The Mitchels walked beside her along the dock to the row of parked motorcars.

"Where are you going, Miss Delafield? May we give you a lift?" Mrs. Mitchel said.

"I'm going to *The Ledger* to write this story for the morning edition before my assistant sneaks in and steals my column space for the Wanamaker wedding," Louisa said.

"And why do you have a thief in your employ?" Mrs. Mitchel asked.

"Unfortunately, she's good at the job," Louisa said.

Behind her Louisa heard the pealing laughter of a young woman. She refused to turn around and hurriedly got into the back seat of the Ford with the mayor and his wife. As the car pulled away, she glanced out the window. Forrest was smiling indulgently at the young woman, who leaned against him. She had obviously drunk a bit too much of Morgan's fine wine.

Louisa huffed, settled back into the automobile and told herself she had made her choice — job over marriage. She must live with it, but it felt as though something sharp were stuck in her throat. She turned and forced a smile.

"What should I do if I need to talk to you or Tunney?" she asked the mayor.

He rubbed his chin, thinking. Mrs. Mitchel leaned over and put a white-gloved hand on hers.

"Why don't you mention orchids, dear? I notice that you often talk about flowers in your column," Mrs. Mitchel suggested. "An upcoming orchid show, perhaps. And then I'll invite you to tea and you can relay your message."

"Brilliant," Louisa said with a smile.

The Mitchels' driver pulled up to the building that housed *The Ledger*.

Inside the sprawling newsroom, a copy boy played with a paddle ball, a night clerk filed stories from the wire, and Billy Stephens pecked out a story on his typewriter. Most of the other reporters worked business or national politics, so she and Billy were often the only writers in the newsroom at night. He looked over as she settled down at her desk.

"Got anything for me?" he asked.

"No," she said, curtly.

"Don't be sore at me, Toots. This wasn't my doing," he said.

Louisa knew he was right, but she couldn't bring herself to respond.

"You know the boss is right," Billy continued.

"Maybe he is," Louisa finally responded. "That doesn't mean I have to like it."

She pounded out her story — dresses, canapés, the guests with their gold-plated names, and a few atmospherics, sunset, gentle waves, etc. She admonished herself to remember that she'd had a lovely evening and to be grateful she had a job that entailed drinking the finest wine, eating marvelous food, and admiring the latest fashions. She would not mention the crimson dress with the plunging back that revealed a certain young woman's winglike shoulder blades.

She finished her story, jerked it from the typewriter and handed it to the copyboy to take to the typesetter. Then she gathered her cloak and her purse and went out into the night, hoping to find an empty taxi.

She stepped outside, looked down the street first one way and then the next. Then she saw the blue Packard, engine running. Forrest stepped out of the car.

"Louisa," he called. She froze momentarily. She took a step in the other direction but then immediately wheeled back around and marched toward him. She wanted to slap him, but as she had never slapped anyone before in her life, she kept her hands to her sides.

Besides, she was the one who had given him up. She must not show anger.

"Where is your date?" she asked coolly.

"I took her home," he said.

"How honorable of you," Louisa said. "She did seem a bit under the influence."

Forrest reached out and took her hand. His fingers felt warm and strong. She thought about how his hands had made her feel in the not-so-distant past.

"Louisa," he said, tugging her toward him, his voice insistent. "I miss you. Come home with me tonight."

She stood indecisively, a battle raging inside. She wanted to run away. She wanted to fall into his arms.

"No. This back and forth can't go on any longer. You were right. I should either marry you or we should part. As friends, I hope. I thought that I would marry you. I thought that I would say yes, but if I did, I would no longer be myself. I see that now. I am born to do this," she said and pointed to the newspaper building. "So much more is at stake than one man and one woman's happiness."

She noticed a taxi coming down the street and raised her hand.

"At least let us take you home," he called to her.

She shook her head and hurried over to the taxi. As soon as the door slammed shut, she slumped into the seat, closed her eyes and used every ounce of her willpower not to weep.

Chapter 20
Ellen

Ellen had never been to London before, and since she had a day to kill before taking another train to the port at Tilburn for the ship to Amsterdam, she decided to explore. The first thing she saw upon exiting the train station was a huge sign that read WE NEED MORE MEN! It took her a moment to realize it wasn't a plea from lonely women but that the authorities were trying to recruit soldiers. Another sign read TO ARMS! TO ARMS! YOUNG MEN, YOUR COUNTRY NEEDS YOU TODAY!

She sighed and thought of Martin. Everyone seemed so eager to spill the blood of young men. *Why worry? Plenty more where they came from,* she thought bitterly. As she wandered through the city, she made comparisons with New York. London felt older, more imposing, something about its dark history seemed to ooze from the cracks in the sidewalks. She was walking among a besieged and beleaguered people. Some of them would be all for the war; others were encased in a cocoon of dread. Some scurried about. Others wandered aimlessly.

If Hester were with her, they would be charging off to find Mrs. Emmeline Pankhurst and her suffragettes, which is what they called themselves in London after some newspaper columnist thought he was being cheeky. Ellen wasn't sure where Mrs. Pankhurst might be ensconced. Surely, the war had rendered their efforts beside the point. From what little she did know, there was a battle within the movement between the women who supported the war effort and those who urged peace talks. She thought back to those evenings on the *Lusitania* and that fiery couple she and Hester had befriended, neither of whom had survived, their bodies lost at sea. Elbert had been adamant that the war was a colossal waste of money and humanity. He had even mentioned a women's peace conference. Ellen felt sure he was right, but when one side of a conflict put a torpedo into the hull of a ship full of civilians, how could you not fight back?

She came to a street of stately old buildings, each with a wide awning to protect pedestrians from the drizzling rain. The street was crowded with horse-drawn carriages, many more than you'd see in New York where the motorcar now reigned, but the horses looked old and tired. She supposed the younger ones, like the younger men, had all been sent to the front. She looked for a newspaper to tent over her head as she crossed the street and found a stack in a box on the corner. She took out a paper and as she was unfolding it, she read the banner: THE WOMAN'S DREADNOUGHT. When she looked inside, an article caught her eye. "*Let Us Not Be Cowards*" the headline read. It was about the *Lusitania*. She stood on the crowded sidewalk as pedestrians flowed around her like a stream around a rock and read avidly.

> *"The destruction of the Lusitania and the drowning of the people aboard her has shocked our nation more than the loss of far greater numbers of lives upon the battlefield could do. And this is natural, for the men, women and children on the Lusitania were not soldiers who had gone out to fight and to be fought, and to take the chances of mortal combat, but were harmless voyagers, destroyed without even a chance of surrender to superior force. It is a ghastly, cruel happening, an unjust catastrophe brought down upon the innocent and helpless people who are living in our midst and who are no*

more to blame, whether for the sinking of the Lusitania or for the war itself, than we ourselves."

The article went on to recount the wanton destruction of property belonging to Germans currently living in England. One British woman apparently had her entire home destroyed by a mob simply because she was married to a German man.

> *"Her husband, her young son and her daughter disappeared. She came to us distracted; she could find no trace of her dear ones, she knew not whether they were killed or injured, or in prison."*

Ellen hadn't thought of other innocent people who might have had their lives destroyed by the torpedo. She continued reading. The article contained another example of the heinous destruction of an innocent German-British family's home and then ended with an exhortation to the readers: "*Let us not be cowards*."

That final sentence seemed to be aimed directly at her. She caught a whiff of lavender in the air and thought of Hester, beautiful, brave Hester. Hester never backed down from a fight in the name of justice. But which was the just side, Ellen wondered. A voice in her head said, "Go meet her."

Meet her? Meet who?

She looked closer at the article. It was signed E. Sylvia Pankhurst. One of Emmeline Pankhurst's daughters! Just above the article was an address for the paper.

On an impulse she hailed a hansom cab and hopped inside. The driver stood on a platform just behind the carriage itself.

"Where to, miss?" he asked, leaning down to speak through a slot in the back.

"400 Old Ford Road," she said. Wouldn't Louisa find it ironic that Ellen, on her one day in London, was headed to a newspaper office? And wouldn't Hester be thrilled that she was going to see a Pankhurst woman.

The cab rolled on iron wheels into an area of London that reminded Ellen of the Bowery in New York.

"What is this part of town called?" she called up to him.

"This is the East End," he shouted over the sound of horses' iron-shod hooves. "Where the working man lives. Or used to. They've sent so many of them off to fight, it's mainly poor women and children now."

He stopped in front of a storefront. The rain had slowed to a drizzle. After she paid the fare, she looked around. A sign reading THE WOMAN'S DREADNOUGHT hung over the doorway. Posters for a woman's exhibition and flyers for various lectures filled the windows. Across the street stood a munitions factory, and next door, a building with a bright green awning that bore the sign ARBER'S PRINTING SERVICE. That's convenient, she thought, and went inside the newspaper office.

Unlike *The Ledger* where she and Louisa and a receptionist were the only women, this room clamored with feminine voices. A pink-cheeked woman about her own age looked up from a desk near the front and asked, "May I help you, Miss?"

"I would like to speak with Miss Sylvia Pankhurst," Ellen said.

"She's not here," the woman said.

Another woman, who looked to be around 60, eyed Ellen over her spectacles and said, "What would you be needing her for?"

Ellen wasn't sure how to respond. All she knew was that she had to talk to the woman who had written this article.

Ellen held up the newspaper and pointed to the article.

"I was on the *Lusitania*," she said. Both of the other women gasped simultaneously. "And I need to speak to the person who wrote this article."

The older woman walked over and took Ellen by the elbow.

"You poor dear. I'll take you to her."

She led Ellen outside.

"Where are we going?" Ellen asked, looking about in confusion.

"The Mothers' Arms," the older woman said. "She'll be there."

Her mother's arms? Ellen let the woman lead her down the street to another storefront.

"This looks like a pub," she said, looking at the brick exterior.

"Used to be one. It was called the Gunmakers' Arms because all the men from the gun factory came here after work. But it went out of business. Sylvia got the lease and turned it into a center for helping poor women. Now it's the Mother's Arms."

The woman led Ellen inside where it was cheerful and bright and nothing like a pub. Bright chintz curtains hung on the windows. The walls were painted white. A few women tending to babies gossiped at tables. Children in clean clothes played in another area near a row of cots with handmade quilts. A woman wearing a white coat stepped out from behind a folding screen and signaled a boy to come into what Ellen assumed was some sort of clinic. As they walked through the long room, Ellen tripped over a toy train. She picked it up and handed to a little girl who thanked her and ran off.

"We have our own toy factory not far from here," the woman told her.

"A toy factory?" Ellen asked. "Why?"

"It provides a living wage to the women who work there. Something they can't find elsewhere. Since the war started, so many women lost their jobs *and* their men. The ones whose husbands have gone off to war are supposed to receive checks from the government, but that's a big, fat lie. The police are busy tracking women for 'morality violations,' so the government doesn't have to pay 'em," she said. She stopped in front of a woman who sat in an armchair, sewing trousers. A pile of them sat in a heap beside her. "Hello, Mrs. Thompson. How are you?"

Mrs. Thompson looked up and sighed, "As well as can be expected."

Ellen's guide, whose name she still didn't know, turned to her and said, "Mrs. Thompson is just one example of the terrible low wages that women get paid. She gets two and a half pence for every pair of soldiers' trousers that she completes, and it takes most of an hour to do one."

Mrs. Thompson's hands were gnarled, her eyes pink and swollen, and her back bowed.

Ellen felt a surge of anger. The real border isn't between countries, she thought. It's between us and them. Rich and poor. The anarchists weren't wrong about that. Her thoughts were interrupted by a woman's melodious voice, cultivated and yet with a slight (but common among the upper classes, Ellen had noted) speech impediment.

"Have you brought me another volunteer, Lola?" the woman asked. She didn't pronounce her r's so "brought" sounded like "bwought."

Ellen looked into the clearest, deepest gaze she'd ever seen. The skin was fair and without a blemish, the expression exuded confidence, and the full lips were just a little crooked. A slight diminishment of the chin softened her face and a slightly raised eyebrow revealed a curious, bemused nature. Her hair was tied back in as plain a style as possible.

"Sylvia, this young woman... I didn't get your name, dear," the older woman said.

"Ellen. Ellen Malloy." Ellen said.

"She was on the *Lusitania*. She said she wanted to see you, and I couldn't bear to turn her away. She read your article, apparently."

"The *Lusitania*!" Sylvia said. "I'm so sorry. And yet you survived. Yes, you have the look of a survivor. How may I help you?"

Ellen caught her breath.

"It's a long story," she said.

"Let's go to the restaurant, Miss Malloy. I'll spot you a bite in the cheapest joint in town," Miss Pankhurst said.

"Please call me Ellen."

"Fine. And you can call me Sylvia. I prefer not to be confused with my war-mongering mother and sister," she said.

"War-mongering?" Ellen asked.

"As soon as the war started, the needs of women simply weren't all that important to them," Sylvia answered with a shrug.

The canteen was at the back of the building. It smelled of beef stew and bread and the sweat of people who worked hard and yet barely survived.

"It seems there's no business you're not involved in," Ellen said as they entered. "Whether it's publishing, child care, or restaurants."

"There's so much need, Ellen," Sylvia said and put her hand on Ellen's arm. "We have three canteens where the poor can get a meal for two pence or a cup of soup and piece of bread for one pence."

They sat down in the crowded little eatery at a corner table. The stew was scrumptious and nutritious. And the bread wasn't too bad though a little tough on the teeth.

"Why did you come to see me?" Sylvia asked, curiously.

"Because of what you wrote. About courage," Ellen said. "I'm in a situation, you see."

"What kind of situation?" Sylvia asked, resting her chin on her clasped hands.

Ellen shook her head. She couldn't tell her yet, so she turned the conversation around.

"I'm sorry to hear of your falling out with your ma. She was a great hero to my...friend, Hester French."

"Was?"

"Hester drowned," Ellen said, keeping her voice steady. "And I didn't. For some horrible reason, I survived." Ellen felt the guilt pounding in her temples. "And I don't know why. Why did I live?"

"She must have been very important to you," Sylvia said. Ellen nodded. They sat quietly for a moment, the sound of forks and spoons and idle chatter like a buffer around them. "I understand your feelings. I lost my father when I was sixteen. He was the world to me. He was sick, but when I tried to get help, I was ignored by the only adult available, our cook. That's when I learned never to trust authority."

"I didn't know that," Ellen said.

"And then last year, my younger brother..." Sylvia didn't finish.

Ellen felt a wave of sympathy wash over her. She knew how she'd feel if she lost one of her brothers, especially Martin.

"I'm not a big believer in Providence," Sylvia said, finally, casting her eyes down at Ellen's knotted fingers.

"But I do believe that when life gives you a second chance you must do something important with it. You must not throw it away."

Something important? Ellen wondered if going to Berlin was important or simply an exercise in futility.

"Tell me about your ma," Ellen said. "Why are you no longer close to her?"

"It's no secret. She wants to empower middle class and wealthy women, women of substance. She doesn't care about the poor. Not like I do. I want all women to vote. All women to have equal pay. All women to feel safe."

"Are you a pacifist? Some people I met on the ship — Elbert and Alice — they were pacifists."

"I do support peace, but right now I'm so busy trying to keep the women and children of East End from starving that I can't do much for the peace movement. That and for the past two years I keep getting thrown in jail."

"Jail? For speaking your mind? Was it horrible?"

"Beyond horrible. Each time, I go on a hunger strike, and each time, they force raw eggs down a tube in my throat," Sylvia said grimly. "To this day, I have to eat soups and soft food."

Ellen realized that for all her hardships at least she'd never had to endure anything as cruel as being forcibly fed. As she finished her stew, she knew she could trust this woman who had turned her back on her own family to stand up for the poor and downtrodden, this woman who had refused to eat in defiance of the authorities.

"You mentioned a situation?" Sylvia said. Ellen cleared her throat.

"What do you know about the Irish rebellion?" Ellen asked.

"My speech two years ago in support for Dublin workers was the reason my mother and sister turned against me in the first place. You know, they're much too cozy with the Labour party, who don't care a whit for Ireland's problems."

"Then you know *Sinn Fein,*" Ellen said. "They want to involve Germany in Ireland's struggle with England, but I don't think that's the way to victory. It would be trading one master for another, worse one. To aid Germany after what they did off our very own coast makes me want to scream with rage."

"What do you propose to do about it?" Sylvia asked.

"One of the leaders asked me to go to Berlin and deliver a message to the fella who's trying to make a deal with the Germans. I said I would. In fact, I volunteered. But I'm thinking maybe I could talk some sense into him instead. Either that or somehow sabotage the unholy alliance," Ellen said.

"You're going to Berlin? In the middle of a war?" Sylvia asked with concern.

"It's crazy, but the idea of Germany helping Ireland has got me all moidered. I feel like a traitor to my brother and my father, the both of them staunch Irish Republicans, if I don't help them. But if I do help them I would be betraying the memory of someone I loved dearly and putting Ireland in an even worse spot."

Sylvia reached over and took her hand.

"Ellen, I haven't known you long but I feel you're a kindred spirit. And I can tell you this: nothing that promotes peace is a betrayal. If you can stop needless bloodshed from happening, you are helping all humankind. You're right. If Ireland helps Germany commit more murders in the name of war, then that defeats their whole fight for justice at home."

"Do you think I can do any good?" Ellen asked.

"Your venture sounds dangerous, but I do know others who are doing it. My friend Jane Addams and some other ladies are going to Germany on a peace mission for the Women's International Peace Conference. When do you leave for Berlin?"

"Tomorrow morning."

Sylvia broke into a wide smile. "That's perfect. Jane and Alice are leaving tomorrow as well. They're Americans. They'll be a great help to you."

For the first time since that awful day when the torpedo landed in the side of the *Lusitania* and knocked her world out from under her feet, Ellen felt not quite so alone.

Chapter 21

Louisa

Louisa sat at her writing desk in the parlor, rereading Ellen's letter. Ellen had sent it by mail rather than cable, which was much slower but more private. The letter said Ellen was going abroad to see her fiancé. Puzzling. What could that mean? Ellen did not have a fiancé. She'd also included a message for Paddy O'Neil, but it was in Gaelic! So Louisa had no idea what it said. Ellen was certainly being cagey. She'd ended the letter with the German words for good-bye: *"auf Weidersehen."* Louisa was stumped.

She put the letter away and stared out the window, pondering her situation as raindrops slid down the glass in rivulets. She had offered to help Tunney by buttering up Count von Bernstorff and finding out anything she could about the sabotaging of American ships, but she had no idea how to begin. According to her sources, the man divided his time between Washington and New York. When in New York he and his wife sometimes stayed in Cedarhurst, a quaint little village on Long Island that was just beginning to become fashionable with several charming shops. But what excuse would she have for going there? She doubted he was at the top of anyone's guest list in the aftermath of that ghastly German slaughter of some 1200 men, women, and children. In fact, the social season was in a bit of a lull. Most people weren't in the mood for celebration.

The best venue to get to know von Bernstorff would be something small and intimate. A dinner party would be perfect. Certain locales on Long Island were becoming the haunts of new money, mainly from the Midwest, but she didn't know that set at all. The only people she knew who had a "cottage" there — complete with two wings, a rose garden, and a separate abode for the gardener — were the Murphys. But the same problem arose. How could Katherine be expected to host von Bernstorff after losing Hester to a German torpedo?

"What country are you visiting?"

Louisa snapped out of her reverie and saw Suzie standing in the doorway, with her sewing basket and an armful of fabric.

"Pardon me?" Louisa asked.

"You were miles away," Suzie said. She walked in and put the fabric down on the sewing table.

"I was lost in thought, I suppose," Louisa said.

Suzie sat in the chair by the fireplace and opened her sewing basket, digging around for needles or thread.

"What are you mending?" Louisa asked.

"Not mending anything. I'm creating," Suzie said.

Louisa's curiosity was piqued.

"Looks like something... lacy?"

"I'm going into business," Suzie said. "I'm going to earn some money."

Louisa's curiosity turned to alarm.

"Why do you need money? Am I not paying you enough?"

"Louisa, you do the best you can, but I need to keep busy," Suzie said, pulling a long piece of thread from a spool and breaking it with her teeth. "And someday I want to travel. Maybe go down south for another visit to my family."

Louisa's mind reeled.

"So what exactly are you making?" she asked.

"Delicates," Suzie said.

"Delicates?"

Suzie held up the beginnings of what looked like a silk camisole.

"Oh!"

"You should go to the cinema more often. Ladies want to look like motion picture stars even under their clothes. If they buy from me, they won't need to go to a store. I'll go to them. It's more discreet that way."

"How will you get the word out?"

"Through the servants' network, of course."

Louisa realized she should never underestimate Suzie. Before Louisa got her syndicated column, Suzie's budgeting skills had saved them from financial ruin while her sewing skills had been put to ample use, retrofitting Louisa's mother's old gowns into something more contemporary for Louisa to go to social events. Now, it made perfect sense that she would use those same skills for her own benefit.

"I'll make something for you," Suzie said. "Only charge you for the cost of the material."

"I have no need for any finery under my dress," Louisa said drily.

Suzie gave her a sympathetic look.

"I'm sorry that this war ruined your marriage plans. Are you sure you did the right thing?"

"Of course I am," Louisa said. Then she slumped. "No, I'm not sure. But I've promised to help Captain

Tunney uncover the saboteurs who are setting fire to American ships and poisoning American horses. I can't do that and plan a wedding."

"Uncovering saboteurs sounds dangerous," Suzie said. "You sure you should be getting involved? And without Ellen here to watch out for you?"

"I won't be doing anything too risky," Louisa said. "Just keeping my eyes and ears open at parties and that sort of thing."

"Well, let me know if I can help," Suzie said. She took out her pin cushion and laid a pattern on the coffee table. Louisa thought her offer was sweet, but couldn't imagine what Suzie might do to help.

Suddenly a loud crash sounded from upstairs.

"Lord, what has that clumsy girl broken?" Suzie put down her sewing and hurried out of the room to locate the disaster.

Louisa sighed. She rose and paced by the fireplace, Suzie's words echoing in her head: "Let me know if I can help." They were the same words Katherine Murphy had said that evening when they suspected Hester was truly gone. *Perhaps, Louisa thought, if I confide in her, Katherine might be willing to help.* Hester had been a fairly convincing performer in the few skits and tableaus that Louisa had seen — all in the service of some reform or another. What if Katherine had a little bit of that acting talent as well? What if she were not only willing but eager to put a stop to these murderous acts?

There was only one way to find out.

***

Katherine was more than willing to host a dinner party.

The Murphys' driver turned down the long driveway, drove past a brick two-story cottage where the gardener and his wife lived, through a row of maple trees to the portico where he stopped the car to let her out. He took her valise and her evening dress bag out of the trunk, handed them to a footman, and left her in the butler's charge. Katherine and John Murphy might not be old New York money, but they still knew how to play the lord and lady of the manor with all their housemaids, footmen, and other assorted servants.

The footman delivered her bags to an elegant room on the second floor, windows looking out on the sound, and a moment later the housekeeper arrived.

"Would you like me to send one of the maids to help you dress for dinner?" she asked.

"That's very kind, but I think I can manage," Louisa said. When her father died, she'd only been twelve so she'd never had a lady's maid. It seemed pointless to start now.

"As you wish," the housekeeper said but stopped at the door. "I could send Sarah to do your hair. She's quite good with the combs and so forth that everyone wears these days."

Louisa started to reject the idea out of hand but then caught a glimpse of herself in the mirror. That beastly hair of hers was like a wild animal. And she needed to impress von Bernstorff.

"That's probably not a bad idea," Louisa said. The housekeeper nodded her approval and left.

It seemed Louisa had just lain down and shut her eyes when the door opened. In fact, it was almost dinner time, and Sarah had arrived to help with her hair. Louisa rose and put on her dress. Her gown was an aquamarine crepe Georgette with voile trim. She wanted to look elegant and attractive, but not "available." She'd read about women spies and how they sometimes got their information. She would not stoop so low. Mayor Mitchel had said they wanted favorable press. All right, she thought, but how would that enable her to get information about the sabotaging of ships? Not to mention the fact that he would surely suspect something if she suddenly offered to write his propaganda.

Sarah was young and plump with large teeth and soulful eyes. Louisa sat down at the vanity and handed over the hairbrush. She enjoyed feeling pampered.

"Do you know anything about our guests?" Louisa asked as Sarah brushed her hair and expertly twisted it around her fingers.

"Oh yes, ma'am. There's some wild doings at their house. Drinking and all night orgies," Sarah whispered.

"Orgies?" Louisa exclaimed. "At Count von Bernstorff's house?"

"Oh no, Ma'am," Sarah said. "I thought you meant that young couple. No, the count is a very respectable personage. And the countess comes from a distinguished American family. Her daddy is a silk merchant. Her lady's maid says she has the most beautiful clothes of any woman in New York."

"I see," Louisa said. That could be the way in, she thought, through the countess.

"Well, now, you're all done," Sarah said.

The housekeeper was correct. Sarah had tamed the beast and dressed it up with pretty gold combs.

At the top of the stairs Louisa encountered Katherine's husband, John Murphy. He had a forthrightness that Louisa had always liked.

"You look enchanting," he said.

"Not too enchanting, I hope," she said.

"Oh, not dangerously so," he said with a half smirk. Then he rested a hand on her arm and said, "Miss Delafield, a word, please."

"Yes?" she asked, curious and a little concerned by his suddenly serious visage.

"I know a bit about your mission tonight. You know the German Chancellery is throwing buckets of money into these sabotage efforts, don't you? I mean, *buckets.*"

She hadn't thought much about the finances behind the German enterprise and she wasn't sure what his point was.

"I suppose so," she said.

"They assume they'll find people whose love of the coin is greater than their love of their country. If you want to be their friend, you need to have a price."

"A price?" Louisa mused. The idea would have been preposterous if she had a fortune. But because she didn't, she understood his meaning well. "I should let them know I can be bribed. That's what you're saying."

His response was a penetrating stare. He was close enough that she could smell the astringent scent of his aftershave.

"Thank you," she said. Well, now she had the beginnings of a plan.

Count and Countess von Bernstorff were certainly impressive – both of them tall and long-necked. He had a high domed forehead and a thick waxed mustache curling across his cheeks. She had silver hair and wore a dazzling diamond choker. Her skin glimmered in the light of the chandeliers, and she looked every bit the beauty she'd been in her youth.

A young couple, the Buchanans, had also been invited. The man, Tom, spoke in a loud, brash voice, and his wife, a ravishing young thing from the Midwest, laughed uproariously at everything he said. Neither of them paid her a bit of mind. They weren't "Old New York" and didn't care a thing about being mentioned in her column.

Louisa was seated next to the count, who regaled her with stories of his British childhood while Katherine kept the Buchanans distracted. Neither the count not the countess seemed especially German. They were more citizens of the world. No one at the table mentioned the *Lusitania* or the war. It was not until dessert of poached pears that the count leaned over and said, "I am sorry we were unable to attend the opera. That was an unfortunate day."

"Indeed," Louisa said. "Most unfortunate."

"The terrible part is," he confided in a low voice, "we put ads in the papers, warning of the German government's possible response to violations of neutrality by any ships, even passenger ships. How was our submarine commander to know that the British admiralty wouldn't be there to save the passengers? Gross negligence on their part."

Louisa was flabbergasted, but stifled her response. He continued, leaning so close she could smell the wine on his breath.

"German women and children are starving thanks to the British blockade of food and imports. But no one reads about that in your American press. Our women and children don't seem to matter to the world, but when your women and children die, we are portrayed as monsters. If we are monsters, Miss Delafield, we are not the only ones," he said and forked a slice of pear into his mouth.

"But to torpedo a passenger liner?" she asked, unable to contain her incredulity.

"I'm sure the commander who ordered the strike assumed that a modern liner would remain afloat long enough to allow the rescue of her passengers. The speed with which the ship went down and the death toll was surely caused by the explosion of the ammunition in the cargo hold. Yes, the *Lusitania* was a wolf in sheep's clothing. Now America condemns us wholeheartedly as murderers of women and children, but the victims of the submarine campaign are far less numerous than the German women and children dying of slow starvation because of the English blockade."

He had a point, but if she appeared too agreeable, he would surely suspect her of disingenuousness.

"I sympathize with the women and children of Germany who are victims of this awful war and, yes, of the blockade," she said. "But there is the not-so-small matter of Germany's invasion of Belgium."

He scoffed and launched into one of Germany's modern-day fairytales.

"You Americans fail to understand the full extent of the peril to the very existence of the German Empire. This peril compelled our rulers, much against their will and with heavy hearts, to have no other recourse but to invade Belgium," he said. Then he spread his hands to indicate the lavish table. "You live in perfect security and under such pleasant conditions that you can't possibly realize the position of the Germans, surrounded by greedy foes, and straightened within narrow frontiers. Contrary to the generally accepted view, Germany is quite as much sinned against as sinning."

Louisa digested this trumpery along with her poached pears.

"You do offer an interesting perspective," she said.

He grinned and shrugged. The next thing she knew they were talking horse racing, and he was marveling at Whitney's filly and her recent success at the Derby.

After dinner the men went outside to the verandah to smoke, and Louisa had an opportunity to speak to the countess. Now was the time for her to set her bait.

The countess looked like a woman who would be influential in her husband's affairs.

"I understand you were educated in Paris?" Louisa said to the elegant woman as they drank coffee from paper-thin China cups and stood underneath a misty Turner.

"I was. I adore Paris and miss it dreadfully. I can't wait for this absurd war to be over," she said with a wave of her bejeweled hand as if it were no more than a pesky fly.

"I would love to travel. Unfortunately, after the war, I will still have to earn a living, writing about tea parties and soirées when this is all over," Louisa complained.

Countess von Bernstorff frowned.

"It's a terrible thing to lose one's fortune. I've often thought of your poor mother. We came out the same year. I remember when she met your father. Oh, and her wedding! She was stunning and so happy. Then... that tragedy," she said with a sigh. She looked at Louisa and brightened. "Yet what a brave creature you are. You're a modern woman. Able to make your own way through life. I quite admire you for it."

"Oh, I love my work. I only wish the pay were equal to my passion for it," Louisa said with a laugh. "Tell me about your plans for the summer."

The rest of the evening talk was as light and airy as the night breeze. The guests finally departed, and

Louisa walked upstairs with John and Katherine Murphy to retire.

"Those Buchanans certainly lead a racy life," Katherine said, referring to the young couple who had sat at her end of the table. "He's never had to work a day in his life and never will. I'm not sure it's good for one's character to live such an easy life."

Louisa felt it best not to mention that Katherine Murphy herself was an heiress and had never worked a day in her life either. But at least she'd married a working man. John Murphy had been born the son of an immigrant street sweeper. He was now president of the Pennsylvania Steel Car Company.

"He'll come to a bad end someday," Mr. Murphy predicted. He turned to Louisa and asked, "How did your evening fare?"

"It was lovely," she said and winked to let him know she'd heeded his advice. He nodded in approval and put his arm around his wife as they walked toward their respective rooms.

Chapter 22
Ellen

Legs trembling, Ellen stood on the deck and stared out at the gray waters of the North Sea. In the distance she heard the faint thudding of cannon fire while on the water the battleships of the English navy prowled like sharks. She'd been assured that sailing under the neutral Dutch flag guaranteed protection from U-boat attacks, but she trembled with every distant boom. She was getting sores in her mouth from biting the inside of her cheeks. Every bird shadow on the sea looked like a torpedo.

"Let us have courage," she whispered, echoing the words of Sylvia Pankhurst. She looked up and saw something large and silver in the sky. The sight shocked her, and then she realized it was a dirigible, probably looking for submarines. She'd only seen pictures of them before. What an odd slow-moving thing it was like a glistening, flying whale. She had no idea if it was German or British. What if it had a bomb on board? Why had she thought this was a good idea? Why had she gotten on board another steamship? Her knuckles turned white as she gripped the rail and her breath grew shallow.

"Young lady, are you all right?" an American-accented voice asked.

Ellen turned and found a woman in her mid-forties with a solemn school-teacher face, deep-set eyes and a firm, slightly jutting jaw, staring at her curiously. She had the air of someone who was never wrong about anything.

"I'm fine," Ellen said and forced a smile.

"You look white as sheet and about as substantial as a ghost," the woman said, scrutinizing her.

"I'm not happy being on the water is all," Ellen said.

"No doubt the sounds of war don't help." The woman looked grimly at a nearby battleship. "Tell me, what's an Irish girl doing out here while there's a war going on?"

"I could ask you the same question," Ellen said. "But I think I know the answer. You're with the peace envoy, aren't you?"

"I am indeed," the woman smiled and held out her hand. "Alice Hamilton. I'm the personal physician to Miss Addams."

"Ellen Malloy," Ellen replied and shook the proffered hand.

"We've been looking for you. Miss Pankhurst called our hotel last night and told us to keep an eye out for you. And now here you are."

"Sylvia mentioned Miss Addams, but didn't explain exactly who she is," Ellen said.

"Miss Addams? Why, she's a notorious peace monger," Alice said. "Let's commandeer a couple of deck chairs and get to know each other." Her speech had a crisp, refined quality that reminded Ellen of Louisa. "It will take your mind off whatever has you feeling so uneasy."

They whiled away the afternoon as clouds gathered and dispersed like sheep on a blue hillside. Alice told her all about Jane Addams and the women's peace conference at the Hague, how the Belgian and German women had stood shoulder-to-shoulder, how the police stopped coming when they realized there'd be no violence for them to quell, and how they'd come up with a manifesto and this peace mission.

"I myself am not an official member of the delegation. I'm a doctor," Alice said. "Jane's good friend Mary is paying all my expenses to make sure Jane is safe and healthy. I can't guarantee her safety, of course, but her health will not be a problem as long as I'm around."

"Is she sick?" Ellen asked.

"No, but she's had health problems in the past. Tuberculosis of the spine when she was young. At any rate, Mary is taking no chances."

"So Mary is ...?" Ellen asked.

"Her life companion," Alice answered and then said in a lower voice, "Her lover." She glanced at Ellen. "Does that shock you? There's nothing unnatural about it no matter what the quacks say."

Ellen took a deep breath. No one had ever said to her that there was nothing unnatural about one woman's love for another. Was it true, she wondered. Had her love for Hester been something to celebrate in the open light of day? Well, it didn't matter now. Hester was gone and with her any hope for happiness.

Alice went on to talk about all the new things they were discovering in the world of medicine. Ellen listened until she dozed off.

"Miss Malloy," the American woman said, shaking her. "The bell has rung for dinner. Would you like to join my companions and me?"

Ellen was mortified that she'd fallen asleep, but Alice said it looked as though she probably needed it. So Ellen found herself at a table with five gregarious women — Alice Hamilton and Jane Addams, both

Americans; an Italian woman, named Rosa; a Hungarian woman, and a British woman. Jane Addams was a stout, vivacious woman. Alice had explained earlier that Miss Addams had founded Hull House in Chicago, a "settlement house" where immigrants, poor people, and middle-class people lived and worked side by side. It was also the meeting place for socialist organizations. She was both widely admired and widely loathed in the United States. Hester would have adored her.

"If only the newspapers would stop fanning the flames of hatred with their stories of atrocities," Jane said. "The British swear the Germans are killing Belgian babies, and the Germans claim the Russians are killing Hungarian babies, and it goes on and on."

Ellen ventured to ask, "Shouldn't the people know the truth?"

"Certainly they should," Jane said. "But the whole truth. Not half the truth. They only tell of the other side's atrocities, not their own. And not all of those stories of atrocities are true. It's also not true that everyone is delighted to be at war."

The Italian woman said in a morose tone, "If peace is not somehow negotiated, we're facing a century of war."

The British woman raised a glass and said, "Here's to the peacettes."

The others laughed and raised their glasses.

Alice then explained to Ellen, "The British press believe they're somehow diminishing us by calling us peacettes."

"Just like they did by turning suffragists to suffragettes, but we embrace these terms. So much better than bigot, bully, or war monger," the British woman added.

"They prefer bloodshed and mayhem to rational thought and negotiation," Jane said.

"I believe the arts are the way to reach people," the Hungarian woman said. "Music, dance, and poetry."

The comment about poetry sparked a memory for Ellen, and she said, "When I was on the *Lusitania*, my friend Hester and I often dined with Elbert and Alice Hubbard. I remember he recited Walt Whitman right there at the table the night before we were sunk by the Germans."

The women at the table froze, forks and glasses in mid-air, their eyes pinned on Ellen.

Finally Alice asked, "You were on the *Lusitania*? How did that not come up before now?"

"I'm not after talking about being sunk by a torpedo while I'm standing on the deck of another ship," Ellen said.

"You saw dear Elbert and Alice before they died?" Jane asked, tears brimming and then spilling from her pale blue eyes. Ellen should have known those people moved in the same small circles. It was no surprise that Miss Addams would have been acquainted with the famous pacifists from New York.

"They were fine folk," Ellen said. "Hester and I were in complete agreement with their views."

"I knew you were one of us," Alice said and squeezed her wrist.

Then the Italian woman leaned over. She smelled like flowers and cigarette smoke.

"But who was Hester?" she asked.

Ellen stammered and then answered, "An American woman who hired me to be her companion. We were quite close."

Her eyes met the eyes of the elegant Italian woman, and they held each other's gaze for a moment. But it was Jane, who surprised her.

"I'm so sorry for your loss, Miss Malloy," Jane said. "I don't know what I'd do without my dear Mary."

Ellen looked around the table and saw nothing but sympathy in the faces looking back at her. They understood, and they did not judge.

They arrived in Amsterdam after dark, and all stayed in a small hotel by the train station. There were no more night trains thanks to the war.

The next morning Ellen traveled with the "peacettes" to Berlin. As the train hurried through the countryside, she looked out the window at the passing fields. It didn't look like a country at war aside from the fact that the only men in the fields were very old.

When they arrived at the train station in Berlin, she was despondent as she realized her new-found companions would no longer be with her. With these women she had felt so confident in her own peacekeeping mission, but now the companionship was at an end.

They stepped off the train into a gigantic cathedral of a cacophonous train station and went to retrieve their bags. Light poured in from a row of high arched windows.

"We're only here for a short while, my dear. We go to Venice in a few days," Miss Addams said to her, gathering her suitcase. "But I hope we'll see you again sometime."

"Maybe you'll come to visit us in Chicago," Alice said with a smile that lit up her usually serious face.

"I'll be sure to," Ellen said "And if you're in New York..." Ellen gave Alice the address of her rooming house though she wasn't sure if she'd ever get to America again.

After they had gotten their luggage, Ellen searched through her bag and found the address that Mellows had given her: The Hotel Excelsior on Potsdamer Platz. According to her map, she should be within walking distance. When she looked up, the Americans were already piling into a taxi. She gazed around. Here she was in a new city, looking for a man she'd never met before, surrounded by the babble of a foreign language.

Ellen took a deep breath, hefted her portmanteau, and strode outside.

Chapter 23

Louisa

The hand-written invitation came on monogrammed linen paper from Countess von Bernstorff.

> *Would Miss Delafield do us the honor of joining the count and countess for a picnic lunch, followed by a polo match on Tuesday afternoon at the Meadow Brook Club on Long Island? The Meadow Brook Magpies will be playing against Point Judith.*

The invitation also offered to have their driver pick up Louisa from the train station and bring her to the German Embassy in Cedarhurst. They could all ride out to the club together. Louisa immediately accepted the invitation. Being a society writer also entailed knowing how to write about sports to some degree.

On the appointed morning, she took the Long Island railroad for the short trip. They were close to the Cedarhurst stop when she looked out the window and saw two enormous towers with cables running down to the ground as if they were circus tent poles. A huge sign beneath the tower read: TELEFUNKEN SAYVILLE NEW YORK. A German company with a wireless station so close to the coastline? Was this why the Germans moved their embassy from Newport to Cedarhurst, she wondered. It seemed the German scientists were ahead of everyone else in this new field of radio waves. She still didn't understand how it worked. How could people send invisible messages through the air? And if the Germans were using it, what information were they sending?

When Louisa arrived at the German Embassy in Cedarhurst, she was surprised at the weather-beaten, old two-storey house. It wasn't grand, but she supposed that was not their chief concern. They were close to the Atlantic Ocean, and if America did join the war, German submarines could patrol the coast to prevent American ships from leaving. That radio tower would make communication so easy.

She assumed a pleasant smile as she walked up the porch steps to the house. A butler showed her into a study where Count von Bernstorff, wearing a French serge suit, offered her a drink.

"The countess is still upstairs getting ready. You know how women can be," he said. "What will you have to drink?"

"A lemonade for now," Louisa said. "I have to be on the clock for the match." In truth, she wanted to keep her wits about her.

"You are writing an article for your paper about the match?" he asked.

"Of course," she answered. "It's my job."

"That's right," he said. "You are the esteemed society columnist."

"Are you living here for the summer?" she asked, looking out the window at the rolling green lawn outside.

"No," he said. "The countess stays here quite often. She likes the bucolic atmosphere. I prefer the Ritz."

The house maid brought in a tall glass of fresh lemonade.

Louisa thought of the mayor's comment about von Bernstorff's philandering and realized his wife's absence would make that quite convenient in the city.

Unlike the glamorous Ritz, this room smelled of pipe tobacco and dusty books. In the corner stood a knight's shell of shiny armor complete with a helmet and a long spear-like weapon with an axe head on top.

Louisa stared at the hollow knight and wondered if the count had brought it all the way from Germany. Had it belonged to some long-dead ancestor?

"What in Heaven's name is that weapon?" she asked.

Von Bernstorff looked in the direction she was pointing, then went over to the suit of armor, and pulled the spear-like thing from its grip.

"This is a halberd," he said, holding it aloft. "Fascinating device. See this hook on the back of the axe head? It's for pulling your opponent down from his horse. One of these actually ended the Burgundy Wars. A peasant managed to get the spear end through a chink in the armor into the flesh of Charles the Bold. And with his bloody death, so ended the war."

He mimed stabbing an invisible opponent, and for an uneasy moment, Louisa imagined the sharp end of the frightful thing piercing her own soft flesh and spilling her blood all over the Persian rug. She reined in her imagination.

"It's rather terrifying," Louisa said.

"I have a proposition for you, Miss Delafield," von Bernstorff said, returning the weapon to its rightful owner.

Louisa took a sip of the lemonade.

"A proposition?" she asked.

"A decent proposition," he said with a slight chuckle. "My wife has taken to you. She's under the impression she should improve your lot. Loyalty to class or something like that."

"That's very kind of her. What is the proposition?"

"We would like you to write some articles for us," he said.

"Articles about what?"

"About Germans and Germany," he said.

"Favorable articles, of course," she said.

"Yes, but I'm not asking you to write anything that isn't true. Americans are only getting one side of the story. Everything they read tells them that the Germans are the aggressors in this war. So much nuance is omitted. There's a terrible prejudice against what you in the press call 'hyphenated-Americans.' But millions of German-Americans live peacefully in this country. Why not write stories about them and their accomplishments? Why not remind Americans of all the things they love about German culture? German music, for instance. German beer. And why not tell the stories of those women and children starving to death because of the British blockade? Oh, I don't expect you to explain the subtleties of European politics to your readers. How can they understand that France's encroachments along the Mediterranean are an obvious threat to us and that a Russian-French alliance could squeeze us out of existence?"

"Much too difficult for the American brain," she said. If he noticed her sarcasm, he didn't mention it.

"But a writer like you, someone with your gifts, could show them the human side of the story. What do you say to that?"

Louisa didn't answer him right away.

"I'm not sure I would know how to write propaganda," she said finally.

"Really? Aren't you constantly writing propaganda for the upper echelons of New York Society? Always showing them in the best light? You never write about J.P. Morgan's affairs or the abuse of workers by men like Carnegie. Do you?"

"No," she admitted.

"There is nothing either immoral or illegal about what I am asking you to do. And, I might add, for which I am offering to pay you quite handsomely."

"I already have a job, Count von Bernstorff," Louisa objected. "And they don't take kindly to reporters moonlighting."

"How would they know of our arrangement? You can write some favorable stories in your paper, and perhaps you could write some articles for other publications under a pseudonym," he said.

Louisa finished her lemonade and put the glass down on a silver tray.

"I'm sorry," she said. "It's too risky. I can't afford to lose my syndicated column."

Von Bernstorff inhaled and then conceded defeat — at least he appeared to. She was sure this was simply the first round of negotiations.

"I understand. I won't press you further," he said, picking up his Panama hat. "Come. My wife must be ready by now."

In the car on the way to the polo grounds, the countess kept up a lively banter about social seasons of the past. Then she gave Louisa an appraising look.

"You're wearing such a lovely frock, my dear," she said and reached into her bag. "I brought something for you to complement it. Open your hand."

Louisa complied, and the countess dropped a pair of exquisite pearl earrings into her palm. Louisa gasped.

"I can't wear these. They're much too valuable," she said.

"Nonsense. I have so many baubles I don't know what to do with them all. Besides, it's only for the afternoon. You can return them on the way home," the countess said with a knowing smile.

"Well then," Louisa said and put the earrings on. "How do they look?"

"Stunning," the countess said and laughed. "Doesn't she look stunning, Johann?"

"Oh, yes, indeed," he said.

The game would not begin until four p.m. They arrived an hour early along with a few hundred other spectators, all setting up picnic parties with hard-boiled eggs, ham or roast beef sandwiches, and drinks. Souvenir vendors hawked pennants and other polo memorabilia from booths near the entrance to the stands.

Their driver set up a folding table and brought a picnic basket from the trunk of the motorcar as well as four folding chairs.

“Are we expecting someone else?” Louisa asked.

“The German military attaché is joining us. Have you met Herr von Papen?” Count von Bernstorff asked.

“I have not, but I gather that’s him approaching,” Louisa said, looking at the tall figure striding toward them. He was alarmingly handsome with fierce gray-blue eyes under heavy eyelids, strong features, and a neatly trimmed mustache forming a half moon over his upper lip. There was something solid about him, and at the same time he exuded an aura of excitement and danger. She imagined he was quite popular with both men and women.

“Franz, so good to see you. This is Miss Delafield,” the countess said. Louisa offered her hand, which he kissed gallantly.

"His full name is Franz Joseph Hermann Michael Maria von Papen," the countess said, teasingly. "And his family goes back to the stone age."

"That's quite a mouthful," Louisa said.

"You may call me Franz," he said, his eyes glinting like glass in the sunlight. "Or else we'd be here all day." He had to be joking, she thought. She might be a working woman, but she was also a lady, and a lady did not call a man she'd just met by his first name.

"Are you a polo fan?" he asked.

"Being a polo fan is part of my job description, Herr von Papen," she said. "I cover several matches every season."

"But are you a fan?"

"Who wouldn't adore the sport of kings?" she asked. "To watch a pony charge down the turf while the rider readies his strike is always thrilling. I think it's the sounds of the battle I love the most."

"I agree," Herr von Papen said. He gazed at her for a moment and then said, "Lovely gold tint to those pearls. South Sea?"

Surprised, she reached up and touched one of the earrings clinging to her ear lobe. She'd completely forgotten about them.

"I'm not sure. You'll have to ask the countess."

After the food was laid out and drinks served, von Papen and Count von Bernstorff sat at one end of the table and conversed while the countess diverted Louisa. Louisa tried to listen to the men, but their talk consisted of obscure, incomprehensible facts — the price of cotton in Italy, how many sugar factories there were in Holland, that sort of thing. Occasionally they lapsed into German and shared a laugh.

"Franz never once mentioned those earrings when I was wearing them," the countess whispered.

Louisa glanced over at the military attaché.

"Don't worry, Louisa," the countess continued. "I'm not trying to set you up with Franz. He's already married to a German heiress."

"Thank goodness," Louisa said. "He seems rather larger than life."

"However, if you're looking for someone interesting to write about...," the countess said.

"Countess, I'm afraid I've turned down your husband's generous offer," Louisa said.

"Of course you did," the countess said and patted her on the hand. "Smart move."

After she'd eaten, Louisa took out her notebook and jotted notes, writing the names of ladies she knew and describing their dresses. Before long it was time to go into the stands.

Count von Bernstorff had purchased box seats, and she found herself sitting next to von Papen with the count and countess directly behind them. It was a cloudless afternoon; a gentle breeze carried the scent of horse sweat, leather, and manure. Before the game could begin, the saddled ponies were led past the stands, their legs swathed in protective bandages.

He leaned close to her and said, "That's a nice gray."

For a moment she thought he was referring to her dress, and her mind whirled in consternation until she realized he was looking at a lively gray pony on the field. He continued speaking to her as if they were old friends.

"I am passionately fond of horses and have been all my life," he said. "Not to brag, but I won a few steeplechase cups when I was younger."

"Steeplechase? That sounds like a fun pasttime," she commented.

"More than fun. Steeplechasing requires considerable self-discipline, endurance, and powers of decision as well as a fine contempt for broken bones," he said and held up an arm that he must have broken in his adventures. "I went to England some years back to find horses for the Kaiser. I remember I saw a gray horse that looked very much like that one..."

His self-centeredness was beginning to get on her nerves. It was time to shake things up, to see just how agile his mind was.

"I've heard, Captain von Papen, that you were involved in a forgery scheme," she said. The story had appeared several months ago in her own paper as well as *The World, The Herald,* and *The Times.*

He bent his head and gazed at her through thick dark lashes. The man had no sense of subtlety.

"It's true. I admit it. But I'm not worried about going to...what is that lovely place, Riker's Island?" he said and waved his hand. "Nothing can be done to me. I have diplomatic immunity, and besides, your government has put a stop to it."

"So you admit it?" she asked.

"Why not? It was the right thing, the moral thing, to do. Thanks to Britain's blockade, thousands of German nationals cannot return home. So we hired someone to forge passports. Passports, not dollar bills. Why shouldn't loyal men and women be allowed to return to their homeland? How would you like to be stranded in a foreign country while your home was besieged on all sides?"

"I should not like it at all," she admitted.

"The humane thing to do was to help my countrymen return home to their wives and children," he said and stroked his mustache. He was utterly convincing.

"And to fight in the German army," Louisa said.

"Only if they choose to do so. Would you deny a man the right to fight for his homeland?"

"I suppose not," she said. She had to admit his arguments were not without some foundation.

The conversation ceased as they watched the polo match. The Point Judith team had been given a ten-point handicap which they had steadily eroded through errors and penalties. Now they were at eight and a half points while the Magpies had already scored three goals in the first few minutes of the game. The crowd held its collective breath as one of the Magpie players hooked the ball out of scrimmage near his own goal and galloped down the field with the ball, his opponents chasing him the whole time, but after that heroic charge, he missed the goal, and there was a collective groan. Not that it mattered. The Magpies went on to score another goal soon after.

She wondered who, in the game of war, were the Magpies and who were Point Judith. She had a feeling that so far the Germans were the Magpies.

"A complete rout!" von Papen exclaimed at the end of the game.

The Meadow Brook Magpies had won the game twenty points to seven and three-quarters. Louisa felt rather sorry for the Point Judith team which had lost its handicap points a fraction at a time. She made a few notes in her reporter's notebook, including the names of the star polo players, their horses, and some quick descriptions of the game.

"The Magpie goals came so fast toward the end it was hard to keep up with them," she wrote.

On the way back to Cedarhurst, the countess asked Louisa what she thought of the German military attaché.

"Quite a charmer," she said.

"Did he tell you how he faced down Pancho Villa in Mexico?"

"No, we talked about horses," Louisa said.

"Well, get him to tell you about his exploits. I think it would make a fascinating story."

Louisa decided not to take the bait. Yet.

"Oh, here are your earrings," Louisa said, plucking the pearls from her earlobes.

"Keep them, please," the countess said. "Franz was right. They look lovely on you, and I never wear them."

Louisa knew that if she kept the earrings, she would be sending a clear message to the German count and his wife. She held them in her hand for a moment, looked down at the lustrous glow against the pink skin of her palms and then dropped them into her purse. As she did so, she noticed she still had the Gaelic letter from Ellen. She would need to contact Paddy and schedule another meeting.

Count von Bernstorff cleared his throat to get her attention.

"Shall we have another conversation soon, Miss Delafield?" he asked.

She nodded perfunctorily and then looked out the window at the passing fields. She had just sold her soul, or at least her pen, to the devil. Or so she thought.

Chapter 24

Ellen

Ellen gazed up at the linden trees as she strolled through the Tiergarten with Joseph Mary Plunkett at her side. She'd finally managed to find him that morning, having coffee at the Hotel Excelsior. Of course, he wasn't staying there, which she'd discovered when she went there the night before. That place was much too pricey for the likes of them, but apparently he had breakfast there every morning.

"All the cable said was that my red-haired fiancé was coming to visit," Joe said. "I thought they meant Grace, which surprised me as there's been no formal announcement of an engagement between us and her hair isn't red. Not to mention, she knows very little of my activities for the Brotherhood. I told everyone, including her, I was going to Jersey for my health."

"You did seem a wee bit disappointed when you saw me," Ellen said. "Is Grace your lady love?"

"I had my heart broken by another, but it's on the mend. I've known Grace for years and I'll admit I think of her more and more often these days," he said with a dreamy-eyed look.

They passed a giant white statue of a tempestuous-looking man in a chair and two figures below, one with a stone harp.

"Who might that be?" Ellen wondered.

"Richard Wagner, the composer," Plunkett said. "We should go to an opera while you're here. There are still a few city entertainments. Light entertainments. No Wagner. No one here wants to think about war."

They came across a disheveled, one-legged young man, holding out a tin cup to the passersby. Ellen didn't have money to spare but she put a coin in his cup anyway.

"I'd like that," she said once they were past the maimed man. "I've not been to many operas."

"I would have thought you'd seen plenty in New York," he said.

"No," she admitted. "When I wasn't working with Miss Delafield, I usually helped out with the suffrage movement. For entertainment, I would go sometimes to the art museum with my friend, Hester."

They walked in a comfortable silence for a bit longer before he asked, "Will you be coming to mass with me?"

"Mass?" she asked, surprised. She wasn't quite on speaking terms with God or any of his representatives, especially after the *Lusitania*. "I don't think so."

"I never miss a chance to pray for Ireland," he said. They came to a rose garden and he asked, "Would you like to hear one of my poems?"

"Mr. Plunkett, you are full of surprises," she said.

"You didn't think a revolutionary could also be a poet?" he asked.

"I didna think you'd have the time what with all your scheming with the Germans and so forth," she said.

Plunkett stopped at one of the rose bushes, burdened with lush red flowers, and recited, "I see his blood upon the rose and in the stars the glory of his eyes. His body gleams amid eternal snows. His tears fall from the skies."

"Why, that's lovely," Ellen exclaimed. "Your still waters run fathoms deep, don't they?"

It was impossible not to admire the gaunt, bespectacled young man no matter what she thought of his mission. Not only did she admire him, she enjoyed his company, which only compounded her guilt for she did not actually want him to win over the Germans though she still had no idea how she might thwart those plans.

The garden was beautiful, but after they'd traversed it, Plunkett showed her a less salubrious version of Berlin.

"The streets are lousy with women in black," he said as they passed a middle-aged woman in a long black dress over her thin frame. "It's not a fashion statement. This war is destroying the society. They used to post the lists of the dead, but they don't do that anymore. Too many."

She had noticed the black attire of so many of the women and the lack of young men except for the maimed ex-soldiers who loitered in doorways or the occasional officer in tall black boots. She wondered if this is what the Brotherhood wanted for Ireland? But she said nothing.

Everywhere they went, they saw long queues of women with cheekbones sharp as knives, clasping ration cards in front of shops and market halls. Gangs of truant children loitered in alleys. Everyone looked hungry and deprived as if it were a city of stray dogs.

"All the food is rationed but the restaurants that cater to the tourist trade still have food. So there's more than a little resentment between the common people and the foreigners."

"And what about the rich Germans?" she asked.

"They're not going hungry," Plunkett said with a smirk. "But then the rich never do, do they?"

She wondered about this sentiment coming from him. It was no secret he came from well-to-do land owners back home. Yet every last member of his family was a rebellious Republican.

They walked for miles before hopping on a tram back to the center of the city.

"Spies lurk everywhere in Berlin," Plunkett said as they settled themselves at a corner table in a dark little restaurant on the Kurfurstendamm. "British spies. Russian spies. Germans who spy on the spies. As I don't speak German, I'm leery of being suspected myself."

"But you've been in contact with the Foreign Office, haven't you?" Ellen asked.

"I have, but getting them to take us seriously is a hard task," he said. "They all think Roger is a spy."

"Sir Roger Casement? He's here?" Ellen asked.

"Right behind you," Plunkett said.

"Hello, Plunkett. Is this the girl Liam sent?" a tall fellow in a brown trilby with a pointed beard and feverish eyes said as he sat down.

"'Tis," Plunkett said. "A Galway girleen." Ellen felt sure he was poking fun at her rustic roots, but from him the words seemed affectionate rather than cruel.

"I turned 25 this past April, hardly a girleen," she said and held out a hand to Sir Roger. "Ellen Malloy."

"Roger Casement," he said, shaking her hand.

They ordered spatzel and pork chops. Ellen felt guilty getting such fare when she knew there were hungry German women and children, but she ate the food when it came.

"Did the German people have no idea what was in store for them," Ellen wondered aloud, "when their beloved Kaiser decided to go to war with the rest of the world?"

Casement and Plunkett glanced at each other, and she worried she'd said something wrong.

"Are you not married?" Casement asked, changing the subject.

"She's one of these modern women, aren't you, Miss Malloy?" Plunkett said. "She's been working at a newspaper in New York."

"Oh," Casement said. "That's why Liam recruited you. But what use are you to us here?"

"I brought some papers from Mr. Meadows, detailing how a certain bay might be..." she stopped short when Plunkett vigorously shook his head.

"The walls have ears," he said. "I'll look at those papers tonight and see what I can do with them. Tomorrow I can take them to Captain Boehm."

After they ate, the men each ordered a large stein of beer. Ellen contented herself with a cup of coffee as she never liked the bitter taste of German beer. The bar had filled up with Germans and foreigners, and it sounded like the Tower of Babel inside. The wall of noise around them must have made the two men feel safer because they began to talk more freely. Or perhaps, Ellen thought, the beer had loosened their tongues.

"Roger had this idea he was going to create an Irish Brigade from the lads in the prisoner of war camp," Plunkett said under the cover of noise.

"I thought it would work until I learned what cowards they all are," Casement said, morosely. "They were already trained, and the Germans said they'd let them go back home as long as they'd fight the British. But they'd rather remain prisoners. I was up against a wall of obstinate stupidity."

"I can see why Germany would have been for that idea," Ellen said. "They wouldn't have to house the prisoners, and they could harass Britain at the same time."

"We'll do more than harass the Brits. All we need are German arms," Plunkett said.

"And Irish bodies," Ellen said.

Casement leaned over, his dark beard pointing at her. "If you're not on our side, what are you doing here?"

"Leave her be, Roger," Plunkett said.

"How do we know she isn't a spy sent by the Brits?" Casement asked, glaring at her as if he could unseal the secrets of her heart.

"Because my grandda and three of his babes died in the Great Hunger," Ellen said bitterly. "How many kin did you lose? My gran only survived when she was taken in by strangers. And still no matter how much food is on her plate, she never gets enough to eat."

After a moment of silence, Plunkett said, "That's as good a *bona fides* as I need."

Casement relented and looked at Plunkett.

"Fine," he said. "We've other things to concern us. The Germans will not help you, my boy. They will not provide the arms you seek. However, if you are bent on this act of idiocy I will join you," Casement said. "Only I regard it as the wildest form of folly."

Ellen thought she detected something in the way Casement looked at Joseph. He did seem truly saddened by his determination to go through with his plan to get arms, but she saw something else in those pale eyes of his, roving around like the searchlights outside. Fear.

They left the restaurant, the two men slightly drunk and singing sea shanties.

"Oh the times were hard and the pay was low. Leave her, Johnny, leave her," they sang. Ellen smiled. She couldn't deny it was fun to be with a couple of her countrymen doing what they did so well: drink and sing.

Plunkett told some silly story about two men in an Irish pub in London, who discovered they were both from Ireland, both from the same city, and even from the same school. He continued: "'Mother Mary and Begora,' one says to the other. 'We even graduated from school the same year. It's a small world, 'tis.' Lucy, a newcomer to the pub, asks the bartender what's going on. He shakes his head and tells her, 'For the love of Mike, the O'Connor twins are drunk again.'"

Ellen burst out laughing. Such an Irish story, and the way Plunkett told her going full tilt with a thick brogue struck her as hilarious.

She was the first to notice the group of soldiers coming along the sidewalk toward them. She tried to shush the two men, but they laughed and sang, "I thought I heard the old man say, you can go ahead and take your pay."

She watched with dread as the soldiers got closer, and then in the next moment the soldiers surrounded them and screamed at them in German, pointing rifles into their faces. Fear flooded every cell in her body. Her muscles contracted as if she were trying to shrink into nothing. Plunkett and Casement stood gape-mouthed, staring at the soldiers.

One of the soldiers yelled at Plunkett, "English? Are you English spies?"

Plunkett shook his head.

Casement said, "We're here at the behest of the German government. Sektion..."

But a second soldier slammed the butt of his gun into Casement's belly, and he doubled over in agony.

"Americans!" Ellen yelled. "We're Americans!"

The soldiers turned and studied her. She reached into her bag for her passport but the soldier nearest her — a boy, really, with angry blue eyes — snatched the bag from her and shoved her to the ground while another placed his boot on her chest and leveled the rifle at a spot on her forehead between her eyebrows. She whimpered, hating herself for her fear. Her stone heart had shut out grief, but fear suffered no such impediment.

The boy dug through her bag, found her passport and looked closely at it, then at her. The leader of the soldiers took the passport and studied it. Then he said something to the soldier who had his foot on her chest. The soldier stepped away, and she exhaled.

"Why are you here?" the leader asked her in heavily accented English.

"We're news reporters," she said.

"News reporters?" he asked as if he had no idea what she meant.

"We write for the newspapers," she said.

He looked at Plunkett, who nodded.

The leader's lips curled into a frown, but he dropped Ellen's passport onto her chest.

"Get home. Obey the curfew," he said. Then the soldiers walked on, talking and laughing among themselves as if the encounter had never happened.

Plunkett helped her to her feet, and they both helped Casement stand upright, but no sooner had he stood than he vomited on the sidewalk. They staggered away as quickly as possible, Ellen trembling in fear.

"How do you have an American passport?" Plunkett asked.

"Before I left New York, my employer insisted I take American citizenship and get an American passport. She thought I'd be safer if my passport was from a neutral country," she said. "After the *Lusitania* sank, the American consul gave me a new one."

"My passport is American, too, but it's fake," Plunkett said.

Casement turned on her.

"You're not even an Irish citizen anymore?" he asked, incredulously.

"I'll always be Irish," Ellen retorted. "No matter what a piece of paper says."

Casement scoffed, but he held his tongue.

The two men delivered Ellen safely to the women's boarding house where she was staying, along with several Hungarian factory workers. No men were left to work in the factories so Germany brought in the women.

That night she slept fitfully in a room she shared with two of the Hungarians. In her dreams she found herself lost in a recurring loop, running through a forest searching desperately for Hester. She'd waken and then fall right back into the same dream.

After the third time, one of the Hungarian women shushed her, and she lay back down to wait for morning.

Chapter 25
Louisa

Louisa entered the Old Cathedral and saw Paddy standing in one of the chapels, holding a lit taper in his hand. He reached forward and touched it to the wick of a candle, muttering a prayer. When he saw her, his whole face brightened.

"Louisa," he said. "I was just lighting a candle for the victims of the *Lusitania*. What news do you have of my old friend Ellen?"

"She sent me a rather strange letter," Louisa said. "Part of it is in Irish. It's a message to you."

"You don't say?" he said and guided her to a pew at the back where they both sat. Louisa took the letter out of the envelope and read it to him.

"Dear Louisa,

I'm beginning to finally recover from my dunking in the Irish Sea though I'm sure my heart will never recover. I know I mentioned to you the boy and his granny that I met on the ship and how I helped reunite them in the aftermath. The boy's parents lived in New York. His mother died, and his da was too busy working the docks to take proper care of him so his granny, Mrs. McNabb, had to go and get him. A very brave boy, I might add. And full of questions. Mrs. McNabb told me that his da had a fiery temper so she couldn't leave the boy with him as his da was known to explode for no reason at all.

I won't be coming back for another few weeks. I'm going abroad to see my fiancé, a fine Irish lad. Speaking of the Irish, will you give this message to my friend, Paddy?"

She handed him the letter and asked, "What does it mean? A man with a fiery temper? And a fiancé? This is some sort of coded message."

Paddy studied the letter, his fingers rubbing his chin.

"Interesting choice of words. I wonder if this Irish fella who works on the docks is somehow involved in the ship fires and explosions," he said. "As for the 'fine Irish lad' she could be in deep with the Brotherhood. Her da was a true believer."

Louisa's heart lurched in her chest. She knew Ellen loved Ireland deeply. Would she put herself in danger for it?

"What about the part that's in Irish?" Louisa asked.

"I hate to admit it, but I only took a couple classes from the Gaelic League in my teens and I've forgotten most of it," he said and scratched his head.

"What should we do?"

"We'll take it to someone who knows the Irish language inside and out," Paddy said, folding the letter and putting it back into the envelope. "My wife, Paula, was steeped in Gaelic when she was a wee thing. Her grandparents refused to speak the language of the oppressors. She would love nothing better than to be our translator."

"Thank you," she said.

He squeezed her hand and said, "We're all in this together."

After she left the church, Louisa took the subway to the newspaper office to catch up on her work. She did still have bills to pay, after all. Phyllis sat at the society desk in a canary yellow day dress, laughing at something Billy Stephens must have said, for he was leaning toward her with his Cheshire cat grin. Louisa felt a pang at the sight — not because Phyllis and Billy were so chummy but because Ellen wasn't sitting in that chair, Ellen who wouldn't have been caught dead flirting with Billy Stephens.

"Good morning," Louisa said. Her tone was a bit frostier than she'd intended so she smiled, but the smile felt more like a grimace.

"Miss Delafield," Phyllis said, sitting up a little straighter. "How lovely to see you. The polo match you wrote about sounded like fun."

"It was splendid," Louisa answered. "And you did a fine job with the wedding. Thank you for covering it."

"Who woulda thought we'd have two society writers now," Billy said. "And I'm still the lone police reporter. Hey, got anything for me, Delafield?"

Louisa glared at him. Their arrangement was supposed to be secret, and she had no intention of keeping him updated on her activities. She would give him a story when she had one and not before. It still grated on her that he would get her byline.

"Why would I have anything for you, Mr. Stephens?" she responded curtly.

Billy glanced at Phyllis and must have realized his mistake.

"No reason," he said and sauntered off to get some coffee and a stale pastry.

"What an odd thing for him to ask," Phyllis mused. "How are you feeling? Worrying about your friend must have taken quite a toll."

"I'm fine," Louisa said and handed Phyllis a stack of invitations. "Will you type up these wedding announcements, please?"

While Phyllis typed, Louisa looked through her correspondence and found another invitation from Count von Bernstorff. This one was for lunch at the New York Yacht Club next Friday.

She rose and headed into Thorn's office. It was time to let him know her progress and to show him the earrings the countess had given her. She supposed she would get to keep them for a while, which didn't bother her at all.

"I'm going to agree to write a profile on von Papen," she said. "That should mollify von Bernstorff, and make him think I'm willing to help."

"Good. Stay on it," Thorn said.

"There was something else," she said. "On the way to Cedarhurst, I saw a huge radio tower in Sayville on Long Island. It's owned by a German company. I don't know much about the science of such things, but perhaps someone should look into it."

"Maybe you should tell British intelligence," he said.

"I don't even know who that is," she answered.

He turned his hard gray eyes on her.

"Last time I checked you were a reporter. It's your job to know who is who, isn't it?"

"That it is, boss," she said and went back to her desk. At least he let her keep the earrings.

***

Friday at noon Louisa took a cab to Clubhouse Row for her luncheon with Count von Bernstorff. Aside from the annual regatta, Louisa had rarely been to the Yacht Club and somehow had never ventured inside the extravagant Beaux-Arts building with its limestone facade. She asked the doorman for directions to the "model room" and was astounded when she entered. Models of all sorts of ships covered the aquamarine walls and an enormous gilt-framed painting of sailing ships hung over a stone mantel, complete with carved sea monsters. She felt rather like a minnow in this oceanic room. The floor with its shiny parquet wood might have been the ocean bottom.

Within moments of her walking in, Count von Bernstorff was at her side. Smelling of peppermint and pipe tobacco, he gallantly took her elbow and guided her to a sitting area where von Papen sat next to a man in a plain frock coat and an expression as placid as a dinner plate. They both rose when she approached.

Captain von Papen kissed the backs of her fingers and then said, "Miss Delafield, this is Herr Albert."

The second man bowed. His deferential demeanor undercut his bulky size and the lightning-bolt scar on his face, which looked as if it were the result of a duel.

All the men sat back down when she seated herself. Von Bernstorff and von Papen chatted for a while about yachts and New York and even about President Woodrow Wilson and his wisdom in staying out of the war while the other man watched them. Louisa couldn't help but wonder what the third man was doing there, and she surreptitiously glanced at him to try to gauge his expression, but it never wavered. He could have been watching paint dry.

"I see Boy-Ed's British counterpart is here," von Papen said to von Bernstorff, pointing his chin at a robust-looking man in a seersucker suit at the bar. Louisa had seen the man recently at a few society gatherings and knew he was the British naval attaché but she had not been introduced. The British man seemed to be regaling an audience of admirers. Was he the British intelligence man Thorn had said she should know?

"Mr. Grant is always busy, trying to paint us as the bogeymen while he sends flowers and champagne to the ship captains who keep our steamers trapped here." Count von Bernstorff sneered and then turned to Louisa.

"My dear, I have a list of topics you might cover for us," he said and handed her a sheet of paper with names and events with Franz von Papen's name at the top of the list.

"I've already spoken to my editor and he's approved an interview with Captain von Papen," she said.

"Splendid," von Bernstorff exclaimed.

He turned to Herr Albert and signaled him. The big man slid an envelope across to her. She slipped the envelope into her bag nonchalantly. It felt hefty. Now, she understood why he was there. He was the money man.

"I'm ready whenever you are," von Papen said, gazing at her with a slight smile. Charm mixed with arrogance bubbled forth from him like spring water. "We could even meet tonight."

"Tonight?" she said.

"At my office. For my interview," he said. "Then we can go get dinner."

"I'm afraid I have to cover the new Gilbert and Sullivan Revue at the Cort tonight. Most evenings I'm on one assignment or another," she said. The last thing she wanted was to have dinner with this man. Once one saw past the veneer of his charm, he was repulsive.

"Then tomorrow? My office is located at 60 Wall Street," he said. "Come at 4:30 and please be prompt."

The next day Louisa arrived at 60 Wall Street and took the elevator to the 25th floor where the office of the Bureau of the Military Attaché — replete with leather and teakwood furnishings — afforded a splendid view of the city and the harbor. Captain von Papen invited her to sit down on one end of the couch. He sat at the other and crossed one leg over the other as he puffed on a slender cigar and regaled her — as promised — with stories about his brush with the Mexican revolution. Here was a man who thought so highly of himself and his potential that he would never suspect she might not actually be in thrall to him.

"Truthfully, my visit to Mexico was a farce," he said and waved his hand. "The local 'general' was no more than 25 years old, and his troops looked more like a musical comedy chorus than a military detachment. At one point I was chased down a hill with a fusillade of shots, which fortunately missed me."

Louisa laughed in the right places, took copious notes, and appeared duly impressed. Papen gave her plenty of information, but none of it useful. This was a fool's errand, she thought.

She asked, "Do you feel left out of the action here in America while your country is at war?"

He smiled slowly and looked at her with an unwavering gaze.

"Would I rather be in those god-forsaken trenches with the rats and the tear gas and the exploding mines?" he asked. "No, a man of my talents has better uses."

"Such as?"

He wasn't going to fall for it, but she had to try.

"We'll leave that for our next interview," he said. "Perhaps at my apartment?"

"I think not," Louisa said. She wasn't going to fall for his ruse either. She made her exit, saying that she had to go to the paper and type her story so it would appear in Sunday's paper.

"I look forward to reading it," he said. "Von Bernstorff will be especially pleased."

Once outside, Louisa ducked into a nearby flower shop and waited for von Papen to leave his office. It was the end of the day and she doubted he was the sort of man who worked late. She bought some carnations and then stood at the door, peering out. There he was! She stepped out of the shop and followed at a distance. He had long legs and a military stride as he headed uptown along Fifth Avenue. She struggled to keep up with him, losing him momentarily and then spying his figure among the pedestrians. He stopped and hailed a taxi. She quicky did the same.

"Where to?" the driver asked.

"I don't know," she answered. "I have to catch up with that man. He...he left his wallet in the flower shop."

After a good twenty minutes, they reached the south end of Central Park, and von Papen got out of the taxi.

She paid her driver, but when she reached the corner, she found that he was gone. Had he crossed the street and walked into the park, she wondered. She examined the nearby buildings. A granite building stood directly to her left. It had faux balconies on the front and the occasional architectural flourish but nothing to make it stand out. Then she saw the sign: *Deutscher Verein*. This must be the German Club von Bernstorff had mentioned.

She crossed the street and bought a copy of the *World* from a newsstand and found a bench to sit upon. She held the paper in front of her face, glancing over the top to observe the entrance to the building from a distance. A number of different men entered the place, often in pairs. Occasionally someone came out, sauntering off in no hurry. At one point a large black car pulled in front, and Count von Bernstorff stepped out and bounded up the steps.

This was the place, she thought, where all the planning and scheming happened. They could network safely there and speak in their own language. And a woman would never be allowed to enter.

Several taxis were parked along the sidewalk on the other side of the street, waiting for customers. There was not much else she could do. She couldn't go into the club, and the men could be there all night. She could take the train home, but it might be easier to take a taxi. She crossed the street and got in the back of the closest.

She was about to give him her address when she saw von Papen exit the building with a tall handsome man in a crisp be-medaled blue uniform.

"Where to?" the cabbie asked.

"Would you mind waiting a bit?" she asked. Fortunately, she still had the envelope filled with cash that Herr Albert had given her at the Yacht Club.

"The meter's running," he said. "It's your dime."

She slunk low in the back seat and watched the two men get into the taxi at the front of the line.

"When that taxi leaves, follow it," she said.

The driver chuckled.

"You suspect your man's going to see another dame?" he asked.

Louisa sat up and said, "I think that's exactly what he's doing. Seeing another dame."

The taxi with the German men drove down 9th Avenue for several blocks before crossing over to 7th. Her driver easily followed as it turned down a tree-lined street in the West Village. When the first taxi stopped in front of a three-story brownstone, Louisa slunk down again as her driver went past.

"Lady, if he's visiting this establishment, he could have his pick of dames," the cabbie said.

"Really? What is it?"

"It's a house of ill repute," he said. "Mainly for Germans, though. I hope I'm not offending you."

"I'm not offended," she said. "Thank you. You've been very helpful."

It was late by the time she got back home, and Suzie was already in bed. Louisa was tired. She warmed a pot of milk, added some cinnamon and poured it into a glass. Then she sat down at the table to assess her progress. It didn't seem like much but it was early yet, she reassured herself. Paddy had told her that Ellen's Gaelic message indicated that Irish longshoremen were involved in the sabotage efforts. "The enemy of our enemy is our friend is their thinking," he'd said. He'd talked to Tunney and was going undercover to learn what he could. He wondered if she might check in on Paula as he wouldn't be able to go home possibly for weeks. Since then she hadn't heard from him. And what had she gotten from von Bernstorff and von Papen? Not much. Not anything really. They spent their evening in a German Club and von Papen frequented some sort of fancy bordello.

She finished her milk, trudged upstairs and noticed a chill in her bedroom. The window was wide open. Pansy must have forgotten to close it after airing out the room this morning. Louisa pulled it shut. She was so tired that at first she wasn't sure what she was seeing when she looked in the mirror and saw the man in the reflection behind her. Before she could do anything, he had one arm wrapped around her waist and another clamped over her mouth.

"Shhhh," he whispered, his breath hot against her ear.

Chapter 26

Ellen

It took several days for Plunkett to get an appointment with Captain Boehm of the Abteilung III b. While they waited, Ellen traversed the streets of Berlin by herself, spent afternoons listening to Plunkett recite his poetry, and dined in the evenings at one cafe or another with Plunkett and Sir Roger Casement with Casement growing increasingly paranoid. He worried he was being followed by British spies, and he was sure he would hang someday. Plunkett tried to calm him, but to no avail.

The weather was splendid, and she enjoyed wandering the city. Even when it was overcast, which was often, the daytime temperatures usually lingered in the mid-20s Celsius. One morning as she wandered the streets, she was struck by the sight of three robust-looking women striding purposefully near the Brandenburg Gate, carrying handbags in their white-gloved hands. She immediately recognized Jane Addams, Alice Hamilton, and Aletta Jacobs from the peace mission. Miss Hamilton was the first to notice her.

"Miss Malloy! What a pleasure," she said when they were all face to face.

"The pleasure is all mine. How are you ladies faring in your mission? Have you knocked any sense into these warmongers?" Ellen asked.

Jane Addams laughed, "We're not here to knock anybody. We're on a mission for peace, which everyone says they want. And yet they're not willing to do what needs to be done to get it."

"Everyone who's not involved in the military tells us it's an old man's war for which young men are expected to die," Alice said. "And how is your mission?"

"I don't know yet," Ellen said. "I'm worried my countrymen will get in cahoots with anyone they think will help them overthrow the British."

The women didn't have long to chat, but just seeing them gave Ellen at least a small hope that there were enough people of good sense in the world to end this senseless slaughter. No one else should have to lose someone they loved. As she watched them walk away, grief snuck up and settled its cold hand on her heart. She clenched her fists. I've no time for you, she told it.

At lunch she learned that finally, Plunkett had gotten word Captain Boehm would see him and the fiancé who had brought news from Ireland.

That afternoon they walked into the offices of the *Sektion Politik Berlin des Generalstabs* where a secretary showed them into Captain Boehm's office.

"Is this your fiancé, Plunkett?" Boehm asked, standing and coming around his desk. He was a broad-shouldered man with a square head and large ears but handsome features — blue eyes, silver hair, and a clean-shaven face. He maintained a slight smile as if he found everything a little droll.

"I'm afraid that was just a ruse, Captain," Ellen said. "I'm Ellen Malloy. The Brotherhood sent me with a message for Mr. Plunkett so he could prove just how eager *Sinn Féin* is to help in the war effort."

"Is that so? What can your little island offer our mighty empire?" He crossed his arms and studied her with that amused expression.

Ellen cleared her throat. She looked at Plunkett, but he remained impassive. She needed to give the man enough information to appear legitimate. She also needed to make him trust her — and then somehow convince him to withdraw his support from the rebels. But that could come later, if at all.

"First of all," she said, "many Irish want Germany to win. They're dead up against the British. Secondly, the Republicans have identified a bay on the Western Coast that has the capacity to serve as a harbor for your U-boats. Thirdly, I've been asked to inform you that the Irish Republican Brotherhood believes that with sufficient arms, they could turn out forty to fifty thousand volunteers." She knew that figure was an exaggeration, but that's what Liam Meadows had claimed and she had to play her part.

"What can you tell me of the British presence in Ireland?" the captain asked, leaning casually against the desk and glancing at his fingernails.

"It's small," she said. "Perhaps five thousand troops with little heavy artillery."

Boehm nodded.

"I see. Are you a soldier in this Brotherhood, Miss Malloy?"

"I am not. I emigrated to New York a couple of years ago and was home visiting my sick father. My brother is a member of the Brotherhood. In fact, my family have been fighting the British for generations. I am merely doing my duty to my family and my country," she said. "The enemy of my enemy is my friend."

For the first time since she'd entered the room, she had fully caught his attention.

“New York?” he asked, leaning forward, his eyes focused on her. “And what do you do there? Do you work? Are you married?”

“I am not married. I work for a society writer at a New York newspaper. I’m her assistant,” Ellen said.

Captain Boehm stepped closer to her.

“A newspaper?” he asked, no longer smiling. She nodded. He turned and paced around the desk. “I spent many years in America. I lived in New York, Chicago, and even all the way out west in Oregon,” he said. His voice was filled with excitement. “It’s a magnificent place. The forests in the northwest are like cathedrals.”

“I haven’t been out west,” she said, “but what I have seen of the country is impressive.”

He stopped his pacing and put an avuncular hand on her shoulder.

“Miss Malloy, I’d like to speak to you further. Would you join my wife and me for drinks tonight?” he asked. “She’s an American and would love to talk about her home country. Especially New York society.”

Ellen glanced at Plunkett. His eyes were wide with surprise.

“I’m afraid my wardrobe is quite limited,” she said.

“That’s not a problem. There’s a dress shop not far from here where my wife has an account. Go there and pick out a couple of dresses,” he said. “I’m afraid all of the French *vendeuses* have fled the country, but the store is adequate."

"But I've no way to pay for them," she said with more than a little dismay. Why did rich people think everyone else had money?

He smiled broadly.

"Miss Malloy, my main goal in this war is to secure a solid Irish-American link in America. America may pretend to be neutral but as long as she manufactures weapons for the allies, she is not neutral. Our plan is to stop the pipeline of resources from that great but misguided nation. Would you be interested in being part of that plan?"

Ellen tried to understand what he was saying.

"Do you want me to return to America?" she asked.

"Yes, and once you are there, we will find ways you can be useful," he said.

She let the idea register. He wanted her to be a spy in New York?

"How?" she asked.

"You let me worry about that," he said.

She realized this could be the perfect opportunity to discover just what the Germans were doing in New York, but she knew better than to appear too eager.

"I'm not sure," she said.

"Get some dresses. I will pay for them," Captain Boehm said. "My secretary will give you the address and will call ahead. Tonight, we'll have drinks. Tomorrow, I will convince you of the justness of our cause just as you and your compatriots have convinced us to help the Irish rebellion."

"Speaking of the rebellion," Plunkett interjected. "You do know that the 20,000 rifles promised to us will not be enough. We need at least five times that."

Boehm nodded.

"As soon as we capture them from the Russians, we will put them in a warehouse for our Irish friends. We'll have enough when the time comes. Don't worry," Boehm said. Plunkett, in fact, looked very worried, but he said nothing.

***

While Plunkett sat at the table in his apartment, writing his infernal poetry, Ellen stared at the piece of paper with the dress shop's address on it and brooded over her next move. It felt as if she were in a pitch-black room groping her way forward. What was she doing, she wondered, going out with a German military man and his wife? Was she still hoping to interfere with this German-Irish alliance? It was ridiculous to think she could somehow shape events so far out of her control. Or was she actually trying to help Plunkett? What did it even mean to be loyal to one's country? If she were truly loyal, wouldn't she happily join the fight to liberate Ireland from the English tyrants even if it meant death for so many of them? And why was this captain suddenly so interested in her?

"What're ya thinking about?" Plunkett asked.

"I'm wondering what I'm doing," she said and sighed. "May I have a cigarette?"

Plunkett cocked his head.

"I didn't know you smoked," he said.

"I don't. But it's time I learned a great many things, don't ya think?"

He handed her a cigarette and lit it for her. It felt dry against her lips, and the tobacco smelled like earth after a hard rain.

"Don't suck it in," he said. "You'll make yourself sick. Just lightly puff on it."

She puffed on the thing, feeling ridiculous, but it did have a calming effect, and she saw why people smoked. It gave them something to do with their hands. It wasn't something ladies did, but she wasn't a lady. She didn't know what she was. With Hester gone, it didn't seem to matter. The loss, the confounding realization that she would never see Hester again, not once in her whole life, colored her whole world in shades of gray. She stared at the smoke snaking up from the cigarette.

When Captain Boehm's driver picked her up, she was wearing a simple black evening gown that she'd gotten from the dress shop. Black seemed appropriate.

She got in the back seat with the Captain and his wife, who wore a shiny red dress with an incongruous matching red homburg perched on her stylish black hair. She immediately clasped Ellen's hands and exclaimed that she couldn't wait to "talk shop" whatever that meant.

Ellen had assumed they were going to one of the fancy hotels on Potsdamer Platz but instead the driver took them down a series of dark narrow street until he finally stopped in front of an inconspicuous looking building with a hand-painted sign above a stairwell going down to the basement.

"What is this place?" Ellen asked.

"A *kabarett,* my dear," replied Frau Boehm. "Not as much fun as the ones in Paris. Too much censorship in Wilhelm's Germany, but it's better than nothing."

They descended the stairs and found themselves in a dark room with candles on the tables. Unusual paintings hung on the wall unlike any art she'd ever seen before — all sharp lines and angles in violent blacks, reds, and grays. They sat at a small table near the stage. Ellen accepted a cigarette offered by Captain Boehm and leaned forward so he could light it for her. She was glad she had learned to smoke earlier that day. A waiter brought a bottle of Riesling to the table, and Frau Boehm proceeded to pump Ellen about New York society. Fortunately, Ellen remembered enough of Louisa's columns that she could satisfactorily relate several of the more outstanding events from the previous season. She found herself mimicking Louisa's arch tone as she described the Annual Charity Ball at the Knickerbocker, the dance contests at the Freddy League Entertainment, and Mrs. Vincent Astor's final entertainment of the season before setting sail on the family yacht for warmer climes. Frau Boehm listened raptly.

When the performances began, Ellen was spared from the recitation of society names and parties. First dancing girls in feathers and sequins pranced on the stage for a bit. Then two men came out and performed a comedy sketch, one dressed as a clown wearing a lady's hat complete with veil and black eyelashes painted on his white face and the other a German general. Ellen couldn't understand what they were saying, but the comedy was broad enough with pratfalls and exaggerated screeches that she managed to force a few laughs. Then a beautiful woman with kohl-lined eyes and a glittering gown, slit to show her shapely legs took the microphone. The spotlight played across her mournful face. Ellen was puzzled by the deep gravel of the singer's voice as she sang her torch song. Then Ellen looked closer at the hands holding the microphone. They were large, knuckly hands. The hands of a man. She glanced quickly at the captain and his wife. They either didn't see the charade or they didn't care. In fact, they both laughed giddily when the singer came over to their table and mussed Captain Boehm's hair.

Ellen noticed a man by himself at a table in a dark corner of the room. She wasn't sure what drew her attention to him. He was so still she didn't notice him for a good long while. But once she did, she found it hard to take her eyes away. He was rather ordinary looking but he held himself as if he were poised to pounce at a moment's notice. At one point he turned and looked directly at her. His stare made her skin crawl.

She was glad when the show was finally over, and they were back in the car. The wine had gone to her head, and she felt unsteady in the heels that the dress clerk had convinced were "*de rigeur*."

"Tomorrow, Miss Malloy, we'll find you a suitable place to live," Captain Boehm said.

"But, sir, the Brotherhood doesn't have unlimited funds," she objected.

"Not to worry. There are many empty apartments now that the French and English have fled the city. They're even still furnished," he said with a shrug. "War destroys some but makes opportunities for others."

That's why powerful men wage war, Ellen thought, for the "opportunities."

At least the night had not been a waste. She'd have time now to suss out Germany's true position with regards to Ireland, but it was obvious that Captain

Boehm wanted something in return. She wished she could talk to Louisa about all of this.

"Who was that man in the corner of the club?" she asked. "He seemed to be watching everyone."

Captain Boehm and his wife glanced at each other and didn't say anything for a few moments. Then Captain Boehm said in an offhand manner, "That was Nicolai. You'll meet him one of these days."

Ellen shuddered at the thought.

Chapter 27

Louisa

"You?" Louisa sputtered when the man slowly released his hand from her mouth. She was staring at the reflection of the British Naval Attaché, the same man she'd seen at the Yacht Club in a seersucker suit. Now he was wearing a black overcoat and a fedora.

"I'm with Section Five," he said in a low voice. "British Secret Intelligence."

"What are you doing in my bedroom?" she hissed at him. She couldn't control the trembling in her legs or hands. Whether from anger or fear, she wasn't sure. "And how dare you put your hands on me?"

"My apologies," he said. "I had to make sure you wouldn't scream. I need to speak to you."

"I am not a difficult person to find, for God's sake," she said. "You could have found me at the paper or the theater or the opera, for that matter. You didn't have to scare the wits out of me." She grabbed a shawl from a hook and threw it around her shoulders.

"It would not do for anyone to see us talking, Miss Delafield," he said, his voice soft and low. "The Germans know who I am. And I do not want them to suspect you just when you're starting to gain their trust."

"Am I? They haven't told me anything useful," she said.

"These things take time. And patience," he said. He lit a cigarette and wandered about her room, stopping to examine the paintings on the wall and her books on the night stand. Now that she got a good look at him she saw that he was tight-lipped and tough. He had strong features, a large nose, and eyes like blunt instruments. He fairly crackled with energy. And that accent?

"You don't sound British," she said, suspiciously.

"Australian. Grew up in the gold fields," he said with a glint in his eye. She handed him a teacup to use for an ashtray. "Thank you."

"How do I know you are who you say you are?" she asked. "I don't even know your name."

He stopped his exploration of her room and looked at her.

"Can anyone else hear us?" he asked.

"My mother sleeps like the dead and Suzie's room is at the other end of the house, but if I screamed, yes, she would certainly hear it."

He nodded.

"My name is Reggie Grant, and I know you're in cahoots with Tom Tunney to try to find out how the Germans are sabotaging American ships. Something I'd like to know as well," he said and sucked on his cigarette. The smoke rose and snaked around his face. "I rather doubt you'll be able to find out anything, but I could be wrong. You're a fairly resourceful woman from what I understand."

She wasn't sure if he was insulting her or complimenting her.

"Why do you need to speak to me?" she asked.

He took a deep breath, flicked the ashes from his cigarette into the tea cup and said, "Your friend Officer Paddy O'Neil is dead."

He might as well have punched her. She gasped involuntarily. Stunned, she found her way to the vanity and sat in the chair.

"I don't understand. I just spoke to him..." she said. "How? What happened?"

"Bad luck. Someone he once arrested saw him at the piers and blew his cover." He went to her window, opened it, and tossed out the cigarette. "It's a terrible blow, I'm sure. But I'm here to tell you, Miss Delafield, that you cannot go to the man's funeral no matter how fond you were of him."

Louisa covered her mouth with a hand. She took deep breaths until she felt she could speak.

"How did it happen? Please tell me," she said.

"He went to the docks and got a job as a stevedore. Those fellows are all itinerants anyway. No one bothers to check the references. They come and go. But he was recognized. It was an easy matter to have a pallet fall just when he was underneath it. Too bad. I understand he was a hero. Stopped an anarchist bombing in a church or something a while back."

"Yes," Louisa said. "A hero, but also a husband and a father. Oh, poor Paula."

"This is a much more dangerous game than your previous adventures. Yes, I know about your exploits as the muckraker Beatrice Milton," Reggie Grant said. "But now you're one of the players. It's not too late for you to get out. Simply tell Bernstorff you've changed your mind, return the money, and go back to your life."

"The money? How do you know so much?" she asked.

"It's my job," he said, turned to look at her, and stuffed his hands in his pockets as he leaned against the window sill. "Where did you go tonight?"

"I followed Franz von Papen and some other man to a brothel," she said.

“What did the other man look like?”

“Very brash and handsome like some Nordic god. In a blue uniform,” she said. “German Navy, I suppose.”

“Of course. That would have been Karl Boy-Ed, the German Naval attaché,” Grant said.

“Are all you attachés spies of some sort?” she asked.

“Of course,” he said. “I’m surprised you haven’t met Boy-Ed at one of your society shindigs. I hear he’s on the hunt for an American heiress.”

“Well, he won’t find one at the house where I saw him go tonight,” Louisa said, rising. Now it was her turn to pace the room.

“Was it on Fifteenth Street?” he asked.

“How did you guess?”

She studied his face. He was arresting in the light from the Tiffany lamp, his cheekbones illuminated and his green eyes shining.

“That’s Martha Held’s place.”

“Martha Held? The opera singer?” Louisa asked in surprise.

“The very same. What I wouldn’t do to get inside those walls,” he said and looked up at her own walls. The wallpaper was dingy, she thought with an embarrassment that in turn made her angry. He had no business being in her room in the first place.

“Well, I certainly can’t get in there,” she said, curtly.

He gazed at her and said, "No, I suppose not." Then he sighed. "I'll let you get your beauty rest. But we'll see each other again."

"Surely not here?" Louisa said.

"Where else?" he said and grinned at her before slipping out the window to stealthily make his way down the ladder of her fire escape.

She shut the window and locked it, then undressed and got into bed. But she couldn't sleep. Paddy dead? How would she ever forgive herself for getting him involved? And Ellen would feel just as culpable. Damn this war. Damn it to hell. She was not a woman who cursed out loud, but she allowed herself the thought. She realized just as she was finally drifting off that she had forgotten to tell him about the radio towers in Sayville.

The next morning, she struggled out of bed. It had taken hours to fall asleep. When she woke up, she remembered the conversation with Grant the night before. He had said she couldn't go to Paddy's funeral. He was right, of course, but she couldn't bear to have Paula think she didn't care. And with Ellen not here, she couldn't even get a message to her. She didn't know whom to trust.

Paddy's death weighed on her like a lead cape, and the morning sunshine felt as inappropriate as wearing a camel skin to the opera. She was in mourning but did not want it to appear that way, so she wore dark blue instead of black. She hadn't written her piece on the Gilbert & Sullivan Revue yet. Fortunately, she only had to cover the society angle and not evaluate the merits of the performance, which was mediocre at best.

She opened her purse and saw the packet of money that Herr Albert had given her. She wondered what to do with it.

Phyllis blew in, wearing summer green, a cheery straw hat, a smile, and rose-scented *eau de toilette*. She carried her parasol in one hand and a small white pastry box in the other.

"Good morning, Louisa," she said. "I brought us some Sally Lunn buns from the Knickerbocker."

Louisa's stomach felt like rocks were jostling inside it so she declined on the excuse she'd already eaten.

"Maybe later then," Phyllis said. "What can I do this morning?"

Louisa looked at the meager pile of invitations. It was summertime, and everyone who was anyone was somewhere else. She should probably head to Saratoga or over to Newport herself if she wanted anything of note to put in the column.

"There's not much," Louisa said. She didn't have the energy to make work for Phyllis. "If you want, you can take the day off."

"Surely, there must be something I can do," Phyllis said.

Then the thought that had been nagging at Louisa became a full-fledged idea.

"There is something you can do. But it's not the usual sort of assignment," she said.

Phyllis leaned across the desk and asked in a hushed voice, "Are you investigating something criminal, Louisa? I'd love to help with that. Billy told me about your Beatrice Milton stories."

"Beatrice Milton has been fired," Louisa said, annoyed with Billy for his blabbering mouth. "A police detective I know recently died, and I'm unable to go to the funeral. His name was Paddy O'Neil."

"You want me to go to a funeral?" Phyllis asked, leaning back with a less-than-eager expression.

"No. I want you to take something to his widow. She lives in the Irish section north of the Bowery along the Hudson. I can't go see her, and don't ask me why, please. But you could go. You can offer my condolences and give her this," Louisa said and pulled the package of money from her desk drawer. She wrote down Paula's address on the package and handed it to Phyllis. "Tell her it's from a fund to honor fallen officers."

"Is it?" Phyllis asked.

Louisa didn't answer.

"You should go home and change into something else first," Louisa said. "Perhaps a little less chic."

"Something drab?"

"If you have it," Louisa said.

"All right," Phyllis said with a reassuring smile. She gripped the packet of money and sailed away, taking summer with her.

Louisa did not know how much to trust Phyllis. The fewer people who knew what she was up to the better, and the list was already rather long: Captain Tunney, Virgil Thorn, Billy Stephens, Forrest Calloway, the Mayor, J. P. Morgan, Jr. and now that British spy, Reggie Grant. Phyllis probably suspected something was going on, but so far she had proven to be discreet. She did not gossip or find fault with others, which was an anomaly among their set. And she did seem devoted to Louisa if a bit ambitious, so Louisa rested easy that she had put this task in capable hands. As for the money, well, what better place for it than Paula's family coffers?

Giving the money to Paula did nothing to assuage her sense of guilt, but she understood that even though America was not technically in the war, they would still suffer casualties. German bombs and incendiary devices regularly killed Americans at sea. German torpedoes took down ocean liners and merchant ships. Even the horses hadn't been safe. The world was going mad, and she'd better find a way to cope or it would drive her mad, too. The way she coped was to do something. Something to help stop it. And yet she'd come up with absolutely nothing. Reggie Grant already knew about the brothel. Did he know about Herr Albert, she wondered. That quiet, scarred man who held the purse strings? She would have to tell the Australian about him the next time he made an appearance in her bedroom, and she was shocked to discover she looked forward to their next meeting.

Chapter 28

Ellen

Captain Boehm was relentless. He took her to a poor house and showed her the children, spindly-legged and hollow-eyed from hunger. He took her to the hospital and showed her the wounded soldiers, their limbs stinking of gangrene. She'd already seen the long lines of hungry families outside the markets, but she hadn't seen the city streets at night where gaunt women in tattered finery tried to sell themselves for a loaf of bread.

"In America they speak of the German atrocities," Boehm told her, "But here you see what our people suffer."

One day he even took her to a prisoner of war camp where she met Irish soldiers, who greeted her with indifference. They would not be joining Casement's Irish Brigade, they told her. They'd had enough of war and didn't want to go home and find more of it.

She asked Boehm if the Germans really intended to help the Irish rebellion. He said, of course. But later in his office, she found the report that Plunkett had worked so hard on — crumpled, stained, and forgotten. She hoped this meant the Irish men would come to their senses and abandon this idea of aligning themselves with what would only be yet another tyrant.

When Boehm wasn't bludgeoning her with the sufferings of the German people, he was showing her how to shake a shadow and conversely how to follow someone. They went in department stores, up elevators to one floor, took the stairs to another, down the elevator to a third. They went in restaurants and out the back door. He gave her a coat that could be turned inside out and told her to always carry a scarf to cover her hair. He told her that incendiary devices could be powered from ordinary household items such as sugar and chalk. You can transmit messages anywhere there are numbers, even in the price of bread, he said. One of his assistants, an expert in ciphers, showed her the technique of chemical writing. But the most memorable lesson came from a short, blond man with a broad smile, who spent two days teaching her about chemical warfare.

She met him at a laboratory on the outskirts of Berlin. He greeted her effusively and took her inside to his work room. There among petri dishes, beakers full of liquids, glass vials, an incubation oven, and cages of guinea pigs, he showed her a vial full of yellowish liquid, which he told her was a bacteria called glanders.

“Just one small swab of this can kill a full-grown horse,” he said.

“A horse? Why do you need to kill a horse?” she asked.

“Horses are still the best method to transport machinery at the front. The fewer horses the enemy have, the less artillery they have. Eliminating horses coming from America is one of our top priorities if we’re to win this.”

“I see,” she said. “And what does it do to them?”

“Come here and I’ll show you.” He took her around the table to a set of cages in the corner. In the bottom row of cages lay the little guinea pigs. Some of them were listless. Others were dead.

“How awful,” she whispered.

“Not as awful as men dying,” he said, cheerfully. He seemed to love his work and spent the rest of the day showing her the various means of transporting and delivering the deadly bacteria to its intended recipients.

He made sure she wore gloves when handling it, and he even had her inject one of the guinea pigs.

"You must have no pity," he told her. "No pity at all."

***

At night she went back to the apartment, which Boehm had provided for her. She slept hard in the massive bed every night and had no dreams to speak of. She wasn't sure who was in charge of her body anymore. She moved her feet. Her hands and her mouth managed to feed her. Otherwise, she was like one of those machines she'd seen in a museum once — an automaton. You wound it up and it wrote or it danced or it turned its head clockwise.

Sometimes she ate dinner with Plunkett and Casement. A few nights she went out to the Kabarett with Boehm and his wife. One night in particular she would never forget. The skit had shown a couple in outlandish clothing, standing at a railing. They smiled in exaggerated happiness. Then the drummer in the band banged his bass drum once loudly and the couple fell down and writhed. When they fell, they revealed a round white life saver with the words "*Lusitania*." The drunken crowd laughed uproariously. Ellen made her way to the water closet and vomited.

That night she promised herself she would do whatever Boehm asked her to do. She would go back to

America and work with the Germans, who were sabotaging the American supply line to the Allies. She would find out everything she could about their activities, and then she would destroy their plans the way they had destroyed hers. While she admired Jane Addams and her group of "peacettes," — peace was a worthy goal, after all — Ellen admitted to herself that she was in this for revenge.

***

"Do you think you're ready to go back to America?" Boehm asked her one afternoon after she'd successfully shaken off the man he'd assigned to tail her. She'd made it back to his office in a record twenty minutes.

"Sure, I am. But I've no idea what you're asking me to do," Ellen said from the leather chair across from his desk.

"First of all, you will make a delivery of glanders for us. To Herr Paul Koenig. The bacterial preparation loses its potency over time so I'm afraid we can't allow you to go back to Ireland first."

"I understand," she said. She didn't need to go back home. She'd gotten a telegram earlier in the week that her father was dead. He would be buried before she could get there. She was already so numb she barely registered the loss. At least they'd reconciled before his death.

"Who is Paul Koenig?" she asked.

"He works at the Hamburg-American ship line. He's in charge of security for all of our operations. He will be your handler so you might as well know that we trust the man thoroughly," Boehm said, twirling a pen in his fingers.

"What sort of work will he have me do?" she asked.

"Oh, there's all sorts of uses for a woman of your talents. Koenig will know where to put you," Captain Boehm said. "I knew the moment you walked into my office that you would be a valuable asset."

"What do you mean by my talents?" she asked.

"You're smart and brave and you can be inconspicuous, even with that red hair," he said. "And of course, women have ways of getting information that men do not. Sometimes, the only way for you to ingratiate yourself will be — how to put this? — unsavory."

His eyes traveled up her body, and then he brought his gaze up to her eyes.

Ellen understood his meaning. Women sometimes had to use sex to get information.

He continued, "We need to know if you're up to the task."

"How?" Ellen asked.

"You must pass muster with Nicolai," he said.

"The man in the Kabarett?" Ellen asked. A hollow pit yawned in her belly.

Captain Boehm nodded curtly and looked down at the desk.

"It's not up to me," he said. "Once Nicolai has given the go ahead, there will be nothing in your way. Here is the address. Go there tonight at ten. He's expecting you."

"For what?" she said.

"You're a woman of the world," he said. "You should know what's expected."

"Captain Boehm, I am not a woman of the world," she said. "I've been sullied by no man."

He looked at her in surprise. A moment of anguish flittered over his features and then disappeared behind a placid mask.

"Then it is all the more important for you to visit Nicolai. If you do not, we cannot use you," he said.

***

Ellen knocked on the door and a moment later, it swung open. The man stood tall and burly in the doorway while he appraised her. He had the cruelest eyes she'd ever seen. He stood aside and gestured for her to enter.

The room smelled unlived in, like a museum — no food odors or soapy bath smells. Another abandoned apartment? Velvet drapes covered the windows. The furniture was plush and heavy. Flowered wallpaper created a cluttered feel. On the walls were framed posters featuring half-clad women. One of them showed a reclining woman wearing only a pair of black stockings and a smile. Above her the words *"Die Verbotene Venus."* These pictures, she thought, were probably a recent addition. They didn't go with the stuffy Victorian decor of the rest of the place.

"Fraulein Malloy, good of you to come," he said in a gravelly voice. He offered her a drink. "Irish whiskey. Just for you." He handed her a glass of amber liquid.

She did not care for whiskey, but she drank anyway. It felt like burning coal on her throat. She knew what was coming by the hard and hungry curve of his lips. She knew better than to fight it, to scream, or to try to run away. She drank another and another.

He pulled the pins from her hair and let it tumble over shoulders. She forced herself not to jerk away from his touch. Then she let him take her into the bedroom and roughly undress her. Like the guinea pigs in the glanders lab, she lay there listlessly while the German man gyrated above her, Ellen remembered the last morning she had with Hester, how the ship's engines hummed underneath them as Hester softly caressed her face, her neck, her breasts, her thighs with a tenderness such as she would never know again.

Remember why you are doing this, she told herself. *You must avenge Hester and the little girl with the bow in her hair and even Lord Fatlip.* She shut out the calls of the drowning people as they begged for help and the screeches of the crazed seagulls. Ignoring the sharp pain in her womb, she reached around the man's compact body and dug her fingernails into his flesh.

Chapter 29
Louisa

Suzie had transformed a corner of the parlor into a small sewing factory. Silks, satins, and laces covered the sofa. A dress form with a white lace contraption around the bust occupied the middle of the room. A Singer sewing machine sat on top of a second-hand table. And in the middle of the room stood Pansy in a red satin corset and bloomers.

From her invalid chair, Anna watched. Louisa would have thought her mother would be scandalized, but she only seemed mildly curious.

"I thought we hired Pansy to help out around the house so you could take it easy," Louisa scolded. "Now you're working harder than ever, and Pansy is your model?"

"I've got to keep up with my orders, and not everybody is the same size," Suzie said, tape measure draped over her shoulders. To the girl, she said, "Thank you, Pansy. You can get back to work now."

Pansy stepped behind a screen to change.

"Are you actually making money?" Louisa asked.

"I am. I have an 'in' with the servants at all the big houses," Suzie said. "I give them my samples to show the ladies in the house, then the ladies make their orders and I deliver."

Louisa examined one of the satin corsets.

"They do look well put together."

"Have you noticed that corsets are a little longer this year? And roomier. And every woman wants one of these new brassieres," Suzie said as she pinned a pink bow to the front of the lacey white creation on the dress form. "Why did it take so long for women to figure out they need to be able to breathe? You know, I could use a model about your size. Are you free?"

"I am not," Louisa said. She turned and headed toward the kitchen. She found some lukewarm coffee on the stove.

She poured herself a cup of coffee and took it outside to their miniscule backyard. The ginger tabby followed her and rubbed against her ankles, mewling. She bent down to scratch her head, and her mind wandered to Reggie Grant. How his presence had filled her room that night. She replayed their conversation. He seemed to know a lot about the Germans, but just like the police, he didn't know how they were blowing up or setting fire to the American ships. And if he didn't know, how could she expect to find out?

The littleleaf linden was in full summer regalia, and up in the branches Louisa saw a flash of red. Was it a cardinal? She gasped in delight. She couldn't remember the last time she'd seen a cardinal, his red plumage like a flame in the green. He made a loud cheep-cheep, and after a few moments, he took wing. As her eyes followed the bird's trajectory, she saw his reflection against the upstairs window. Once he was gone, her eyes remained on the window. The red cardinal was the same color as the satin corset Pansy had been modeling. The color looked exquisite on the bird, but rather tawdry on a woman, she thought. Then Reggie Grant's words after she'd told him about seeing the German men enter Martha Held's place floated through her mind: *What I wouldn't give to get inside those walls.*

She nearly dropped the China coffee cup in her haste to get inside.

"Suzie!" she called, dashing into the parlor.

Anna looked up startled.

"Why are you making such a fuss?" she asked querulously.

"Suzie," Louisa said again.

"What is it?" Suzie mumbled around the pins tucked between her lips.

"I need your help," Louisa said.

***

Usually, Louisa would be in Newport for the various yacht racing festivities, but this year she would file a report from the Manhattan side for the simple fact she had a hunch that Reggie Grant would be at the Yacht Club again. As a navy man, he would be fond of events that involved boats.

There were any number of races in the summer, and with so many Americans staying home because of the war, the after-parties were becoming famous. Louisa got to the club at the tail end of the race, just in time to see the last of the sloops gliding in with their billowing white triangle sails against the azure sky. She stood for a moment with the crowd to soak in the moment. It was as if nothing at all was wrong in the world. Maybe someday it would be so.

Once inside the club, Louisa searched for Commodore Harold Vanderbilt to get the pertinent details for her column. She'd already asked Thorn to send a photographer to take photos of the rich and frivolous, and she found him, snapping a photo of the winner and his wife. Then she found the Commodore at the bar. He was happy to pontificate for the paper, and it never hurt to have the name Vanderbilt in the column.

"The knockabout sloop Dandelion won today's race," he said.

"And how many yachts competed?" she asked, notebook in hand.

"We had seven yachts ranging in length from forty feet to sixty feet. They had a light northeasterly breeze for most of the course," he said and handed her a fluted glass. "Have some champagne, Miss Delafield. It's in short supply these days."

The Commodore was then swept away by his sister and some others while Louisa mingled with the crowd to collect quotes and get the names of the notable. She finally saw Reggie Grant surrounded by admirers — mostly female. He wore his full naval uniform and was the embodiment of dashing. No wonder he was becoming this year's toast of the town. She edged close enough to hear what he was saying.

"Sure, Wilson used strong language in his message to the Kaiser after the *Lusitania*, but do you think the Germans are afraid? Not a chance. My London source told me they've deciphered cables showing that the embassy plans armed insurrections on your city streets should America enter the war. Think about that for a minute," he said. Louisa watched the reactions of his listeners. He'd hit his mark. They were aghast. One man in a dark suit looked especially concerned.

"They've got enough hyphenates to do it," the dark-suited man said.

"Indeed they do, old man. And their propaganda machine is running at top speed," Grant said.

Louisa tried to catch Grant's eye. With a slight lift of an eyebrow, he indicated he had seen her. She wandered over to the winner of the day's race and took down some more quotes. She turned to the ladies in the group to admire their attire. Some of them complained that they had to wear last year's dresses, thanks to this silly war. She had just picked up her second glass of champagne when a waiter brought a note to her on silver tray. She stepped away from the crowd to read it. "Meet me outside one block north in ten minutes. R."

Five minutes later she strolled nonchalantly away from the club. No one paid her any mind. When she reached the corner a block north of the club, a sleek gray automobile with what looked like a metal fairy perched on the front pulled up to her. Reggie Grant sat behind the wheel, grinning. She didn't wait for him to come open the door for her, but instead immediately slid into the two seater, and they went roaring off.

"What kind of motorcar is this?" she asked.

"A Rolls Royce Silver Ghost," he said.

"Ghost? I don't imagine you're too invisible in this. It's gorgeous," she said.

"I had it sent from home. It impresses people much more than a mere Packard. And that's what I need to do. Impress people. Especially American people," he said.

"You seem very good at your job. Who was that man in the suit back there?" she asked.

"A member of Wilson's cabinet. Everyone in that crowd is eager for America to join the war. I drop little pieces of information and those tidbits find their way into the president's ear," he said.

They drove across the Tappan Zee Bridge and north along the Hudson River.

"The Germans don't realize that most of their servants work for us. They think anyone who speaks German believes in *Deutschland uber alle*. But the 'Bohunks' come from countries that have been oppressed by the Empire for centuries, and they have no love for the Prussians or the Germans. They call Bernstorff 'the Barber' as in the Barber of Seville, only he's the Barber of Sayville, New York. Lecherous old goat."

"Sayville is where I saw two enormous radio towers, which are owned by a German company, Telefunken. Doesn't that seem suspicious to you?"

"It does," he said.

The sun was setting as the car climbed through the hills.

"Where are we going?" she asked.

"Nowhere," he said, and a few minutes later he pulled onto an overlook. He turned off the Rolls and came around to let her out. They stood on the cliff and looked at the Hudson River cutting through the valley below, glimmering with the last rays of the sun.

"This is lovely for Nowhere," she said.

"You have a beautiful country," Grant said with a satisfied nod. He lit a cigarette, the flame briefly illuminating his face.

"How did you get involved in all this?" she asked.

He took a deep inhale of the cigarette before he responded.

"About three years ago, I was to be the captain of the HMS Centurion, a super-dreadnought, nearly six-hundred feet long. She was to be the dragon of the sea. But we had a little problem on a test run of the turbines out on the Channel. I was below deck, changing out of my wet shoes and socks of all things. She had no heating yet, and it was freezing. That's when I felt the tremor. A few minutes later I heard the call to collision stations. I ran upstairs and saw an injured steamer just off the aft tunnels. I called down to the skipper to stay put, telling him we'd lower boats, but there was no reply and then we lost sight of them. It was only later that we learned all were lost."

"Lost?" Louisa asked. Grant stood next to her, staring out into space, his cigarette glowing. The sun had disappeared, and stars poked through the dark curtain overhead one by one.

"We had no idea what had happened at first. We hoped for the best, but..." He hesitated. His voice sank as he continued, "We'd hit an Italian steamer. All thirty-five men aboard died."

He dropped his cigarette and ground it out with his shoe. Then he looked at her with his hands in his pockets. He grimaced helplessly. She could not imagine the guilt he must feel.

"So they sent you to America as your punishment?" she asked.

"Exactly. I wound up in what I thought was some backwater post. I had no idea that I was finally in the very spot where I could do the most good with whatever odd talents Providence had granted me. And now here I am, under a starry sky with a most intriguing woman."

They stood close to each other and were silent for several long minutes. She felt a chemical interaction in the air between them.

"Perhaps you should take me back to the city, Mr. Grant," she said. The break up with Forrest had been too painful. She didn't want to go down that road again.

"Only if you promise to call me Reggie," he said.

"All right, Reggie," she said and smiled.

They got in the motorcar.

"Don't worry about directions," he said. "I know where you live."

"By the way," she said. "I think I know how to get into Martha Held's."

***

The advertising artist at the newspaper had happily obliged Louisa with a flyer showing a variety of corsets and brassieres. The styles were racier than what would appear in the newspapers, with sheer busts and shorter corset lengths, and the female figures were posed more seductively. "Not available in stores. Private showings available." She'd had to get assistance from the mayor to have a new phone installed in her house with a different number, registered to a Mademoiselle Couture's Fine Lingerie. Suzie said she was sure they would call and she was right. The call came the day after Suzie hand-delivered the flyer to the butler at the house on Fifteenth Street. Martha Held herself made an appointment for noon the next day.

"The girls are never up before then," she'd said.

Louisa and Suzie arrived shortly before noon with a hired boy to help carry the trunk.

An elegant Negro man opened the door for them.

"Come in, ladies," he said. "Frau Held is expecting you."

Louisa couldn't help but notice that his eyes lingered on Suzie, who wore a purple dress of her own creation that flattered her buxom figure. Suzie was over sixty, but she had a big smile and bright eyes, and Louisa realized that this man considered her attractive. The butler showed them into the parlor and invited them to have a seat.

The hired boy brought in the trunk and placed it in the parlor, which Suzie opened to display the wares inside. Martha Held, the former opera singer, came in the room, wearing a long negligee with feathers on the sleeves and collar. She was tall and grand with glossy black hair and bright blue eyes, and her voice resonated in the room the way it once had on a stage. Covering the walls were pictures of her in various operas.

"That will be all, Sweet," she said to the butler. He bowed and left the room but not without another glance at Suzie.

Frau Held looked from Louisa to Suzie and back again. As a European she didn't seem to have the prejudices that many white Americans had toward Negroes. She shook both their hands. Louisa explained that

Suzie was the seamstress while she was in charge of the business end of things. Of course, when it came to business, Suzie needed no one's help, but how else could Louisa explain her presence?

"The girls are on their way down. Lazy sluggards," the madam said. "They don't all sleep here so I'll buy a few extra for the ones who haven't come in yet." She thumbed through the selection as the "girls" piled in, sleepy-eyed and gossiping. As soon as they saw the trunk, they crowded around. Suzie pulled out garments and placed them strategically on the couch or hung them from the standing lamps so the women could see them amid the laughter and demands for coffee.

"This design," Suzie explained, showing off the corset cover, "flattens the back and slims the hips. Notice the lace in the front and the back. You might not be able to see your backside but others can." She winked at the women when she said this. Louisa was amazed at Suzie's powers of persuasion.

Martha Held left Louisa and Suzie alone with their customers. The women admired the fabrics and declared the look quite "modish." Louisa had been afraid she would be uncomfortable around women such as these, but they were good-natured and a few were even shy. She soon had no qualms about being amongst them and realized she'd have to get them talking if she was going to find out who could be helpful to her. She targeted the one she thought men would find most beautiful — a blonde with flawless skin and striking blue eyes surrounded by a forest of thick eyelashes. She could be in the motion pictures, Louisa thought.

"Pink is a very popular color this year," Louisa said, approaching her. "And goes well with your complexion." She held a pink corset up to the woman's chest.

"Does it show off my assets?" the blonde asked with a laugh.

"Indeed it does," Suzie interjected. They all chuckled.

"How much?" she asked.

"Five dollars," Suzie said. Louisa's eyebrows lifted at the price, but the blond woman pulled a five dollar bill from her bosom and handed it over. Then her eyes lit up and she picked up a black satin corset with a low bust.

"Captain von Papen will like this," she said. Louisa's breath caught. She had guessed correctly, but instead of taking the corset herself, the blonde tossed it to a dark-haired girl with olive-toned skin who smoked a cigarette in an armchair across the room. Then she turned to Louisa and said, "Carlotta is the favorite of the German military attaché."

Louisa looked over at Carlotta. She was probably not more than seventeen, but she had the bored worldly expression of a woman far older. Carlotta looked at the black corset and seemed to approve. She rose and tossed a ten dollar bill on the coffee table. "I'll take a red one, too."

Louisa turned to the blonde and said, "And what about you? Whose favorite are you?"

"Karl, of course. The German naval attaché. He's handsome and charming and...," she said, glancing at the dark-haired girl, "easily satisfied, unlike some." Then she leaned close to Louisa and whispered, "That Captain von Papen fellow is an arrogant prick, pardon my French."

Louisa had never heard that term before, but she was pretty sure she knew what it meant.

The blonde woman then turned to the girl and said, "Carlotta knows how to handle him. Don't you?"

The dark-haired girl's expression was inscrutable as she squinted her eyes against the smoke seeping from her lips.

Louisa needed to find some way to talk to Carlotta.

"I have told you, I don't let girls smoke in here!" Martha Held had returned and now glared at Carlotta. "Take that outside."

Carlotta strolled out of the room, the cigarette lodged between her fingers. Louisa worried that she'd lost her chance, but a minute or so later, Louisa saw her through the window on the back porch.

"Suzie, I need to get a little fresh air if you don't mind. Can you handle the rest of the sales?" Louisa asked.

Louisa came onto the porch just as Carlotta was stubbing out her cigarette.

"Carlotta," Louisa said. "May we talk?"

"You want to talk to me?" Carlotta said. Louisa looked into her face. She was so young it made Louisa want to cry.

"I can't really talk here. Can you get out sometime? And meet me somewhere?" Louisa asked.

"Sure. We're not slaves, you know," Carlotta said.

"Of course not. Do you know the ladies' lounge in Grand Central Terminal?" Louisa asked.

The girl nodded.

"Do you think you could meet me there? Say around 4 o'clock this afternoon?"

"Why?" the girl asked. "What's in it for me?"

"Money," Louisa said. "If you'll help me."

"How much?"

"Plenty."

The girl thought about it for a moment and then shrugged.

"Sure. I'll be there. As long as this isn't some trick..."

"It's not a trick. I promise," Louisa said.

In the taxi on the way home, Suzie counted her money.

“How many of these houses of ill repute do you suppose there are in the city?” Suzie asked. “This is so much money.”

“A lot,” Louisa said. She was remembering when a couple of years ago she herself had been abducted and held against her will in such a place. Fortunately, she’d been rescued before any damage had been done. It would have utterly destroyed her and yet these women acted as though there was nothing wrong with how they lived. It baffled her. Perhaps for some, such as the pretty blonde, it would all work out. Someone would not mind her past and would marry her, but the young ones like Carlotta. Something in her eyes said her very soul was disintegrating.

“That butler sure was looking you over,” Louisa said.

“Was he? I didn’t notice.”

***

When Louisa met with Carlotta in the ladies lounge at Grand Central later, she realized she was even younger than Louisa had first thought.

“How old are you?” Louisa asked.

“Old enough,” Carlotta answered.

Louisa had no business judging the girl and proceeded to enlist her help in uncovering Papen’s plans.

***

"Did she agree?" Reggie asked as he lounged in the arm chair in her room after Louisa told him the story.

"Yes, I told her I would pay her for every bit of information she could get out of von Papen," Louisa said. "She was agreeable. I got the feeling he was cruel to her."

"It's true then," he said. "You are a resourceful woman."

"I'll expect you to provide the money," she said.

"Of course," he said. He rose and approached her, placing his hands on either side of her waist. Then he bent close to her and kissed her softly on the lips. "Not only resourceful, but beautiful, too."

"I prefer being resourceful," she said and drew away from him. The kiss had happened so quickly that it had caught her off guard. The other night she'd worried about getting entangled with another man, but now she wasn't sure what she wanted.

"Forgive me for being forward," he said. "I gathered my attentions were not unwanted. I must have gathered wrong. I'll make sure you have the money to give to Papen's girl. Goodbye, Miss Delafield." He smiled at her, tipped his hat, and walked toward the window.

"Stop," she said. Her uncertainty had vanished.

He turned and looked at her and slowly blinked like a watchful cheetah. She didn't say anything. She didn't need to. He crossed the distance between them in one stride, his hat tumbling to the floor, and took her in his arms. This time when he kissed her, she didn't pull back. His arms encircled her, and all her armor fell away.

Chapter 30
Ellen

Ellen rose early to meet Plunkett one last time at the cafe in the Excelsior. He was already seated at a corner table when she arrived. Only a handful of patrons occupied the other tables. Plunkett's hat was shoved back on his head, revealing his high forehead. Dark pouches hung under his eyes as if he'd been looking up a chimney. He'd admitted to her earlier that he had contracted tuberculosis as a boy, and that he was often ill. But his hollowed-out look was due to more than just the ravages of disease. To Ellen, he looked like a man condemned to die.

"So you're going to New York to help the Germans?" he said.

She didn't answer him. She simply gazed at him and saw a good man, dedicated to a righteous if misguided cause. She took a sip of the hot coffee and looked out the window.

"I've something to tell you, Joey," she said. "I didn't come to Germany with the intention of helping you or your cause."

"Why did you then?" he asked. The morning sunlight streaming through the window glinted off his spectacles.

"I wanted to stop you," she confessed. "Then I saw there wasn't any need to be stopping you because the Germans don't plan on helping you. They aren't the least bit concerned about Irish independence, and they don't have any faith in Ireland's ability to help them. I've learned that much."

"I don't believe you," he said. "They'll come around. They've promised us guns."

"They don't keep their promises, Joey. Why don't you get out while you can? Don't ask all those Irish lads to break their poor mothers' hearts for such a futile cause. Violence won't get us what we want."

"So you're a peacette, are you?"

"No. I'm just a woman who already lost one person I love to an unholy war, and I don't want to lose another," she said. "It's bad enough that our boys are dying on these bloody European battlefields. Don't take the war into their homes. I beg you."

"Ah, girleen, what can I do now? The wheels are already grinding forward. There will be an uprising whether the Germans help us or no," he said.

Ellen had known he would not be convinced. What man who was determined to go to war had ever been convinced by a woman's pleas?

"I will do this for you though," he said and leaned across the table, taking both her hands in his. She noticed how soft his fingertips were. These were the hands of a thinker, not a laborer or a soldier. "I'll tell Liam when the time comes to send your brother away from the fighting on some sort of errand or another."

"Martin won't fall for that," she said.

"He will if we convince him that it's absolutely vital to the success of our cause," Plunkett said.

"Can you do that?"

"I'm a military strategist, aren't I?" he said and grinned at her. She squeezed his hands in gratitude.

***

Captain Boehm came over to the apartment as she was packing. He'd brought a packet of papers and a leather "make up" kit for her. Underneath the rouge pots, tubes of lipstick, tins of face powder, and jars of face tonic was a sealed compartment.

"What's in the compartment?" she asked.

"Glanders," he said. "Don't touch it. And don't make any friends on board. Keep to yourself as much as possible," he told her.

"That will be easy," she said. It had been five weeks since the sinking of the *Lusitania*, and she didn't relish the idea of being on an ocean liner once again. She'd be happy to hide away in her cabin for the whole trip. She could even feign seasickness and take her meals in her cabin.

The night train took her to Amsterdam. The next morning, she embarked upon the *Nieuw Amsterdam*. As soon as the ship pulled away from the docks into the North Sea, the captain assembled the passengers and explained that the trip would cover almost four thousand nautical miles and would take about two weeks. He went over the safety instructions, telling them the locations of all the lifeboats and promising the passengers there were enough of them and that they were seaworthy. *That's what they all say*, she thought.

Afterward she retired to her small second-class cabin. It was nothing like the luxurious stateroom she'd shared with Hester on the *Lusitania*, but it suited her purposes. What she needed to do right now was to sleep, to dream away what had happened to her in that stuffy apartment where Nicolai had "tested" her. She hadn't passed with flying colors, but apparently she'd done nothing to scratch her off the list of would-be spies. From what she understood, she would be surrounded by a nest of them.

On the second night of the voyage, she woke up in a panic. It felt as if she couldn't breathe. She threw the covers off and dressed quickly. Finding her way through the narrow hallways of the vessel, she located the stairs to the deck and went up into the balmy night air. A full moon shone a bright path on the water. She stood at the railing and realized they were in the same waters where Hester had drowned. What if Hester was calling her? It would be so easy to join her, to simply slip over the rail and plunge into the water. This time there would be no child to save and no life raft to keep her alive until the rescuers came. This time it would just be her and the dark and the water. And Hester. She knew her thoughts were crazy but she kept thinking of that man on top of her, grunting and bucking. She remembered how the drops of his sweat fell on her skin. She remembered the ripping sensation inside her. And then she thought of Hester. Was she lonely? Did she want her to come to her? She could hear her, she thought. Crying. She felt the cold rail under the palms of her hands, felt a pull stronger than anything she'd ever known. She stepped up and put one foot on the rail. Below her the dark beast nuzzled the side of the ship. She could hear the crying of those drowning souls. She heard it now clearly. Just as she put her second foot on the rail, she realized the crying was not in her head.

She looked around and saw a child, standing about ten feet away, sobbing — a lost little girl in a pink flannel nightgown. Ellen lowered herself back down to the deck.

"What are ye doing out here, wee one?" Ellen said as she walked over to the child.

The girl continued to cry, her mouth agape, tears rushing over her cheeks. Ellen knelt beside her.

"Aw, come here," Ellen said and took the child in her arms. "We'll find your mam. What's your name?"

"Sarah," the little girl said, between sobs.

Ellen took the child to the captain's station and volunteered to stay with Sarah while a steward went to find her parents. She lifted the little girl onto her lap and began to sing the lullabies her own mam had sung to her when she was wee.

"Too-ra-loo-ra-loo-ral,
Too-ra-loo-ra-li,
Too-ra-loo-ra-loo-ral,
Hush now don't you cry!"

Soon the girl placed her head on Ellen's breast, and her tears subsided. It was a good twenty minutes before the steward came back with an hysterical American woman and her chagrined husband. It seems they'd gone to sleep and neglected to lock the door to their cabin. The little girl had gone exploring. Ellen handed over the little girl, who was smiling now, happy to be in her mother's arms, oblivious to the fright she'd given them.

"I can't thank you enough," the mother repeated over and over.

"Can we give you a reward?" the father asked.

"No, sir, you may not," Ellen said.

"Then will you sit with us at dinner tomorrow night?" the mother asked.

Ellen thought about her promise to Captain Boehm not to make any friends.

"I'll be happy to join you," she said.

She went back to her cabin and fell fast asleep. For the rest of the trip, she ignored Captain Boehm's instructions and ate with the American family every night. She enjoyed their company and they seemed to enjoy hers. Sometimes she offered to sit with Sarah while the parents went off to enjoy the entertainments.

One evening a Canadian soldier joined them at their table. He was on his way home on a medical discharge. He looked quite stalwart in his uniform and cap. He had a big square head and stiff shoulders. But she recognized something in him. Like her, something inside was damaged. She saw it in the way his eyes roved unsteadily around the dining room.

"Have you seen battle?" she asked gently.

"I was at Ypres," he said in an oddly raspy voice that didn't match his robust appearance.

One of the men at the table looked up sharply, but Ellen knew nothing of that particular battle.

"In April the Germans came at my battalion. Not with artillery. We were expecting the sounds of guns and canons. Instead it was eerily quiet, and on the back of the wind, a smell came. A smell I'll never forget. So harsh your tear ducts sizzled."

"Chlorine gas," one of the men at the table said to the others in a low voice.

The mother of the little girl took her daughter from the table, but everyone else sat motionless, raptly listening to the soldier.

"In minutes men were sprawled in the trenches, coughing, crying, screaming. I felt like someone had jammed a flame thrower down my throat. I couldn't breathe. I couldn't see. I knew at that moment exactly what hell must be like. I thought I'd be fighting men but you can't fight what you can't see. This wasn't battle. It was horror. That's all. Didn't matter how good you were with a rifle or how tough you were in hand-to-hand combat. The gas overpowered us all. Those of us that could retreated. Those that couldn't died."

Ellen felt a shiver travel down her back. It was the same with the torpedo that sank the *Lusitania*. They'd been helpless to stop it. She wondered if the Canadian soldier, like herself, felt guilt for having survived.

"I'm lucky," he said. "Some of those men will never be able to see a sunset again. Me, I spent a couple months in hospital. My eyesight came back, but my lungs are shot. Don't know if my vocal cords will ever be the same."

At that moment, someone at a nearby table popped the cork on a bottle of champagne. The soldier flinched and knocked over a glass of water. His hands shook.

"Sorry. I'm not fit company," he said. He stood and left the room. He wasn't so lucky after all, she thought. None of them were. She never saw him at dinner again.

On the last night on the ship, when Sarah crawled onto her lap while her parents danced to the music of an orchestra, Ellen realized Hester would never have wanted her to leap off the ship's deck into those cold waters. Hester would want her to live, and it was up to Ellen to make it mean something, even if that something was only revenge. She leaned her chin on the top of Sarah's head and watched the dancers as they held each other, twirling across the floor.

Chapter 31

Louisa

Louisa had put a notice in her column about an orchid show and the next day she met with Olive Mitchel, the mayor's wife in an elegant tea room, which was furnished with painted tables, hickory chairs, and botanical paintings of flowers on the walls. They ordered heart-shaped waffles with strawberry jam and talked about the things women were supposed to talk about. Then Mrs. Mitchel, a stout woman with an egg-shaped face and shrewd eyes, mentioned the recent article on Franz von Papen.

"Yes," Louisa said, wiping strawberry jam from her lips. "The count is very happy with me. Did you also see my story on the popularity of biergartens?" She glanced around to make sure no one could overhear their conversation and leaned forward. "I'm afraid they are getting more out of me than I am from them. I had hoped that I might get more information from a 'good friend' of Herr von Papen, but nothing so far."

"Patience," Mrs. Mitchel said. "Patience."

Louisa didn't feel patient, but at least her nights had grown considerably more entertaining.

***

Reggie's fingers caressed the back of her neck as they lay together in her four poster bed. Making love to this handsome, virile man had certainly soothed the sting of losing Forrest. While Forrest had been a gentle, careful lover, Reggie was youthful and energetic. They tried various positions, and he had found places inside her that made her bury her moans in her pillow. He had also directed her to a certain Fifth Avenue doctor for a Dutch pessary and some spermicide so she wouldn't get pregnant. Birth control, as Margaret Sanger called it, was illegal, but there were a few doctors who cared more for the welfare of women (as long as they could pay) than they did about the law.

"It's been two weeks," Louisa said, "and I've heard nothing from Carlotta."

"Perhaps it's not so easy to extract information from the great Franz von Papen," Reggie said. "He may be arrogant, but he's not a complete fool. You said so yourself in that lovely write up you gave him."

"You know why I wrote that," Louisa said and turned to face him. He kissed her lightly on the lips.

"Why have you never married?" he asked.

She sighed.

"I almost accepted a proposal," she said.

"From whom?" he asked, curiously.

"I thought you knew everything, Mr. Spy," she teased.

"No. Whoever he was, you've been most discreet."

"Then it will stay that way."

"At least tell me what changed your mind," he said.

"Two reasons," she said. "The first is that the *Lusitania* sank and I realized I had more important things to do than plan for a wedding."

"And the other?" he asked.

She sighed again.

"My father was murdered when I was twelve. In a seedy hotel room in Greenwich Village."

"I did know about that," he admitted. "I also know that your blood is as blue as the ocean."

"For all the good it does me. When I was at my father's graveside, I promised myself I would find out what happened. I wouldn't marry until I understood what had destroyed my parents. What happened to the fortune? Who killed my father? Why? These questions haunt me. I know there are answers out there."

"And who has the answers?" he asked.

"I believe that our former attorney, Mr. Herbert Markham, knows something. His wife, Julia, was going to tell me, but then she clammed up as they say in the dime novels. When I call on her, she's too sick to see me or out of town. If I see her socially, she's always very polite but close-lipped. So I'm at an impasse. And now I don't have the time to think about it," she said, as he ran his fingers through her long, loose hair.

He kissed her bare shoulder. The edges of her window around the shade had turned gray.

"It's almost morning. You should leave."

"But it's so nice here with you," he said.

"I know, but really, Reggie, you must," she said. She gave him a little shove, and he complied. He dressed quickly and kissed her on the forehead.

"Don't get into any trouble," he said.

"You either," she said. Then he was gone and she lay in bed, thinking about this new relationship. War did indeed make strange bedfellows. She thought of Forrest and wondered if he was still seeing that little floozy. Then she berated herself. Who was she to talk about floozies when she was sleeping with a man whom she had no intention of marrying? Then she paused and wondered, did she really have no intention of marrying

Reggie Grant. She certainly had feelings for him. She shook her head. A ridiculous idea for all the aforementioned reasons and then some.

***

She stopped by Thorn's office to tell him that she'd gotten nothing so far. They'd printed two stories favorable to the Germans — the profile on von Papen and a story on the biergartens. Now she planned another on Countess von Bernstorff's favorite family recipes. But she had absolutely nothing to give to Captain Tunney.

She went to her desk where, to her surprise, Phyllis was typing a story.

"I thought you'd still be in Newport," Louisa said. "Isn't Mrs. Berwind hosting her annual luncheon at The Elms?"

"She got a summer cold and cancelled," Phyllis said. "Not to mention, I was getting tired of the fare at the White Horse Tavern."

"I understand perfectly," Louisa said. "Too much mutton."

"I wondered if you'd like me to go to Saratoga for the week. I hear the scene is quite lively this year."

"That's not a bad idea," Louisa said.

"You usually go there every summer, don't you? Why not this year?" Phyllis asked.

Louisa didn't have an answer. She hadn't even thought to have an excuse ready. What an oversight. Of course, Phyllis would want to know why the society writer was sticking so close to the city when society had fled.

"I may as well tell you the truth," Louisa said. "Thorn has asked me to stay in the city this summer. He wants me to write some political stories. Apparently, the mayor is starting a new initiative, and Thorn wants me to follow it."

"Louisa," Phyllis said, drawing out her name. "Are you getting a promotion soon? Are you grooming me to be your replacement?"

"Indeed not!" Louisa exclaimed with a bit too much indignation, considering that she had actually intended to do just that.

"Forgive me for being presumptuous," Phyllis said, hastily.

"Never mind, Phyllis. You've done an exemplary job and you've been invaluable to me. I shouldn't have snapped at you."

Phyllis smiled at her affectionately, then pulled the piece of paper from the typewriter.

"You were perfectly in the right," Phyllis said. "I'll just take this to the typesetter."

She hadn't gotten far when she turned.

"By the way. You had a phone call. From someone named Ellen? Is that the lady who used to work for you?" Phyllis looked crestfallen. "Now that she's back, will she want her job back?"

"I don't know," Louisa said, stunned and excited and apprehensive. What would she do about Ellen? Ellen was a good soldier. But she was no society writer, and right now Louisa needed someone to cover the stories she couldn't get to. "Don't worry. I meant it when I said you were invaluable to me."

"I hope so," Phyllis said.

Louisa wasted no time getting over to Mrs. Cantor's rooming house to see Ellen. A maid sent her up to Ellen's room. When she opened the door, the two women stared at each other, momentarily speechless. Ellen looked just the same and yet also somehow different.

"You're back," Louisa said.

"'Tis I in the flesh," Ellen said.

Louisa entered the small room and hugged her, eyes watering, unable to speak.

"I spoke to your new assistant," Ellen said, pulling out of her arms. They weren't accustomed to hugging. "She sounds quite hoity toity."

"Phyllis is only temporary," Louisa said.

Ellen pointed to a stack of newspapers on her desk.

"I've been catching up. She even got her own byline a few times."

Louisa felt at a loss.

"Since I started helping Captain Tunney, or I should say, trying to help him since so far I haven't uncovered a thing, I can't cover all the society events, and it turns out she does a fairly good job of it. But as soon as this business with the Germans saboteurs is over, I'll go back to my regular duties, and you can have your old job back. Everything will be just as it was."

"Ah, Louisa," Ellen said, sinking onto her bed. "It will never be as it was."

Louisa watched the dust motes dancing in a stream of sunlight, coming through the window. She went over to the bed where she sat next to Ellen and clasped her hands in her own. "I'm so sorry about Hester."

They sat in silence for several minutes before Ellen murmured thank you and gently extricated her hands.

"So tell me about these German saboteurs," Ellen said, rising and going to look out the window.

"There's Count von Bernstorff, the German ambassador. Loves to be in society, and from what I understand is frequently unfaithful to the countess. There's also Captain Franz von Papen, the military attaché, an incredibly arrogant fellow. I wrote a profile of him and Thorn actually published it. Fortunately, I was able to couch it in society terms. Next is Karl Boy-Ed, the naval attaché. I haven't met him yet. I have, however, seen him going into a brothel that caters to Germans. The

British Naval attaché, Reggie Grant, thinks the spies trade their information in that brothel. Suzie and I got in there under the guise of selling underthings. I may have made a contact there. Finally, Heinrich Albert. He's the accountant. Strange and quiet. I have a meeting with him later today."

"Why?"

"To pick up my bribery payment and get another assignment. Can you believe it?"

"Oh, yes, I can. I've learned a lot about their tactics," she said. "I've got another name for you. Paul Koenig. He's their head security fella. Works at the docks. One of his underlings met me at the dock, took some things from me, and said 'P. K.' would be sending me a message soon."

"What things did you bring?"

"Letters from the German General Staff to your friends, Count von Bernstorff and Franz von Papen. They were sealed and probably in German so I couldn't read them. And I delivered some glanders bacteria, also sealed, in a makeup case."

"Glanders! How awful. I saw what it did to a shipment of horses. So gruesome," Louisa said, remembering with horror the roan mare, lying on her side, so very still.

Then Ellen filled in Louisa on the other details of her trip to Germany, with the exception of her "training" from Nicolai.

"They gave me plenty of U.S. currency before I left so you needn't worry about giving me my job back yet," Ellen said. "It's better if I'm at loose ends right now."

"I suppose if we accomplish nothing else, at least we're taking some of their money," Louisa said. "Money they might be spending on real spies."

"Oh, we'll accomplish something. Don't you worry," Ellen said. Louisa smiled and felt a wave of gratitude. Phyllis might be able to write about society, but Ellen had the courage of a lioness, and that's what Louisa needed. Courage. Then she remembered...

"Ellen, I have some terrible news for you," she said. "It's about Paddy."

Ellen's body went rigid before Louisa even had the chance to tell her what had happened. These days one could always assume the worst, but Louisa had at least expected Ellen to cry. It was as if something had died inside her friend.

***

Louisa took the train to the Hamburg American Lines office building at 45 Broadway. It was later than she intended, and when she found Herr Albert's office, he was already packing up his briefcase.

"I'm so sorry I'm late," she said.

He pursed his lips, but said it was no matter. He opened his top desk drawer and handed her an envelope.

"This is your assignment from Count von Bernstorff," he said. "If you'll wait I'll give you the payment. Do you have an expense report?"

"Expense report?" she asked.

"Yes, any expenses you incur in the service of the Kaiser will be reimbursed but we must have receipts," he said. Louisa glanced at the file cabinets. He must keep records of everything, she thought. Then she looked at the briefcase. It would contain his most important records, the ones he keeps with him at all times.

"My expenses are covered by my newspaper," she told him.

He opened a small safe in the corner. She glanced inside and saw stacks of bills. He quickly shut the door, turned, and handed her fifty dollars — a tidy sum of money! She tucked the money into her purse.

"Now, if you'll excuse me," he said. "I want to try to catch my train and get to my hotel in time for dinner."

"You take the train?" Louisa asked. "Surely a man of your stature..."

"I do not believe in wasting money, Fraulein Delafield," he said. "I'm an accountant."

With that he picked up his briefcase and showed her out the door.

As they took the elevator down to the first floor, she asked him, "Are you staying at a hotel, Herr Albert?"

"Yes. The Ritz Carlton, of course," he said. Well, at least he wasn't scrimping on his accommodations, Louisa thought. It seemed the Ritz was the German's preferred choice. She watched as he lumbered across the busy downtown street, his bulging briefcase at his side, and then climbed the steps to the Sixth Avenue Line. The train came barreling down the tracks, clattering loudly. No one seemed to notice the noise. It was part of the landscape.

Meeting Herr Albert had caused her to miss going to the Grand Central Terminal to see if Carlotta was there, but as she hadn't seen her since their initial meeting she doubted she'd missed her today.

Instead she took a cab back to the paper, reading von Bernstorff's note on the way.

My dear Miss Delafield,

You might want to interview our naval attaché, Karl Boy-Ed. He has a very interesting mother. Her name is Ida, and I think your female readers would love to learn about her. She's a writer and a great supporter of women's issues. She just published a book called Soldiers' Mothers. She wrote it after Karl's brother died. A mother's sorrow is surely something any woman can understand.

How many more of these propaganda pieces could she possibly write without her readers beginning to think she was a German sympathizer?

Phyllis was still at the office when she returned, making a list of possible Saratoga stories. Louisa sat down at her desk and pretended to look at her correspondence, but she was too distracted.

"Phyllis, when you were in Germany did you hear of an Ida Boy-Ed?" she asked.

"The writer?" Phyllis said.

"Yes, and mother of the current German naval attaché," Louisa added.

"She's a journalist, I believe," Phyllis said. "And a great patron of other writers. I never met her but I heard about her. My husband was an artist, and we socialized with the Bohemian set."

"Maybe you should do this assignment instead of me," Louisa said, more to herself than to Phyllis.

"What assignment?" she asked.

"Well," Louisa hesitated. "I'm trying to help my American readers understand who the Germans really are. How can we understand the war if we don't understand the people? Most Americans don't know much about Germany."

"I wondered why you wrote a profile of Franz von Papen," Phyllis said. "I thought perhaps you found him dashing. He is quite handsome."

"Oh dear me," Louisa said, not willing to admit even to herself that she'd found him attractive the first time they met. "I'm not his type. He doesn't care for women."

"You aren't saying..." Phyllis said with a shocked expression on her face.

"No, it's not that," Louisa said. "Instead of women, he likes girls."

Phyllis craned her neck forward and asked, "How do you know this?"

Louisa searched her mind for the right lie.

"I'm afraid I've been listening to gossip," Louisa finally said. "Please pretend I never said anything."

"About what?" Phyllis asked. "Weren't we just talking about *fashion*?"

"Indeed we were," Louisa said. "By the way, your job here is safe for the time being. I believe Miss Malloy has found another position."

"I must admit I'm happy to hear that," Phyllis said. "My parents have not been as welcoming or as generous as I might have hoped."

Louisa gazed at her protegee, for that's how she'd begun to think of her. She certainly still dressed the part of an heiress. Perhaps she had a patron?

Chapter 32

Ellen

A piece of black crepe hung on the door. Ellen knocked and after a moment, Paula stood in the doorway, wearing her black widow's weeds. The rosy glow was gone from her cheeks, but she managed a smile and invited Ellen in.

"Sorry I didn't get here sooner. I only got back to New York yesterday. Louisa told me about Paddy's passing this morning," Ellen said, placing the flowers she'd brought in the center of the kitchen table and then handing over a bag of candy she'd brought for the kids.

"You came when you could. That's all that matters," Paula said and put the kettle on for some tea. Ellen sat down at the table.

"Where are the little ones?" she asked.

"Michael's taking his nap and Tommy's off somewhere playing," Paula said as she spooned tea leaves into a China teapot. Ellen thought of those two boys, growing up now without their father.

"How will you manage, Paula?" Ellen asked. "Will you go back home?"

"New York is my home," she said. "I've got Paddy's pension from the Force. It's not much but it's something. And your friend Louisa sent us a packet of money from a fund for fallen officers. I was quite surprised by that, I don't mind saying. If I'm frugal we can get by for a good while, and then I'll work in a factory or maybe a department store."

The kettle whistled, and Paula poured the hot water into the teapot. While they waited for the tea to steep, Ellen told her about the ordeal of the *Lusitania* and then her visit with her family in Galway.

"Most of the men are gone to fight in the war," she said. "The ones that are left are all for having an uprising. Some of the them are off killing the Germans. Others are wanting to invite them into their homes for a pint."

"It's the same here. If you read the *Gaelic American Newspaper,* Germany is Ireland's great friend. But not all of us fall for that line. Paddy didn't. That's why he went undercover, you know." Paula poured the tea through a strainer into Ellen's cup.

"I'm afraid I'm responsible for that. I wrote a letter to Louisa with a message for him about what was going on at the waterfront," Ellen confessed. Her chest felt like it was in a vise as she said these words to Paddy's widow.

"Ellen Malloy, do you think there's a force on all God's earth that could have stopped my husband from doing his job? It was his duty to expose the malcontents who are sabotaging those ships. Captain Tunney personally sent him in there. And when I married him, I knew the risks. I married a hero. I'll always have that," she said. She had tears in her eyes, but at the same time, she was smiling with pride.

Ellen watched Paula wipe away her tears with something like envy. Perhaps if she could just cry and then go on with her life, her chest wouldn't feel so heavy she could barely breathe.

They talked of other things then: the two little boys, Paddy's wake, the encroaching war.

Ellen finished her tea, and before she left, she reached for Paula and hugged her fiercely.

"I'm after following in Paddy's footsteps," she whispered. "I only hope I can be as brave."

Two days later she received a message at her boarding house. The typed message read: "*Be at 2nd Ave and 59 St today at 3 pm. There's a telephone pay station there. When the telephone rings, pick it up.*"

That afternoon she found the telephone on the corner. It was in a large iron box on top of a three-foot high pole. She opened the box and at precisely 3 p.m. the telephone rang. She picked up the receiver and put it to her ear.

"Miss Malloy?" a man's voice asked.

"Yes," she answered.

"I'd like to meet you."

"All right."

"Tomorrow morning, say 11 o'clock. I prefer to meet somewhere in the open. Do you know Penn Station?"

"I do."

"I will be in the waiting area by the stairway to the incoming Long Island trains."

"How will I know you?"

"I'll know you."

That evening Ellen spotted a man loitering near Mrs. Cantor's boarding house. It was the same one who had met her when she got off the boat. Koenig must have sent him to check up on her. She waited until ten that night to slip out the back door of the house and make her way to the subway. She took the downtown train to Union Station, got off the train and then immediately jumped back on just before the doors closed and took it to the next stop where she switched to the Uptown train. A ten-minute walk had turned into an hour-long trip before she finally wound up at Louisa's door, but she was sure no one had followed.

"Ellen Malloy!" Suzie said, eyes wide. "As I live and breathe."

"In the flesh," Ellen said and stepped inside the house.

"What are you doing here so late?" Suzie said, cinching the tie around her flannel robe. Before Ellen could answer, Suzie appraised her and said, "You don't look like you were hit by a torpedo."

"Oh, Suzie," Ellen said. "I've missed ya."

The two women hugged awkwardly but with genuine warmth.

"Is Louisa still up?" Ellen asked.

"Her light's on. Go on upstairs. She won't mind," Suzie said.

When Ellen opened the door to the bedroom, Louisa was sitting up in her elegant mahogany four-poster bed, reading a book. She set down the book and stared at Ellen in surprise.

"In the neighborhood," Ellen said. "Thought I'd drop by. What are you reading?" She picked up the book. "*The Thirty-Nine Steps*?"

"Have you heard from Paul Koenig?"

"I have. I'm supposed to meet him tomorrow morning," Ellen said. "You look nice for someone going to bed. Lovely nightgown."

"What does he want you to do?"

"No idea. But I aim to make sure that the New York police know whose side I'm on. I don't want to hang when this is all over. When do you talk to Tunney again?"

"I never talk to Tunney," Louisa said. "But I have a contact in the British Secret Service. And he's in regular communication with the American Secret Service and the New York Police Department."

"Then you and I need to establish some means of communicating," Ellen said. "Since Koenig's already got somebody checking up on me."

"You can come back to the paper, can't you? We can find you some sort of clerical work," Louisa said. "And then when I'm no longer helping Tunney we can let Phyllis go and—"

"I'm not sure that's a good idea," Ellen said. The last thing she wanted was to have some crummy desk job while she watched fancy Phyllis work as Louisa's assistant.

"Then I suggest you wait here for a bit. There's someone you should meet. He may have some ideas."

"Here? In your bedroom?" Ellen was incredulous.

"It's private," Louisa responded.

"I'll say," Ellen said.

"Are you working for the morals police now?" Louisa said.

"Excuse me, but I used to work for a *society* writer, so I know a bit about propriety," Ellen said.

"Then you also know something about discretion."

Ellen sat down on the bed, crossed her arms, and grinned. "I am the very embodiment of discretion."

The man showed up shortly after midnight. He was tall and rangy with keen blue eyes and a clean-shaven face. The air fairly crackled with energy as soon as he entered through the window. He stopped short when he saw Ellen sitting on Louisa's bed, but recovered himself within seconds.

"Reggie Grant, British Naval Attaché," he said bowing to her.

"You don't sound like a Brit," Ellen said, suspiciously.

"By way of Australia," he said. "And you must be the intrepid Ellen Malloy."

Ellen nodded.

"Tell me, Ellen. How is *Sinn Fein* these days?"

"Well, if the Brits would get their boots off our necks, so many of our misguided members might not be cozying up to the Germans if that's what you're asking me," she said.

"Fair enough," he said. "And where do you stand?"

"I want self-rule. That means no Brits and no Germans," she said, lifting her chin. She thought of all the women she'd met in the past month: Sylvia Pankhurst, Jane Addams, and Alice Hamilton, the so-called "peacettes." She continued, "Germany has been the aggressor in this war, and they need to be stopped. I'm willing to lay my life on the line to help do that."

"Good girl," Grant said. "Though I hope it won't come to that. Louisa tells me you were on the *Lusitania*."

"I was," Ellen said, not wanting to go into any details.

"I lost a good friend," he said. "Alfred Vanderbilt. Wonderful fellow."

"I saw him before he boarded. Apparently, someone sent his mother a telegram saying he should not board the *Lusy*, but he went anyway."

Ellen felt a vague suspicion.

"Was it you that sent the telegram? Did you know the Germans would sink the ship?" Ellen asked. "I've heard rumors munitions were on board that shouldn't have been there."

"I promise you. I knew nothing," he said. "I'm sorry you went through that terrible ordeal."

Ellen studied him. He possessed the self assurance so many rich and handsome men had. They also were excellent liars, and as a spy he was in the business of lying. He might be genuinely sorry for those who did go through that "terrible ordeal," but she doubted that he "knew nothing." It was his job to know everything.

"Ellen has a meeting with Paul Koenig tomorrow," Louisa informed him.

"Abteilung III b sent you to meet him?"

"They sent me with letters and glanders," she said. "One of his men took both from me when I first arrived."

"Did you see what was in the letters?" he asked.

"No," she said. "The packet was sealed. The case with the glanders was also sealed."

"She doesn't know what Koenig wants her to do yet," Louisa said.

Reggie paced the room like a tiger.

"Does Suzie know about this?" Ellen whispered, nodding toward the pacing man. Louisa's brow furrowed, and she shook her head. Ellen thought she was kidding herself. Of course, Suzie knew.

Grant suddenly turned to face her.

"Do you know shorthand?"

"No. I'm a pretty fair typist though," Ellen said.

"More than fair," Louisa interjected.

"Learn shorthand. Immediately," Grant said. "And let Koenig know about your skills when you talk to him. Koenig is a wily bastard. He doesn't use operatives more than a few times, but he'll always need a secretary."

"I'm sure he already has a secretary," Ellen said.

"Not for long he won't," Grant said. Ellen didn't want to know how he planned to accomplish that.

An awkward silence ensued. Ellen noticed the way the two of them kept looking at each other. She had become invisible. Quite a trick, she thought.

"I'll be going then," she said. "I'm sure you two have some other business to discuss. Goodbye, Louisa."

"Goodbye, Ellen dear," Louisa said and walked with her to the bedroom door.

"How will I get a message to you?" Ellen asked.

Louisa looked down the dark hallway.

"We can always meet for lunch at the Automat," Louisa said. "There is nothing remarkable about two old friends having lunch or if that doesn't work, contact Suzie. *Au revoir,* my friend. Be safe."

Then the door shut, and Ellen made her way downstairs, quite sure that those two had forgotten her already.

***

On the way to Penn Station the next morning, Ellen stopped at a bookstore and picked up a book on shorthand. She walked down Seventh Avenue to the train station, though the word "station" hardly described the magnificent building. It was only five years old, and she thought it every bit as impressive as Grand Central even if it was smaller. She entered the light-filled building and found the wooden benches near the stairwell for the Long Island railroad. It felt like being in church only without the annoying priests. She sat on a bench and opened the stenography book. To her surprise, it was fascinating — another kind of cypher.

"Are you learning shorthand?"

She looked up. The man was big with long, thick arms and a jowly face. He had a receding hairline and a small black mustache. He frowned at her with an odd schoolboy sort of pout. He was most likely menacing even as a baby.

"Just brushing up on my skills," she said. "I'm looking for a secretarial position. Maybe at the *Gaelic American*. I do have some experience at a newspaper, and I like the philosophy of the *Gaelic*."

He sat down next to her. He smelled of garlic and onions.

"The *Gaelic* is a fine paper," he said. "You type, too?"

"I do. Are you Herr Koenig?" she asked.

He answered with a brusque nod.

"One of my men saw you visiting a policeman's widow," he said.

"Paula is a girlhood friend of mine from Galway," she said.

"Her husband died in the line of duty, I hear," Koenig said. "Unfortunate accident."

"I didn't know him well," Ellen said. "But poor Paula. Her mother back home died while I was there. I brought her a necklace her mam wanted her to have. Not worth anything, but of some sentimental value."

Koenig seemed to be registering this information.

"How do you feel about horses, Miss Malloy?" he asked.

"I can't ride if that's what you're asking me," she said.

"But could you kill one or two? Or a hundred?" he asked.

Ellen swallowed.

"I can do whatever I have to do," she said.

"Good," he said. "We'll return your make up case to you in a day or so. Then you'll make a trip to Hoboken. I take it you already know how to administer the drug."

"I do," she said.

"No one will suspect a man and a woman together," he said. "That's how we killed the last bunch. I'll be in touch."

He stood up and walked away nonchalantly. Ellen felt the blood thrumming in her veins. Not only had she brought the glanders over, now they wanted her to kill horses with it. Grant had said Koenig was a wily bastard. Evil bastard was more like it.

Chapter 33

Louisa

"Telephone for you, Delafield," Billy Stephens said. He indicated the table near his desk. She didn't get many calls at the office. The subjects of her column still preferred hand-written correspondence, preferably on cream vellum.

"Hello?" she said.

"Louisa, you need to come home."

"Suzie? Is everything all right?" Louisa's pulse quickened. She hadn't known Suzie to pick up a phone and make a call in her life.

"You have a guest. A young lady who needs to speak to you right away," Suzie said.

Louisa spent the extra money on a cab rather than take the train home. She was at her doorstep twenty minutes later. Inside the parlor, perched primly on the settee sat Carlotta, the girl from Martha Held's. She wore a demure white dress with a pretty sash and looked nothing at all like the trollop she'd been the first time they saw her.

"I've got some information for you," Carlotta said.

Louisa felt a rush of excitement as she sat down to hear her out.

"What is it?" she asked.

"Money first," Carlotta responded.

"Of course." Louisa dug through her purse and pulled out a ten-dollar bill.

"I was thinking more like twenty," the girl said.

"All right," Louisa said and extracted another ten-dollar bill from the packet Herr Albert had given her. Carlotta tucked the money into her own purse.

"I heard him and the other one talking in the parlor last night," she said. "They were saying something about sugar shipments. At first I didn't think nothing of it. But then Boy-Ed starts laughing and says 'there's a sweet surprise in those bags.' And Franz is laughing, too, and makes this motion with his hands. Like something exploding. I figured this was the kind of thing you wanted to know about."

"You were right," Louisa said. "This is very helpful. Sugar is extremely flammable. It makes perfect sense."

"I gotta go," Carlotta said, standing up. "Mrs. Held will dock my pay if I'm not on the job when the men start arriving."

"Franz von Papen is not your only customer?" Louisa asked.

"No. But he pays the best," Carlotta said. Her face clouded over. "And he makes me earn it."

Louisa's heart sank as she stood in the doorway and watched the girl walk down the street back to that life, a life as wretched as any factory girl's in spite of all the finery that came with it. She found Suzie in the parlor also watching her through the window.

"That poor girl," Suzie said.

"Indeed. How did she find her way here?"

"Henry called me. Said she wanted to talk to you. He didn't know how to reach you so he called me."

"Henry?"

"Mr. Sweet. The butler at the brothel," Suzie said. "You remember him, don't you?"

"I do. How well do you know him?" Louisa inquired.

"We've been to the Nickelodeon a couple of times," Suzie said, trying unsuccessfully to hide her smile.

"Suzie," Louisa said in astonishment. "You've been out with a man? Can we trust him?"

"I trust him," Suzie said. "You aren't the only one with secret admirers, Louisa."

Suzie looked at her with a piercing gaze. Louisa felt her face flush with embarrassment. Of course, Suzie must know about her midnight visits from Reggie Grant. Suzie waved a hand. "Never mind. I also got a message from Ellen today. They want her to put some kind of bacteria up in the noses of horses."

"My god," Louisa said.

Louisa called Reggie's office and pretended to be from a florist shop as he had instructed her to do. "Trust no one," he had warned her. "Leave a message that the flower orders are ready for pick up."

"Do you order many flowers?" she asked.

"Indeed. We send them to the officers' wardrooms on the ships. Along with beer, mineral water, and books." Then he explained that Britain kept cruisers outside the harbor in case any of the German liners tried to slip through the blockade.

"I'm sorry, Mr. Grant isn't available," the secretary said. "And I don't have authority to pick up flowers."

"Where is he?"

"He's at the — " There was a pause as the secretary sounded out the name of Wyandanch Club on Long Island. "He's sport shooting."

It would take too long to get the information to Tunney through Olive Mitchel, and she believed there was no time to lose. Any day another ship might go out carrying sugar and bombs. She also admitted, it would be nice to see Reggie somewhere outside of her bedroom. And she hoped at the exclusive club they might be away from prying German eyes.

The Wyandanch Club was for members only at the hefty price of two hundred dollars a year, so Louisa called the manager on the pretext of writing a story.

"But I don't understand why lady readers would care about sport shooting," he said after she explained her idea.

"Every once in a while I do an educational column for women so they can know what men do when they're off on their own and as a primer so the women can talk to them about their interests," Louisa said.

"Well, I suppose it can't hurt," he said.

She arrived that afternoon on the Long Island Railroad and took a cab to the club.

Along the way, she relished the sights of the countryside. She'd been trapped in the city for too long and had missed the wide open sky. They passed a man in a fedora fishing in a creek that wound along the road, and it made her wish she were a painter. But her sense of peace vanished when they passed a pasture where some horses grazed and she remembered Ellen's horrid task. This was such a dangerous game they were playing.

The club was in a huge rambling building.

"They don't go out till the morning," the manager told her.

"That's fine," she said. "I'll have dinner with the guests tonight. I believe my friend Mr. Reggie Grant is here. Please make sure I'm seated at his table."

With that she settled herself in the large library under a stuffed mallard with its wings outstretched as if in mid-flight and read a treatise on fly fishing.

***

The dining room featured more taxidermy and a painting of two hunting dogs over the stone fireplace. In the corner, a hound slept peacefully ignoring the babbling diners and the waiters hurrying to and fro. Reggie was indeed surprised to see her when she sat down next to him. He appeared to be delighted as well. He introduced her to the Treasury Secretary, a thin fellow with a hawkish face named McAdoo, who also just happened to be Woodrow Wilson's son-in-law. The British desperately wanted America to join the war. Reggie's job was to charm, cajole, and curry favor with anyone close to the president. For her part Louisa asked McAdoo some questions about his wife, the president's daughter, and their social life in the capital to include in her column. He was flattered and only too happy to talk about his wife's charity work. They'd only been married a year and he seemed very much in love.

The multi-course dinner consisted of various salads and appetizers, pheasant, potatoes au gratin, rice pudding — much more food than they could possibly eat. While McAdoo and Reggie talked about their favorite hunting grounds, she thought of Count von Bernstorff's comment about Germans starving because of the blockade. Hungry people didn't care who's to blame for their plight. They just wanted to eat. The sooner this war was over the better it would be for all of them.

Later Louisa joined Reggie in his room after dinner for brandy to brief him on the latest developments. But when she got there, he immediately took her in his arms and kissed her ravenously. His hands found their way under her dress. As his fingers stroked the warmth between her legs, she decided her news could wait until the next day. She lay back and let him have his way.

***

An insistent knock awakened her. For a moment she wasn't sure where she was. She glanced out the window and saw red streaks in the sky. She was in her own room at the hunting club.

"Who is it? What do you want?" she called.

"Your wake up call, Miss," a voice on the other side of the door said. "Sport shooting starts early around here."

She roused herself, cleaned up quickly and dressed in an outfit she'd purchased from Wannamakers just before boarding the train — brown tweed jacket with green trim on the collar and sleeves, flared skirt for easy movement, boots, and a green felt hat with green plumage.

"Aren't you a vision?" Reggie said when she appeared downstairs. He didn't look bad himself in his cap and dark green vest.

"Perhaps we're all still dreaming," she answered. "What an ungodly hour. Nice vest."

"Thanks. It's McAdoo's. Lots of pockets. He's not coming, by the way. A few too many cocktails last night."

They walked through some woods and then into a dew-spangled field. Birds fluttered up from the grasses as they passed, and a few clouds floated overhead, their underbellies glowing in pinkish orange light. It was as if the whole world were having a conversation with itself before the noisy day took over. A wooden platform occupied one end of the field. A few hounds had followed them out. The dogs nosed around for a minute or so before settling patiently at their feet. She looked at the other end of the field and saw what looked like a trench where a young man could be seen next to some sort of metal contraption.

"Why do they call it trap shooting?" she asked.

"In the old days, and in some places still today, they used live pigeons. They kept them in a trap and as soon as the birds were let out, they immediately flew up in the air. Some traps even had spring floors to propel them toward the sky. But the bleeding hearts didn't like all that bird killing," he said.

"It does sound rather barbaric," she says.

"What we do to young men is barbaric," he answered. He positioned his legs wide and held a Remington rifle at the ready. At his signal, the young man in the trench pulled a release and a round disc flew up into the air. Reggie, expertly, followed the arc of the clay pigeon and fired. It burst into dust.

"Impressive," she said.

"You know you still haven't told me why you've come," he said.

"Carlotta visited me."

"Excellent." He smiled at her and said, "You can tell me all about it over breakfast, my little spy."

He shot several more times and then to her surprise he held the rifle out to her.

"Me?"

"You didn't buy that sporty outfit just so you could watch, did you?" he asked with a challenging glint in his eye.

"I don't know what to do."

"Then you need to learn. In case you need to shoot a Kraut." He showed her how to hold the gun tight against her shoulder and how to aim. Then standing close against her, he held her arms, signaled for the release and swung her arms up.

"Fire," he whispered.

She pulled the trigger and the clay pigeon burst into bits.

She whooped in exultation.

"Let me try it by myself," she said. He gave her some pointers and then stood back to watch.

Of course, she missed each target by a mile. He gave her more pointers and she actually nicked one. Her shoulder was getting sore but she couldn't give up without hitting at least one squarely. And when it finally happened with a burst of dust, she laughed in triumph and handed him the gun.

He gazed into her eyes and for a moment she felt as if she were sinking. Oh no, she thought. She didn't want to be falling for him, but she feared it might be happening.

As they walked back to the club, he said, "So tell me what you've found out."

"It seems they are getting the bombs onto the ships in — " A blast cut her off, and she screamed as Reggie fell to the ground. Blood seeped from a hole in his back.

Chapter 34
Ellen

A messenger brought the makeup case to her rooming house.

"I never knew you to wear makeup," Mrs. Cantor said.

"I don't. It belonged to Miss French," Ellen lied. "Her sister wanted me to have it." She took the case quickly up to her room and opened it. The concealed compartment was no longer sealed. Inside, she found four large tubes of the curdled yellow substance and several long swabs along with instructions: "Insert swab into tube. Insert infested swab into nostril of every third horse. Wear gloves, keep mouth and nose covered. Take apple slices or carrots to coax the animals."

She calculated how long it had been since the bacteria had been first produced in the lab, less than a month — not long enough to lose its potency. She knew she had to prove herself to Koenig, but she couldn't bear to be the instrument of death for the warhorses. She remembered her lessons from the chemist in Berlin. He had said that oxygen would eventually render the bacteria ineffective so it must always be tightly sealed. She opened the tubes and placed them upright in the makeup case. He had not said how long it would take to destroy the bacteria, so she could only hope that a few hours would be long enough.

She used the phone downstairs to call Louisa's house. She couldn't say anything over the phone since Mrs. Castor or one of the other lodgers might overhear her. But Suzie answered and agreed to meet her at the market.

Ellen walked the aisles of the Astor Market on Broadway. She saw Suzie at the end of one of the aisles, examining loaves of bread. Ellen made her way to the fruit stall. She purchased a bag of apples, but she was nervous and the money slipped out of her hands and onto the floor. She bent down to pick it up and quickly glanced around to see if she were being followed. Down at the far end of the aisle she saw Koenig's man, pretending to examine some dead chickens hanging by their feet. He was the same furtive blond man she'd seen before. Suddenly, she heard Suzie's voice behind her.

"Some of those strawberries, please," she said to the man behind the counter. Ellen stood up and placed the money on the counter along with a note. Then she moved quickly away with her package and hurried out of the market.

***

At eleven that night, she left the house and met Koenig's man on the street. She carried a satchel with the tubes of glanders and small flat sticks. Up close she saw that the man was just about her height, had a face as narrow as an axe blade, and looked to be in his early thirties. He told her everyone called him Freddy. He looked down at the ugly brogans she wore and complimented her on her choice of footwear.

"The last time a woman did this, she wore high heels. Nearly broke her neck, climbing over the fence," Freddy said.

"You mean I'm not the first?" Ellen asked, pretending Koenig had told her nothing.

"There was one other. Pretty girl. She was familiar with horses, so she did okay even in the heels," he said.

A dull ache throbbed in her gut. Other than a few old nags that pulled the drays back home, she wasn't at all familiar with horses.

"How do we get to their stalls?" Ellen asked as they waited for the train.

"Stalls?" he asked and laughed. "They're not in stalls. They've been sent from all over the country. They keep them in big corrals until they're ready to ship them overseas. Here, give me those apples."

They took a late, nearly empty train to the Bronx. Their stop was near the end of the line, and as they swayed back and forth on the long trip, Freddy cut the apples into slices. She put some into the pockets of her jacket. She wanted to ask if horses bit but was afraid to show her ignorance.

"Freddy," she asked, "is your name really Friedrich?"

His thin lips spread into a smile.

"Ja," he admitted.

"I thought so," she said.

They rocked back and forth, jostling against each other once in a while.

"How did you come to be here?" she asked.

"Trapped," he said. "I'm a sailor aboard the *Vaterland.* We've been stuck in port at Hoboken since the embargo started. There's thousands of us. All out of work. I was lucky Mr. Koenig hired me."

"It's because your English is so good. I didn't even notice your accent at first," she said.

"Before I joined the navy, I worked in a hotel for English tourists," he said. And now here he was, she thought, on his way to kill horses.

He was silent for a few minutes as the train stopped at a station and passengers got off. They were alone in the car when the doors closed. The train hurtled down the tracks again.

"I would do anything to stop the English from invading my homeland. I have a girl back home. Her name is Liesel. She's not the prettiest girl in Dusseldorf, but she's a good girl, a hard worker, and smart. She's saving money for our wedding." His fingers knotted together.

"You miss her," Ellen said.

He nodded and looked out the windows though there was nothing to see in the dark.

"If they were to touch her . . ." he said quietly and shook his head.

She hadn't thought about what war means for the women left behind, and she felt sorry for him. She felt sorry for everyone caught up in this bloody mess.

The train screeched to their stop, and they trotted quickly down the steps of the platform to the street level.

"Where are they?" she asked, looking around.

"Van Cortland Park," he said. "It's just a few blocks."

She followed him up a hill and down another street to a large expanse of field and wood, silhouetted in the half-moon's light. They followed a path along the field. Ellen shivered though the night was not cold.

"There they are," Freddy whispered as he put on his gloves. She already had on hers, and she covered her mouth with her scarf.

She peered through the dark and saw a mass of forms in a paddock. There must have been fifty horses in that enclosure alone. Ellen thought of herself as someone who did not frighten easily and perhaps if this were daytime and she could see what she was dealing with, she would not be afraid, but it was night, and the darkness made her feel as if the ground was shifting under her feet. They waited in a copse of trees until the night watchman made his rounds. Then they dashed over to the fence. It wasn't particularly high and Ellen had no trouble getting over it, but once she was in, she immediately wished she had said no to Koenig, no to Captain Boehm, no to the whole thing. She should be home in her bed right now.

Instead, she was surrounded by the smell of hay, horse sweat, and manure. In the moonlight she could see that some of the horses were lighter colored than others. One had spots on its back. Another was as black as the night. The horses whinnied and jostled each other nervously. Freddy took one of the tubes from her and jabbed the stick inside the tube.

"Go on," Freddy whispered. "Stick some up their noses."

Ellen's hands shook as she inserted the stick into the tube and pulled the curdled goo out. It was dark, and the smell was overwhelming. The horses knew she didn't belong there. When she tried to reach for one of the horse's heads, it jerked back and gave her a wild-eyed look. Its hooves danced around her feet. Surely it was going to stomp on her toes. She found herself squeezed between two of the beasts as they neighed and turned about.

"Aw, watch me," Freddy said and snatched the stick from her hand. He yanked one of the horses by the mane, tried to stick it in the nostril but only smeared the stick across its nose. If a horse could be said to scream, this one did. Ellen hoped her ploy to destroy the bacteria had worked, but she could not be sure.

"Ach du schieße," Freddy muttered.

Ellen turned her back to him, wound through the large, warm bodies, and found one of the smaller, more docile beasts. She pulled a slice of apple from her pocket and laid it flat on her palm. She shivered as the horse's soft fat lips pulled the slice from her hand. Ellen surreptitiously turned the stick around and smeared the harmless end of the stick on the quivering nostrils.

The horse pulled away and moved into the crowd. She pulled out another apple slice, and a horse beside her pushed forward, startling her. She dropped the slice. The other horses soon smelled the apples and crowded around her, whinnying, tails slapping their rumps. Tossing the apple slices into the air, she hoped to distract them. She stumbled against the heaving chest of one of the creatures. Her feet tried to find purchase but the horses were stirring around faster now. A large brown horse with fire in its eyes turned its nose toward her and nipped her arm.

"Ow," she screamed.

That's when they heard the whistle.

"Stop! Police!"

Ellen dropped the tubes on the muddy ground and tried to wend her way through the crowd of horses. Lights flashed here and there. The horses whinnied and pranced in agitation. Their warm thick bodies jostled all around her. She couldn't get out. The horses smelled her fear, she was sure, and she smelled theirs. She felt herself being squeezed between the flanks of two of the panicked beasts. She could barely breathe.

"Help!" she called. The horses became more and more agitated, pushing against her as they shoved each other.

"Don't scream," Freddy hissed at her as he wormed through the horses toward her. Then like a vengeful white Pegasus, one horse reared high, its hooves striking the air. Ellen cowered, sure he was going to pound her into the ground. She screamed, but as the horse came crashing to the ground, its hooves missed her. Instead, she heard a terrible crack followed by a groan. The next thing she knew Freddy was sprawled on the ground and the big white horse's hooves pranced on his body.

"No," she screamed. Strong hands grabbed her, dragging her through the maze of horse's bodies. "Stop, you've got to help him!"

"He's beyond help, lady," a voice told her.

The police helped her back over the fence and left her as they went back in. She watched as they got control of the horses. Finally, two men brought Freddy's broken body to the fence and clumsily shoved him over. He fell on the ground and lay there silently. His skull was smashed. An eyeball had gotten loose from its mooring. Blood oozed from the wounds on his chest, and a white rib bone had broken through his torn and bloodied shirt as if in surrender.

"Christ on the cross. He's nothing but a bloody pulp," a voice said.

She turned to find a large man with a mien as solemn as a judge. She tried to speak, but her mouth had not a drop of moisture, and she couldn't stop trembling.

"Miss Malloy," he said. "I'm Captain Tunney. I got your message from Miss Delafield's servant."

She nodded and looked down at poor Freddy.

"I'm afraid you'll have to spend the night in jail if you want to maintain your cover," he said. Her blood felt like liquid lead in her veins. Jail? She couldn't just go home? Home to her warm bed? Home where she could forget this night? He went on, "They'll charge you with vagrancy. It's the best I can do. Where are the vials?"

She pointed into the corral where the horses milled about, calmer now.

"In the mud," she said.

"All right," he said. "You did good, lass."

"How can I get hold of you to get information to you, Sir?" she asked.

"There's a candy shop on Broadway not too far from the Hamburg Building. You can leave a message for me there. Be sure to buy the lemon drops."

Then he walked away.

An hour later she sat on the cold metal bench of the jail cell. A woman with greasy gray hair who smelled like she'd pissed herself sat down next to her. Ellen turned her head away and scooted as far away as possible. A wild-eyed drunk woman veered from one corner to another, alternately crying and laughing. And a prostitute in a shabby satin dress leaned against the bars and hummed "Oh Susanna."

The stink woman reached a claw over and touched Ellen's knee and launched into a tedious story about her mother dying of consumption.

Ellen thought it best to ignore them. She crossed her arms, closed her eyes and thanked Mother Mary she hadn't had to kill horses that night. But she couldn't stop seeing the image of Freddy's split skull and his eye dangling from its socket.

When morning came, a jailer let her out, saying she was free to go. The vagrancy charge had been dropped, but they'd better not see her in the Bronx again. When she stepped out into the light of day, it felt like she'd been locked up for a decade rather than a single night. She'd only had a few dollars in her pocket when she'd been apprehended and the jailer kept that, saying it was for her room and board for the night though they hadn't given her a thing to eat. She'd found one last apple slice in her pocket and eaten it. She'd have to walk to Manhattan, and she had no idea how far that might be.

She looked shabby and odd in her old boots, her dirty dress and no hat. She'd had one earlier but must have lost it in the corral. The people she passed avoided looking at her. The worst part was walking by the diners and food carts, the smell of food wafting past her. At one point she tried to hail a cab, thinking she could pay them when she got back to her room, but not one would stop for her. She couldn't blame them.

Unlike Manhattan, not every square foot of the Bronx had a building on it. Trees crowded along some of the lanes. Motorcars passed but not in a steady stream. She found the elevated train and decided to follow its path.

The long walk gave her a chance to think. She was hungry and tired, but the movement of her legs cleared her head, which had been filled all night with the remembered sensations of horses' bodies, Freddy's cry, the sound of his skull as it was crushed by the horse's hooves, and those big blinking black eyes of the terrified horses. All night she imagined their steaming breath on her neck and the sound of whinnying woke her sporadically. But now she was awake and the sky above coated a sharp blue. Her blood was warming, and her skin tingled in the sunlight. The fear that had gripped her from the moment they slipped over that fence into the corral was turning from a quivering liquid thing into something solid and angry.

She walked over a steel bridge crossing the Harlem River Canal and looked down at the water churning below glittering like thousands of blades. That could just as easily have been her skull under the horses' pounding hooves. She wondered what Captain Boehm would think if he knew she'd been placed in such a precarious position. He hadn't trained her for this.

The journey took more than two hours, and her blistered feet ached by the time she reached the westside of Manhattan. She thought of going home, of paying Mrs. Cantor an extra fifty cents for a long hot soak in the tub since it wasn't her bath day. She thought of lunch, of a meat pie and a berry tart. Mainly, she thought of her bed, soft with clean sheets, the window open beside her to let in a breeze. But all that could wait.

She kept going, past the familiar markets of Harlem, walking steadily, purposefully. She couldn't stop now if she was hit with a brick. She walked down Broadway through midtown to downtown until finally she stood in front of a large stone building where a sign above a doorway read "Hamburg-America Line." Underneath it, painted on the windows were signs for "Pleasure Cruises, Nile Service," and "Hamburg to London, Paris, Mediterranean." Of course, the shipping line had been effectively shut down with the blockade and now there was nothing much for its workers to do except think of ways to sabotage the Allies. She imagined that kept Koenig pretty busy.

She entered the lobby of the building and perused the sign that indicated the location of the different offices. The one she wanted was on the third floor. Rather than bother with the lift, she climbed the stairs. The fatigue had left her. She felt as strong as one of those steamers out on the water.

The sign on the door read, “Security.”

She opened and entered. No one was at the desk which had a large typewriter on it. She saw wooden file cabinets, a cup of pencils, a stack of paper by the typewriter, and a water cooler. On the other side of the room another door. She went to the door and pressed her ear to the smoked glass. Koenig’s voice.

“Why should I pay you? Your mission was a disaster,” he said. She heard the click of a telephone receiver and then some muttering. So she and Freddy weren’t the only ones who had failed at their assignment.

Ellen sucked in her breath. She started to walk in on him, but then noticed a list of names on the secretary’s desk. She went over and looked at the list. They were all German names, men’s names like Franz, Friedrich, and Hans. Hundreds of them. After each name were some initials, and it immediately became clear. These were the German sailors stranded in America by the embargo. Each of them a potential conspirator for the Fatherland. Freddy’s name was probably in that list.

“What the devil?”

She wheeled around and saw Koenig standing in the doorway to his office.

"Top of the morning, P. K.," she asked. "Are you surprised to see me?"

"A bit," he said, gathering his surprise back under the mask of his stony facade.

"I'm wondering. Did you set us up?" she asked. "Did you call the police on me and Freddy? Because if you did, you made a mash of things."

"Why? What are you...? Where is Freddy?"

Ellen laughed bitterly and shook her head. His cool reserve crumbled as he grabbed her by the arm and shook her.

"Tell me where he is," he growled.

"Hell," she said. "That's where people like us go when we die, isn't it?"

He dropped her arm.

"Dead?"

"That he is. The peelers showed up not too long after we got into the paddock. The lights and the shouting frightened the horses. Freddy fell, and he never got back up."

Koenig spun around and strode over to the window. She imagined his face conveyed a storm that he needed to hide.

"And what about you?"

"I spent the night in the Bronx jail on a vagrancy charge," she said. "They let me go this morning, hoping I wouldn't raise a fuss about Freddy's death, I guess."

"Did they find the vials?"

"No," she said. "It was dark and muddy. The horses' hooves smashed them to bits, I imagine."

He strode over to her and leaned his face close to hers, breathing loudly. He smelled of coffee and sauerkraut.

"Are you lying to me? Why wouldn't they suspect what you were there for?" His voice had grown low and rumbled out of his chest.

"I told them Freddy was my boyfriend and he was trying to steal a horse," she said, jutting out her chin. If he wanted to act tough, she could, too. "I said he told me he wanted one and that's how I knew where to find him."

Koenig stepped back, his composure firmly fixed like a shade pulled tight over a window. She sat down in the secretary's chair and felt the fatigue creeping up her body. She pulled a sheet of paper from her bag and handed it to him. He read it over.

"Vagrancy," he said. "You're lucky they didn't try to charge *you* with stealing horses."

"I'm luckier than poor Freddy, that's for certain," she said. She continued, "I do not think Captain Boehm would be happy to know you have endangered a valuable asset."

"This is America and I'm in charge here," he said, puffing out his chest.

"No you aren't," she said. "Count von Bernstorff is in charge. Franz Papen is in charge. Possibly even someone else. But not you. And what you don't seem to realize is that the woman I used to work for at *The Ledger* is a very close friend of the count." She turned and gazed up at him. "Very close. I'm of a mind to let him know the toll of your bad judgment. You lost one good operative. And you nearly lost me. Those are costly mistakes."

Koenig backed away and seemed to consider her words.

"I could easily have you disposed of, Malloy," he said.

"But you won't," she said and sat up straight. She fed a sheet of paper into the typewriter and continued, "I don't see a secretary around here. Have you managed to lose her, too?" Then she typed the sentence, "The quick brown fox jumped over the lazy dog," three times, pulled out the sheet of paper and handed it to him.

"I'll take the job," she said.

He stared at the paper and then at her. Outside the sun shifted in the sky and sent a spear of light through the window. Koenig's hostility transformed into something almost like admiration. Then he guffawed loudly — a startling sound completely out of place in this orderly room.

"You'll start tomorrow," he said when he finished laughing.

"Fine," she said. "But I'll be paid today for last night."

"You didn't do the job," he said.

"Consider it a loss," she said and held out her hand.

He reached into his pocket, pulled out a couple of dollar bills, and thrust them into her hand.

When she looked down at the money, her stomach growled in anticipation. The door to his office shut, and she was alone. She glanced once more at the list of names on the desk. Then she thought of Freddy's fiancé, a girl named Liesel in Dusseldorf, saving her money for a wedding that would never happen.

Chapter 35

Louisa

Reggie's face was as pale as a gin and tonic, but his hazel eyes were clear and alert. The wound to his shoulder had not injured him seriously according to the surgeon who removed the bullet. He lay in his bed in the lodge, his head propped up on a stack of pillows, white gauze wrapped around his shoulders.

"I heard they've already caught the fellow who shot me," he said. "He thought I was McAdoo."

"Apparently, a lot of these assassins and saboteurs are amateurs. He didn't realize that if he killed Wilson's son-in-law that would only hasten our entrance into the war," Louisa said. The man had been found at the train station and confessed almost immediately in the hopes of a lighter sentence.

"They aren't all amateurs," he said. "Or else they wouldn't be able to sink so many supply ships. Our men are dying by the dozens for lack of munitions, medical supplies, even food."

"Carlotta said they are smuggling the bombs on board in bags of sugar," Louisa said.

"Makes sense. Those bags are supposed to be sealed before they're loaded. But that could easily be faked."

"I don't know how to verify this information," she said.

"It's not your problem. I will give it to Tunney, and his men will check it out," he said. "The New York Police Department takes this threat seriously even if your federal secret service is about as effective as the Keystone Cops."

She gazed out of the window at the afternoon sunlight spreading over the woods in the distance.

"I should try to catch a train back to the city," she said. She stood near him and gently touched the unbandaged shoulder. "Though I hate to leave you here. Perhaps you should go to a hospital."

"Death traps, those places," he said with a shake of his head. "I'll be fine. The surgeon said no vital organs were damaged."

"What if there's another shooter out there?" she asked.

"He was probably lone wolf, and he's safely locked up. Besides, he wasn't even after me. A day or two in bed is all I need." Then he grinned and brushed his fingers along her hip. "It would be more fun if you were in bed with me."

She blushed and said, "That's the last thing you should be thinking about."

The sound of high heels furiously clicking on the wood floor in the hallway interrupted them and then the door was flung open. An elegant woman in a black and white chemise dress and a cunning little black toque sporting a diamond and ruby brooch stood in the doorway. She didn't even glance at Louisa, but instead flew across the room and threw her arms around Reggie's neck.

"Darling, what happened to you?" she asked breathlessly. Louisa stepped back.

"Just a flesh wound, my dear. Nothing to fret about," he said.

"Nothing to fret about? I've been fretting ever since I got off the boat yesterday and was told you were unavailable. Those wretches at the embassy didn't tell me where you were or even that you were shot until this morning," she said. The accent was British upper crust, aristocratic.

Louisa had no idea what to do. She had a sinking feeling this was no loving sister. How had she been such a fool? And how could she save face? Should she quietly steal out of the room? She stood there, unable to decide. The question resolved itself when the woman looked up and said in an utterly confused tone, "Oh. Hello?"

The expression on the woman's face went from surprise (though Louisa wasn't sure it was genuine) to suspicion (which she was sure *was* genuine) to that plaster-of-Paris mask all wealthy women assumed when in the presence of someone they considered an inferior.

"Millicent, this is Miss Delafield, who has been good enough to stop by to see if I needed anything. Miss Delafield, this is my fiancée, Lady Millicent Fairchild," Reggie said.

Fiancée? He might have said something before now. He might have saved her this utter humiliation. Her sight grew blurry. She curled her fingers into her palms and squeezed to keep from feeling the pain that banged on the inside of her chest like a lunatic in an asylum. She surreptitiously leaned back against the wall.

"I didn't expect you until next week, darling," he said to the woman now perched on the side of his bed like a woman who had been bred to the side saddle.

"You do lose track of time, don't you, love?" Millicent said and then turned to Louisa, "I'm much better now that I see this rascal is alive and survived yet another scrape." She looked at him fondly, but Louisa sensed something of a performance.

"His would-be assassin wasn't much of a shot," Louisa said, trying to sound perfectly normal.

"Have you been taking care of Reggie for me?" she asked.

"No, I merely came to check on him before I return to the city. I was accompanying Mr. Grant and Mr. McAdoo on their sport shooting expedition when he was shot."

"Oh, I didn't realize McAdoo was with you, dear," she said.

"He was supposed to be," Louisa covered. "You see, I cover society for *The Ledger*, and the opportunity to write a story about the son-in-law of the president was one I simply couldn't pass up. Besides, my readers love to learn what men are up to when they go off on their jaunts." Louisa couldn't believe the control in her voice when inside she was shaking like a toy rattle in a baby's hand.

"Yes, I wonder myself sometimes," Lady Millicent said.

"But now you're here," Louisa said with an expansive smile that felt as if it would break her cheeks. "And you can take care of any needs he has."

Her eyes sliced over to his of their own accord. A half smile was etched on his face as he blinked up at her. She took a step toward the door and then as if she were an actor who suddenly remembered her role, she stopped and turned to the woman.

"Lady Millicent, I hope you don't mind, but my readers would love to know... Well, your dress. It can't be easy to dress so fashionably in wartime and yet..."

Was there a woman in the world who could resist a compliment to her sense of *savoir faire?*

"Oh, I don't mind at all. There's a charming young French designer who's set up shop in Biarritz. Her name is Coco Chanel, and everyone adores her. Biarritz is on the coast so it's out of harm's way so far. My buyer braved the U-boats and went over there and picked up an entire wardrobe for me."

Louisa nodded thoughtfully. Not even war could stand between a wealthy woman and her clothes.

***

She was numb on the train ride home. Why didn't he tell her? Then again, why hadn't she asked? For all she knew, he could have had a full-fledged wife back in England. She had known what she was doing, and she had enjoyed it. But now she felt sordid. If she were going to live her life as a single woman devoted to her career, she realized she would have to guard her heart better — and her reputation. She couldn't bear to ache like this.

Work was the antidote to aches of the heart, she reminded herself. Work gave one purpose. Work gave life meaning. She almost had herself convinced by the time she got to the office.

"Got something for me, Delafield?" Billy Stephens asked, coming to lean against her desk.

"Oh, yes, the whole frightening affair of the assassination attempt on the British Naval Attaché. It turned out to be some sort of German freelancer. Long Island is crawling with them apparently. These stranded men go to von Papen or one of his minions, spout their crazy ideas, are given a gun and then troop out to cause mayhem. They caught him, of course. Turns out he thought he was shooting at Wilson's son-in-law."

"Got any quotes for me?"

"Sure," she said. "I wrote it all down for you."

She handed him the notes she'd taken. This was a story she was glad not to have under her byline. Instead she'd write something about the fashionable Lady Millicent Fairchild. The taste of crow would cure her.

Billy took her notes over to his desk while she rolled a sheet of paper into a typewriter and started pecking away. She had hardly typed two sentences when a shadow fell across the paper. She looked up and found

Forrest Calloway standing at her desk, his hat in his hand.

"Forr...Mr. Calloway. What a surprise," she said. "What brings the publisher of *The Ledger* to my humble corner?"

"Miss Delafield, I wanted you to be the first to know," he said, the words tumbling out of his mouth. "I'm engaged to be married."

He might as well have doused her with a bucket of ice water. She looked down at the flimsy paper in her typewriter. Her eyes lost focus. She could clearly hear her mother's voice: "chin up, don't show a thing, remember who you are."

For the second time that day, she dragged a smile onto her face. She steadied herself and then looked up into the deep brown eyes of her erstwhile lover.

"I'm delighted to hear it. That lovely young woman whom you brought to the party on Jack Morgan's yacht?" she asked, her stomach churning.

"No, of course not. I'm marrying Sadie Treadwell. The widow," he said. She knew immediately whom he meant. An attractive, respectable woman in good standing with society. Not at all showy. She'd been married to a banker who died two years ago, and she had a couple of fatherless young sons. Ah, there it was. Sons.

"Will there be an engagement party?" she asked in a voice so bright it almost erased the quaver.

"Yes, we haven't set a date for it yet. I hope you'll come and not just in a professional capacity but as my guest, Louisa," he said gently. The kindness in his voice was like an ice pick to her chest. How much more could she take?

"If I'm not available, I'm sure my assistant Mrs. Wolfe would love to attend," she said. "If you'll excuse me..." She stood and crossed the room because she knew that she could not force that smile for another second — not for all the money in J.P. Morgan's bank. She felt like a trapped animal. She thought about hiding in the teletype room, but instead she took the stairs to the first floor. When she opened the heavy door to the pressroom, sound engulfed her.

Inside, the giant presses rumbled as they flung out sheet after sheet of *The Ledger*. The clanking of machinery, the smell of ink and paper, and the warm yellow light pooling on the floor embraced her. She found a stool in the corner of the large room, sat down, and wept. She knew she was being ridiculous. She had turned down Forrest Calloway's offer of marriage. She had slept with a British spy without even wondering if he was spoken for. She told herself that she loved her work. She cherished her independence. But she couldn't deny that she also wanted love. And she couldn't understand why she couldn't have both. She covered her face with her hands as she wept.

Sensing someone nearby she looked up. Billy Stephens stood in front of her, holding out a handkerchief. Another helping of humiliation, she thought, as she took the handkerchief from him and wiped her eyes.

Chapter 36
Ellen

Ellen was beginning to think this was all for naught. Koenig invented meaningless tasks for her to do each day: typing manifests for ships going nowhere, taking dictation for innocuous letters about his security concerns, adding and re-adding figures which she assumed to be payoffs but to whom and for what she didn't know, and typing nonsense that might be coded notes or might be something he put together to confuse her.

She had to figure out a way to earn his trust.

"You know you're not making the best use of my talents," she told him one morning.

"And just what are your talents, Miss Malloy? I already have a wife," he said with a sneer.

Ellen stifled her disgust.

"I've noticed a clicking sound on the telephone line whenever I put a call through to you. I don't believe this is normal," she said.

A look of consternation crossed his face.

"What are you implying?" he asked.

"The police probably have a wiretap on your phone. Captain Boehm told me the New York Police Department is notorious for using them, and the telephone company does whatever they ask," she said. "You should be careful what you say on the phone."

"I'm always careful," he said with a snort. "But I will be even more careful now."

The next day as she sat at her desk and typed an inventory, Koenig leaned in his doorway and studied her.

"What is it?" she asked without looking up from her typing.

"Can you spruce yourself up a bit?" he asked.

She stopped typing and stared at him. He had a toothpick lodged in the corner of his mouth.

"Excuse me? I look perfectly respectable. This is a new dress I bought especially for summer. And my hat isn't that old either."

"But you look like a secretary," he said.

"I am a secretary," she said.

"I need you to look like the sort of high-class woman that might be found waiting for a friend at the Ritz-Carlton," he said.

"Oh? And why might I be going to the Ritz?"

"You'll be making a delivery to one of my operatives. My best operative, and she can't be seen coming here," he said as he moved the toothpick from one side of his mouth to the other.

"I can find suitable attire," she said.

Koenig smiled at her. He had a ghastly smile, his teeth small and yellow, his cheeks straining. She looked the other way until she was sure he was gone.

***

That night she donned her men's clothing, slipped out the back door of the boarding house, and walked to Louisa's. It was after ten, and she hoped Louisa wasn't at some society event.

When Suzie opened the door, she stared at Ellen with a puzzled look.

"Oh, it's you, Ellen," Suzie said. "Come on in. Louisa just got in herself. She's upstairs. Why are you dressed like Louisa's father?"

"Safety. Isn't that why you gave them to me?"

Ellen bounded up the steps, eager to see Louisa again. She knocked on Louisa's door and identified herself. Louisa's voice beckoned her inside.

Louisa sat at her vanity, still wearing a sparkling evening dress and a pearl necklace that looked very old. Her shiny auburn hair hung down past her shoulders. She looked so pretty, Ellen thought. Pretty and sad.

"Are you feeling all right?" Ellen asked.

"I'm fine," Louisa said and turned to face her.

"Looks like you just got back from somewhere fancy," Ellen said and sat down in the arm chair by the writing desk.

"Fancy and dreadful," Louisa sighed. "Miss Spence's School had a benefit for tubercular and crippled children. Not that the cause isn't worthy, but a bad orchestra playing Irving Berlin tunes isn't my idea of a good time. But it's summer so what can you expect? I really need to get out of Manhattan."

Ellen glanced over at Louisa's open wardrobe. It was crowded with dresses.

"I need a dress," she said. "I'm meeting with one of Koenig's operatives at the Ritz to deliver a payment. And I can't look out of place."

"Koenig trusts you?" Louisa asked.

"I think so."

"Who is the operative?"

"A woman. I don't know anything else," Ellen said. "Have you learned anything from Papen or Bernstorff?"

"No, but I did learn something from a girl that Papen sees at Martha Held's. They're transporting the cigar bombs in sugar bags. That's how they're set to go off in the middle of the sea where the ships can't get any help. Because it's in the cargo hold, all the cargo is destroyed even if the ship isn't."

Ellen rubbed her hands together.

"I bet Captain Tunney loved that piece of information," she said. "Hey, is your spy coming by tonight?"

Louisa shook her head. "He won't be coming back. His fiancée arrived from England."

Ellen was only a little surprised. It didn't seem to be a topic Louisa wanted to dwell upon.

Louisa continued, "Anyway, now that I've found out about the sugar bags, I don't know what there is left for me to do. The only reason I got involved is because the mayor and Captain Tunney wanted to solve the mystery of the sabotaged ships, and I believe we've done that. Now, I can get back to my job. Otherwise, I'm afraid Phyllis Wolfe will take it right out from under me. She's getting all the good Newport and Saratoga bylines."

"But, don't you think there's more you can learn? More you can do? There's a war going on, Louisa. People are dying. One of my brothers is fighting in it right now," Ellen said.

Louisa shook her head.

"I didn't tell you this, but Forrest Calloway made me give all my material to Billy Stephens. No more Beatrice Milton. She's been fired."

"Why? I thought Thorn loved your Beatrice Milton stories," Ellen said.

"Thorn is just the editor. Forrest has the final word, and he believed that I was sullying my reputation. He's probably right. The only way I was able to do this investigation is because I promised to give any story unrelated to society to Billy Stephens," Louisa said. "I'm done, Ellen. I need to wrest my beat back from Phyllis. If I don't, I'll lose my job and I'll be a pauper."

Louisa turned back to face the mirror over her vanity. Ellen stared at her profile. She had been born to money, and it showed in her bearing, the straight line of her shoulders, the tilt of her chin, the high crest of her forehead. Ellen would never be able to reclaim her place as Louisa's assistant, not if Louisa was only writing society news. Perhaps, Ellen thought, their friendship had been a sort of mirage. A friendship of convenience. She felt as if someone were tightening a screw in her chest.

"Are you willing to lend me a dress?" Ellen asked.

"Certainly," Louisa exclaimed. She went to her wardrobe and opened it, pushing through the dresses. "This one is old, but still nice." She pulled out a rose-colored dress with gray piping along the collar and held it out to Ellen.

"Thank you," Ellen said. "I'll bring it back in a day or so."

"No need," Louisa said. "It's too small in the bust so it should fit you perfectly. It will be a few inches short, but that's the style now anyway."

Ellen sensed something else in the remark. Was Louisa really saying there was no need for her to come back. If Louisa wasn't working for Tunney anymore, and she had a new assistant, what did she need Ellen for?

Ellen let herself out of the house and felt an annoying pressure in her chest. As if the stone in her heart had somehow gotten even heavier. Hester was gone, and now it seemed Louisa was moving out of her life as well.

Chapter 37

Louisa

The letter came to her house, not to the office.

Dear Miss Delafield,

Please come to the Morgan estate on Matinecock Point on the morning of July 3. It is a matter of some urgency. About your father. An early train will get you there by 8. It's a short taxi ride to Morgan's estate, except for the absurdly long driveway. The British lords have nothing on your American aristocrats. Physick, the butler, will have instructions for you.

Yours truly,

Reggie

Louisa was dumbstruck. What was he up to? Should she just ignore him? No, she couldn't. What if he had actually found out something about her father.

The Morgans held a small party every Independence Day weekend, and this year they would be entertaining the British ambassador. J.P. Morgan was now the sole munitions supplier to the British and French, so it made sense that Reggie would be there. But why couldn't he tell her what he had to tell her here in the city?

She folded the letter, put it in a drawer and overheard Suzie grumbling.

"Where is that girl?" Suzie asked, one foot on the stairs.

"I'll go get her," Louisa said. "She probably can't hear you. You did send her all the way up to the attic, didn't you?"

"That was thirty minutes ago. I swear she gets so distracted. She's probably reading one of those magazines about the moving pictures," Suzie said as she walked back to her sewing corner where a pile of corsets, brassieres, and camisoles waited.

Louisa climbed to the second floor and saw the pull door to the attic open and the rickety stairs reaching down to the ground. Hanging on to the sides, she climbed up the steps and poked her head in the attic. Electricity had not been installed up here, but she saw

Pansy sitting on the floor in a puddle of dim light from a kerosene lamp. The girl was thoroughly engrossed in reading something so she didn't even notice her until Louisa asked, "Find something interesting?"

Pansy yelped and jerked up. She clasped her chest and said, "Oh my goodness, Miss Louisa, you like to make me jump out of my skin."

"I'm sorry. I didn't mean to startle you. What is so absorbing?"

Pansy looked down at the book in her hands.

"Oh, this? It's nothing. I'm... well... I know I shouldn't have..." she looked up at Louisa with a guilty grimace. "It's somebody's diaries, but it's so interesting. Every dress is described, the food, even what people said. And it's full of gossip. Somebody named Alva was trying to wiggle her way into somebody named Caroline's party."

"Really?" Louisa asked. "Let me see?"

Pansy handed over a leather-bound volume.

Louisa looked at the front page and saw a bookplate reading "Property of Anna Adams."

"It's my mother's," Louisa said. "Her maiden name is Adams."

Louisa had never imagined her mother keeping a diary. She had never seemed interested in anything but going to parties and gossiping with her friends before she became a widow. And after that, well, she did like to read the newspaper but that was about it.

"What is going on up there?" Suzie called from below.

"You better head down," Louisa said to Pansy.

"I'll leave the lamp up here if you want to read them," Pansy whispered before going to the opening and lowering herself down the wobbly ladder.

Louisa stared at the book and then looked into the chest where Pansy must have found it. There were more! Louisa collected all of them and dropped them one at a time through the opening. Then she climbed down the ladder and shut the overhead door to the attic.

She sat down on her bed and opened one of the diaries. Would it be wrong to read them? What could it hurt, she thought. She doubted her mother had kept any great secrets, and maybe there was a clue in there as to what had happened to her father. After the first one, they were all "property of Anna Delafield," and the dates went all the way up to 1901, the year her father had been killed.

The doorbell rang.

Louisa heard voices, put the diaries under her bed, and went downstairs.

Mr. Sweet, the butler from Martha Held's brothel, stood in the foyer holding onto a woman in a large brown coat.

Suzie looked at Louisa with a stricken expression and said, "It's Carlotta."

Louisa rushed over to the girl. Her face was swollen, her eyes a deep purple color. Her nose lay flat against her cheek and her bottom lip bled.

"What happened?" she asked.

"Papen happened to her," Mr. Sweet said.

"It was a trap," the young woman said. "They don't use sugar bags. It was all a lie. He knew!"

"How did he find out?" Louisa asked.

"Someone named P. K. told him the police were nosing around the docks, opening up sugar bags and searching for bombs. Franz said I turned him in for money," she said. "He said he never trusted me to begin with. He was right about that."

"Bring her into the parlor," Suzie said.

"Who is it?" Anna asked, eyes wide with alarm when they came in. The ginger cat dashed under the couch.

Suzie gave Louisa a look. If a lie was going to be told, Louisa would have to tell it.

"This gentleman is a friend of Suzie's, Mother. This young woman is a maid at the hotel where he works. One of the guests was drunk and did this to her," Louisa said.

"She's going to bleed on the fabric," Anna said as Louisa led her over to the sofa.

"Mother, remember Christian charity?" Louisa asked.

"Isn't that what churches are for?"

Louisa opened the coat to take it off Carlotta and saw she was wearing only the black corset that Suzie had sold to her. She also saw that her ribs were black and blue. She quickly closed the coat.

"I have to get back to ... the hotel," Mr. Sweet said. "Can you take care of her?"

"Yes," Suzie said. "She'll be fine. You go on."

Mr. Sweet left. Pansy brought in some clean rags and a basin of hot water. She gently wiped Carlotta's face.

"I'm going to call for a doctor. Her nose is obviously broken, and she seems to be bruised all over," Louisa said. She bent over Carlotta and touched her arm. "I'm terribly sorry this happened to you, Carlotta."

This is my fault, Louisa thought. She reminded herself that people were dying as a result of the sabotages, but this failure felt like a punch in the stomach. No, she told herself, Carlotta was the one who had been punched and more than once from the looks of it.

The doctor arrived and looked Carlotta over.

"She's suffering a nasal fracture," the doctor said. He gave her something for pain. Louisa turned away while he readjusted the bone or cartilage or whatever noses were made of. He stitched her lip and said, “I’m afraid this is going to leave a scar.”

Carlotta didn’t utter a word. Anna had wheeled herself over to the group to see what was happening.

“She’ll be able to breathe through her nose once the swelling goes down but I’m afraid I can’t make it look the way it did. It will always be crooked,” the doctor said. “She needs to rest. These other bruises and cuts are quite severe. If she bleeds when she relieves herself, call me again. That will mean there may be some internal damage.”

Louisa gasped.

When he left, Carlotta said, “He said he would make sure I could never make money again.”

“Who cares what a maid looks like?” Anna asked.

“Von Papen said that?” Louisa asked, ignoring her mother’s outburst.

“He did,” Carlotta answered.

“What do you plan to do with her, Louisa?” Anna asked, anxiously. “You can’t leave her here in my parlor. What will I do?”

Louisa exchanged a glance with Suzie, but Pansy was the one who answered.

“I’ll put her in my bed and I’ll nurse her till she’s better,” she said.

“Pansy, you’re an angel,” Louisa said.

Pansy put her shoulder under Carlotta's arm and gently guided the girl upstairs.

***

That night Louisa waited, sitting at her vanity table, dressed in a severe dark green dress buttoned up to her neck. The window slid open and Reggie stepped inside.

"I understand there's an order of flowers for me," he said.

"I have information, and it isn't good," she said. "The sugar bags story was just a ruse. Von Papen suspected that Carlotta might betray him so he set a trap for her."

"I see," Reggie said. "He's no novice to the craft."

"He beat her up. Badly," Louisa said.

"Where is she?"

"In Suzie's room."

"In this house?"

"Martha's butler told Martha he would take her to another brothel, one where the clientele would not be so picky. Instead he brought her here. She has nowhere else to go."

"Keep her out of sight then. I suppose we're back to square one," Reggie said. "I'll let Tunney know."

She couldn't bear it another second.

"Are you not even going to apologize to me?" she said.

"For what?" he asked.

"For failing to mention you were engaged." Fury built inside her.

"I didn't know it mattered," he said.

"It does matter," she said through gritted teeth.

"Then I apologize for failing to mention it."

"Why did you sleep with me?" Louisa asked. "That wasn't necessary."

"I slept with you because you are beautiful and intelligent, and I'm attracted to you. I'm engaged to Millicent because she is rich and an aristocrat. How can a society writer such as yourself not know the way the world works?" He looked genuinely mystified.

"I suppose I have a blind spot when it comes to the matter of my own heart," she said.

He stepped closer to her.

"I really am sorry, Louisa," he said gently. "I did not mean to hurt you."

"Thank you," she said and turned away from him. She looked down at her hands. "What news do you have of my father?"

"You'll have to wait until Jack Morgan's party," he said.

"Why?" She wheeled back around to face him.

"You'll find out." He kissed her forehead and went back out the way he had come in.

Chapter 38
Ellen

"And don't you look pretty as a tea rose," Koenig said when he saw Ellen at her desk the next morning. Ellen had never been remotely compared to a rose before. "Take the train to the Ritz around lunchtime. Go to the Grill Room, order lunch and wait for her."

"What is this woman's name?"

"Her code name is *Die Wolfin*. She'll have one of those umbrella things — the kind ladies carry but to keep off the sun."

"A parasol?" Ellen asked.

He nodded. It was odd how much his face looked as if it were made of plaster.

"When she approaches you, hand her this bag and say, 'I believe you left this at dinner last night.' She will thank you, take the bag, and that is all. Take your time going and coming back. Stop in stores. Make sure you aren't being followed. We cannot be too careful."

"I understand," Ellen said.

He handed her a Macy's shopping bag. Inside was an evening clutch. He also gave her two dollars so she could have lunch at The Ritz. It seemed an extravagant amount.

On the way to the hotel, Ellen stopped at Grand Central Terminal and ducked into the lady's lounge. She entered a stall and extracted the beaded evening purse from the Macy's shopping bag. Opening it, she found an envelope. Inside were five crisp ten-dollar bills. A lot of money.

She took a circuitous route to the hotel, and thirty minutes later she arrived at the Madison Avenue entrance of the Ritz Carlton. Louisa had told her it was the finest hotel in the city, designed by the same architects who designed Grand Central. It was especially known for its gardens. Unlike the enormous Grand Central, however, the lobby of this hotel felt intimate, welcoming, and luxurious without being oppressively opulent. She crossed a large Persian rug to reach the concierge's desk and asked for directions to the Grill Room.

"Right down those stairs there, Miss," he said.

She thanked him and headed for the stairs, which were lined on either side with fresh flowers. The carpet was a dark red, bolts of velvet cloth swooped from the ceiling, and since there were no windows, light emanated from sconces around the room. Though it was a fairly large room, the tables were clustered around the edge. The place had a clandestine feel to it. She realized why Koenig had staged the meeting here instead of the main dining room upstairs or the rooftop garden.

A maitre'd showed her to an out-of-the-way table, and within minutes a waiter had come to take her order. She ordered the simplest thing on the menu, a chicken pie and a cup of coffee. She sat waiting, wondering where the woman was when she heard a low, melodious voice.

"Why, hello, my dear, I didn't expect to see you here."

Ellen looked up and saw a woman, impeccably dressed with a veil over her face, carrying a black and white parasol tucked under her arm. Ellen could tell she was young and rich by her smooth elegant hands, by the resonant tone of voice, by the perfect diction, and the way her sentence ended on a high note as if she were the most delighted person in the world.

"You left your bag at dinner last night," Ellen said, knowing that her own voice and accent revealed her to be nowhere near this woman's class. She reached into the Macy's bag and pulled out the evening bag.

"Oh, silly me. How good you were to bring it," the woman said and deftly took the bag. Then she was gone in a swish of fabric.

Ellen hadn't gotten a good look at the woman's face, but she knew one thing for sure, *Die Wolfin* was a member of society — born and bred.

Chapter 39

Louisa

She had been putting off the promised interview with Karl Boy-Ed, the German Naval Attaché who could pass for a Nordic god, but she could wait no longer. Von Bernstorff was starting to sound skeptical about her devotion to their little project though he had arranged for another payment to her, which she promptly used to buy some new clothes for poor Carlotta who had left the brothel with nothing but the dress on her back. Fortunately, the girl did not seem to have sustained any serious injuries but her misshapen nose and missing teeth would always be a reminder of von Papen's brutality.

Louisa agreed to meet Boy-Ed at the German club across from Central Park in the evening as it was too warm during the day to do much of anything. A fat German man in a suit showed her into a lounge where Boy-Ed sat laughing with some of his compatriots. When he saw her, he leapt up and took her hand, bowing to her with a click of his heels. If von Papen thought he was a charmer, he had absolutely nothing on Karl Boy-Ed. She remembered the bubbly blond-haired "lady of the evening" at Martha Held's who was his regular consort. At least, it seemed he treated her well.

Louisa and Boy-Ed sat in comfortable chairs in a corner of the room near the window so they could feel a breeze.

"Your country's independence day is this weekend," he said. "Though sometimes we Germans wonder if America truly is independent."

"You are speaking to a member of the Daughters of the American Revolution, Herr Boy-Ed. I assure you we are a sovereign nation. But I did not come here to talk politics with you. I came here to talk about your mother," she said.

"You cannot talk about mothers without talking politics, I'm afraid," he said. "For it is the mothers who raise the boys who die on the battlefield. Such as my poor brother."

He proceeded to tell her about his mother, who actually did sound like a remarkable woman and Louisa found that she enjoyed the conversation in spite of herself.

That is until Franz von Papen walked up to them and bowed to her.

"Miss Delafield, what a pleasant surprise," he said. Her mind flashed to poor bruised and battered Carlotta and her stomach squeezed. Do not give yourself away, she said to herself. She took a deep breath and willed a smile onto her face.

"Captain von Papen, how delightful to see you," she said.

"And you, Miss Delafield," he said, taking up her hand to kiss it. "I see you have been talking to this blond rascal. Don't let him worm his way into your heart."

"Not to worry. My defenses are up," she said, meaning every word of it.

Papen turned to Boy-Ed and spoke to him in German for a few minutes. Her German was rudimentary at best and even if she could understand she knew they would couch anything of import in some sort of code, and yet one word stood out. "Maverick." That was not a German word as far as she knew.

"I apologize, Miss Delafield," von Papen said. "It is easier and quicker for me to communicate in German.

And I needed to convey some information to my naval counterpart."

"It's time for me to leave anyway," she said.

"Herr von Papen, your guest, Mr. Hoadley, is here," the fat German man interrupted them to say.

"*Danke,*" von Papen said curtly.

A tall man strode into the room with a swagger that only an American could pull off. Finally, she had two pieces of information that she could give to Reggie when she saw him tomorrow at Jack and Jane Morgan's estate: Papen was meeting an American named Hoadley and the word 'maverick' must mean something.

***

The train arrived before eight the next morning, and Louisa emerged into the mid-summer warmth.

"The Morgan Estate?" the taxi driver asked. "I'm surprised they didn't send one of their men to come get you. I don't mind the drive. Place was built only a couple years ago. Real castle-like. A hundred and forty acres! And 57 rooms. Sheesh, what I wouldn't give for a tenth of what that man's got. You must be rich yourself to be invited there."

"No. I'm but a lowly reporter," she said.

"A reporter? Say, do you know what happened in D.C. last night? Some kind of bombing?"

"I only know what I read in the paper this morning. No one was injured apparently," she said. A bomb had been set off after hours in the Senate building. The saboteurs were getting bolder and bolder.

"These Germans are spoiling for a fight, aren't they?" he said.

"They are indeed," she said.

"You know what they say about sleeping tigers," he said.

"Indeed."

"We're here," he said after a short drive though she couldn't see the house yet. They puttered down an absurdly long tree-lined drive, just as Reggie had reported, until suddenly the trees parted and there stood a magnificent building — castle-like indeed. They pulled into a circular driveway lined with flower-filled gardens. He stopped the car in front of a magnificent wooden door, and a footman rushed to open the taxi door for her.

"Miss Delafield?" the footman asked.

"Yes," she said.

"Physick is expecting you."

Physick waited for her in the foyer. A British butler, he had probably been trained in one of the great British estates — the sort of butler who would lay his life on the line for his employer if called to do so, she thought. Later she would remember that thought, but now she just wanted to speak to Reggie and get to the bottom of this.

"Mr. Grant has asked that I show you to his room, Miss Delafield," the butler said.

"His room?" Louisa asked and glanced around the empty hallway. "That hardly seems proper."

"Mine is not to question why," Physick said without the slightest hint of irony. "The family and guests will breakfast at nine. You are more than welcome to join them."

Louisa followed Physick up the wide polished staircase past enormous portraits of stern-faced men and American landscapes. Nothing at all modern. They walked down one long hallway after another, their footsteps cushioned by Oriental carpets. *I should have left bread crumbs,* Louisa thought, wondering how she'd ever find her way out. Finally, Physick stopped in front of one of the doors and knocked softly. It opened at once, and there stood Reggie in his dressing gown. He pulled Louisa inside and shut the door.

"What on—" Louisa exclaimed, but Reggie held a finger to his lips. He pointed to a figure sleeping in the large canopied bed.

"I thought your fiancée was in Boston," Louisa said. "Why would you—?"

"She is," Reggie said. "That is not my fiancée. If you'll excuse me, I'm going to shower."

He picked up a toiletries bag and then pointed to the sleeping woman.

"She's all yours," he said and headed into the bathroom.

Who? Louisa wondered. She circled the bed and peered at the face half buried in a pillow. Even sleeping, Julia Markham, wife of attorney Herbert Markham, reminded her of a Kewpie doll. Julia had been dodging her for a year. No more dodging.

"That Lothario," Louisa said, wondering if Reggie slept with every woman he met as a matter of course.

Julia's eyes opened. She stared at Louisa and Louisa stared back, watching the realization dawn on Julia's face.

"He's quite the seducer, isn't he?" Louisa asked.

"Louisa Delafield? What? Where is—?"

"Reggie is taking a shower. He wanted to give us some privacy," Louisa said.

A look of disappointment and shame passed across Julia's face. It must just be dawning on her that Reggie's interest in her had been a ruse.

"Where's your husband?" Louisa asked.

"On a business trip," Julia said, sitting up in the bed. "Hand me my negligee, please."

Louisa picked up a filmy negligee from the floor and tossed it to her. Julia put it on and sat on the edge of the bed.

"I've been wanting to ask you some questions," Louisa said. "But you've managed to avoid me for over a year now."

"Oh, Louisa, you don't want to know."

"But I do, Julia. I really do," Louisa said. She sat down in an armchair by the window. Outside was a gorgeous view of the Long Island Sound — blue and glittering like sequined silk in the sun.

Julia sighed.

"This is about your father, of course," she said.

Louisa nodded.

"Well, this all happened before Herbert and I married so I've had to piece it together over the years," she said.

"How did you do that?"

"I overheard things he said to his mother. I looked at his financial affairs, and I gazed into that dark heart of his. He tried to have you killed. He gave money to that woman anarchist and sent her to Florida after you last year."

"I assumed as much. Why did he give up?"

"Because once I found out about it, I told him I would expose his illicit doings if one hair on your head was harmed," she said.

Louisa studied Julia. All this time she had thought Julia was afraid of her husband. In fact, he was probably afraid of her.

"Why get rid of me?"

"He knew you were trying to find out what happened to your father, asking questions," she said.

"And what did happen to my father? Who murdered him? Why?" Louisa asked, tension building in every muscle of her body. Was she finally going to learn the truth?

"I don't know exactly. I do know that Herbert was blackmailing him," Julia said, running a hand through her mussed hair.

"Blackmailing him for what?" Louisa asked, leaning forward.

"Infidelity," Julia said with a shrug.

"Men are unfaithful all the time."

"It was a different era then. And I think your father genuinely loved your mother. He didn't want to lose her. Unfortunately, he wasn't the only one in love with her."

"Who else loved her?" Louisa asked.

"My husband," Julia said.

This was a shock.

"Did he kill my father?"

"Heavens, no, but he knows who did. Try as I might, I've never been able to get it out of him. When I saw what he was willing to do to you, I decided to stop asking and hoped you would eventually give up your quest. I see that was a vain hope," she said.

"So Herbert Markham was blackmailing my father? Did he also mislead him into making those terrible investments?"

"I believe your father did that all by himself. Much of the fortune came from your mother's family. Once he started losing money, he made riskier and riskier investments, trying to get it back. It didn't help that he had to pay exorbitant sums of blackmail money to Herbert. Herbert hoped to ruin him so your mother would divorce him. However, after your father was killed — presumably by the husband of one of his lovers, your mother went into seclusion. A year later, Herbert and I married. I had no knowledge of this sordid history at the time."

Louisa sat, mystified, wondering what it meant. Why had her father behaved so badly? Why would he cheat on her mother if he loved her, which evidently he had. She'd always thought him at least honorable.

"I suppose I should let you get dressed," Louisa said and rose.

"Yes, it's time for me to sneak off to my own room."

"Thank you, Julia," Louisa said. "I needed to know this."

"For all the good it will do you," Julia said. "You won't be able to prove anything."

Julia left Reggie's room and Louisa waited for Reggie to return, which he did shortly, full of vim and vigor.

"Did she spill the beans?" he asked.

"She did indeed. That was very kind of you to put her in such a compromising position," Louisa said, sarcastically. She was both grateful to him and horrified by his cavalier use of poor Julia.

"You're welcome."

"I have something for you, too. Last night I interviewed Karl Boy-Ed. Von Papen was there, meeting an American named Hoadley. And while von Papen was talking to Boy-Ed, he mentioned something about a maverick?"

"The *Maveric* is a ship," Reggie said. "Off the West Coast. But who the devil is Hoadley?"

"I thought you might wonder that. I went to the paper after the interview and looked through the business section morgue. He's a Connecticut businessman, owns a company called Bridgeport Projectiles."

Reggie blew out a long breath.

"So that's what the bastards are up to."

"What?"

"They're buying up American munitions so the allies can't have them and shipping them on the *Maveric* to Mexico. This is very helpful, Louisa. Thank you. What we really need now is some proof."

"I'm willing to bet that the proof is in Herr Albert's briefcase," she said.

"I don't suppose you could get your hands on that," he said.

"*I* don't sleep with everyone I meet," she said, "or perhaps I could get my hands on it."

"Touché, old girl. It's all part of the game."

Louisa declined to stay for breakfast even though Jane insisted she was welcome. Louisa did not want to sit at the same table with Reggie and the mortified (she hoped) Julia Markham. Besides, she had an idea about what to do next.

As she waited outside for a taxi to take her back to the train station, a strange little man approached the front door.

"Good morning, sir, I am from the Society Summer Directory," the little man said when Physick asked him his business. Louisa noticed a faint European accent, and the little man looked vaguely familiar — something about his narrow, vulpine face. A shiver traveled down her spine.

The taxi pulled up, and Louisa got inside. She turned back and saw the stoop was empty. Physick had obviously trusted the man enough to let him inside.

On the train, she thought about what she had learned. If Julia had not been able to get the identity of her father's killer out of Herbert Markham, Esquire, then she surely would have no luck with him. Was there some other way? Perhaps she could find out with whom her father had been having an affair. Did her mother know?

As soon as Louisa arrived home, Suzie met her with a worried look.

"Mr. Grant called. Said someone tried to kill Mr. Morgan right after you left," she said.

"Is he all right?" Louisa asked, alarmed.

"He's going to be fine. The butler saved him," Suzie said. "The man is in jail right now. He confessed right away. Turns out he was in Washington the night before. He's the one who set off the bomb in the capitol!"

"You got a lot of information out of Mr. Grant," Louisa said.

"I know how to interrogate," Suzie said.

Louisa found she wasn't particularly surprised by this development as shocking as it was that the man had been brazen enough to go right into the house. The Germans hated Morgan for supplying the Allies. And there were so many of these loose cannons running around the country unable to get back home because of the blockade. Of course, being the exemplary butler that he was, Physick had been the one to save the day. She was halfway up the stairs when she had a sudden realization. Several years ago, a German professor had poisoned his wife and then effectively disappeared.

There'd been a picture of him in the papers. She remembered being fascinated by the story because the man taught at Harvard, but no one could find him.

She went back downstairs and jotted a quick note to Captain Tunney.

"Pansy, would you find a messenger to take this to Captain Tunney's office," she said.

"Why don't you just call him?"

"I try never to say anything on the telephone these days," Louisa said. "You never know who's listening."

She went upstairs and reached under her bed for her mother's journals. It was time to do some light reading.

Chapter 40

Ellen

Finally, she thought, she had something to deliver to the candy shop. A fellow had come by with a scheme to blow up a Canadian railroad. Koenig had sent her upstairs to Herr Albert for money to give the man, dictated a coded letter for Franz von Papen and then left her in the office to type it, which she did, making a carbon copy.

When he unexpectedly returned, she managed to slip the copy into a McClure's magazine.

"Why are you dressed up?" he asked. Ellen was wearing the same dress Louisa had given her instead of her usual brown or gray suit.

"Jane Addams is giving a lecture in Carnegie Hall. I met her when I was on my way to Berlin. I plan to hear what she has to say if it's any of your business," she said.

Koenig sneered.

"You're going to hear a pacifist lecture?" he asked. "Will a pacifist ever wrest Ireland from the clutches of the British? What sort of a coward must one be to be called a 'pacifist'?"

"I don't think there's anything cowardly about being a pacifist," Ellen said, replacing a file in one of the cabinets. "Don't you want peace?"

"I have never felt so alive in my life, Miss Malloy," Koenig said, taking a long inhale from his cigarette. "But as long as Miss Addams' aim is to keep America out of the war, well, then, I suppose we are on the same side."

"Agreed," Ellen said. He handed her a cigarette, and she let him light it for her. In his mind, this little ritual seemed to unite them so she kept up her habit of smoking though she didn't like the way it left her hair and clothes stinking.

Before going to hear Jane Addams speak, Ellen stopped off at the confectionary on Broadway and bought a bag of lemon drops. She left her magazine on the counter before exiting the store.

The real reason she wanted to hear Jane speak wasn't to hear her thoughts on the war, for she knew exactly what Jane and her friends thought of that. No, it was because of something Alice had said on the boat — that there was nothing unnatural about a woman who loved another woman. Ellen wanted to be around women who believed that even if it was from a distance. She also hoped she would have a chance to speak to Alice again and Jane, as well. They were so much like Hester in their passions. She immediately stifled the memories that lingered like a mob on the outskirts of her mind. Must everything lead her back to Hester? Must everything be a reminder of what she had lost? She placed a hand on her chest. Yes, her heart was still as hard as a stone. She must keep it that way.

Carnegie Hall was a huge and ornate venue for a speech, but the large and enthusiastic crowd, which had come to hear the speech about Jane Addams' work at the Hague and in Europe, filled it. Ellen thought back to her time on the ship with Miss Addams and her entourage — the camaraderie among them, the hopefulness. Koenig was wrong. They were an incredibly courageous group of women.

She had splurged for a first-row seat in the lowest balcony. She settled in and observed the audience. It seemed every sort of New Yorker (except the very poor) was represented — old and young, rich and not-so-rich.

Addams was introduced shortly and took the podium. She seemed daunted by the size of the crowd, but she quickly gained confidence as she began to speak of her experiences. She talked about the women's conference at the Hague, how German women and French women and British women and Russian women and Belgian women and American women all came together to share their stories, to create friendships and to make resolutions, demanding peaceful negotiations among the combatants. Her voice gained strength as she became more impassioned.

Toward the end of the speech in a ringing voice, she said, "The old notion that you can drive a belief into a man at the point of a bayonet is in force once more. It is quite as foolish to think that if militarism is an idea and an ideal, it can be changed and crushed by counter-militarism or by bayonet charge!"

The audience hung on every word, nodding in agreement among themselves, but the next thing she said caused a strange hush to fall over the audience.

"And the young men in these various countries say of the bayonet charges: 'That is what we cannot think of.' We heard in all countries similar statements in regards to the necessity for the use of stimulants before men would engage in bayonet charges – that they have a regular formula in Germany, that they give them rum in England and absinthe in France; that they give them the 'dope' before the bayonet charge is possible. Well, now, think of that."

A shift happened in the room — low murmurings, a few scowls. The accusation of doping soldiers seemed to give them pause. Ellen, on the other hand, did think of it. What would it take to stab someone with a bayonet? She tried to imagine what it must feel like to push the sharp blade into a man's chest. The thought of her brothers ever having to do such a thing made her shudder.

The moment passed, and when Addams finished her speech, she was given a rousing applause. Ellen rose to leave the auditorium, but on her way out, she spied Alice Hamilton, Miss Addams' doctor, and went to say hello.

"Miss Addams looks to be in great health," Ellen said and grinned. "You must be doing your job well."

Alice insisted that Ellen join them for a late-night meal at a nearby diner.

"Jane will be disappointed if she misses you. She hoped you would come tonight."

So Ellen joined Jane and Alice and two other women in an eatery next door to the Wellington Hotel. Jane was a little giddy from her speech.

"You don't think it was too much?" she asked. "I don't have any expectations of convincing an audience of that size of anything."

"It was a wonderful speech," Alice said.

Ellen did not mention the strange lull in the audience when she had spoken of the soldiers. Ellen ate her cream of tomato soup and listened while they dissected the speech. After they'd all eaten, Jane turned to Ellen while the others were engaged in talking about their further travels.

"Dear, how are you? I know you must feel the loss of your beloved Hester most keenly."

"I try not to feel much of anything," Ellen said. "And yet I will admit to ugly, wrathful feelings about this vile and senseless war. I've not the foggiest idea how you keep your composure."

"Oh, my dear Ellen, I also feel anger, I feel helpless, I feel grief for the terrible loss of life, but I allow myself to have those feelings, and then I channel them into action. Positive action."

"I am also channeling my feelings, Miss Addams, I promise you that. I can't discuss what I'm up to, but you ought to know I'm doing my part," Ellen said.

"That's fine, Ellen, but don't forget to grieve. If you don't, that buried pain will cause you to sicken and die," she said. "I've seen it happen."

Ellen took a sip from her tea cup. She didn't mention that getting sick and dying sounded fine to her. She didn't want to admit it to herself, but there it was.

"Would you like a lemon drop?" she asked.

Jane smiled and said, "I'd love one."

***

One of Ellen's jobs for Koenig was to peruse the New York papers every morning to hunt for favorable or disfavorable press about Germany. He was also interested in any news regarding anything remotely related to the military. But this morning's papers held nothing that would interest Koenig. Instead, all she found were the swift and vicious reprisals to Jane Addams' speech the night before. The writers all seemed to be focused on her comments about soldiers being doped in order to use their bayonets, as if she had called them cowards for not wanting to kill.

They called her a "silly, vain, impertinent old maid." Theodore Roosevelt was quoted as saying she was a member of "the shrieking sisterhood." The insults and indignation sprouted like weeds in all the major publications. Ellen's head throbbed and she covered her eyes with her hand.

"Are you ill?" Koenig asked.

She hadn't realized he was standing there.

"Just resting my eyes," she said irritably. She looked up at him. "Do you think it's true that soldiers are given stimulants before battle?"

He grinned. "Of course, they are!"

She returned her gaze to the article in front of her. What ignorance, she thought. A woman who had the nerve to speak out against killing was being pilloried as if she were the most vile thing to walk the earth. She wished she were a publisher. She would tell the public the truth — all of it. She would have a publication like Sylvia Pankhurst's, one for women, something that would educate and inspire them. Not like these insipid papers and magazines that pandered to women. And then it hit her — her publication would be something that Hester would want to read.

Ellen did feel ill. This constant stifling of her anger and her pain had begun to eat at her insides. She hadn't even had her monthly all summer.

"Go up to Herr Albert's office," Koenig said. "And get the weekly payments."

Ellen took the stairs up two flights to the accountant's office. He was an officious man with the cleanest office she'd ever seen. He barely looked up at her as he handed her Koenig's payroll. One thing was certain, the Germans were sparing no expense when it came to their American endeavors. She noticed a large leather briefcase beside the desk. Every time she saw him, he had that briefcase clutched in his hand or at his side.

In the afternoon storm clouds assembled in the sky. When it was time to leave, she got on the elevator down to the ground floor and found Herr Albert inside, wearing a big black raincoat, his leather briefcase at his side.

"Fraulein," he said and nodded.

As soon as they were off the elevator, she stopped, pretending to get something out of her purse. She didn't want to get stuck riding the train at the same time as Herr Albert. He strode out the door and she followed a minute later. He walked down the block to the platform for the train and climbed it. He had loads of money, but he took the el after work. She was across the street but rather than run to catch the approaching train, she decided she would wait for the next one. A woman hurried toward the steps. She carried a cane and wore a hat with a veil, and yet, she ran up the steps, quite spritely, not using the cane. Her veil blew upwards and revealed her face for a minute. Looking up at the platform from across the street, Ellen stared at the woman as she suddenly hunched over and hobbled onto the train, leaning on the cane.

That was no old woman, she thought. That was Louisa Delafield.

Chapter 41

Louisa

Louisa dropped her notes on Billy Stephens' desk. She had called Jane Morgan and gotten the full story of the assassination attempt. And Captain Tunney had sent a note, thanking her for the tip. She had been right. Frank Holt, Morgan's would-be assassin, had once been a Harvard professor and was indeed suspected of murdering his wife.

"You didn't write out the story for me?" Billy asked.

She frowned at him and said, "I'm afraid you'll have to do some work on your own. It's all there. I even included a quote from Mrs. Morgan."

Billy glanced over the notes.

"So the butler didn't do it," he mused.

"Oh, for heaven's sake," Louisa said, sailed over to her own desk and sat down to type up her interview with Karl Boy-Ed. By the time she was finished, Phyllis had appeared, wearing a lovely straw hat bedecked with flowers.

"How was Saratoga?" Louisa asked.

"Lovely," Phyllis said as she sat down. "I have oodles of stories. What are you working on?"

"I interviewed Karl Boy-Ed about his mother. It seems she's written a book about losing her other son in 1914. She's quite a fanatic. She says, and I quote, 'A mother is only dust on the road to victory.' If all German mothers are like that, the Allies don't stand a chance," Louisa said.

"Louisa, correct me if I'm wrong but it seems this is the third or fourth article you've written this summer about Germans. I know these aristocrats are quite popular among society members who seem to value class above country, but I wonder what our middle-class readers think," Phyllis said as she jostled some typing paper in her hands.

Louisa had no idea what to say. For one thing it seemed highly impertinent. For another, Phyllis was right. She wondered if she should take Phyllis into her confidence, but too many people already knew about her subterfuge.

"Phyllis, I know your dismal experience with a German husband has perhaps colored your viewpoint, but I won't give in to the prejudices of the American people who are constantly being riled up for a war," she said. "They should hear another point of view."

"Are you a peacette then?" Phyllis asked.

Louisa stared at her.

"You are awfully bold this morning, aren't you?"

Phyllis blushed and looked down at her desk.

"My apologies. I was out of line," she said.

"It's all right. We all get heated up over this war," Louisa said. "You may use the typewriter this afternoon. I'm doing some interviews for that political story I told you about."

In actuality she planned to park herself across the street from 45 Broadway in a cafe and watch for Herr Albert.

Then that evening there would be another dreaded task, a social event that she truly did not want to attend.

***

"Put away your notebook, Miss Delafield," Forrest said. "You are here as my guest."

"What about my readers? I can't leave them disappointed," Louisa said. "I would be remiss not to record every glittery detail."

The engagement party was held at Delmonico's, which Louisa realized was where she and Forrest were supposed to meet for dinner the night she was to tell him that yes, she would be his wife. Now, he had commandeered the whole place for his engagement party to another woman. The guests comprised a glittering collection of new money wealth, publishers, Broadway producers, and the occasional gangster who had pulled himself up into society through gambling enterprises. (Forrest did love his baccarat.)

Forrest looked vaguely guilty, and she didn't think it had anything to do with the fact that he was marrying another woman.

"Tell me, Forrest. Do you love her?" Louisa asked. They stood near a table where a chef carved a juicy haunch of roast beef for guests. The din of the place kept their conversation private.

"I sense you aren't really asking whether or not I love her, but whether I feel passion for her," he said, leaning close to her ear. "The answer is no. True passion — what you and I had — is rare, but it does not last forever. I respect her and admire her, and I enjoy her company immensely. Those things, it turns out, add up to love in the long run."

He looked up.

"And there she is," he said.

Sadie Treadwell approached with a broad smile. She obviously had no knowledge of the relationship between her fiancé and the society writer at his newspaper. Louisa was glad. She realized that considering her own affair with Reggie Grant, she had no business feeling any jealousy or animosity for this woman. Forrest had made his choice, and Louisa must graciously accept it.

"Miss Delafield, I'm delighted that you could make it. I do hope you have some wonderful plan for your future. You're such a talent," she said.

"My future?" Louisa asked. She wondered for a moment if Forrest's fiancée was being snide, but from the pleasant, kindly look on her face, she knew that wasn't the case.

"My dear, I believe the photographer is waving at us. He must be ready," Forrest said, taking Sadie by the elbow.

Louisa watched, puzzled, as they walked away. She looked around the room, and saw Virgil Thorn against a wall with a glass in his hand and a grimace on his face that was attempting to be a smile. Something was afoot.

She wended her way through the crowd and reached Thorn's side.

"Hello, Thorn," she said. "Is it difficult to breathe here?"

"What do you mean?"

"You look like a fish out of water," she said.

"True. We don't see each other outside the confines of 34th Street," he said, frowning. "And now we won't even see each other there."

Confused again, Louisa asked, "Why not? You aren't leaving the paper, are you? What's going on?"

He looked at her with a closed-lipped, pained grin. "We are all leaving the paper," he said. He nodded toward Forrest Calloway and his future bride staring at the photographer as a bright flash exploded. "He sold it."

Forrest had sold the paper? The photographer's flash might as well have been a bomb. So that's what Sadie had been referring to.

Thorn continued, "The new publisher intends to turn it into a stock listing with perhaps a page of Wall Street news. Everything else is off the table. Sports, politics, and, of course, the women's page."

"Why would he do that to us?" Louisa asked, staring across the room at Forrest.

"We weren't getting any more subscribers, and he's got other interests. Look around the room. How many newspaper folk do you see? Not many. It's all Broadway directors and stars. Isn't that George Cohan over there?" He pointed to a handsome, voluble man surrounded by a galaxy of women.

Louisa feared she might throw up.

"I have to go," she said, holding her hand over her stomach.

"Miss Delafield, don't take it so hard. We've got at least a month left. You have some time to find something else."

She took a gulp of her drink. "The syndicate won't want me anymore if I'm some sort of freelancer. They liked the prestige of the association with *The Ledger*," she said.

"You're right, but you'll find a place somewhere. The city is full of papers."

"All of the big ones already have a society columnist," she said and drained her glass. Suddenly, she couldn't catch her breath.

"You're panicking, Miss Delafield," he said.

On the other side of the room, someone had started playing a piano while Cohan sang "Give My Regards to Broadway" to the delight of everyone in the room with the exception of Louisa and Thorn.

"What about you? What will you do?" she asked. "I don't imagine there are many openings for a managing editor in New York right now."

"I might go to a smaller market or back to London, I suppose," he said with a shrug.

She clasped his arm and gave it a sympathetic squeeze.

A few minutes later she was out the door and in a taxi on her way home. Her job, her livelihood, her reason for getting up every morning — gone. Had Forrest done this to spite her? She'd refused his proposal because she put her work above him. She shook her head. It was her fear talking. She knew Forrest. He was not a cruel man. He wouldn't put an entire company out of business for some petty revenge. He'd never been all that interested in the paper, and if it wasn't making money, why should he keep it?

When she got home, she found Carlotta on the couch in the parlor, stroking the ginger cat. The swelling in her face had finally gone down, and the bruises had faded. Her crooked nose marred her pretty face, and one of her front teeth was missing thanks to von Papen's fist. He had done what he intended. Carlotta would not be in demand at any high class brothels. Louisa felt a camaraderie with her. They'd both had their professions taken from them, the rug pulled out from under their feet, so to speak, by a man.

Anna sat in her invalid chair, knitting.

"I'm sorry I've been a burden on you. I'll be leaving tomorrow," Carlotta said to Louisa.

"Where will you go?" Louisa asked, surprised by this sudden announcement.

"I'll find something. Factory work maybe."

"You can't work in a factory," Anna said, setting down her knitting.

"What do you suggest she do, Mother?" Louisa asked, surprised that her mother wasn't ushering the girl out the door. She'd been horrified when Carlotta showed up at the door, scragglier than the ginger cat had been when they'd first found her.

"I don't know, but we can't let her go work in a factory. She's not used to such hard work," Anna said. Louisa stared at her mother. She thought Carlotta was a maid, but she obviously had no idea just how hard servants did work. Wealthy people thought their servants were fortunate to have their positions. No one had ever disabused Anna of that idea. But her mother did have a point. Louisa couldn't let Carlotta wander off without some sort of plan. On the other hand, they might all be working in a factory once *The Ledger* closed down.

"She's right, Carlotta. You'll stay with us for now," Louisa said.

"Are you sure? I hate being a burden," Carlotta said.

"We're certain." Fortunately, Suzie's business in delicates was going well, so at least there would be food on the table.

"Help me upstairs, Louisa," Anna said. "The girl can sleep on the sofa. Let Pansy have her bed back. We have quite a full house, don't we? It's like in the old days. Remember all the servants we had?"

"Yes, Mother," Louisa said. As she helped her mother up the stairs, she said, "Pansy found some diaries up in the attic from those old days. I hope you don't mind. I looked at some of them. You're a good writer. So many details, the flowers, the dresses, and even snippets of gossip. You could have been a society columnist yourself."

"I would never —" Anna responded abruptly. "That's all nonsense anyway. Bring them downstairs tomorrow, and we'll burn them."

When they reached the top of the steps, Anna pulled away from Louisa and hurried into her bedroom without even asking for Suzie to come help her to bed. She's not as helpless as she pretends, Louisa thought. She wondered if there was something in those diaries that her mother didn't want her to read.

Chapter 42

Ellen

Ellen arrived at the office first that morning as she often did. She tidied up the room a bit. Germans were a fastidious bunch as a rule, and Koenig was no exception. As she tidied, she snooped around, which she had been doing ever since Koenig hired her. As she dusted furniture and looked in drawers and filing cabinets she wondered again what Louisa had been doing, pretending to be an old woman and getting on the same train as Herr Albert. The last time they had spoken Louisa seemed to have washed her hands of the whole endeavor. Anger pricked at her. Had Louisa lied to her? Didn't she trust her anymore?

She wiped a rag over Koenig's desk absently while looking into the bottom right-hand drawer, one which she hadn't explored yet. Since she'd become his secretary and had to type up everything anyway, Koenig trusted her with a key to his office. Inside the drawer she found something interesting — a carbon copy of a report to Captain Boehm in Berlin, dated April 30. She glanced through it quickly and saw it was from Franz von Papen. It was in German, but she noticed a list of numbers and she recognized one word: Lusitania.

The door opened. She dropped the pages in the drawer and slid it shut.

"Fräulein Malloy, what are you doing?" He stood in the doorway to his office, holding his homburg in one hand and a briefcase in the other.

She held up the rag and said, "What does it look like I'm doing?"

He tsk-tsked and smoothed his mustache.

"You do not show the proper deference, Miss Malloy," he said. "I have put the newspapers on your desk. Go through them." He added in a sarcastic tone, *"Bitte!"*

She brushed past him and went to her desk. The stack of papers awaited. She wondered if there would be more attacks on Jane Addams or if the baying hounds would have found a new victim.

She began to sort through the papers. She read all about the attack on J. P. Morgan, Jr. at his country estate and cut it out. Koenig would want a record of this.

"This fella who tried to shoot Morgan on your payroll?" Ellen asked, dangling the piece of newsprint in one hand as she leaned in the doorway. "He doesn't seem very bright."

Koenig shook his head and sneered in disgust.

"Nein," he said. "That bungling fool needed no incentive. Some of my compatriots are a bit too zealous."

She went back to her desk, put the story in a file, and turned to the business section of *The Times*. What she read made her heart stand still: "Ledger Sold to Case & White." Ellen read the short article three times. Forrest Calloway had sold his newspaper to a Wall Street firm, who planned to turn it into a stock sheet. What would Louisa do now?

She skipped the next two papers in the stack and went directly to *The Ledger*, which only mentioned the sale in a one-paragraph story on page two of the business section. She turned to the women's section. Louisa had written a story about a German woman, a writer who lost one son in the war and whose other son was the current German naval attaché. So Louisa was still in the game, writing flattering stories for the Germans. Perhaps it was time for a talk.

***

Ellen complained of a toothache and told Koenig she had to leave early that day. He glanced at her suspiciously, but he always did that. He was the most suspicious man she'd ever met.

"You could send Freddy to follow me," she said. "But Freddy's dead."

Koenig scoffed at her and waved as if she were an annoying fly. She was, frankly, amazed he put up with her insolence, but she thought that in a way he liked it. Men like Koenig hated the meek.

"Go on," he said. "But you will stay late Friday and hand out the payroll."

She was sure that Koenig did not have her followed anymore, but to be careful, she found a dentist's office and went inside. She sat down in the small waiting room. There was no receptionist, and she could hear groaning from behind a closed door. She was fortunate that her teeth were strong, and she rarely had toothaches. After a good ten minutes, she left and took a circuitous route to the back alley behind the building that housed *The Ledger*. She had used this alley many times last year when she was being watched by a couple of anarchists and didn't want them to know where she was employed.

She entered through the back doors to the presses. The big machines were silent, and she wondered if they'd already begun closing down the paper. Climbing the stairs to the lobby of the building, she took the elevator to the morgue on the second floor where a clerk was filing papers as if nothing had changed.

"Miss Malloy, what a surprise," he said.

"Hello," she said with a cheerful smile. She had often come to the morgue when she worked for Louisa to find stories that might be useful for the syndicated column. "I'm supposed to meet Miss Delafield here. Could you get her a message and tell her I've arrived?"

"Sure, Miss," he said. He scribbled something on a piece of paper and sent it whooshing up through a pneumatic tube. "I know she's here today because I saw her earlier."

Ellen busied herself looking through recent papers while she waited. The papers in front of her had been printed shortly after the Lusitania was sunk. In the third paper, she saw an article with a picture of Hester French. Ellen felt a lump forming in her throat. She forced herself to stare at the picture and to read the words. It was a test. Could she keep the pain at bay? Could she will her eyes to stay dry? Had she turned her heart into stone permanently?

"Ellen," Louisa said.

Ellen wheeled around — eyes dry as paper.

"Louisa," Ellen said.

"Why are you here? Is everything all right?"

While the clerk busied himself at the other end of the room, Ellen studied Louisa. Her skin was still luminous but a couple of wrinkles were beginning to form between her eyebrows. She's worrying too much, Ellen thought.

"I thought you'd washed your hands of all this business. Then I see your column about the German naval attaché and find you following Herr Albert. What are you up to?" Ellen asked. "Don't you trust me anymore?"

"I was too hasty in giving up," Louisa admitted. "And my heart was a little broken by my Australian friend. But Count von Bernstorff still believes I'm willing to help him out, and I have learned a few morsels of information. Unfortunately, it's not enough. I believe that the real secrets we need are in Heinrich Albert's briefcase."

This still didn't explain why Louisa hadn't told Ellen about her suspicions.

"Why didn't you just tell me? Here I was thinking you were done with all this spying business," Ellen said. "You obviously no longer need me."

"What could possibly make you think that?" Louisa asked.

"Well, you've got your fancy society assistant. You're no longer writing your Beatrice Milton stories. In fact, from what I understand this place has been sold. What would you need me for?" Ellen asked.

Louisa stepped close to her and said, "You're the one person I trust with my life. I do need you. We need to somehow get that briefcase."

We? Ellen was both surprised and relieved.

"It won't be easy," she said.

"Let's meet for lunch tomorrow," Louisa said. "As long as I'm in Count von Bernstorff's good graces, your boss shouldn't care if we meet."

Ellen agreed.

As she left through the press room, the machines started up again. Ellen inhaled the scent of ink and paper. She would miss this. At least as long as the Germans were sabotaging American ships, she would have a job. What would she do when the war was over, she wondered. It was all a blank. She had no future. In truth she wanted no future without Hester in it. She could think no farther than the next day. And tomorrow she would get into Koenig's desk drawer and have a closer look at that report from Papen.

As she made her way back to her boarding house in Harlem, she felt a tenderness in her breasts and noticed that they strained against the buttons of her white blouse. Was her monthly finally coming on?

Chapter 43

Louisa

The atmosphere in the newsroom was that of a funeral parlor. Everyone knew by now that the paper was to be no more.

From the newspaper telephone she called Ellen.

"Let's meet for lunch," Louisa said. "You know where."

They met at the automat in Times Square. Louisa gave four dimes to one of the nickel throwers, who tossed eight nickels back across the marble counter. The nickel throwers were usually women and they were amazingly fast and accurate. Louisa handed Ellen four nickels, and they went to the vending machines, dropped their coins into the appropriate slots, extracted their food from the small compartments and then went to sit at one of the round tables with their food. Louisa got a corn casserole for two nickels, a cup of coffee and a piece of peach pie, each for a nickel. Ellen had a tomato sandwich, a cup of coffee and a piece of carrot cake. This had been a weekly ritual of theirs when they had worked together. The food was delicious and quite fresh as the kitchen was right behind the bank of food slots.

"So, what have you found?" Louisa asked.

"Not much. But what I have found has struck me to my core," Ellen said.

Louisa gave her a quizzical look.

"I found a report that von Papen sent to Berlin. He told them that the *Lusitania* was carrying a half million dollars' worth of detonators, bullets, military equipment, and motor car wheels. That's why they torpedoed us. That's why they killed all those people," Ellen said, fiercely.

"Do you think it's true?" Louisa asked.

"I don't know. Probably. They are so methodical, these Germans," she said, shaking her head.

"It's still no excuse to kill civilians, but it won't help if we publicize the report," Louisa said. "The Germans will just say it proves that the United States is not neutral. Not worth destroying your cover."

She felt an overwhelming sense of frustration.

"It's been almost three weeks since the July Fourth assassination attempt on Jack Morgan's life, and I'm beginning to think it's impossible to outsmart the Germans. Tunney is frustrated. The Mayor positively raves. And Reggie smokes his cigarettes, smirks and makes snide comments about the bumbling American secret service. We need to act quickly," Louisa said. "We have to try to get the briefcase today. Do you still have those clothes that belonged to my father?"

Ellen nodded.

"I'll go home and pick 'em up before I go back to Koenig's office," Ellen said.

Louisa reached over and squeezed Ellen's hand.

Louisa was at her desk when Phyllis, who had spent the weekend in Newport at Louisa's behest, sauntered in.

"How was it?" Louisa asked.

"Livelier than this graveyard," Phyllis said, looking around the nearly empty newsroom. "I went to one of Mrs. Belmont's afternoon picnics and ran into Countess von Bernstorff. When I mentioned I was working with you, she sneered, said something about wanting her earrings back, and then cut me. Why did she do that?"

Cutting is what society women did when they were displeased. They simply cut the offender out of the herd and pretended she didn't exist.

"Perhaps she has discovered I am not so sympathetic to their cause, after all," Louisa said.

Phyllis rolled a sheet of paper into the typewriter and started punching keys, then she stopped and looked sadly at Louisa.

"I suppose this will be my last story," she said. "Have you any more you plan to write?"

"I have an interview with Harry Payne Whitney at his horse farm in New Jersey. That's the last one," Louisa said.

Phyllis leaned forward and asked, "Will you be seeing the filly, Regret?"

"Of course. That's the whole reason for going."

"Lucky you," she said. "Have you found another job yet? And what about your syndicated column?"

"Since I will no longer be the society columnist for *The Ledger*, they've decided to look elsewhere for a syndicated columnist. I didn't have anything more to say to those women anyway. Frankly, I'm tired of society stories," Louisa said.

"Oh my word," Billy said in a falsetto, fanning himself.

Louisa cut her eyes at him.

"That's my cue to leave," she said. "Don't worry, Phyllis. I'll write a glowing review for you should you need it."

Phyllis stopped her.

"Louisa, I saw you at the Automat, having lunch with a red-haired woman. Was that Ellen, the woman who used to work for you?"

"It was," Louisa said, surprised that Phyllis had seen her and Ellen.

"What is she doing now?"

Louisa shrugged.

"She's got a job with the Hamburg American line, believe or not. But I doubt she'll be there long," Louisa said.

"I hope not," Phyllis said. "For her sake."

***

Louisa wore a gray wig, spectacles, a rain cape, and a black hat with a veil. She carried a cane in one hand and a large flowered carryall in the other. She got on the el one stop before Herr Albert's stop and found a seat at the front of the streetcar. She'd been watching Herr Albert for weeks. At exactly 5 o'clock in the afternoon, Albert would board the train which took him from the Hamburg Building to the Ritz. A week ago, she started donning her disguise to get comfortable in it, riding a few seats behind him, waiting for him to make a mistake, but the German finance man never dropped his guard.

Today as usual Herr Albert stepped into the train car and lumbered down the aisle. He was a wide-shouldered man with sad, sloping eyes. This time she'd parked herself closer to the front of the car. She stared out the window as he passed her and then glanced surreptitiously over her shoulder. He sat down several seats behind her with a sigh and placed the briefcase on the seat beside him.

At the next stop, a slender young man, homburg pulled low over his brow, got on the train. Louisa looked away as the young man approached and passed her. Louisa noticed her hands were shaking. They had talked the plan over and over. But would it work? Louisa stared out the window and saw a cinema where Charlie Chaplin's new motion picture "A Woman" was playing. How simple life was for the people going in there to laugh and while away a half hour. As they approached the next stop, she picked up her large carry all and shuffled down the aisle towards the doors at the back. As she got close to Herr Albert's seat, she yelped and tripped, sprawling on the floor of the train, hanging on to her hat so it wouldn't fall and reveal her face.

"Help!" she called out. Herr Albert leapt out of his seat and bent over to help an old woman get her bearings. He knelt down and got her cane, which had skittered under some seats. The train screeched to a stop, and in a squeaky voice, Louisa thanked him profusely for his help.

"It is nothing, Madam," he said. "*Bitte*, be careful." He made sure she got to the doors before turning back to his seat.

Open, she thought. Open! Just as the doors slid apart, she heard him yell, *"Nicht wahr!"* She glanced back as she got off the train and saw him staring at the seat where his briefcase had been.

The doors shut and as the train car passed she saw him through the windows looking around with a wild expression on his face. He glanced out the window and saw her. Understanding lit his eyes. Then he saw the young man in the Homburg, grinning and holding a briefcase, approaching her as the train pulled away.

Louisa hurried toward the steps with Ellen, dressed as a young man, at her side.

"Here, let me help you," Ellen said and took her elbow. She leaned in close and whispered, "He'll get off at the next stop."

"He looked right at me," Louisa said.

"Did he know it was you?"

"I don't think so. He probably believes we're just run-of-the-mill thieves."

At the bottom of the platform, they dropped the briefcase into the carry all. Louisa dumped the hat and wig in as well and handed her rain jacket to Ellen, who draped it over her arm and sauntered off.

Louisa raised her hand to hail a taxi, but they were all full. Taxi after taxi passed her by. Perspiration trickled along the side of her face. She glanced around. The next stop was only a block away. If Albert caught a taxi...

Finally, a yellow taxi pulled over for her and she dove inside.

"Where to?" the cabbie asked.

"*The Ledger* on 34th Street," she said. That had always been the plan. But all of a sudden she knew that was a mistake. The paper would be defunct soon. This information needed to get out to the public in a much bigger way. Forget *The Ledger,* she thought. Joseph Pulitzer's paper wouldn't hesitate to publish whatever might be in this briefcase.

"Stop. Wait. Take me to *The New York World.*"

"Where's that?"

"It's—" She looked out the window and saw Heinrich Albert jump out of a taxi and whirl around, searching. Then his eyes met hers. A look of fury exploded across his features.

"Oh no," Louisa muttered. "Newspaper Row at Frankfort. Hurry."

The taxi pulled away from the curb. She turned around and saw another taxi behind them with Herr Albert gesticulating wildly in the back seat.

When her driver pulled up in front of the building of *The World*, she threw a dollar over the seat, not waiting for change, and dashed into the building, clutching the carryall. She ran past the guards to the elevator. She pushed the button nervously, glanced over her shoulder, and saw Albert entering just as the elevator doors opened. She stepped in quickly.

The elevator operator held the door open for the waving man.

"I'll give you five dollars to shut that door right now," Louisa said in a steady voice.

"What?"

"You heard me," she said.

The elevator operator clanged the door shut. Louisa stared at Herr Albert through the caged door as up she went.

Chapter 44
Ellen

When Ellen woke up the morning after the briefcase theft, she knew she was with child. She'd missed the earlier signs, but this morning she felt nauseated and woozy, and her monthly had not come for two months. She would have to find an abortionist for she would never give birth to something that came from such an abominable union. It would be unthinkable to be reminded of it every time she saw the creature. Of course, she knew what can happen when one of those quacks got their hands on you. She'd seen her dear friend Silvie expire on the table two years earlier. But that was a chance she would take. Besides, what did it matter whether she lived or died?

She got to the office at her usual 8 A.M. and found Koenig already there. He stared out the window and said nothing. He didn't even acknowledge her. She could feel him seething. She glanced at the newspapers on her desk. The story had not yet broken. No matter, the theft of the briefcase was a devastating blow.

"Do you want to tell me what has happened?" she asked, sitting down at her desk and leaning back in her chair.

"I do not," he said. "Fortunately we already have this week's payroll. But that fool Albert will be expelled from the country soon enough and then, Fraulein Malloy, none of us will get paid."

He stormed into his office and slammed the door.

Ellen smiled with satisfaction.

He opened the door, and she erased her smile.

"You will stay late and give out the payroll. Say nothing."

"I don't even know what's happened," she said.

"What's happened is that tomorrow or perhaps the next day, von Bernstorff and von Papen will be exposed. Our entire financial enterprise will be exposed. All because a fool decided to help an old woman off the bus!"

He shut the door again.

***

She took an apple out of the drawer and stared down at the dwindling pile of envelopes. She'd stuffed them with money and labeled each one that afternoon. Stevedores had been dropping by ever since 5 o'clock, smelling of oil and dirt and sweat. The monthly payments to most of them were small. An incentive to keep their traps shut and their eyes open, Koenig had said. She wondered how much he had paid the men who'd killed Paddy O'Neil.

A few were larger payments, including one for the man she was waiting for. He was one of the ones trusted to put the bombs on board. She ate the apple and waited.

The door opened, and a big, dark-haired man strode in.

"Name?" she asked, looking down at the ledger before her.

"O'Reilly," he said in a gruff voice. The name she'd been waiting for!

With a bored air, she took an envelope out of the top drawer and handed it to him, holding on for just a moment as he grasped it. She looked up into his dark brown eyes, and realized she could have been looking into the eyes of the boy on the *Lusitania*.

"Here ya go, O'Reilly," she said with a smile.

He held her gaze for a moment.

"I wouldn't expect an Irish woman to be working in the office of the Hamburg American line," he said. "What happened to the old sourpuss what worked here before?"

"Gone," she said with a shrug. "Where ya from?"

"County Cork? You?"

"I'm a Galwegian," she said. "My brothers are still over there, fighting in the war."

"For the British?" he asked.

She scoffed. "Not at all. There's more than one war going on, you know."

"Aye, there is," he nodded. He started toward the door, and she felt a sense of urgency. She needed to keep him there, keep him engaged. What could she say?

"I suppose I should be angry at the Germans for torpedoing the Lusitania," she said. "But they wouldn't have done such a thing if America wasn't sneaking munitions over to the Brits."

He stopped with his hand on the door.

"What do you know about the Lusy?" he asked.

"Just that I was on it with my fiancé when she went down. I survived, but my future husband did not. He was too busy saving the lives of others," she said, allowing a quaver in her voice.

"You were on her?" he asked, astonished. He came quickly toward her. "My boy was on the ship, too. He and his grandmother survived by the grace of God."

She tilted her head at him.

"I s'pose we have something in common then," she said. "What was her name, the boy's granny?"

"Nella McNabb. Did you meet her?"

"I did, indeed. Good Irish woman. She told me that ya lost yer poor wife," she said, laying it on thick.

He nodded.

It was time to pretend to be someone other than who she was. She wasn't a pretty, delicate thing like appealed to men of means, but an Irish longshoreman would have no use for a frail flower. He'd look for a woman of substance, one who could take care of a household and give him children. She held his gaze and saw a change come over his face, a softening.

"And how did you wind up here working for Koenig?" he asked.

"It's a long story," she said.

"How 'bout we get a bite to eat when you're done here? I'd like to buy you a dinner and a pint," he said.

Ellen pretended to think about it for a moment and then said, "I don't suppose it could do any harm. Where?"

"The Fraunces Tavern on Pearl Street," he said. "Say, seven-thirty. I need to clean up first. No rest for the wicked."

"I'll see you then," she said. After he left, she had the satisfied feeling of one who finds a fox in the trap. At the same time, she wished he had been a different O'Reilly, for she hated to hurt the father of young Seamus. Why did war have to come along and make enemies of us all, she wondered. She dismissed the thought. If she had qualms about what she was doing, she shouldn't have gotten involved in the first place.

***

The Fraunces Tavern held a couple of centuries' worth of smells. After all, it had been around since the American Revolution. The bill of fare displayed a wide selection. Ellen ordered a plate of little neck clams at a quarter each and some fresh green turtle soup for forty cents. O'Reilly ordered the roast spring lamb with mint sauce and roasted new potatoes.

Ellen listened to him talk about his dreams of going home to a free Ireland. The food came and he ate like a starving man, not bothering to close his mouth while he chewed.

"There's them that plan to stay here in America and die here, but I'm not one of them." He winked and added, "I miss the rain too much."

"You must be doing some very important work for Mr. Koenig," she said when she thought it might be appropriate to broach the topic.

"What makes you say that?" he asked.

"I know how much money was in that envelope," she said. "I don't blame ya. We have to do whatever we can to help the Brotherhood. I've met Joseph Plunkett and Sir Roger Casement, you know."

"You don't say," he said, leaning forward with interest.

"I was in Berlin with them when they were getting guns for the cause," she whispered.

"Shite!" he exclaimed.

"England will lose to Germany, I'm sure of it," she said.

"How did you wind up working for P. K.?" he asked.

"I was sent by the *Abteilung III b* itself," she said. "He could hardly say no."

"Ya were not," he said, peering at her as if seeing her for the first time.

"'Tis the God's truth," she said. "After the Lusitania sunk, I went over there on behalf of the Brotherhood with Plunkett. When the Germans learned I'd been living in America, they decided I could be useful. So here I am filing and typing for Koenig. I'm not nearly as useful as I could be," she said. "Not like you, I'm thinking."

O'Reilly grinned. She hoped by spilling some of her own secrets, he would share his.

"Thanks to me, them supply ships never make it," he said in a low voice and chuckled.

"Koenig told me you got the bombs on board, but how do you do it? Aren't they dangerous? I knew some anarchists that blew themselves up trying to build one last year."

"These don't use dynamite. I had the chemist explain it to me. See, you have a tube about ten inches long, made in two parts with the elements separated by a thin piece of aluminum." He used his hands to demonstrate. "One side has sulphuric acid and the other some kind of explosive liquid. The two liquids don't combust until the acid eats through the aluminum. Takes anywhere between a few days and a couple of weeks."

"Clever," she said. "Then it's quite easy for you to get them on the ships, isn't it, being a longshoreman?"

"Yeah, but I do it at night just to be safe. Matter o' fact, I've got a meet up tonight with the chemist, otherwise I might be asking you to come home with me," he said and reached under the table to touch her thigh.

"And what makes you think I'm that kind of girl, Mr. O'Reilly," she scolded, pulling her leg away from him.

"I was only teasing ya," he said. "I think more highly of you than that."

"You might want to keep your mind on more important things," she said, but there was no harshness in her voice. She would use everything at her disposal to learn what she could from him.

"Right you are, Miss Malloy," he said.

They finished their meals, and he drained his pint.

"I'll be walking you home," he said. "It's not safe down here at night."

"Thank you," she said. "But I live in Harlem so you might want to walk me to the subway instead, else you'll miss your appointment."

"I've got time," he said. "The meeting's not till midnight."

"Well then, I suppose I would feel a bit safer," she said. She didn't want him to know where she lived, but it was better to keep him close, she thought. She might even learn where he was meeting the chemist. The most important thing would be to discover which ship they planned on destroying. Then she could tell Captain Tunney, and they could search the ship, arrest O'Reilly, and get him to turn on the chemist.

As they walked down 116th Street toward her rooming house, he talked about his wife and how they had met. Like so many couples, their courtship seemed not to be about love so much as a way to help each other survive in a hard world. Wealthy people married each other so as to keep hold of their wealth; poor people married each other just so they might not starve.

They came in sight of her rooming house.

"How far do you have to go for your meeting?" she asked.

"The Battery," he said. "Don't let Koenig know I told you though."

"Loose lips sink ships," she said.

"That's not all that sinks a ship," he said with a laugh.

She shook his hand and thanked him for dinner and then watched him turn and walk back the way they had come.

Chapter 45

Louisa

Louisa had somehow gotten lost in the pressroom. She couldn't get out. She was screaming but no one could hear her over the constant banging of the presses. She ran from door to door, banging until finally she woke up and realized she wasn't in the pressroom. She was in her bed and someone was banging relentlessly on the door downstairs.

She got out of bed, threw on a robe, and went into the hallway where she found Suzie and Pansy wrapping their robes around themselves.

"Who could that be?" Suzie asked.

"I think I have an idea," Louisa said.

"You stay here," Suzie said to Pansy. "Look after Mrs. Delafield in case she wakes up."

Louisa and Suzie cautiously made their way downstairs. Carlotta stood in the doorway of the parlor where she'd been sleeping with a terrified look on her face.

Louisa flung open the front door and there stood a glowering Franz von Papen and his sidekick, Karl Boy-Ed.

"How may I help you gentlemen?" Louisa asked.

"You have something belongs to us, Miss Delafield," von Papen said. "We want it back."

"I can't imagine what you are talking about, Captain von Papen," Louisa said.

"We are prepared to pay a substantial sum of money for the return of the briefcase," Boy-Ed said.

"Oh, the briefcase? You mean the one that belongs — or belonged — to Herr Albert?" Louisa said. "I don't have it. If you want it, you'll have to go to the office of the *New York World.*"

"The New York World?"

"Yes, it's a newspaper. One of the biggest in the city," Louisa said and smiled cheerfully.

Boy-Ed laughed.

"My mother would admire you, Fraulein," he said.

But von Papen was not amused.

"You have no idea the enemies you have made," he growled.

"Is that a threat, Franzie?"

Louisa wheeled around and saw Carlotta standing in the hallway holding a gun. She stepped forward and pointed it directly at von Papen's nose. His eyes went wide and he took a step back.

Boy-Ed patted von Papen's shoulder.

"Let it go, Franz. All's fair in love and in war," he said. "There's nothing to be done now."

Von Papen sneered at Carlotta, but her hands were steady. All the fear that Louisa had seen on her face earlier was gone. Von Papen turned to Louisa and slid a cloak of charm over his visage. He bowed.

"*Auf Weidersehn,* Miss Delafield," he said. He flung one more look at Carlotta, turned on his heel, and marched down the steps with Boy-Ed at his side.

Louisa shut the door and heaved a sigh of relief. Then she turned to Carlotta and asked, "Where did you get a gun?"

"Mr. Sweet met me in the park yesterday and gave it to me. He thought I might need it," she said.

"How thoughtful." Louisa glanced at Suzie who stood in the doorway of the parlor with the fireplace poker gripped in her hand.

Chapter 46
Ellen

Ellen waited until 11:30 and then slipped out of the house. Dressed in her men's clothing with her hair tucked under a longshoreman's cap, she walked quickly in the brisk night air, crossing the city to take a different train down to the waterfront. Once she got there, she huddled in a doorway of the Seamen's Church across from the Pier Gate and watched. During the day the harbor hummed with activity. Motorcars and trucks clogged the roads, longshoremen came into their shifts, and trains full of supplies chugged out of the warehouses. She knew the names of the German ocean liners and other vessels with their red-white-and-black flags, waylaid by the British blockade. Koenig was in charge of security for the Hamburg-American lines, after all, which meant he also looked out for any other German ships and their stranded crew members. But while the German ships sat like docile cows in pasture, the steamships, and even the occasional schooner, flying the flags of neutral and allied vessels busily moved in and out carrying an enormous volume of trade. Anyone who owned a cargo ship had the potential to make a lot of money. These were also the ships mysteriously catching fire at sea.

At night, the place was deserted except for the few policemen patrolling the streets. Unlike the rest of New York, there were few lights down here and the whole place was drenched in a murky darkness. She smelled the briny scent of the water but she couldn't see it for the long brick halls and warehouses lining the street. She waited, wondering if she were on a fool's errand until finally she saw him. She recognized the broad shoulders and the nonchalance of his stride. O'Reilly entered through the pier gate and went inside.

Ellen quickly crossed the street and went to the gate. A bored nightwatchman told her to sign in. She signed Frederick's name, keeping her shoulders hunched. The nightshift was a skeleton crew and she saw no one else. She crossed through the cavernous building and made her way out to the piers. It was quiet except for the sound of the water going about its brisk business, and ships' flags flapping in the wind.

She walked quickly, hands in pockets, glancing around for O'Reilly. She knew he would go in the opposite direction of the German ships. The heat of the day had slipped away and the night air felt balmy. She looked down one pier after the next and then she saw a figure heading up a gangplank. She edged close enough to see the name on the ship. That's all she needed. The name. Tunney and the bomb squad could do the rest.

A blow to the head knocked her to the ground. She grunted, rolled over and looked up. There stood Koenig holding a gun. Next to him *Die Wolfin* held up her black and white parasol, aimed to deliver another blow.

"Time for a little journey, Miss Malloy. I'm afraid you won't be so lucky this time," Koenig said.

The throbbing began at the base of her skull and radiated outward. It had a rhythmic beat, and for a moment she imagined she was on a French battlefield with artillery shells pounding the earth around her, but the explosions were coming inside her head, she told herself, and she was not on a battlefield. She was in a box. She could smell the pine, feel the rough wood against her cheek. She kicked a foot toward the back and surmised her enclosure was about the size of a rifle box. She lifted her arms to feel around and realized her wrists were bound together, and her hands were in the prayer position. If she were to meet her maker, at least she was in a suitable posture.

Snatches of memory came to her. Koenig berating O'Reilly. The woman's creamy voice saying, "we can't let her live." And O'Reilly promising to take care of it. Then the stench of ether and blackness.

Now she was here in a box.

She wasn't alone, of course. Fear took up the leftover space. A thick, black fear. In fact, she couldn't tell any difference between open eyes and closed eyes. It was as if someone had dropped her in a bottle of India ink. She tried to roll and felt something next to her thigh. She touched it with the backs of her hands. Metal. The bomb. He had put the bomb in the box with her! The throbbing instantly got worse, accompanied by lightning bolts of pain dancing from one temple to the other.

The air was thin and close. Panic wrapped a cold hand around her throat and she found herself shivering uncontrollably. She screamed but soon realized it was useless. Even if anyone could hear her, they wouldn't help her. She hated this closed-in feeling. It was so hard to breathe. Oh, God, she was going to vomit.

Think of something good, she told herself. Maybe she would suffocate in here. Suffocation would surely be a better death than whatever that metal container had in store for her. Would it explode? Or would it burst into flames and burn her to death? Fire had to be the worst way to die.

Her mind took a sharp turn and she thought of Hester, the last kiss they'd had on the deck of the Lusitania. And for the slimmest second she felt those lips on her own. Then she saw those lips open in surprise as the lifeboat upended and she was suddenly in the air.

Ellen had never allowed herself to think of Hester's death, not the actual moment of it. But now she could think of nothing else. Had she been terrified? She must have been. The swift impact when she plunged down into the icy water. And the force of the ship going down had surely sucked her with it. She imagined Hester gasping for air, but instead the Irish sea rushed into her lungs. How long did it take to drown, she wondered. She hoped it was quick.

Finally, after all this time, she felt the full horror of her loss and she began to sob.

"Hester, I miss you," she said to the darkness. She wept like an abandoned child. She wept for Hester and wept for herself and wept for the little girl with the white bow in her hair.

After a while, she became drowsy. Her brain grew cloudy. She was no longer sure if she was awake or asleep. The thing inside me will die, too, she thought, as everything faded.

Chapter 47
Louisa

The headline in *The World* was a long one. It read: "HOW GERMANY HAS WORKED IN U.S. TO SHAPE OPINION, BLOCK THE ALLIES, AND GET MUNITIONS FOR HERSELF." Louisa sat at her desk and read the story with satisfaction.

"I wonder how *The World* got the scoop," Billy Stephens mused, leaning against one of the big square pillars in the room.

"Have you got a new job yet?" Louisa asked.

"Yep. I'm moving to Chicago to work at the *Tribune*. Should be fun. Just as much crime as New York," he said. "What about you?"

Louisa shook her head. She hadn't looked anywhere else. She didn't have the heart for it. At least she was off the hook now with Count von Bernstorff. In fact, she'd met with Captain Tunney that morning.

"You did fine work, Louisa," he had said in his avuncular manner. "If we weren't keeping your identity a secret, the mayor would probably give you the key to the city."

"There's still the matter of the bombs on the ships."

"True, but mark my words, Bernstorff, Papen and Boy-Ed will be booted out of the country before the year's end. They're the real trouble makers — financing the whole shebang, as we know now from Herr Albert's meticulous records."

"I hope so," she said. "And I hope America doesn't have to get involved in this war."

"That, I'm afraid, is another matter," he said. "Anyway, the mayor sends his thanks for your service."

"What about Ellen?" Louisa asked.

"She'll need to keep working for Koenig for as long as she can. She's been feeding one of my men information. Why? Do you want her to come back and work for you?"

"No," Louisa said. "There's no job for her at *The Ledger*. Mr. Calloway has sold the paper."

Captain Tunney was shocked at first, but then he had wished her the best of luck and gone on his way.

He still had his hands full with the German saboteurs. Apparently now someone was trying to blow up the railroad near Niagra Falls.

Louisa put the paper down and went to the telephone. She asked the operator to connect her to Koenig's office but Ellen didn't answer the phone. Instead it was Koenig himself.

"P. K. here," he said.

Louisa lowered the receiver and broke off the connection. She wondered where Ellen was. Herr Albert had recognized Louisa, but she had been sure Ellen was in the clear.

Louisa took the subway up to Harlem, but instead of disembarking at her own stop she got off at 116th Street and headed toward Ellen's boarding house.

When she knocked on the door, Mrs. Cantor's maid showed her into the parlor. A few minutes later, Mrs. Cantor bustled in.

"Miss Delafield, I'm so glad you came. I've been worried sick and wasn't sure what to do."

"Worried? Why?"

"Ellen didn't come home last night, and I don't trust that German man she works for. She's involved in something, isn't she?"

"I don't know," Louisa said. "I'm sure she's just trying to make a living."

"I found a letter addressed to you," Mrs. Cantor said. "I was going to bring it to you this evening if she didn't come home."

Louisa took the letter and opened it.

> *"L,*
> *I've found Mrs. McNabb's son-in-law. I'm after following him to the shipyard to see where he's planting bombs. Let Tunney know. Most ships leave by noon. I'll meet him at the pier first thing in the morning. E"*

"May I use your telephone?"

Mrs. Cantor showed her to the telephone in the hallway. She asked to be connected to Tunney's office and prayed he would pick up.

"Tunney here," he said.

"Captain Tunney, you must stop the ships from leaving the East River piers. Ellen wrote me a note that she was following one of the saboteurs last night. Now, she's missing. You're the only one with the authority to stop the ships from leaving."

"You think she's on one of the boats?" he asked.

"That or in the river, but they wouldn't want a body to be found in the river," Louisa said this as dispassionately as she could. She couldn't bear to think that having survived the *Lusitania*, Ellen had come home to die in the East River. And yet she had to acknowledge it was a real possibility. She knew how ruthless these men could be.

When she got to the pier, she found Tunney had already ordered that no ships were allowed to leave. His men were systematically searching the ships.

"As soon as Koenig heard we were closing the shipyard, he took off," Tunney told her. "And who knows where this O'Reilly fella is. We're searching the pubs along the waterfront. Not that he'll talk when we do find him."

Louisa gazed around at the longshoremen standing in idle groups, arms crossed, throwing hard glances at the police. Then she looked at the rows of ships.

"How many are there?"

"Eighty," Tunney said.

Louisa was heartsick. She walked along the pier and remembered this had been the place where poor Paddy O'Neil had died, crushed under a loaded pallet. Would this be where Ellen would die, too?

Chapter 48
Ellen

She had no idea how long she'd been out. Darkness surrounded her, and her little prison smelled of her own piss. But something was different. In spite of everything, the fear was gone. She felt lighter. She'd been carrying a heavy stone in her chest for months now, a stone that had finally been dissolved by her tears. Then she smelled something sweet. Lavender. She felt a presence there in the darkness. Mother Mary, is it you? she asked, knowing it wasn't Mother Mary but Hester. Hester's warmth. She was no longer in this makeshift coffin. Instead, they were walking in a field with sunlight drenching them, hand in hand, Hester chattering away about the flowers and how very lovely everything was.

Then she felt Hester's hand on her womb. Let this be our child, Hester whispered. Let this be our little girl.

She wanted to do what Hester asked. But she didn't see how it would ever happen. She was going to die an awful death in the middle of the ocean.

The lavender scent grew stronger. Sing, Hester whispered. Sing for me. And so Ellen sang in the dark.

Too-ra-loo-ra-loo-ral,
Too-ra-loo-ra-li,
Too-ra-loo-ra-loo-ral,
Hush now don't you cry!
Too-ra-loo-ra-loo-ral,
Too-ra-loo-ra-li,
Too-ra-loo-ra-loo-ral,
That's an Irish lullaby.

When she tired of that song, she sang another and another. She sang away the hours and she didn't stop.

Chapter 49

Louisa

Captain Tunney's men had been searching for hours with no luck. He told Louisa he would not be able to hold the ships much longer. He had other men combing the saloons to try to find O'Reilly.

"We're spread pretty thin," he said.

A breeze wandered up from the water as she walked along the wharf. Louisa shivered in spite of the day's heat. Glancing up at the deep blue sky — the same color as Paddy's eyes — she took a deep breath. Instantly, she knew where an Irish longshoreman would hole up. It wasn't in a saloon.

She hurried back through the pier gates and found a taxi.

“Houston and Mulberry,” she said.

The taxicab, driven by a woman wearing a leopard-print hat, had her there in minutes.

“Wait for me, please,” Louisa said.

She looked up at the church window and said a prayer for Paddy O’Neil. Then she went inside and walked down the aisle along the center of the nave.

A man sat in a pew in the middle of the church, his head bowed.

“Mr. O’Reilly?” she asked.

He looked up at her with a startled scowl.

“Who the devil are you?” he asked.

“I’m a friend of Ellen Malloy,” she said.

His eyes darted back and forth.

“Don’t know her,” he said.

Louisa sat down next to him.

“You know who she is,” she said. “Ellen Malloy saved your son’s life.”

“Yer lying,” he said.

“No, sir, I am not,” Louisa said stiffly. From her bag, she took out a newspaper clipping from the *Irish Times* and showed him.

“Jesus!” he said. “Seamus’ gran told me a woman had saved his life but she didn’t give me a name.”

“Mr. O’Reilly, where is Ellen?” Louisa asked. “The police already know that you’re involved in the sabotaging of American supply ships. You could go to federal prison for a very long time. However, if you tell me where Ellen is, you will be sent on the next supply ship to Ireland. At least that way, they'll know there are no bombs on it."

"I could disappear," he said. "No one would find me."

"And let the woman who saved your son's life die? Tell me now."

To her surprise, tears sprang in his eyes.

"They wanted me to kill her, but I couldna do it. She's tied up in the hold of the Anaconda."

"Along with the bomb you planted."

He stared down at his hands.

"Yes. She'll die anyway."

Louisa thought of all the lives his bombs had destroyed. Somehow it wasn't so easy to accept when you knew the person you were killing.

"You won't find her," he said. "Not unless I tell you how."

***

Louisa hurried out of the church and climbed into the back of the cab. She handed over some money, not even waiting to see the fare on the taxi meter.

"Back to the pier, and hurry. A woman's life is at stake."

The driver put the motorcar in gear and they sped through the dark streets of the city. Louisa couldn't stop the trembling in her legs. What if the bomb went off early? What if they couldn't find the box? What if she didn't have enough air to breathe in the box?

After what seemed an eternity, the taxi pulled up to the brick terminal, and she leapt out. She ran past the security guard, through the terminal and out onto the wharf.

She saw Tunney standing at the end of one of the piers.

"Captain!" she yelled. "She's on the Anaconda. The Anaconda!"

Captain Tunney blew loud and long on his whistle. His crew of policemen stopped what they were doing and hurried over to him. Louisa was out of breath by the time she got to the gathering crowd.

"She's in a box," Louisa said. "In a cargo hold of the Anaconda With the dry goods. That's all he would tell me."

"Let's go," Tunney said and marched along the pier to the gangplank of the Anaconda. They climbed up the wooden plank and onto the deck of the ship with its complex arrangements of derricks and winches for loading and unloading cargo. The ship's deckhands watched them curiously as Tunney led the charge across the deck with Louisa on his heels.

"What is the meaning of this?" a man, wearing a cap with some sort of insignia, called to them.

"I'm Captain Tunney with the New York Police Department. Get me your captain!"

"I'm the first mate, sir. I can help you," he said. He was a round-face man with a trim beard that circled his jawline like a dinner plate.

"You have a bomb on this ship. I need to see your cargo plan," Tunney said.

The man's eyes widened. He abruptly turned and went to the bridge of the ship. A few minutes later he emerged with a multi-colored map of the various cargo holds on the ship.

"Where do you keep the dry goods?" Tunney asked.

"All over the ship."

"Where would a box be that was large enough to hold a woman?"

"A woman? I thought you said it was a bomb you were looking for."

"Both. A woman and a bomb."

"Could be here in the 'tween deck, sir," the man replied and pointed to the map.

"Take us there."

The first mate led them into the forecastle and down a narrow stairway. Their footsteps banged loudly as they tromped along the cramped halls, past doors to accommodations for the sailors, Louisa imagined. They then had to climb down a ladder to a hold, filled with barrels, sacks and crates. She smelled coffee and coal.

"This way," he said. He took them through another passage and then into a large dark room. He held up his lamp so they could see. It was filled with stacks of large rectangular boxes.

"What's in the boxes?" Tunney asked.

"Machinery parts," the man said. "For the allies."

"All right men, start opening," he commanded.

Louisa balled her fists and held them close to her chest as the men began pulling boxes down. With pry bars they opened each one. And in each one they found screws and ball bearings and pistons and all sorts of things but no Ellen and no bomb.

"We've been taken on a wild goose chase," one of the men turned to Tunney and said.

Desperation took hold of Louisa. Paddy, if you're in heaven, will you help us, Louisa thought. She didn't know about or care much for the Catholic faith except that they were big on saints, and if anyone should qualify for sainthood, she thought it would be Paddy O'Neil.

Then she remembered something. The police had not found bombs in the canvas sugar bags, but Reggie had said sugar was highly inflammatory and it would make sense for the bombs to at least be placed near the sugar shipments.

"Where's the sugar?" she asked the first mate.

"That's in the aft hold," he answered.

"Let's go," Tunney said.

As they hurried down the hall toward the back of the boat, she heard something quite faint.

"What is that sound?" she asked.

"I don't hear anything," Tunney said.

Louisa took the lamp from the man and went back into the hallway.

"Someone is singing!" Louisa said. She pushed past the first mate and pulled open the door to the cargo hold.

The first mate held up his lantern. Next to the huge canvas bags was a rectangular box. The singing faded away.

One of the men pried open the top of the box, looked down, and said, "We've got her."

"Careful," Tunney said. "The bomb should be in there too."

Louisa pushed past the men and looked into the box. Ellen blinked in the light of the lantern and then she passed out.

"Stand back, Miss Delafield," Tunney ordered.

He peered into the box and then lifted a cigar-shaped object and held it up.

"Here we have the culprit," he announced. "Now get this poor girl out of that box."

Two of the men lifted Ellen out of the box and set her down, so she was sitting against some cargo. Louisa knelt beside her.

"Ellen," she whispered. "Please tell me you're all right."

She cradled her head and noticed her hair was damp with blood.

Ellen moaned.

"She's hurt," Louisa told Tunney.

"We've got a doctor outside. I thought we might need one," he said. The two men who had lifted her out of the box took her between them and carried her off the ship.

Louisa had almost lost her friend. Not once, but twice now. She thought of all the families who had lost someone they loved in this horrid war, which she feared eventually America must join. There would be no choice.

***

It was full daylight outside when Louisa opened her eyes. She'd fallen asleep in the armchair in her bedroom. She looked over at her bed and saw Ellen sleeping with the ginger cat curled up at her feet. The doctor had stitched up her scalp and said she would be fine in a day or so, but Ellen had been groggy and not made any sense when she tried to say something.

"Louisa?" Anna's voice called from the doorway. Anna was usually downstairs in her invalid chair by now, but there she was standing in the doorway, proving once again there was nothing wrong with her legs. "Is Ellen all right?"

"I think so. It's kind of you to ask," Louisa said.

"She has a strong constitution," Anna said. Then she turned and called out, "Pansy, help me down these stairs."

Louisa sighed. She had an interview scheduled with Harry Payne Whitney at his horse farm in New Jersey. She'd planned to leave that morning and spend the day touring the farm and then having a leisurely lunch with Mr. Whitney and his wife, Gertrude Vanderbilt Whitney. She knew that Gertrude would be mourning her brother who had gone down with the *Lusitania*. The horse's success was a welcome distraction. Louisa hated to cancel the interview, but she couldn't leave Ellen. She had already put too many other things ahead of their friendship.

Suzie came in with a cup of coffee for her.

"Would you stay here with her while I make a call?" Louisa asked her.

When Louisa called the paper, she was connected to Phyllis, who would leap at the chance to take her place. "The photographer will drive you, of course. I suppose you ought to be the one who does the interview since you did write the Kentucky Derby piece."

"I'd be happy to do it," Phyllis answered eagerly.

"Thank you. Please give my regards and my condolences to Mrs. Whitney," Louisa said.

"I will," Phyllis said. Louisa knew, at least, that Phyllis could be trusted to be tactful.

She hung up and went back to the bedroom.

"How is she?" she asked Suzie.

"Same as when you left the room. You need to stop fretting over her. Ellen will wake up when she wakes up," Suzie said.

To while away the time, Louisa read her mother's old journals. An hour later Suzie brought up some sandwiches and the two of them silently ate as they waited for some sign of life from Ellen.

When they were done, Louisa took Suzie's plate.

"I'll take these downstairs," she said. She needed to move her legs, which had gotten stiff sitting so still.

She was at the top of the stairs when she heard Suzie.

"Louisa, she's awake. She called out for you," she said.

Louisa abruptly turned around and hurried back into the room, handed Suzie the plates and leaned over Ellen.

"Ellen?" she asked.

Ellen's eyes were half open.

"Lou—," she said.

"I'm here," Louisa said. "Don't try to get up. You have to rest for a while, the doctor said."

Ellen shook her head vehemently.

"It's a society woman," she said in a hoarse whisper.

"Society woman? How do you know?"

"I heard her voice," Ellen said. "And I know by now what a society woman sounds like. She sounds like you. And I met her. She dresses rich and carries a parasol."

"Does she have a name, this society woman?"

"They call her *Die Wolfin*," Ellen said, rising up and clasping Louisa's arm. "She's the horse killer."

Louisa felt her blood turn cold. A parasol? *Die Wolfin?* The she-wolf? Wolf? Wolfe.

"It's Phyllis," she said, and suddenly it all made sense.

Ellen fell back against the pillow and shut her eyes.

"Better let her rest, Louisa," Suzie said.

"Oh dear God," Louisa said. "Phyllis is on her way to Brookdale."

***

Reggie pulled up in front of the house, and Louisa dove into his car.

"We've got to get to Brookdale Farm in New Jersey as soon as possible," Louisa said. "I tried to call Harry Whitney but no one answered."

"I've a better idea," Reggie said and turned his car in the other direction.

"Where are we going?" she asked.

"To the harbor. We can get there much faster by boat," he said.

When they got to the harbor, Reggie commandeered a Hacker-Craft runabout, and he handed Louisa a map.

"These are the fastest boats on the water right now," he said. "Top speed is thirty knots."

She managed to get on board, and soon the boat was skimming over the water. She kept seeing the image of the dead mare in her head. She should have called the police, she thought, but she had no idea what Phyllis planned to do and if the police showed up, Phyllis would know better than to show her cards. They must catch her in the act.

The water sprayed in a mist, and Louisa shielded her eyes against the sun. As they came close to land. Louisa looked at the map and then looked at the coastline.

"There should be a river soon," she said.

After a few more minutes, they saw the mouth of the river, and Reggie turned the boat into it.

"How far down?" he asked.

"A mile, I think," she said.

They puttered past trees, and Reggie carefully avoided the occasional sunken trunk.

"There," she said, pointing to a long fence. "That's a track."

They found a dock and Reggie pulled alongside it. She didn't wait for him to tie the boat before clambering onto the dock and running toward the track. The track was empty except for a trainer walking a white foal. Beyond the track were scattered barns.

The two of them walked quickly toward the elegant stucco barns. The first one they came to bore a sign that said, YEARLING BARN. Regret was no yearling. She had to be three years old to run in the Derby. Louisa looked around and saw a man and a woman outside the next barn.

"Stop!" she called, but they didn't hear her and went inside.

She lifted her skirt and took off at a run toward the barn with Reggie right behind her.

They reached the barn and stood in the doorway.

There were Harry Payne Whitney and Phyllis. Hanging her head over the door to her stable was the chestnut filly, Regret. A young Negro boy was cleaning out a stall nearby.

"Don't let her near that horse, Mr. Whitney," Louisa said.

Harry Whitney turned toward her in surprise.

"Miss Delafield?" he asked. "I thought you couldn't make it. I was just showing Mrs. Wolfe —"

"She's going to poison your horse," Louisa interrupted.

"Hello, Louisa," Phyllis said. She held her open palm toward the horse. "I've brought some apple slices for Regret."

"What's it laced with? Anthrax?" Louisa asked. "Glanders?"

"Cyanide," Phyllis said.

Harry Whitney's jaw dropped.

"No!" he yelled. The horse jerked back in surprise.

Phyllis took a step closer to the filly.

Reggie pointed his gun at Phyllis.

"Don't," he said.

"Is your friend going to shoot me?" she asked Louisa. "An unarmed woman in cold blood? That would be murder, wouldn't it?"

Regret came forward again and stuck out her neck, her nostrils quivering as she sniffed the apple slices.

"Please don't," Whitney begged.

Just as the horses' lips neared Phyllis' palm, the stable hand stepped out and brought the pitchfork across Phyllis' arm. She shrieked, dropping the apple slices to the ground. The startled horse whinnied, backed up, and reared in her stall. The boy dropped his pitchfork and reached for her harness.

"I wouldn't let nobody hurt this horse, Mr. Whitney," the boy said, gently stroking the filly's head.

Phyllis wasted no time but dove for the apple slice and, to Louisa's horror, popped it in her mouth. Reggie lowered his gun and stared at her. Then he crossed the barn in a few long strides and pried open her mouth. It was too late.

"How much did you take?" Reggie asked.

"Enough to kill a horse," Phyllis said.

"We've got to get her to a hospital," Reggie said.

"What about hydrogen peroxide? We could force her to vomit," Whitney said. "It's what we do when a horse has ingested poison."

Reggie shook his head.

"Cyanide doesn't work that way," he said. "It's already in her bloodstream by now, shutting down the absorption of oxygen. A hospital might have an antidote."

Phyllis stared defiantly and said. "I won't take it."

"I'll have my man drive you to a hospital," Whitney said and hurried off to fetch his driver and motorcar.

"It won't do any good," Phyllis said.

"We have to try, don't we, dear?" Reggie said, clasping her by the arm.

Phyllis turned to Louisa, "Come with me, Louisa. I don't want to die alone."

Louisa's emotions roiled — anger and pity and pain.

"I'll come, but you need to tell me the truth," Louisa said. "For once."

The motorcar, large and luxurious, pulled up to the barn. Reggie and Louisa placed Phyllis in the backseat between them, and the driver took off. The effects of the cyanide were not visible yet, and Louisa wondered if this weren't some sort of ruse. Perhaps Phyllis hadn't taken anything and was only hoping to escape once they got to the hospital.

"How could you do such a thing, Phyllis?" she asked. "How could you turn on your country?"

"Louisa, I do admire you, but sometimes you're a blind fool," Phyllis said.

"A fool?" Louisa said, "What about you? Coming here to kill Whitney's thoroughbred all because Count von Bernstorff or von Papen told you to?"

"They didn't," Phyllis said.

"Then why did you do it?" Reggie interjected. "Do you have personal vendetta against racehorses? Did you lose a bet?"

"You, of all people, should know why I did it." Phyllis turned vehement. "You know as well as I do who runs this country. It's not Woodrow Wilson. It's not the parakeets in Congress, chattering about 'the people.' It's them — the Morgans, the Vanderbilts, and yes, the Whitneys. People like my parents. They are the ones who must suffer from this war if we are ever going to get America to rise up and fight the Germans. Something must wake them!"

Louisa was stunned. She leaned forward, looked over at Reggie, and asked, "Did you know about this?"

"No idea. She wasn't working for us," he said. "But I will say she's not wrong. Your industrialists are the only thing standing between Britain and defeat right now. If they were angry enough, they might be able to force the issue. You may not care for her methods but if this really is her motive —"

"It is!" Phyllis exclaimed. "I hate the Germans. All of them."

"But you were working for them," Louisa said.

"So were you, Louisa. Writing those articles to make them look good," Phyllis said. "I know where the money for that policeman's widow came from." She suddenly grabbed her head with both heads and whimpered. "It hurts."

"Hurry," Reggie called to the driver.

"You tried to kill my friend, Phyllis," Louisa said in a low voice. "For that I can never forgive you whatever your motives."

Phyllis pulled her lips in tight, her fists clenched, as beads of sweat popped up on her brow.

"I don't need your forgiveness," she said in a strained voice. "Millions of lives will be saved once

America enters the war. My life, your friend's life, even the life of that magnificent filly, they don't matter."

She groaned again, bent over, and heaved vomit onto the floor of the car.

"Phyllis," Louisa said, her anger turning into fear for the young woman's life. "Hang on, dear. We'll be at the hospital soon."

"Not soon enough," Phyllis said. As her body stiffened, she cried out in pain and gasped for air. She pulled at the buttons along the front of her dress, ripping it open.

"Oh dear," Louisa said. Then she froze. At the top of Phyllis' breast, just above the line of her brassiere, peeked an angry puckering of skin. Phyllis yanked open her dress, revealing the pale skin of her abdomen. Louisa gasped. She wore no corset, and the skin across her belly was covered with round ugly red scars.

Louisa clasped a hand over her mouth as Phyllis convulsed, choking, and crying. She finally slumped sideways onto Reggie. She gasped again, flecks of foam on her lips, and gazed at Louisa with wide panic-filled eyes, breathing fitfully.

"Reggie, do something," Louisa pleaded.

"It's too late," he said. "There's nothing I can do."

He gently wiped the hair from Phyllis' face. She coughed, her skin slowly turning blue. Then she sighed and closed her eyes. A thick silence fell over them.

Phyllis had stopped breathing, mouth open as if still craving air.

Louisa closed her dress, covering up her chest.

"Who do you think did that to her?" she asked Reggie in a trembling voice. "Those scars?"

"Probably her husband," he said. "From what I understand he was a bit of a sadist."

Louisa didn't ask him how he knew this. She took it for granted that he just knew things.

"Poor Phyllis," she said, remembering the warm and witty girl Phyllis had been. "I'm so very sorry."

Chapter 50

Ellen

Ellen leaned forward so Pansy could check the stitches on the back of her head.

"Y'all sure do keep me busy," Pansy said. "You have a concussion, Miss Ellen, so you must rest. You might be confused for a while. Do you have a headache?"

"Where is Louisa?" Ellen asked. She did have a headache but didn't want to admit it.

"I believe she said something about saving a horse from Phyllis. That's her assistant," Pansy said.

"Pansy, don't you have some dishes to wash?" Suzie asked, coming into the room.

"Carlotta's doing it," Pansy said. She turned to Ellen. "I'm gonna make you some of my sassafras tea. That will help you feel better."

Pansy left the room.

"Is Louisa all right?" Ellen asked. "She can't trust that Wolfe woman. She's a killer."

"Mr. Grant is with her. I am sure they can handle one deranged socialite," Suzie said. "Now, try to get some rest."

Ellen laid her head back down on the pillow, but "rest" was not to be found. Instead, she wondered what she would do now? She put a hand on her abdomen and felt the slight swell of her belly. She had made a vow to Hester, but how could she honor it? She had nowhere to go, no livelihood. Koenig might try again to have her killed. And what if Louisa didn't make it back?

Pansy brought in some tea. It tasted like a forest, and Ellen slowly began to relax.

She finally fell asleep, but awakened when the door opened. Louisa poked her head in.

"Hello there," Louisa said. "You're looking much better."

Ellen scooted up in the bed, giddy with relief.

"You're looking fine and dandy yerself," Ellen said. "Turns out we're both alive, after all. Did you stop her?"

"We did," Louisa said. She sat down in the armchair.

"I wasn't worried a bit," Ellen lied.

"How's your head?" Louisa asked.

"Much better. Pansy's sassafras tea has made sure of that," Ellen said.

"When we found you," Louisa said with a half grin, "You were singing a song about 'Old Van Kluck.' Do you remember?"

Ellen's eyes widened.

"Oh, we don't give a fuck for old Van Kluck, and all his feckin' army," she sang, and then burst out laughing. "It's a song my brother sang, and I scolded him for cursing."

Louisa giggled, and for a moment it felt as if there were no war, no German saboteurs, no loved ones to grieve.

"How did your encounter with *Die Wolfin* turn out?"

"Phyllis is dead," Louisa said. She shook her head sadly.

"Did your British spy kill her?" Ellen asked.

"She killed herself. She took the cyanide she had intended for the Whitney's horse," Louisa said.

"Why would she want to kill a thoroughbred? It's not like they were going to send Regret to the front line," Ellen said. "It makes no sense."

"She wasn't really on the side of the Germans," Louisa explained. "She hoped that if it looked as though the Germans had killed America's beloved Horse of the

Year, there would be enough outrage, especially among the upper classes, to force America to join the war."

"I don't know why she would think that. The Lusitania wasn't enough," Ellen said bitterly.

Louisa said, "I'm not sure about that. Sometimes the wheels turn slowly. Every little thing adds up, and eventually we will reach a tipping point. I hate the idea of going to war, but how else will England and France survive?"

"I met some ladies during my travels, who were all about trying to get the countries' leaders to come to a peaceful resolution. No one would listen to them," Ellen said. "Those admirable women ought to be running the world instead of the war-mongering fools."

"You mean Jane Addams?" Louisa asked. "You didn't tell me about meeting her. I agree. She'd certainly do a better job of it than the men. But, of course, women can't vote so they don't get to run anything."

"Now, you sound like Hester," Ellen said.

Louisa sat down on the bed.

"I know you miss her. We should do something to remember her," Louisa said.

"Too bad all that German money has dried up," Ellen said ruefully. "How am I supposed to take care of a baby?"

"A baby?"

"I've got a bun in the oven," Ellen said.

Louisa's jaw dropped.

"How on earth did that happen?"

"Don't you know the facts of life, Louisa?"

"I do. But you...you aren't..." Louisa stammered. She wasn't sure how to say what she was trying to say. "Was it that Plunkett fellow?"

Ellen shook her head.

"This is Hester's baby," she said.

Now Louisa shook her head, "That isn't how it works, Ellen."

"And how do you know?" Ellen said, jutting her chin forward. As far as she was concerned, she and Hester had made the baby. No one else was involved.

Louisa's brow squinched in confusion, but then she said, "I suppose it doesn't matter how it got there."

Suzie opened the door.

"You had a phone call from a Mrs. Murphy while you were gone, Louisa."

"What did she want?"

"She wanted to find out if we knew where to find Ellen. I told her she was here, and she said that she and her husband would be coming over tomorrow morning to talk to her. She asked that you arrange for them to have a private conversation."

Ellen put her hands over her stomach. Did they know somehow that she was pregnant? That was impossible. But it was also impossible that Hester had come to her in that little box. Hester had often mentioned how desperate her sister was for children. Perhaps this was the answer. And yet Ellen's heart shrank at the thought of it.

Chapter 51

Louisa

After dinner, Pansy and Carlotta went to a motion picture show. Louisa got Anna to bed while Suzie cleaned the kitchen, and then the two of them sat at the kitchen table. Louisa told her everything that happened that day, and then told her the most startling news of all.

"A baby?" Suzie said. "I didn't think Ellen—"

Louisa shook her head.

"I'm afraid one of those Germans may have forced himself on her," Louisa said.

Suzie snorted in disgust. "I don't doubt it. How is she going to support a baby?"

"I don't know. She can't have her old job back. I don't even have a paper to write for anymore," Louisa said. "I don't know what we're going to do. The syndicate has let me go. There's not a single society writing job open. I have been making discreet inquiries, but society isn't as important as it used to be. The only thing people care about these days is the war in Europe."

"From what I gather, you have plenty of exciting stories to write about, concerning these sabotage artists."

"Tunney has asked me not to write about any of that. While the contents of the briefcase have turned the tide, the Germans have not yet stopped their activities. He doesn't want to give away any of our secrets."

They sat in silence, both lost in thought. Louisa heard the front door open and Carlotta and Pansy talking and laughing in the hallway. Her mother was right. There were too many people living in the small house. She would have to share her bed with Ellen since she didn't plan on sleeping in the armchair again.

Suzie said, "My business in delicates is doing pretty good. Mr. Sweet knows a few other butlers in places such as Mrs. Held's."

"Is that proper, Suzie?" Louisa asked.

"I don't think we're in a position to worry about propriety," Suzie answered.

They heard a throat being cleared and looked up. Pansy stood in the doorway.

"Aunt Suzie, Miss Louisa, I've been wanting to talk to you, but it's just been so busy around here," Pansy said. Louisa's heart softened at the sight of the young woman. In the year that she had lived with them she'd filled out and looked more and more like her pretty mother.

"Come on in, girl, and sit down," Suzie said.

But Pansy didn't sit.

"Miss Louisa, I want to thank you for taking me on as a servant in your house," Pansy said. "I have sure loved living in New York City, and the work hasn't been too hard. But I know you're in a bind and you probably can't afford to pay me anymore."

Louisa sighed. It was true.

"Do you want to go back home to St. Augustine?" Suzie asked.

Pansy shook her head.

"No, ma'am. I... Well, I want to be a nurse."

Louisa's head snapped toward Suzie, and they stared at each other for a moment in surprise.

"Where did you get a notion like that?" Suzie asked.

"I thought you wanted to be an actress," Louisa said.

Pansy shook her head.

"Not anymore."

Louisa thought about how gently and competently Pansy had taken care of Carlotta when she was injured and how even now Pansy was the one constantly seeing to Ellen's needs.

"What a marvelous idea," Louisa said, "but do they... well, can Negro women be nurses?"

"Yes, ma'am, they can," Pansy said. "There's a training program in the Bronx at the Lincoln Hospital. It's called the School for Colored Females in the Nursing Arts."

"And how are we going to afford to pay for that?" Suzie asked.

"Uncle Lloyd has money, and he's offered to take care of the tuition," Pansy said.

Suzie's mouth dropped open. Louisa remembered Suzie's brother from her own sojourn south. She had no doubt he was bursting with pride over this recent development.

"Will you still live with us?" Louisa asked.

"No'm," Pansy answered. "There's a dormitory right across the street. I spoke to a woman at church, named Nella, and she just graduated. She says it's a lot of work, but she says there's no better profession."

"But how long will it take?" Suzie asked, "and where will you work afterwards?"

"The course is two years," Pansy answered. "If the war is still going on, they're going to need lots more nurses."

"Suzie," Louisa said. "I believe you were afraid Pansy was going to try to be in the motion pictures. Is this not a better outcome?"

To her surprise, Suzie wiped a tear, stood up, and gave her niece a long, hard hug.

***

The house was quiet. Ellen was asleep in Louisa's bed and Louisa sat in her bedroom armchair, reading her mother's diaries. She closed the last one and looked at the clock on her bedside. It was 11 p.m. Her mother would probably not be asleep yet. She often stayed up late re-reading one of her Jane Austen novels.

Louisa went into the hallway and knocked on the door to her mother's bedroom.

"Come in."

Louisa opened the door. Her mother, sitting up in the bed, said, "Suzie, I'm so glad you —" she stopped. "Oh, it's you."

"Yes, Mother. I want to talk to you," she said.

"Do you want to tell me why we're suddenly running a boarding house? It was one thing to have Suzie's grandniece move in, but this is getting to be too much. All these women!"

"I know, Mother. We'll work it out."

"Then why are you here? It's late."

"I've been reading your diaries," Louisa said, turning the vanity chair around and sitting so they faced each other.

"I'm sure it wasn't very interesting reading," Anna said.

"Actually it is interesting. I loved learning about your social life back then, but it's not all parties and teas." She leaned forward, resting her elbows on her knees. "I read about your anguish because Father never touched you after I was born. You longed for him, and you believed he loved you, but there was no intimacy."

Anna's mouth tightened, and she looked away.

"I knew you would have questions someday," she muttered.

"Mother, I need to know the truth. I know you believed he was unfaithful to you. Do you know who killed Papa?" she asked. "Was it another woman? A jealous husband?"

"No, it wasn't." Anna gazed at her, eyes brimming with tears. "I killed him."

Louisa's heart shattered like a crystal glass thrown from a window. As soon as the words had left her mother's lips, Louisa knew it was true. She covered her face with her hands, unable to look at her mother. All these years — the questions, the confusion.

"I don't understand," she said with a catch in her throat. "How? Why?"

"He was cheating on me!" Anna said, growing distraught.

"How do you know that?" Louisa bolted up, hands clenched.

"A woman always knows," Anna said, frightened and defensive. "I asked Herbert to look into it for me, but he already knew. He told me where they met. So I went to that shabby hotel. I took a knife to threaten this woman. I couldn't take it anymore. I found his room and knocked on the door."

Louisa stood up and paced the room. She tried to imagine her frantic mother with a knife. What had she thought she was going to do?

"But, Louisa, he wasn't in there with a woman. It was a man! A burly shirtless man with tattoos on his chest. This man opened the door and asked what I wanted. I pushed past him and saw Richard lying on the bed with nothing but a sheet — a dirty old sheet — covering him, and I screamed. I took out the knife. I was blind with rage. The lies. The deceit! All those years I had wondered what was wrong with me. Why my husband never came to my bed." Tears fell from her cheeks. She wiped them away with the back of her hand.

Louisa had never seen her mother cry before. Not even at the funeral.

"I'm sorry, Louisa, at first I blamed you. He wanted nothing to do with me after you were born. Even before then it was sporadic. Oh, he was always kind to me. Like a brother, Louisa. Can you imagine? You can't. You haven't been married," she said.

Louisa had not been married, but she had known love and intimacy.

"Yes, mother, I can imagine," Louisa said.

Anna peered at her.

"I suppose you know more about these things than you let on," Anna said.

"So you stabbed Father in a fit of rage?" Louisa asked.

"I didn't mean to," Anna said. "I was just so angry. As if I were possessed. Richard was crying. He was so ashamed. The man — he was some sort of longshoreman — grabbed his shirt and fled. There was my husband — my husband! scrambling into his trousers. The knife was in my hand. Oh, I know I shouldn't have brought it. It was insane. I wanted to kill myself right there in front of him, to show him how he had destroyed me. I held it over my breast. He grabbed me, and we struggled. And for a moment, everything went black. I didn't mean to kill him. I didn't. I promise, Louisa—" Her breath stuttered and she began to sob. She looked down at her hands as if even now all these years later, she could still see the blood stains.

"Monstrous," Louisa whispered.

"Yes, I am a monster," Anna said.

Louisa stood still. For a woman who dealt in words, they utterly failed her now. Her lungs felt as if they were collapsing in her chest. She sank down and tried to breathe. For a long, dark moment she just sat there, her knees shaking, her mind whirling. Should she turn her mother into the police? No, she could not do that. What would be the point after all these years?

"What...what did you do then? How did you get away with it?" Louisa finally managed to ask. She strode to the window and stared at her reflection. Behind her she saw her mother, now perched on the edge of the bed.

"I realized what had happened, what I had done. I tried to revive him, but the blood kept leaking from the wound in his chest. In a few minutes he was dead. It was so quick, Louisa. I dropped the knife, went out the back of the hotel and caught a hansom cab to Herbert's office," she said. "He took care of everything after that."

Herbert Markham, of course. Louisa turned and faced her mother.

"According to Julia Markham, Herbert was blackmailing Father. He must have known it wasn't a woman when he sent you to that hotel room," Louisa said. "He had been blackmailing him for years."

Anna looked at her stricken. "No, he wouldn't..."

"He would, and he did. When he realized I was investigating Father's murder, he sent an anarchist to try to kill me," Louisa said.

"Kill you? Not Herbert," Anna said.

"Fortunately, Julia is a decent human being and when she learned what he was doing, she threatened him with exposure if I were harmed."

Anna sighed.

"Herbert was in love with me. I suppose he thought that if I saw the truth I would leave Richard," Anna said and shook her head.

"Only after he made sure to drain us of our fortune," Louisa said.

"I'm sorry, Louisa," Anna said. "All of this is my fault."

Louisa looked at her mother. She had been sitting every day for years in an invalid chair even though she had two perfectly good legs.

"This explains a lot — the belle of the ball turned recluse. It wasn't just about the loss of our fortune. It was guilt, wasn't it?"

Her mother nodded.

"I couldn't bear to see anyone, not after what I had done. After a while, that chair and this house became my prison. I've never been able to forgive myself," she said. "I can't expect you to."

Louisa put a hand to her chest and felt the wild rhythm of her heart beneath her palm. Her mother had been punishing herself for fifteen years for a crime of passion. Louisa suddenly felt so much pity for both of her parents. She wasn't sure she could forgive her mother, but in recent years, she had grown to understand how complicated the heart can be, and she knew she would have to try. She had lived for so long with the not knowing, and now she would have to learn to live with the knowing.

She went to her mother, took hold of her hands, and said, "Mother, you've paid for your crime long enough. It's time to show yourself some mercy. Tomorrow, I'm tossing that invalid chair out onto the sidewalk. No more prison for you. I hereby order your release."

Anna brought Louisa's hand to her face and wept. Louisa felt the tears as they dampened her fingers.

Forgiveness would come with time.

***

The next morning Katherine Murphy and her husband arrived. Louisa showed them into the dining room where Ellen joined them. Louisa slid the pocket doors shut to give them some privacy while she and the rest of the house's inhabitants sat in the living room, each pretending to keep busy. Louisa read a *McClure's*. Suzie worked on her sewing. Carlotta absently stroked the ginger cat, who had taken a liking to her. Pansy had her nose in a nursing book she'd gotten from somewhere, and Anna did needlework.

Louisa could hear murmuring from the dining room, but couldn't make out what they were saying. It was all she could do not to slip over there and put her ear to the door.

Anna whispered, "What could they possibly want with Ellen?"

"Ellen was good friends with Hester, and Katherine is Hester's sister. They may want to ask her about Hester's last days. I don't know," Louisa said. It was really quite mysterious.

"I bet they want to give her something of Hester's, something for Ellen to remember her by," Pansy said.

"Why would they do that?" Carlotta asked. "I promise you rich people never give nobody nothing."

The wait seemed interminable, but finally the scraping of chairs on the floor sounded from the dining room. Louisa rose and went to the parlor door. The Murphys came down the hallway with Ellen following them.

"I hope we weren't much trouble, Louisa," Katherine said with her usual exuberance. "Ellen has some news for you."

Mr. Murphy tipped his hat to the ladies and the stately couple went outside where their chauffeur opened the back door of their Pierce-Arrow.

Louisa shut the door and turned to Ellen. Suzie and Pansy had crowded into the hallway with Carlotta and Anna at the doorway. Ellen's face had gone completely white.

"Well? What did they want?" Louisa asked.

"Hester left me her fortune," Ellen said.

Pansy shrieked and then clapped a hand over her mouth.

"Would you repeat that?" Louisa said.

"Hester left me her fortune," Ellen repeated.

"Oh, my," Suzie said.

Ellen walked in a daze into the parlor and sank down onto the sofa while Suzie and Pansy sat on either side of her. Louisa stood by the mantle, and Anna sat in the armchair. Carlotta leaned in the doorway.

Louisa was trying to hold back the enormous relief she felt. She'd been so worried about what Ellen was going to do with a baby, wondering how she would take care of it. And now, now, fate had intervened. Ellen had a fortune.

"I know what I'm going to do with it," Ellen said, her eyes lighting up.

"Travel the world," Carlotta said.

"Buy a mansion," Pansy said and giggled.

"No, I'm going to start a magazine for women," Ellen said. She looked at Louisa. "I actually have often thought about how I'd like to have a magazine for women. A progressive magazine, full of real stories. It would be a way to honor Hester."

"A magazine?" Suzie asked in surprise.

Ellen nodded.

"I already know a first-rate muckraker who needs a job. And an editor, too. Thorn needs a job, right?"

Louisa tried to absorb this information. The idea staggered her. Ellen would be her boss!

"What about the baby?" Louisa asked. "Who will help you take care of it? A magazine is a lot of work, Ellen."

"If Sylvia Pankhurst can do all the things she does, I can own a magazine and raise a baby. Besides, we'll have help," Ellen said and turned to look at Suzie with a question in her eyes.

"You know I'd love to help you out, Ellen," Suzie said and sighed. "But I've been holding off telling you all something." She took a deep breath and looked at their puzzled faces. Louisa felt a clenching in her chest. Was Suzie ill?

"I'm getting married."

Louisa gasped as the room seemed to spin.

"In case anyone is wondering, I love babies," Carlotta said.

Louisa lowered herself onto a nearby chair. The ginger cat leapt onto her lap. It was too much to take in all at once. Ellen, pregnant and suddenly rich with a former prostitute to take care of the baby while she published a magazine? And Suzie ... Suzie, who had always been there with food, support, advice, coffee, fixing her clothes, cleaning the house, scrimping and saving when they had no money, making sure Louisa went to college so she could support herself. Tears sprang to Louisa's eyes, and she stood up so fast it made her dizzy. The cat tumbled to the floor and stalked off with an angry flick of her tail.

"You're getting married? To Mr. Sweet?" Louisa asked.

Suzie nodded.

Louisa walked over and wrapped her arms around her old friend, her dear companion.

"Finally, after all these years, you're doing something for yourself," she whispered.

As happy as she was for Suzie, she realized Anna must be devastated. She turned and saw Anna standing underneath the family portrait.

"Mother, are you all right?" she asked.

"Never better," Anna said in an imperious tone. "We've got a wedding to plan."

They all turned to look at Suzie, whose radiant smile brightened the whole room.

Author's Note

One morning deep in the pandemic, I woke up and realized my next book had to begin with a ship sinking in 1915. I knew it couldn't be the Titanic because that happened in 1912 and I had no intention of writing a Titanic story. When did the *Lusitania* sink, I wondered. Sure enough it was in 1915. At the time, I knew very little about the *"Lusy."* I didn't know that almost twelve hundred people died after a German torpedo struck the hull of the boat — or that 761 people survived and many of them left first-hand accounts of the tragedy. What I did know is that the event would figure heavily into the investigations of Louisa Delafield and Ellen Malloy.

Thus began the delicious task of researching 1915. Of course, I read the brilliant Erik Larson's book, *Dead Wake: The Last Crossing of the Lusitania,* and I poured over the newspaper accounts of the sinking of the *Lusitania*. I was stunned that the captain had even been put on trial though he was eventually exonerated of any wrongdoing. There is even a film footage on YouTube from 1915 of people boarding the Lusitania before she set off on that fateful trip.

Louisa, Ellen, Suzie, Pansy, Carlotta, Phyllis, and Anna are all fictional, but most of the other figures and events depicted in the book are historical. Martha Held, a former opera singer, actually did run a brothel frequented by the Germans, Chad Millman writes in *The Detonators: The Secret Plot to Destroy America and an Epic Hunt for Justice:*

"During the summer, when windows stayed open and neighbors gathered on their stoops to escape the heat, they gossiped about what was going on inside Held's house. Her singing carried down the block, rising above the din that lingered in the air whenever her door opened and closed. The neighbors noticed that beautiful women would arrive early in the evening and then disappear through the door leading into Held's basement. Hours later, men speaking German, often dressed in German military uniforms, would follow."

Lots of spy activity was going on in New York in 1915. Count von Bernstorff, Franz von Papen, Heinrich Albert, Karl Boy-Ed, and Paul Koenig were all expelled from the country eventually. And Heinrich Albert really did lose his briefcase on the train, the meticulous contents of which were published in *The World*. To this day, no one is sure who actually stole it.

An incredibly useful book in understanding Paul Koenig's operation, including the killing of war horses with glanders, was *Throttled* by Captain Thomas Tunney himself, which I discovered while reading Howard Blum's informative book, *Dark Invasion*. Another extremely helpful primary source was the *Memoirs of Franz von Papen*, who later went on to support Adolph Hitler's rise to power, thinking (absurdly, of course) the dictator could be controlled. On the other hand, the American-born Countess von Bernstorff later famously despised the Nazis and Adolph Hitler.

Reggie Grant is inspired by the real British Naval Attaché, whom I learned all about in *Guy Gaunt: The Boy From Ballarat Who Talked America into the Great War* by Anthony Delano.

Sir Roger Casement and Joseph Plunkett were actual Irish revolutionaries who went to Berlin to enlist German help in overthrowing the British. They were both later executed by the British. Thanks to the *Irish Times, The Independent, Irish Examiner* and Boston College for their many articles on the two men.

I was especially interested in the story of Jane Addams' attempts to broker peace in Europe. Of course, she was pilloried in the press. As she wrote in her book,

Peace and Bread in Time of War, "We were called 'Peacettes' and the enterprise loaded with ridicule of the sort with which we later became only too familiar."

Fortunately, no one ever did attempt to harm Regret, the filly who put the Kentucky Derby on the map.

Regret and owner Harry Payne Whitney, Photo — Public Domain

If you enjoyed this book, I hope you'll leave a review on Amazon, Goodreads, B&N, social media, or wherever you leave reviews. To read more books in this series, go to Delafield & Malloy Investigations. Please also visit my website and sign up for my newsletter to learn more about forthcoming books and offers: trishmacenulty.com.

Coming Soon:

The Butterfly Cage

An elderly blind woman enlists Louisa Delafield and Ellen Malloy's help when her companion is snatched from a Manhattan Street. They soon learn that this young woman is just one of several. While Louisa investigates a New York playboy's possible involvement, Ellen resumes her role as a servant and goes undercover to learn what she can. What the two women discover leads to international intrigue with far-reaching consequences.

Set in the fall of 1913, this story takes place early in the two women's partnership.

Pre-order here:
https://www.amazon.com/gp/product/B0BW6MXS65

Acknowledgments

First and foremost, I wish to thank my husband, Joe Straub, for moral support, technical support and editorial support. Writing this series would not have been possible without him. Much thanks to my writing partner, Tamara Titus, who doesn't seem to mind reading the roughest of rough drafts. Her feedback has always been invaluable, and her stalwart belief in my work has given me the strength to keep going. Of course, much thanks to my team of readers: Pam Ball, Kevin Murphy, Kathleen Laufenberg and Patti Wood who have been with me through the years. They not only provide excellent corrections and suggestions but even more importantly, friendship and support. Thanks so much to P.V. LeForge for his excellent proofreading and to Jenny Q for cover design.

About the Author

Trish MacEnulty is the author of the historical fiction series, Delafield & Malloy Investigations. She has written four other novels, two memoirs, a short story collection, and children's plays (some of these under the name Pat MacEnulty). Her historical YA book, *Cinnamon Girl*, (Summer 2023) is being published by Livingston Press.

She lives in Florida with her husband, two dogs, and one cat and writes book reviews and features for the *Historical Novel Review*.

Made in the USA
Columbia, SC
09 August 2023